PRAISE FOR THE ANATOMY OF EXILE

"A sprawling epic about diaspora, war, immigration and the lasting scars of intergenerational trauma; one that lands with particular power and poignance amid the latest Israel-Hamas war."—*The Forward*

"Shying away from villains and heroes, the novel creates sympathy for a spectrum of individuals trapped by tribalism, land grabs, heartless government actions, and economics. A book to read right now."—*Kirkus Reviews*

"Zeeva Bukai writes as perceptively about romantic love and family life as she does about the wider forces that haunt it: war and exile, love across borders, the long, torturous shadow of the past. The Anatomy of Exile is a compassionate, searing and full-of-life that bears witness in important ways."—Elizabeth Graver, author of *Kantike*, winner of the National Jewish Book Award

"In her tremendous, transporting debut, The Anatomy of Exile, Zeeva Bukai demonstrates the unique power of literature to transcend borders, excavate our shared humanity, and perhaps even heal. . . . This is a vital exploration of what it means to be in exile, and how the loss of an anchor necessitates a reckoning with the self—a self without borders, without country, without land. Bukai writes with lyrical urgency and compassionate insight about identity, belonging, dispossession, and desire, capturing the doomed irony of homeland and the lengths to which people will go to insulate themselves in a false notion of safety."—Sara Lippman, Jewish Book Council

"Bukai is so invested in imagining the impact of the Palestinian-Israeli conflict within the domestic confines of a romantic relationship . . . in her beautifully written, riveting debut novel."—*The Jewish Journal*

"In The Anatomy of Exile Zeeva Bukai beautifully weaves one Mizrahi family's tragic tale of love and loss and deftly illuminates the liminal space between places and languages, Arabness and Jewishness. With great empathy and profound insight, Bukai explores our attachment to place, family, and tradition and the lengths we would go to protect them, showing history repeating itself in inexplicable yet inevitable ways. The Anatomy of Exile is a remarkably assured debut—radiant, intelligent, and deeply moving."—Ayelet Tsabari, author of *Songs for the Brokenhearted*, winner of The National Jewish Book Award and The Sami Rohr prize

"In Zeeva Bukai's stunning debut, the burden of history is masterfully woven into the intimate journey of an Israeli family. With elegant prose and unflinching honesty, this novel about love, betrayal, and exile reminds us of the necessity of storytelling in troubled times."—Amy Gottlieb, author of *The Beautiful Possible*

"The heartbreak of being exiled from the land of your birth is beautifully described in this wrenching novel, a deep dive into the immigrant experience, family dynamics, and the misunderstandings that needlessly divide people. The fiber of loyalty is tested until it frays--yet redemption does come and is sweet. The Anatomy of Exile, both timely and timeless, is a startlingly brave debut."—Chris Cander, bestselling author of *The Young of Other Animals*

"Zeeva Bukai has written a gorgeous, soulful novel whose aching, mismatched characters limp bravely towards love even when it wounds them to the quick. But even more, she's written a portrait of Israel as a young country and reveals the enormous and even magnetic power this sacred ground exerts on those who call it home."—Yona Zeldis McDonough, Fiction Editor, *Lilith Magazine*

"Propulsive and gorgeously written. With meticulous observation that misses nothing, Zeeva Bukai brings to life two worlds and a family torn between them. What is home? Who are we when the ground shifts beneath us? How can we sustain love and hope in the face of betrayal? A richly textured novel brimming with insight and compassion. I was riveted from the first page."—Joan Leegant, author of *Displaced Persons*

"All the more impressive when considering that The Anatomy of Exile is author Zeeva Bukai's debut as a novelist, this is an original, fascinating, deftly crafted novel."—*Midwest Book Review*

"A tight plot woven with complicated moral questions faced by characters willing to confront their circumstances creates a novel that's impossible to put down."—*The New York Journal of Books*

"Its characterizations nuanced and complicated, the novel reflects deep cultural mores and customs from both Palestinian and Israeli cultures. . . .How history is dealt with in the present matters in The Anatomy of Exile, a novel that lays bare human complexities with tentative, wistful hope."—*Foreword Reviews*

THE ANATOMY OF EXILE

A NOVEL

ZEEVA BUKAI

DELPHINIUM BOOKS

THE ANATOMY OF EXILE

Library of Congress Cataloguing-in-Publication Data is
available on request.
ISBN 978-1-953002-66-2

First paperback edition: January 2026

Jacket and interior design by Colin Dockrill, AIGA

For Levi, Shoshi, and Becca

In memory of Rose and Shlomo Bukai, and Yulia Michry Bukai

Part I

ABANDONMENT

One

Tel Aviv, 1967

They were on the beach when they heard the news of Hadas's death. It came over the transistor radio. Her name cut through the surf and salted air that swelled with the gleeful cries of children and ice cream vendors hawking their wares. Salim sank to his knees as the lifeguard's whistle cautioned swimmers to stay close to shore. Tamar drew circles of comfort on her husband's shoulders and whispered that it couldn't be his sister who'd been killed on the bus from Haifa to Tel Aviv.

In a daze, they gathered their things, her feet burning as she stumbled after him. They ran past the water spigot and outdoor showers, stopped to slip on their sandals, and lost their towels along the way. They crossed against the light on Ben Yehuda Street. Cars stopped, drivers cursed and shook their fists at them. They charged through the afternoon heat, their breath loud in their ears.

Salim was the first to reach their apartment on Frug Street; Tamar was close behind. He tried inserting the key into the lock, but it fell from his hands. She bent to retrieve it and fought the urge to glide her hands up over his body, if only to remind him that they were alive. She opened the door and he staggered ahead. The rooms were dim, light beading through the closed jalousies. They didn't speak. They didn't strip out of their damp bathing suits or comb their matted hair. He thrust his legs into a pair of trousers and set off for the police station. She watched him from the balcony, his figure receding, and wanted to call him back, afraid he'd disappear like Hadas. When he was gone, she sought the strip of horizon between the Bauhaus buildings, the fresh scar that separated blue sky from bluer sea, then cupped her hands over her ears and imagined waves tumbling onto the shore. She felt the weight of water, the motion of current, its rhythm a steady pulse. She saw Salim as he was that afternoon—powerful, sturdy as she wrapped her legs around his hips, his feet buried in silt, their kisses a gentle bumping of teeth and salty tongues. Their swim graceful as two seals, their laughter palpating the sky. She tried to recapture the moment before he adjusted the radio dial and then the beep signaling the hourly news, curdling the day like a spoon of vinegar in a cup of milk.

The children came home from camp. Their footsteps landing like firecrackers on the floor tiles. She had no idea what to tell them, how much to reveal, and decided to say nothing. To protect them. To protect herself from the impossible task of revealing that their beloved Aunt Hadas was dead. Ari and Rachel, six and seven, shouted, "Look, Ima," and held a replica of the Temple Mount in Jerusalem they'd built out of tongue depressors and bottle caps. Their hair black as Salim's, sticking to their sweaty faces, their expressions eager and insistent. Ruby, twelve, dove into her room and slammed the door behind her. *Did the driver have the radio on? Could she have heard?* Tamar worried. She wrapped her arms around Ari and Rachel, burrowed her face in their necks and kissed their cheeks until Ari squirmed and wiped his face where her lips had been.

"For you." Rachel held out the city.

"It's beautiful," Tamar said, lifting it in her hands, eyes stinging. "Where should I put it? Maybe on the table so Baba can see it when he comes home. You hungry? I'll get a snack."

She didn't wait for them to answer, merely brushed the hair out of Ari's eyes and walked into the kitchen, the cloud of their disappointment trailing behind her.

Everything was as it always was—the knife in the drawer, the bread in the basket. Someone had put the chocolate spread in the refrigerator again. Didn't they know the bread would tear if the chocolate was hard? Her chest ached. She took a deep breath then sliced the loaf.

"What's the matter with your sister?" She brought the snack tray out to the balcony, careful not to spill the milk.

Rachel shrugged. Ari was preoccupied with a new puzzle. There wasn't room for the tray. A crate of blocks was upended on the floor, a train set knocked on its side. The chaos a wall she couldn't scale. She placed the tray on a stool. "Don't forget to put those away"—she pointed to the blocks—"someone could get hurt."

"You all right, Ima?" Rachel asked as Tamar stepped into the living room.

Startled, Tamar straightened her back and forced a smile. "Of course."

"You've got sand on your face," Rachel said.

"I do?" Tamar said. "That's funny, I hadn't noticed." She looked at her reflection in the vitrine and saw the tangle of light-brown hair that had escaped the long braid, the deep-set brown eyes, and the Slavic cheekbones she'd inherited from her mother, along with the freckles that stretched across her nose. The full mouth seemed to bleed into the rest of her face. How, she wondered, could I look the same as I did this morning? She wiped the sand off. "I'm going to wash up. Thank you, Racheli," she said, and vanished into her bedroom, where she raked her scalp, dragging sand up under her nails, and tried to picture life without Hadas, her dearest friend, her sister-in-law, the family peacemaker, the party coordinator, the light they congregated around. Fifteen years ago, Hadas had introduced her to Salim and had been smoothing things over between them from the beginning, saying and doing things that made Tamar feel valued and wanted. Now Hadas was killed a month after the Six-Day War.

In the weeks leading up to June fifth, when the entire country feared it might not survive, she and Hadas had been inseparable. They shopped for food and necessities though the supermarket shelves were nearly empty, and the Carmel market stalls almost barren. She and Hadas dug trenches in Tel Aviv as part of the city's civil defense preparations. They volunteered at Tel-Hashomer Hospital, rolling bandages, preparing beds. They donated blood. As the war drew closer, the government stockpiled coffins, and rabbis sanctified parks as holy ground for emergency burials.

Each night after they put the kids to bed, she and Salim sat huddled on the sofa, listening to Radio Cairo.

"What are they saying?" she'd asked.

"They're going to annihilate us," he said.

Six nightmarish days of war and then it was over. The borders had shifted. The world had changed. After two thousand years of exile, Jerusalem was theirs again. They were humbled, awed, and triumphant. A month later, their bellies were still full of that triumph. They sang and danced in the Kings of Israel Square. Through it all, she'd been aware of Hadas's unease, the ambivalence of her joy coupled with her sorrow for a peace that would never be and, later, sympathy for those who had believed their leaders and thought this war would see them back in the villages they'd lost in 1948 as if nothing had occurred, the last nineteen years erased.

"Ruby." Tamar knocked on her daughter's bedroom door. She heard a muffled "Leave me alone."

"Please." She thought of Hadas's children, Tehila and Barak, and the air left her in a great whoosh. "Ruby!"

Her daughter snapped open the door, wearing only her camp shirt and a towel wrapped around her waist. Her wheat-colored hair loose around her shoulders. Her cheeks flushed.

"What happened?"

"I'm bleeding," Ruby snapped.

"What?"

"Down there."

Dumbly, she looked on the floor and saw the crumpled underwear spotted with blood. Overcome with relief and a surge of love, she pulled Ruby into her arms. For a moment her daughter returned the embrace. Then as if Ruby remembered she was now no longer a child, hands and elbows jabbing, she pulled away. "Ima, you're hurting me."

Tamar had no choice but to release her. "I'm sorry." She cupped Ruby's face. "There's nothing to worry about. Every woman, every girl . . ." She saw her daughter recoil and stopped talking. Her hands dropped to her sides. Six months ago, Ruby still sat on her lap. Now she considered all affection babyish and rolled her eyes at Tamar's mothering.

"Sorry," she repeated and thought, What bad timing for Ruby to shed her childhood.

"What do I do now?" Ruby asked, gnawing on her bottom lip.

"Come." She led her to the bathroom and opened the cabinet under the sink, pushed aside rolls of toilet paper. "Here are the pads. And here's the belt that holds them in place. Want me to show you how it's done?"

Ruby shook her head. "I can figure it out."

"Any pain?" She peered anxiously at Ruby, who shook her head, her face red with embarrassment.

"Tell me and I'll give you Acamol. Call if you need me."

"Where will you be?" Ruby asked.

"Right outside."

Tamar leaned on the jamb and waited.

Minutes later her daughter came out sporting a look of sheepish triumph.

"My beauty," Tamar said.

"Do I look different?"

"All grown up." Tamar kissed her cheek.

"That's what I thought but I wasn't sure."

"I'm proud of you for handling this so well."

"I'm starving," Ruby said.

Tamar blinked at the quick shift in conversation. "Sandwiches are on the balcony, if your brother and sister haven't finished them all."

"Pigs," Ruby cried, and dashed off.

All afternoon she waited for Salim, running to the peephole whenever she heard someone on the stairs, startling at every sound, distracted and unable to focus on the children. Ari tried to make a game of scaring her by popping out from behind the sofa, screeching as if he'd caught his hand in the door. She finally marched him into the bedroom he shared with Rachel. When evening fell, she heated chicken stew and cut a vegetable salad. She set the table and wondered whether Salim would have an appetite. Her own had vanished. She packed extra food to bring to Hadas's husband, Moti, and the children, and remembered their weekly get-together was scheduled for that night. It was to have passed in easy camaraderie, she and Hadas discussing the kids, the latest book they'd read, a recent scandal. Salim and Moti arguing politics. They often played backgammon and listened to Israeli folk music. Hadas loved to sing and would urge them to join in. When Tamar sang,

8

her voice bell-like, everyone stopped to listen. Salim would smile at her in a way that made her heart skip. The children would clap. She'd grip Hadas's hand in gratitude, knowing her sister-in-law had given her that moment to shine.

Salim came home. His face ashen. "It's really her. My sister." The crack in his voice was a canyon of grief.

She pressed her cheek to his chest, her mind overrun by images of Hadas. Just yesterday they were in Café Casit, the place packed, Édith Piaf bursting from the record player. They drank cappuccino, Hadas smoked a cigarette, staring out at the crowd on Dizengoff Street, her face pale and shuttered.

Tamar leaned across the table. "Is everything all right?"

"I'm sick of Piaf," Hadas said as she ground her cigarette in the ashtray, then gave a tight smile. "Let's get out of here, see a movie. I feel like sitting in a cool dark place where no one knows us, gorging on chocolates. Doesn't that sound lovely? Chocolate and anonymity."

"Sounds like the title of a French film," Tamar said, hoping to lighten the mood, but Hadas was already up on her feet, smoothing the front of her skirt.

They paid the bill and moments later walked arm in arm down the street toward the Chen Cinema.

Now Tamar held Salim in her arms, her body absorbing the hurt until he broke away. She felt something small and fragile collapse between them. After he showered, she spooned stew onto his plate. He hadn't eaten all day and now dipped and lifted his fork mechanically, dragging strips of pita through gravy. His eyes focused on a point beyond her.

"Want more?" she asked when his dish was empty.

He looked at her as though she'd jerked him out of a stupor.

"What did the police say?"

He shook his head, his expression grim, his mouth working as if he were scraping the words up out of a well. "Bullet in the chest, close range."

"Oh, Salim, I'm so sorry." She squeezed his hand. "Is there any information on the killer?"

He took a shuddering breath, "Not yet," and lit a cigarette. "Moti was with me." In the glow of the fluorescent light, his face had a greenish under-the-sea pallor.

"How is he?"

"Devastated." He passed the cigarette to her.

She took a drag then returned it to him, comforted by the intimate ritual they'd developed early on in their marriage of a shared cigarette after the evening meal. Laughter drifted past their window. She removed the plates from the table and wiped down the counter. Their neighbor, Pinchas, called to his wife, Shula. "Keys," he bellowed from the street. A moment later the keys crashed to the pavement.

Tamar filled the *finjan* with water and measured out Turkish coffee and sugar, removing the pot from the stove before the coffee came to a boil. Hadas had taught her to make it strong and sweet the way Salim liked it. She knew nothing about Levantine cuisine when she married. The tastes in her family ran toward European fare like schnitzel and stuffed cabbage. Hadas had proven a good teacher and a great friend. One Rosh Hashanah over a mound of minced beef and sheets of puff pastry, Hadas spoke of their exile from Syria to British Mandate Palestine. In 1944, she and Salim were smuggled across the Golan Heights by the British Jewish Brigade. Salim was ten, Hadas was eight. At first, they were placed on a kibbutz in the Galilee where no one spoke Arabic so they would learn Hebrew. A year later when their parents arrived, the government settled the family in a bungalow in south Tel Aviv where everyone spoke Arabic. In Damascus, Salim fought boys who'd called him *yahudi maloun*, a dirty Jew, and in Israel, *aravi masriach*, a stinking Arab. Sometimes when they were in bed, he'd caress her and say how lucky she was to have been born in Israel, to have Polish parents and milk-white skin.

"No one would ever mistake you for an Arab," he'd say. "You open your mouth, and everyone knows you're a Sabra. You belong."

"So do you," Tamar said.

"Not like you."

On a subterranean level she understood what he said was true, and yet she couldn't help feeling a sense of failure and something else she couldn't reconcile or even admit to, resentment that the home they'd created together wasn't enough to give him a sense of belonging. She knew he loved her. Not only did he tell her so, but his daily attentions were always passionate and tender. Loving him gave her purpose and alleviated the isolation and loneliness she'd felt after her father died. That she couldn't do the same for him troubled her. The only person who gave Salim the profound sense of belonging he needed was Hadas. It was evident when they spoke Arabic together, listened to the Mizrachi music the vendors in the souk played. It was in how they finished each other's sentences and in the undercurrent that passed between them when they experienced a slight or insult in a government office, a bank, or hotel, things Tamar wasn't aware of. Even now she could feel his separateness in the way he held himself, head high, back straight, braced as if waiting for the next blow. With Hadas gone, she could only hope he'd turn to her and the children more.

As she poured the Turkish coffee into a glass, it struck her that from now on she'd prepare the holiday meals alone. There'd be no more laughter while she and Hadas stuffed grape leaves and baked rose-flavored pastries. Hadas's hand delicate and sure, her praise welcome, a balm that stilled Tamar's self-doubt.

They decided to wait until morning to tell the kids about Hadas.

"Tonight, we'll let them sleep like children," Salim said. She fed them their dinner.

Ruby asked, "When are Tehila and Barak coming over?"

Tamar blanched. "They aren't. Moti has to work late."

"That's not fair," Rachel said.

"No, it's not," Tamar replied.

After they ate and played a game of cards, she made sure Ari and Rachel showered, tucked them into bed, then checked on Ruby.

"Aren't you late for the Scout meeting? It started half an hour ago."

Ruby sat at her desk, head bowed, reading. "I'm not going."

"Why not?"

"Everyone will know about me. Meira will tell them."

"How does Meira know?"

"She found me in the bathroom. I hate her." Ruby's voice climbed. "She can never keep a secret. What a *jorah* she has."

"Sshh, that isn't nice talk."

The lamp threw a fist-sized orb on the wall. Footsteps echoed on the street, and in the distance the sea grazed the shore. "All right, *mitukah*." If it were any other day, she would've encouraged her to go to the Scout meeting and make light of Meira's loose tongue. She'd have said the girls who hadn't begun menstruating were envious, but she couldn't summon the energy it would take to persuade her. There was still the funeral to arrange, Hadas's children and husband to visit. Maybe it was time Ruby learned to stand up for herself and confront girls like Meira. Seeing Ruby's confusion, she knew she'd disappointed her for not insisting she attend the meeting.

Like most of their neighbors, they had no telephone in their apartment. She used the public pay phone on the corner and was surprised at how easy it was to make the necessary arrangements. The police had already released the body to the burial society. Two phone calls and everything was taken care of. The funeral was scheduled for tomorrow afternoon, a graveside service at 3:00 p.m. at the Kiryat Shaul Cemetery in northern Tel Aviv. For a few more lira they would post an obituary in the advertisement columns throughout the city, informing people of Hadas's passing, place of burial, and shiva hours. How much easier it was to die here than to live, she thought.

She walked the few blocks to Hadas's apartment, carrying the containers of food she'd prepared earlier. The evening was warm. A breeze rustled the ficus trees that lined the boulevard and lifted the hair off her face. She'd forgotten to tie it back and enjoyed the sense of freedom it gave her. Dizengoff Street was crowded. Vendors sold warm peanuts and spiced chickpeas in paper cones. People sat in outdoor cafés drinking iced coffee and eating Bavarian cream. A middle-aged woman took out a compact and applied lipstick, a young couple kissed. Men whistled at girls in miniskirts. Soldiers made their way home, rifles hanging off their shoulders. Cars honked and Vespas with sidecars wove in and out of narrow lanes. The street throbbed with life.

The temperature was cooler under the sycamore trees, whose air roots dangled like swing ropes. She turned right onto King Solomon Street and smelled the jasmine that grew in the front gardens of the buildings and looked up to find window boxes overgrown with dahlias and petunias. She loved this block. Like Frug Street, it was built in the 1930s when Tel Aviv was new and the most modern city in the world. She entered Hadas's building and pressed the timed light switch in the hall, taking the stairs two at a time to the second floor, straining to reach the apartment before the lights went out. She gave a soft knock, not wanting to wake her nephew, Barak.

Tehila opened the door, her face half hidden behind a curtain of dark hair. Tamar pulled her into her arms, kissing both cheeks. "How are you?" She felt the girl stiffen.

"Abba's sleeping; he took a pill."

"Where's Barak?" Tamar asked, walking into the kitchen with its spring-green cabinets and white Formica countertop. She placed the food containers in the refrigerator.

"Next door with his friend, Ido. He's spending the night there."

"Want to come home with me? Ruby would love it if you did. We haven't told her yet; we can do it together."

"Abba needs me here," Tehila said.

Tamar felt a pang. Tehila was only thirteen and yet hours after Hadas's death, she was already consigned to the role of little mother. Moti would accept the child's efforts without question, believing it his due. For that matter, so would Salim. Tamar planned to do all she could to help Tehila. She prayed she'd live a long life so Ruby and Rachel wouldn't have to serve their father, clean his house, wash his clothes, prepare his meals like little wives. With Hadas gone, her daughter was expected to step into the role of housemaid until she found a husband and even then, Moti would continue to rely on her, unless he remarried. After all, he was only thirty-nine, a few years older than Salim, and still a handsome man.

"I'll just be a minute," Tamar said. "I need to leave your father information about tomorrow. Have you got paper and pen?"

Tehila retrieved a pad from a kitchen drawer. "I'll see he gets it in the morning."

"You're a good girl. Can I fix you something to eat?"

Tehila's eyes filled. "Ima cooked dinner before she left this morning, but I can't eat it, and I can't throw it out. I put it in the freezer."

Tamar hugged her again, frustrated she wasn't able to give her something more substantial, and though Tehila relaxed this time and even allowed Tamar to rock her from side to side, she felt the shame of her own inadequacy. All day she'd had the feeling of not being enough, of not having enough to give to meet the moment. She tried to shake it off, telling herself that it was natural under the circumstances and that she just had to work harder to make up for the loss of her sister-in-law, but a part of her was already retreating to a safe distance, something Hadas would never have done. To Hadas, living life meant being fully engaged; for Tamar, it was enough to watch the pageantry from the sidelines, insulated and protected.

It was a little after ten when she arrived home. The apartment was dark and silent. She heard the kettle whistle in her neighbor's kitchen. Someone in the building had the radio on; an old song she and Hadas used to sing played. The soft hiss of car wheels on Frishman Street, the lonely strike of footsteps on the pavement below, felines caterwauling near the garbage bins; these were the sounds of home.

She found a copy of the preliminary police report on the table. Someone from the station must have dropped it off while she was out, a courtesy to Salim, who worked for the Israel Munitions Industry. She showered, wrapped herself in a towel, and brought the file with her into the bedroom so the kids wouldn't stumble upon it in the morning. Salim lay on his back, staring at the moon spilling through the jalousie. She dropped the towel and snuggled against him.

"I saw the report," she said.

"You read it?" He pulled her close.

"Not yet."

"She wasn't killed in Haifa."

Cocooned in his arms she said, "But that's where she went. To visit cousin Badriya."

"It's not where she died."

"The radio said she was on the bus from Haifa. Didn't it happen on the bus?" She felt his heart pounding and with trepidation asked, "Where?"

He didn't answer.

"Salim?"

"Kafr Ma'an."

Her breath seized at the mention of the Arab village on the outskirts of northern Tel Aviv; she, Salim, and Hadas had lived there more than a decade ago. Ruby was born in Kafr Ma'an.

"That's not possible. The place is deserted, has been for years."

"Police think the killer might have been a resident before the village was abandoned in '48."

Her heart sank. "Have they caught him?"

Salim turned to face the window. "He's dead. Shot himself after he killed her."

Tamar gasped. "Why did he do that?"

"*Majnoon.* He was crazy."

She twisted the sheet in both hands. A headache pulsed behind her eyes. Something was rushing at her, some thought-image she didn't want to see, something she needed to draw a curtain over.

Salim closed his eyes. "What was she doing there?"

"I don't know." She switched on the beside lamp, the lie bitter in her mouth, and lit a cigarette. She took a deep drag and passed it to him. "What do we do now?"

"Nothing." Salim aimed an arrow of smoke toward the ceiling. "It's done."

Two

She was sixteen the first time she heard the name *Kafr Ma'an*. She hadn't known the village existed until she visited Salim and Hadas there. The three had met earlier that summer on Kibbutz Ein Gev, on the shores of the Sea of Galilee. Her scout group was there to pick bananas for export and to meet the volunteers. Hadas was one of those volunteers. Salim was a new army recruit and part of the security detail. She remembered the moment he got off the bus, the way sunlight clung to his hair, turning the black almost blue, the sharp planes of his cheeks, the lean jaw, the hawkish nose, and the warm tone of his skin. She had never thought much about anyone getting off a bus before, or how that moment could upend everything she knew to be true until he descended the stairs with Hadas. A week later, Hadas's invitation to a Shabbat lunch on Kafr Ma'an felt almost inevitable, fated.

Her first impression of the village was that of a dilapidated Eden. Groves of citrus trees heavy with unripened fruit perfumed the air. The stone houses were old and rundown, gardens overrun by weeds.

She said, "How is it that I've lived my whole life in Tel Aviv and have never been here before?"

Salim, painfully handsome in his Shabbat attire, said, "It isn't surprising. All your life you were taught Arabs were dangerous, especially to good Ashkenazi girls like you."

Tamar was shaken, unsure if he was insulting her or speaking what he thought was true.

He reached up, plucked an orange from the tree, and tore it open with his fingers, then offered her a section. When she didn't take it right away, he brought it to her mouth and waited for her lips to close around it, watching as she did so. He then offered a piece to Hadas and took the last for himself before discarding the peel on the ground. He removed a handkerchief from his pocket and wiped Tamar's chin clean. She stood there unmoving when everything in and around her shimmered. That afternoon he would remind her that he and Hadas were Mizrahi Jews from Arab lands and she was not. She didn't know whether he was laughing at her or warning her off, whether he was treating her like a child or a potential lover. She wished she had more experience in these matters and envied Hadas, who seemed confident and unruffled by men. On the kibbutz, Tamar had observed her indifference when young men tried to gain her attention. Instead, Hadas threaded her arm through hers and they simply walked away. Tamar was astonished and grateful Hadas had chosen to befriend her. But it was here in the village that she appeared most at home, her beauty almost incandescent as she filled a basket with oranges, sprigs of rosemary, and wild thyme.

Hoping to make a worldlier impression, Tamar said, "My father had a close Arab friend, a journalist from Jaffa. He and his wife used to come for dinner. But that was before the war in '48. I think they live in Beirut now. When did the villagers leave?"

"March thirtieth that same year," Salim said.

She could still taste the orange on her tongue and feel the gentleness of his touch where he'd wiped the juice from her chin. They stepped onto a dirt road that led to the Yarkon

River, where eucalyptus trees lined the banks, their leaves sweeping the ground, stirring up wheels of dust.

"I'm impressed by your accuracy," she said. "That was six weeks before the War of Independence." Tall rosemary bushes flanked the path before giving way to a field of thistles.

"Now I'm impressed." He took her hand and smiled in a way that filled her with a sad longing because she couldn't imagine someone like him finding her impressive. He was, she thought, humoring her, flirting with her as a way to pass the time.

"Where did they go?" She prayed her hands wouldn't perspire and hoped he wouldn't think her too naive. She had worn her best summer skirt with the eyelet hem and red tricot blouse, which always made her feel just a bit older and more cosmopolitan. She'd copied the outfit from a two-year-old *Cinemonde*, a French movie magazine her mother had.

"Jordan mostly," he said, "Qalqilya, the West Bank."

If she was lucky, the Shabbat afternoon would continue its slow inexorable unwinding, stretching the hours well into sunset. Maybe he would even take her home. "What made them leave?"

"We did. They were afraid we'd slaughter them."

"Us?" she said, shocked.

"Yeah." He dropped her hand and kicked a stone down the path.

She gave her palms a furtive swipe on her skirt, mortified to find them moist.

"Some nights we see them in the *pardes*," Hadas said.

Tamar silently thanked her for steering the conversation in another direction. "Who?" They were almost at the Yarkon River. She could smell the ripe vegetation along the banks.

Hadas turned back to peer into the citrus trees as if she imagined someone there. "Villagers, their relatives."

"Really? Doesn't that scare you?"

"They come for oranges, not for us," Salim said.

Tamar bowed her head.

Hadas squeezed her shoulder. "Don't pay attention to him," she said. "He's a bear when he hasn't had his Shabbat nap."

"Oh God. I'm sorry. I've overstayed. I'll leave now."

"Please don't," Salim said, staring over her head at Hadas with an expression Tamar couldn't read. "My sister's being obnoxious."

Hadas laughed. "You see, I knew it. He doesn't want you to go, no matter how rude he is."

"Was I rude? I didn't mean to be. Forgive me." He kissed Tamar's cheek. "Now you have to stay."

Flustered by his attention, she hoped to put the moment behind them and pointed to an asphodel growing in the weeds. "My favorite. So how did you come to live here?"

"After the war in '48," Hadas said, "the village was empty, so the government settled two hundred Jewish families here. Mizrahi Jews mostly. There's a beautiful poetry collection about this place called *Scenes from a Village*. Every poem feels like it's about us, immediate and alive." She crushed a sprig of rosemary between her fingers. "I'd lend it to you, but it's in Arabic."

How was it, she wondered, that Hadas only two years older seemed so much more sophisticated than her, and Salim was already a man? She knew boys in the army who weren't any different than they'd been in high school, except now they drove tanks and carried rifles. Tamar struggled not to feel like a child around them. Salim had been eyeing her all afternoon as if her visit were a test of some kind, one she seemed to be failing.

Hadas continued, "The government planted us here like trees."

Tamar cocked her head. "Oh?"

"For the same reason they destroyed the wells, so the villagers wouldn't return. Wasn't that smart of them?" Hadas said, her eyes filled with tears. She walked on ahead.

"Is she all right?" Tamar asked Salim.

"Yeah. She gets emotional about these things." He watched his sister reach the river.

On Tamar's seventeenth birthday, Salim proposed. They broke the news to her mother, Miriam. Miriam pulled her aside and said, "Are you sure this is what you want?" and then whispered, "I thought he'd be out of your life by now. You're killing me with this *Arabische Yid.*"

Salim overheard her. He lit a cigarette and passed it to Tamar, who had never smoked in front of her mother before. "Sorry you feel that way," he said then went to her father's liquor cabinet, untouched since his death, and poured three glasses of Stock 84 whiskey. "How about a *le'chaim,*" he said.

"I'm sorry. I can't give this union my blessing. She's too young." Miriam retreated into her bedroom.

Tamar and Salim drank the whiskey on the balcony in silence. She moved out of her mother's house that night and into Salim's, upset when Miriam refused to say goodbye. By then, Hadas was a soldier working at the Tel-Hashomer base, home every night on Kafr Ma'an. Dressed in uniform, she welcomed Tamar with a pot of white asphodel. The flowers looked like stars when they bloomed. The house was old and in disrepair, the roof leaked in one corner of the living room, and the plaster peeled in the bedrooms, but she loved it. She loved that their windows faced the *pardes* and that the scent of orange blossoms filled the house each spring. She loved the

22

lemon tree in their garden and the village's winding streets and alleys, where stray dogs hid from the sun. Each Passover, Hadas painted their front door blue to ward off the evil eye. During the week, Salim was stationed in Beersheva, and for the first time, Tamar knew what it was like to have a sister, someone to confide in and for someone to confide in her. She held on to that closeness and, like the asphodel, felt herself blooming.

Each morning she and Hadas breakfasted together. They drank coffee and ate oranges. Hadas's hair hung down her back, an umbra of kohl beneath her sleepy eyes, a pack of Noblesse on the table, and a cigarette burning in the ashtray.

"I dreamed about them," she'd say. "The family here before us." Sometimes she'd bring out the box with the things they'd left behind. A brass bowl used for shaving, a mortar and pestle for grinding spices, two infant pillows, one with the name *Daoud* embroidered in blue letters across it, the other *Amir*, and a photograph of two young men, one tall with wide dark eyes, the other inches shorter, but handsomer, wearing a *keffiyeh*. They stood against the lemon tree, arms folded across their chests, grinning at the camera. Hadas said each item told a story.

"This was for Daoud, the eldest child. That's his younger brother, Amir." She pointed to the shorter of the two in the photo. "Daoud's favorite season is winter. He loves the harvest and the rain. When he was nine, he stole his neighbor's horse and rode all the way to Yaffa to buy a gift for his mother."

"You sure you don't know him?" Tamar teased.

Hadas turned away to tuck the items back into the box. "Of course not."

"It's unhealthy to dwell on the villagers, to create a biography for people you've never met and will never know," Tamar said.

"You're wrong. We have to remember them."

"Why? We don't know them."

Hadas turned the cup of Turkish coffee over to read her fortune in the grounds. "Because without them, we wouldn't be here. This place wouldn't exist." She put the dishes in the sink. "I hope the family living in our house in Damascus found the spot where Salim and I wrote our names. I hope they didn't erase them, if only to remember that we were there first, that our family had lived in that house long before they did, and that a portion of it would always remain ours, even if it was only the dirt under their feet. We were the giants beneath them."

"But we're here now," Tamar said. "And that's good, isn't it?"

"Yes, that's good," Hadas replied.

On cool December nights when the ground was dry and the moon shone, a handful of villagers returned to harvest what was left of their fruit.

"It's them." Salim pointed into the darkness.

They brought their children. They carried ladders, wooden crates, and pruning shears. They ate beneath the trees. They fed each other oranges. Their words carried on the wind.

"What are they saying?" Tamar asked.

"Remember this sweetness," Hadas said.

Something in her voice made Tamar turn toward her; her face was alight with longing.

The villagers rubbed their hands in the dirt, sniffed the rich soil, wiping it on their vests and pant legs, carrying back a little bit of the earth they'd lost. Come dawn, they disappeared like ghosts in the morning fog.

Three

They told the children about Hadas after breakfast, giving them only the vaguest descriptions: *Killed. Yes, he's dead too.* They didn't tell them what was in the police report, that Hadas had been on the 2:00 p.m. bus out of Haifa, where she'd visited cousin Badriya and had disembarked at the university stop, that she had walked into the ruins of Kafr Ma'an, or that it was a couple with their dog who found her and the gunman in the garden of the old stone house with the blue door. Not even Ruby, who always demanded the minute details of a story requested more information. They didn't want to contemplate what her final thoughts were, or how long it took for her to die, or what loss meant, how it was an acid that ate through stone, or a frozen sea cracking under the weight of a pebble. It was enough to know Hadas was gone.

That afternoon they dressed in somber clothing. Ari complained his shoes pinched his feet. "I'm sorry, Arush." She tucked his shirttails into his pants. "You can't wear your sandals to the cemetery, but I promise you can put them on later."

Rachel wanted to pin a flower to her hair in honor of Hadas.

"Cheli, you look beautiful, but I'm afraid the bees will think so too. What if you get stung? Put it in a cup of water. I'm sure Hadas will understand."

Ruby's eyes were bruised from crying. She wanted to be with Tehila.

"Turn around so I can zip your dress," Tamar said. "This will be a difficult day for Tehila and she'll probably need to take care of Barak."

"Which is why I should be with her," Ruby cried.

"You will be when we get there, and later at the shiva. She'll need you most then." Tamar kissed her. "And Baba will need us today too," she said. "We need to be here for him." After tending to them, getting them out the door, knowing Salim waited impatiently downstairs in a borrowed car, she could feel the rage bleeding into her sorrow. Her dear friend was dead; her sister lost to her.

The children were nervous. It was their first funeral. Salim barely said a word. His anxiety was a barrier between them. She recalled her father's funeral—the ominous strike of the shovel hitting the ground and the dull thud of earth falling onto his body. She had carried the finality of that moment with her until the day she met Salim, until Hadas had showed her that love and friendship made all things possible.

A crowd gathered at the cemetery. The sun swelled into the corners of the sky. Mourners wilted under it. Sweat stained their shirts and glistened on their faces. She and Salim greeted Badriya outside the gate. Salim's cousin was a petite woman. Her chestnut hair concealed beneath a green silk kerchief Hadas had given her on the birth of her baby. She cradled the child against her breast and refused to enter the cemetery, fearing the jealous dead would steal her son's soul. There was a feverish glow to her eyes. She called to Salim with a keening wail. He pulled her into his arms; the infant cocooned between them. They spoke in rapid Arabic, and Tamar felt a wave of loneliness wash through her. The first words he uttered all day were in a language she didn't understand. When he spoke Arabic with Hadas or Badriya, she felt like a foreigner, alien in her body, in her country. On this primal level they were unknowable, distant, hidden from her. *Salim was hidden from her.* She slipped her arm through his, and he withdrew from Badriya's embrace.

Prayers were said. She lost the thread of them. Her intention to remain calm scattered like dust when she saw Tehila and Barak. Hollow-eyed, they looked in disbelief at their mother's body wrapped in a *tallit*. Barak was nine and appeared unnaturally stoic. She wondered if he'd been coached to behave like a man, but just as it seemed he had control of himself, his face crumpled into tears, and Tehila, who appeared to have matured overnight, held him until he collected himself. Moti was a stone block in a folding chair. Salim had to lift him up for the Kaddish prayer and then he fell to his knees. Looking around her, she thought how much Hadas would've hated her funeral. Too solemn, too many people she didn't know, and too many she had disliked.

Grief was a terrain gutted and pocked. There didn't seem to be a solid place to put her feet. Everywhere Tamar looked, especially in the faces of her children and husband, there was Hadas. She wept, but Salim remained dry-eyed throughout the seven days of mourning. The family sat on low stools, the mirrors were covered, friends and family arrived with platters of food and talked in hushed tones. Each day they prayed, imploring Hadas's soul to leave the house and rise to its new home.

A few nights after the shiva, she awoke to find Salim sobbing. The sound like a landslide, like trees torn out by their roots, and houses crumbling to the ground. He wept crouched on their bedroom floor. She tried to comfort him.

"Don't. Touch me. I'll break," he said.

It was nearly dawn when he came to bed. He lifted her nightgown and sank into her. His eyes were closed, his head turned aside as if he were listening for someone. She grabbed his hair in both fists and kissed him. Only then did he see her there beneath him, take her nightgown off, and sigh when her breasts pressed against his skin, the heat rising off their bodies, their movements slow, deliberate. Only then could he sleep, while she watched the morning light bleed into their bedroom.

In the aftermath of Hadas's death, she worried what would become of them. Though he apologized for it, Salim was quick to anger. He brooded. His mercurial moods frightened the children. They cried at every slight. At night while everyone slept, Tamar was assailed by images of Hadas. Hadas tending the garden in the stone house in Kafr Ma'an, running through the *pardes*, Hadas on the bus, gazing at the sea. In her mind, Tamar saw the bus arrive at the intersection of Derech Haifa and Rechov Ha Universita on the outskirts of Tel Aviv. She imagined Hadas descending, then crossing the street, her gait quick as she walked up the hill into Kafr Ma'an. She saw the man as Hadas saw him. His angular face, his dusty shoes, his white shirt torn. She greeted him but didn't see the gun until it was too late. Hadas with her dark-eyed beauty and skin the color of pale earth, the bullet tearing through her heart. How close he must have stood. Her mouth an O of surprise. "Kafr Ma'an," she said as if it were a prayer. "Kafr Ma'an," a sin.

She reread the police report and said to Salim, "What if that man recognized Hadas, knew she'd lived in the village, saw her in the *pardes*, and in the garden, wandering through the rooms of the house? Maybe he wanted revenge. What if they all do?"

"Who are you talking about?"

"The villagers."

"Don't be an idiot," Salim said. "There's no Kafr Ma'an, not anymore. Besides, when people abandon their homes, they get what they deserve."

"But you said they left because they thought their lives were in danger."

"What does it matter now?"

"Why would anyone leave their home?"

"Because they have no choice," he shouted, "because they have to go on living even when they lose everything."

She stroked his cheek. "Don't, *habibi*. Don't blame yourself. You couldn't have known she'd go to Kafr Ma'an when you asked her to visit Badriya. You couldn't have known what that man would do. No one could imagine it."

He sprang back as if she'd struck him. "I have to go. Moti's expecting me."

On the morning after the *shloshim*, the first thirty days of mourning, Salim shaved his bereavement beard. He ate a hearty breakfast and gathered her and the children in the living room. The sun shone on the balcony. Birds chirped and cars hissed by on Frishman Street.

"I've come to a decision," he said in the voice he used when he'd settled something in his mind and there was no turning back. "We're going to America, to New York City."

"What?"

"Five years, that's all I need." He hurried on. "I'm going to make so much money that when we return, we'll have enough to buy a car and a villa on the beach in Herzliya."

Ari and Rachel jumped up from the couch and shouted, "No, Baba!"

Ruby, stricken and pale, said, "I can't. I can't leave Tehila now. What about my friends, school?"

"Your father's joking." Tamar folded her arms across her chest.

"No. I'm not." He took Ruby's hand and sat her down beside him, then drew Rachel and Ari onto his lap. "I need you all to trust me now. I know this sounds hard and in the beginning it might be." He looked at Tamar. "But I promise you, America is going to be good for us. We're going to see things we'll never get to see here, things we cannot describe. Our country is so small and where we're going is so big. We'll have everything there we don't have here."

"Like what?" Ruby asked, her brow furrowed.

"Well, a telephone."

"In our house?" Rachel asked.

"Yes, and a television we can watch movies on in our own living room. We'll learn things, see things, meet all kinds of people, make new friends, and have adventures together. We'll go on a roller coaster and eat hamburgers." He turned to Ari. "You love to build skyscrapers, right?"

Ari nodded.

"In New York there are buildings so tall, they reach the clouds."

Ari's eyes grew wide. "Can we go in them?"

"Whenever we want," Salim said. "And for you, my little dancer"—he kissed the top of Rachel's head—"the best dance companies in the world are in New York, and if you work very hard, you can study with them."

"I've been practicing my twirl," she said, slipping off Salim's lap and lifting her arms into the air. "Want to see?"

"Very much."

Rachel spun until she tumbled onto the rug. Salim clapped and shouted, "Brava."

Then he turned to Ruby. "I love that you care about Te-hila and are thinking about what's good for her, but now we need to think about what's best for our family. We need this change." Ruby shook her head, eyes filling. "Yes, we do, *motek*. What happened to Hadas has made us all so sad, it's hard for us to laugh, to joke like we used to, to love each other like we used to. We have to make a change to protect our family."

Tamar felt the truth of his words.

He continued, "Ruby, before Hadas died, you told me you wanted to learn English, where better than in New York? You'll be fluent in a few months. By the end of five years, you'll all be reading and writing like Americans. Then when we come back, and you go to the army, they'll give you the best positions because of this experience. Afterwards, you'll be able to go to any university in the world. Everything will be open to you. Do you know how rare that is? How special it is to have this opportunity?"

"But what if we never come back?" Ruby wailed.

"Of course we'll come back," he said.

Tamar could see he'd given the children something to think about, maybe even to hope for. "Ruby, take the kids into your room. I want to talk to Baba alone."

She gestured for him to follow her into the kitchen and cleared the table of breakfast dishes.

"If you're worried that I won't get a job, I already have something lined up. Meet the new foreman of Eli Marcus Plastics in Brooklyn, New York City."

Tamar lowered her voice. "You're not thinking rationally. This is your grief talking."

"Rational? How rational is it for a woman to be shot dead in the middle of the day in the garden of the house she used to live in? Hasn't my sister's death taught you anything? People want to kill us here. For what? Land? A house? We can get that anywhere," he said. "We can get that in America."

"Sshh, you'll scare the children." She poured dish detergent onto a sponge.

"They're already scared. Haven't you noticed?"

"I don't think that's true. Did they tell you that?"

"They don't have to tell me. I see it in their faces and in yours. You want the truth? I'm frightened for them, for us."

"Five years, ten years won't bring Hadas back." She ran the water in the sink. He pulled her close. His hands kneading her full hips.

"You're right, *ayouni*." He spoke into her ear. "Nothing will change here except we'll have some distance and plenty of money."

"How can you think of leaving Moti and the kids? They need us now." She gripped the counter. "We need them."

"I've already spoken to Moti. He understands. Who do you think arranged the job for me? Wait and see, they'll follow us. He as much as told me. We'll all come back rich as Herod."

"Are you crazy? Hadas would never have agreed to this. I don't agree to it. Our life is here. This is our home, our country."

"This is your birthplace, not mine, not Hadas's. Think how much of our good life was due to my sister? She was the one who planned all the parties, the outings, the picnics. She held us together." He lit a cigarette and flung the matchstick into the sink.

"But she loved it here."

"I swear on her soul," he said, "five years and enough money to hold our heads up, then we'll come back home. You always wanted to live on the beach. I can give you that."

"We live a few blocks from the beach now."

"I mean a villa on the beach. Imagine it. Where the rich Ashkenazim live." He walked from one end of the kitchen to the other, excitement rolling off him. "Let me give this to you."

"But we don't know anyone in New York. What about the children? A new language, schools?" She was finding it hard to breathe.

"Like Hadas and I learned Hebrew, they'll learn English. With an American education, doors will open for them."

"Even if that's true—"

"They'll be kings and queens here," he interjected.

"What are you talking about? When has that ever mattered to us? We want them healthy, happy, and living here where they belong in their own land. That's what we've always said." She opened the refrigerator and stared at the contents, blinking at the brightness, noting how orderly everything was.

He gave the door a gentle shove. "Tamar," he said, and turned her around. "We have to get out of here."

"You mean you have to," she shot back.

"I'm sorry."

"I'm not leaving our home because your sister died. What you're asking is too much."

"Don't you get it?" He leaned toward her. "We're standing on piles of the dead. My sister's just one more casualty. There'll be others. More innocents in the fields, on buses, in the markets. And the wars, Tamar; they won't stop."

He was so close, she could see the frayed veins in his eyes. Cornered, she said, "What are we, Arabs now? Superstition is going to rule what we do? For that, you want to ruin our lives?"

He shook his head at her. "You forget, I'm an Arab, a Mizrahi. So was my sister."

For the first time in their married life, he looked at her with disgust.

"I didn't mean it. I didn't. I'm sorry."

He picked up his wallet and cigarettes and, without another word, left the house.

She ran to the door. "Salim." His name echoed through the halls.

Four

That night, in a kind of stupor, she fed the kids their dinner. The children fought. She couldn't recall why. Words dropped like pins around her. Ari and Rachel wanted her to mediate their argument, something about the height of the Empire State Building. All she could muster was a vague nod and sent them to bed. Her usual inspection of brushed teeth and clean faces forgotten. She made a half-hearted attempt to tuck them in. When they asked for a story, she stared at them like a hostage, hoping they'd release her. Rachel, always sensitive to her mother's moods, said, "I'll do it, Ima."

She kissed their cheeks, smelled the day's sweat on them, and sighed. They hadn't showered.

She waited for Salim on the balcony. At ten o'clock, people milled out of the Cameri Theatre on the corner of Dizengoff Street. Their laughter rose into the trees. After midnight, she heard the footfalls of a handful of pedestrians going home. There was the gush of a faucet next door, the turning off of a radio on the floor above and then silence. Shades of night went from light to dark to light again. Streetlamps extinguished at the first hint of dawn.

She never realized how raucous birds were, how they swooped in and out of trees like fighter pilots, or the way the sky turned purple before the moon slid into the horizon and in its place rose a blushing sun, or how palm trees stood like giants at a gathering. At six, the garbage trucks groaned to a stop in front of the building, followed by the crash of bins and the stench of yesterday's trash heaving off the curb. Six forty, the junk merchant's wagon plodded down the road. *Alti zachen*, he cried.

The sleepless night left her jittery. She prepared breakfast for the kids before they went off to camp. Ruby was on her way to a weekend in the Ein Gedi Nature Reserve near the Dead Sea. Tamar, glad to have something to do, filled a dozen pitas with tomato slices and yellow cheese for Ruby's scout group. She kissed the children goodbye and held on to them until they sensed something amiss and struggled out of her arms. Ari asked where Salim was.

"Work," she said.

"So early?" Rachel asked.

"Yes. See you later." She shooed them out the door, then charged through the apartment, wiping down cabinets and washing floors and countertops, before pausing at her bedroom, the empty bed a silent accusation. She whipped through the closet, tossing out Salim's clothes. Thoroughly spent, she crawled into bed and pulled his garments over her before succumbing to sleep.

Like in some prophetic dream, she woke midmorning with the image of him reclining on Hadas's balcony. She splashed cold water on her face and bolted out the door. By the time she reached Moti's apartment, sweat and a sharp odor emerged from under her arms. She hoped she wouldn't offend anyone but needn't have worried. Moti answered her knock, his white button-down untucked, his hair on end. The mourning beard, which he hadn't yet shaved, the color of an oil spill.

"What happened?" He blinked into the dim hallway.

"Nothing, I was passing by."

Moti leaned against the doorjamb, leaving enough room for her to peer into the living room. Laundry and bedding piled on the sofa. She wondered if he was sleeping there. Knowing well the loneliness of an empty bed, she couldn't blame him.

"Is Salim here?"

He closed his eyes. "No one's here."

"Moti." She laid a commiserating hand on his forearm. "One day you'll recover. We all will."

He shook his head at the impossibility of it. "If I see Salim . . ."

She turned to leave. Her palm hovered over the light switch. Should she press it now before descending the stairs, so as not to get caught in the dark?

"Don't let him take you to America. You'll never come back."

She gripped her handbag. "We will. He promised. Five years."

"Promised?" He laughed until his eyes welled. She wondered if she ought to call someone. He had a brother in Bat Yam. "Hadas made promises too. She promised we'd have another child. She promised we'd take a vacation abroad. She promised to come home after I asked her not to go. 'Badriya will be fine without you,' I said, 'and if it's so important, I'll drive you on the weekend. The bank gave me a new car.'"

"Oh, Moti."

He rubbed his eyes with the heel of his hand. "You know how she is when she gets an idea in her head."

Tamar nodded, an ache in her chest; he still spoke of Hadas in the present tense.

"Remember the Arabic literature course she took at the University?"

"Yes." She wished he'd stop talking so she could leave.

36

"Then the archeology class at the Eretz Museum, and something called the Alexander Technique that I never understood, at the Kibbutz Seminary."

"But that's what we loved. Her curiosity, her appetite for life."

"Every other week she'd disappear all day, and then the next, and the next. 'Where were you?' I'd say, 'A husband has a right to know.'" His gaze stumbled over her face, landed, flitted again. "'Kafr Ma'an,' she'd say. What did she call it? *Kfar shedim, kfar gagooim*, village of ghosts, village of longing." He swayed on his feet.

"Have you eaten today?" She worried he'd fall. He was too heavy for her to pick up alone.

"'Someone has to remember the village before it disappears.' That's what she said. Now she's gone and what's left of that shithole is still there."

"Moti."

"I'll tell Salim you were here." He shut the door.

The hall light flickered then died. She stood in the dark for a long time before pressing the switch.

Two days and still no word from Salim. They were never apart, except during his annual reserve duty and more recently in the June war. His absence felt like mourning: no appetite, reels of disaster in her head—Salim in a hit-and-run wounded on the side of the road, Salim drowning in the sea, Salim hiking in the desert and falling into a ravine. Salim, Salim, Salim. She ran to the police station. People stared at her as if she were mad, running in the August heat.

The officer on Hadas's case took pity on her and checked the files to see if anyone meeting Salim's description had been arrested or was in an accident. He had the receptionist call the local hospitals and nearby precincts. When she was told that no one named Salim Abadi had been brought in, she sank into a chair, weak with relief that he wasn't injured or dead.

"Give him time. Your man has had a shock." He gave her a glass of water and watched her drink.

She wiped her mouth on the small handkerchief she kept in her bag. Except for two policemen talking near the open window, there was no one else in the room.

"I'm glad you came in," he said. "Maybe you can shed light on this." He slid a picture of Hadas across his desk. The telephone rang and the receptionist answered. A ceiling fan churned.

She touched the corner of the passport-size photo. "Did Salim give this to you?"

"No."

"We have one just like it. Years old." She turned the picture over and saw the photographer's seal on the back and then the inscription in Arabic below. The color left her face, and she slipped her hands into her lap.

"Do you know what those Arabic words mean?" he asked.

"No."

"'For eternity,'" he said.

She emptied her face of expression. "Must be Moti's."

"I don't think so." His eyes clung to hers.

Barely above a whisper, she said, "Where did you get it?" But she already knew.

He leaned back. The blue crocheted *kippah* with the white Star of David in the center slid forward, catching on his ginger hair. "The gunman's wallet."

"I don't understand." She gripped the arms of the chair. "Why would he have it?"

He offered her a cigarette from the pack on his desk. She declined with a tight smile. He took a lighter out of his shirt pocket and snapped it open.

"I hoped you'd enlighten me," he said, drawing on the cigarette, peering at her through a haze of smoke.

"Me?" She plucked at a thread on her skirt. "I don't know anything."

"Weren't you close to her?"

"Very. She was a fine person."

"I never meant to suggest otherwise." He wrote his name and the station's telephone number on a sheet of paper, smoke curling round his fingers. "If you think of anything."

"Detective Dani Itai?" she read.

"Your sister-in-law's case was classified as a terror attack, a suicide mission. Jewish woman comes upon a Muslim man in an abandoned village, a vagrant. Maybe he panicked and so he shot her. Maybe she caught him stealing or digging something up, and so he shot her. But why shoot himself? If this really was a suicide mission, he'd have gone into the Carmel souk or the central bus station and killed two dozen people. What was she doing there? Why did he kill her? There was no sign of a struggle, no robbery, nothing that would suggest rape. And that picture"—he pursed his lips—"speaks of something else. Don't you think?"

She took a sip of water. "Couldn't he have taken it out of her wallet after he killed her?"

"And then put it in his own and follow that with a bullet in his head?"

"I guess not."

He tapped the lighter on the desk. "Did they know each other?" The question pinned her to the chair.

She blinked. "What?"

"Did she know him?"

"How could she?"

"That's the question, isn't it? He's from the West Bank, here illegally, no work permit, and she's married to a bank

39

manager in Tel Aviv." He slapped his hand on the desk, startling her. "It can't be, but it makes me curious. Was she a target?"

"A target?" She clutched her purse. He held her gaze and she forced herself to relax, even to smile, though she wondered if she looked as hideous as she felt. "Aren't we all targets? I mean we're at war and there have been so many attacks. Men infiltrating across the Syrian and Lebanese borders, and now from the West Bank. Believe me, I'd tell you if I knew anything." She traced her sister-in-law's face with a fingertip.

"She was a beautiful woman," Detective Itai said.

"Yes."

"Her husband said she had only friends, no enemies. Your husband said the same. I ask you now, did she have enemies?"

She glanced at him. "No, she was deeply loved."

He nodded then sighed. "Well, it's not like we can interrogate either one of them now." His expression turned almost sheepish. "Sorry. I don't sleep right when things don't fit. My wife says I have an obsessive personality. She studies psychology at Bar Ilan University."

"You must be proud of her."

"Except when she tries to psychoanalyze me," he chuckled.

"Excuse me, Detective, do Moti and my husband know about this picture?"

"Not yet."

"So, you do plan to tell them?"

He steepled his fingers. "I'll leave that delicate matter to you. As far as the police are concerned, the case is closed. We don't have the resources to investigate whether or not your sister-in-law knew her killer. And from our initial inquiries with his family in Qalqilya we learned he spent the last year, if you can believe it, here in Jaffa, working in a restaurant. No papers, no trace of him. Nothing. The man was a ghost." And then he chuckled at the irony.

She bit her lip. "May I have it? I wouldn't want anyone to think.... And there are her children to consider should they ever inquire."

"Quite right." He closed the file. The photograph remained on the desk. "Excuse me, I need to speak to my colleagues."

She waited for him to cross the room then quickly opened the file, searching for the gunman's name, which hadn't appeared in the preliminary report, and found the photos of the crime scene grisly, surreal, and frankly intimate. Something sour rose to the back of her throat seeing Hadas sprawled on the grass near the lemon tree in the garden at Kafr Ma'an, blood staining her shirt and her expression, shock, relief? And then Tamar stared at the man lying beside her sister-in-law, reaching for her, his hand outstretched, the gun on the ground between them.

She snapped the file closed and slipped the photograph into her handbag.

Detective Itai returned.

She stood on trembling legs. "You've been very kind."

"Are you all right? You're pale."

"I'm fine." She took a last sip of water.

"I'll let you know if there's any news about your husband," he said, "but I wouldn't worry. We get a lot of husbands who take a vacation from their families. Just for a few days to clear their heads. He's probably on his way home."

She nodded her thanks and left the station, clutching her bag. The sheet of paper with his name and telephone number on the chair.

Heat wavered over the pavements. She made it halfway down the block before vomiting into a shrub, blinking back tears, then turned onto Dizengoff Square, where the fountain burbled and prisms of light were caught in every droplet. A flock of pigeons pecked at the dry rolls someone had tossed. She saw none of this, only Hadas and the man lying on the grass. A man she knew. A man they both knew—Daoud Hamid. Daoud Hamid, who'd once lived in Kafr Ma'an before the war in '48: translator, engineer, poet, the gentlest of men. For fifteen years he'd snuck across the border to meet Hadas in the groves of the village he and his parents had left behind. And Salim never knew. Hadas had begged her not to tell, convinced her, "You'll only hurt him, and he won't thank you for it. You'll be the messenger that destroyed our relationship," she said. "He won't ever look at you in the same way again. Oh, he'll despise me for dishonoring our family, for being with a man who isn't Jewish and who isn't my husband, but he'll hate you. Remember, you aren't blood."

Hadas was right. She wasn't blood and she wasn't Mizrahi and for that there would always be a part of her that stood outside their golden circle. Salim was a proud man, the head of their family; telling him would only humiliate him and he would hate her for it. He might even blame her for not stopping Hadas, as if she could, as if anyone could when it came to Daoud. She had carried Hadas's secret into her marriage, into her home, where it burrowed in the undergrowth and now rose like a body in a swamp.

It seemed she had always known about Daoud. He and Hadas had met a year or two before she and Salim did. During one of her early visits to the village, Tamar came upon them deep in the *pardes*, close to the river. It was the first time she saw Hadas truly frightened.

"Is Salim with you?" she'd asked.

"No. I'm meeting him at the house. Who's your friend?"

"This is David," Hadas said.

Daoud stiffened.

"How do you do?" Tamar shook his hand. She could see he was upset, though she didn't know why, and Hadas must have sensed it, too, because a moment later she blurted out, "His real name is Daoud Hamid and I love him. He used to live here, that is, we live in his former house. Isn't that funny?"

Daoud kissed her hand. Hadas looked both terrified and defiant.

For more than a decade, Hadas would use her as a buffer, as a means of obfuscating and lying to Salim and later to Moti and her family. And though Tamar hated lying and knew that Salim would find it unforgivable, there was, she admitted to herself, power in the knowledge. She knew something about Hadas that Salim did not.

When Hadas married Moti, Tamar was relieved, sure the affair would end, especially after they moved to Tel Aviv, but Hadas couldn't let Daoud go any more than he could let her go. In his grief, Moti had stumbled upon the truth, but he hadn't pieced it together—the Arabic literature course at the University built on what was once Kafr Ma'an's land, the Alexander Technique she studied at the Kibbutz Seminary at the southern tip of the village, the archeology class at the Eretz Museum, and the class on Myth and the Constellations at the Planetarium, both established on land that was once part of Kafr Ma'an. Year after year she took courses and workshops that placed her near or in the village where she met Daoud. Sometimes she didn't see him for months. Tamar could always tell how long it had been. Everything about her grew brittle, her laughter, her excitement. There were never enough parties. She crowded her house with people, and the arrack flowed, and the music was loud, and no one could tell that she was coming apart. Then she'd get word from an old woman who sold halvah in the souk that he was arriving. The peril of his border crossing subdued her, plagued her. Tamar never understood how Hadas managed her husband and children's expectations while she was with Daoud in the village, creating another home, another life. Even as it disintegrated around them, the village was where time stopped, where they remained in the apogee of their youth, their future inevitable. If only the rest of the world didn't exist, didn't intrude.

When they were together, Hadas lived in a state of anxiety, fearful she and Daoud would be caught. She fantasized about all the ways Moti would find them. "Maybe then it would be finished," she'd say with a fatalistic shrug. "What a relief that would be, for both of us. This isn't easy on Daoud."

"It isn't easy on you either, or on me," Tamar retorted.

Hadas never fantasized about Salim finding them. The idea terrified her.

For years she threatened to break it off, and then in June when the Six-Day War ended and Israel won East Jerusalem and the territories in the West Bank and Gaza, she was determined to end the relationship.

"Why now?" Tamar asked as she slipped another tray of *maamoul*, date cookies, into the oven.

"Everything's more complicated." Hadas wiped flour off her hands. "It's one thing to be exiled because of war, quite another to be occupied by us. Daoud's a lot like my brother, proud. He'd come to hate me. I couldn't live with that."

"But the situation has nothing to do with you," Tamar said.

"Sooner or later, it'll poison us. Come with me to Kafr Ma'an."

"He's there now?"

Hadas nodded. "Please," she said, "I don't want to be alone with him. We'll just talk each other out of it again. With you there, I'll have to go through with it."

She looked so distraught, Tamar felt she had no choice but to accompany her. That afternoon they took the bus. Hadas sat beside her, so pale Tamar worried she'd pass out. They walked up the hill to the village, much of it already gone. They saw Daoud sitting beneath the lemon tree in their old garden, holding what appeared to be a book wrapped in brown paper. His white shirt a beacon in the sun. His face leaner, ascetic almost, and more handsome than she remembered. He greeted Tamar with a look of surprise. They had met a few times in the past. He'd always been kind, courteous, putting her at ease. Now he hesitated, assessing her presence and its meaning. He shifted the package from hand to hand. Besides a brief hello, she couldn't think of anything to say. Hadas stood quietly, unable to lift her gaze. Tamar saw his confusion, his eyes darting between them. She wished she'd stayed home.

"What have you got there?" Tamar asked, pointing to the package.

He looked stricken as if she'd caught him in a private moment. "A book, my book. For Hadas," he said, and gave it to her. "Open it."

She carefully unwrapped it. Her face grew soft, her eyes filled.

She rested her head against his chest. "You did it, *habibi*."

"I said I would." He stroked her face.

"Yes, you did."

"Only took fifteen years," he chuckled.

"Look." She showed the book to Tamar. "*Scenes from a Village*." Daoud's poetry. I've always thought everyone should read it. Now it's translated into Hebrew. One of these days, who knows, maybe French and English."

Daoud blushed.

"I remember you telling me about it." Tamar turned to the inscription page: *To my parents, to Kafr Ma'an that is lost to us, and to H.A, for eternity.* She watched Hadas slip the book into her bag.

"I'll give you time to talk," Tamar muttered, and hurried into the house. She walked through the rooms, unsettled, aware of a sense of imminent loss, as if the house knew it was on borrowed time. Like the others in the village, it would be bulldozed, ground under history's heel, and once it was gone, it would be as if Kafr Ma'an had never existed, living on only in memory. Something new would take its place, something bold and shiny.

The furniture they'd left was still there—a secondhand sofa in what used to be their living room, the kitchen outfitted with a hot plate and wonder pot. The wildflowers and herbs Hadas gathered and dried, hanging from a thin rope nailed to the wall. Books stacked beside the iron bed in the adjacent room, two suitcases at the foot of it she assumed were Daoud's. She sat on the window ledge where she and Salim used to stare out at the groves. Until 1948, Daoud's family had enjoyed this view, had lived in this house, cultivated this land, pruned the trees, harvested the fruit for export, and then abandoned it before the War of Independence began. Now only a few trees remained in the *pardes*. The land was rutted, the fields dug up ready for new foundations to be poured, for apartment buildings to be built. She sensed an anguish seeping out of the ground and imagined Daoud sensed it, too, the way he must have sensed that this time the love he had crossed borders for was truly over and that not even here where they'd met so many years ago, when Hadas was a girl of sixteen and he'd just returned from the University of Cairo, where they continued to meet long after she married, where she cooked for him, where they ate, and slept, and loved, where they pretended this was their home and the village was still vital, and the children they might have had ran through the orchard and dipped their feet in the waters of the Yarkon River, where they imagined that religion and nationhood didn't matter, not even here could he find refuge. Not this time.

On the way home, Hadas bounded with energy. "I'm relieved," she insisted, charging down the street.

"Slow down. What happened?" Tamar was breathless.

Hadas halted beneath a ficus tree. The waning sun slipped through the twisted branches.

"Nothing. Everything. I gave him all the reasons why we shouldn't be together. I told him, 'One day you'll be caught crossing the border, maybe shot, and what of my marriage and children, your elderly parents, your brother, work, and the most obvious reason of all? Even if we managed to leave our families, which neither of us has been able to do, and not because we don't love each other enough but because we love our families too much and couldn't bear their pain and disappointment, where would we go? There's no place that would accept us, not here, not Egypt or Jordan, Lebanon or Syria. They'd stone us for what we're doing. They'd burn down our house. I said to him, 'Daoud, please let me go. Live your life and leave me to mine.'"

"And he accepted that?"

"Of course. He's a rational person. 'You're right,' he said. 'You can't leave your children, and what we're doing here would kill my parents.'"

"So we agree," I said. "You won't put yourself in danger anymore. You won't come back."

Hadas looked haunted. "He pressed his forehead to mine. I thought he was going to kiss me goodbye. But instead he said, 'You took everything from me' he said. 'My home, my future. I never married because of you. You told me to wait and like a fool I waited. Do you know what my family says about me? The ridicule, the laughter behind my back. All of Qalqi-lya laughs at me.' He shook me hard and then said something I'll never forgive myself for."

"What?" Tamar asked.

Hadas closed her eyes. They were on a quiet side street in Tel Aviv. Tamar could smell a beef stew cooking. The aroma sifted out of a first-floor window. She hadn't eaten since morning. Her stomach growled with hunger.

"Tell me," Tamar said.

Hadas whispered, "'I never had sons because of you. I couldn't imagine them with anyone else. But you could. You did.'"

"I tried to hold him." Her face was wet with tears.

"'You're killing us,' he said. 'You know neither of us will survive this.' All I could say was that I was sorry. He shoved me away. 'You're not forgiven.' He said, 'Get out, Get out of my house. I don't want you here.'"

"Oh, Hadas." Tamar put an arm around her. "Do you think he'll be back?"

"No, this time it's really finished." She wiped her face. "Will you come with me to the book stall on Allenby Street?" She patted her bag where Daoud's book was still wrapped in brown paper. "I can't keep it."

The following morning when Tamar stepped out of her apartment building on the way to the grocer, she saw Daoud leaning against a foundation pillar near the front garden. She had no idea how long he'd been there, only that he wore the same clothes she'd seen him in yesterday and that they were wrinkled, the cuffs stained with dirt like he'd been digging in the soil, his hair uncombed, his face unshaven. She pulled him aside. "What are you doing here?"

"I have to speak to you."

"This is dangerous for both of us."

"A few minutes, that's all," he hissed.

"Not here. I can't."

"I'll go to her house. I'll go to her husband's bank, and to your husband's job. I'll tell them everything. How you helped us, how you knew about us and kept our secret all these years."

Tamar's heart seized. "All right. Talk. What do you want to say? Make it fast."

"Invite me up for coffee."

"Are you crazy?"

"If we meet anyone, just say I'm giving you an estimate on work in the house. There are plenty of Arab laborers in Tel Aviv nowadays. We've practically built your city."

"Work?" Tamar repeated.

"Kitchen tiles, bathroom."

She thought for a moment. "All right, but only for a few minutes. My family will be home soon."

He followed her up, his footsteps hammering the stairs. She was sure her neighbors were peering out at them, wondering who she was with. The busybodies thrived on gossip. Thankfully, there were still a few hours before Salim and the children came home.

She opened the door and he walked in, stopping at a picture of Hadas and her family. She saw his shoulders slump before he straightened up and went into the living room. The jalousies on the balcony were open, and sunlight poured onto the clay pots filled with herbs. He looked around the room, at the paintings on the walls, at the family photographs in the vitrine, at a large puzzle the children were working on with Salim.

"So this is how you live, how Hadas lives, too, I imagine. I've always wondered. You have a beautiful home," he said.

"Thank you. Please come into the kitchen. Coffee will take just a few minutes."

He shoved his hands into his pockets. His gaze slid over the cabinets and tiles, the refrigerator in the corner, and the new oven for which they still owed fifteen more payments. His mouth tightened. "My mother barely has an icebox and only a stove top. She uses a wonder pot for baking."

"I'm sorry. That must be hard for her. Until a year ago, it was the same with us," she said. An awkwardness infiltrated the room. This was the first time she was alone with him, the first time he ever shared any information about himself or his family with her. Always Hadas had been there, easing the strained conversation. She hardly knew him, except for what Hadas told her, and now he was here, sitting at her table.

"I don't want coffee," he said.

She frowned. "Then something cold." She poured two glasses of seltzer and added *petel* raspberry syrup, then set down a plate of *maamoul* cookies.

"I assume she told you what happened yesterday." He lit a cigarette.

She pushed the ashtray toward him. "I was there in the house."

"That's right, you were. Did Hadas make these?" He bit into a cookie and closed his eyes.

"We both did. We like to cook and bake together. More pleasant that way." She looked at the wall clock and sighed.

"She really is an excellent cook. One of her many talents."

"Yes," she said.

He gave a joyless smile. "I bet she didn't tell you that before the war we planned to go to France. I had the tickets, the money, everything we needed to begin a new life together. And then war broke out and her husband and brother were called into the reserves. I had to see to my parents, make sure they were safe. I told her I'd return soon and would change the date for our trip. Thought it would give us time to catch our breaths and get organized." He rubbed at a stain on his cuff. "Her ticket's waiting for her at a travel agent in Yaffa. She's supposed to pick it up on the way to the airport. No chance of anyone discovering it or us that way. Her idea. She's good at that sort of thing."

He sipped his drink. "I'm scheduled to leave for Jordan tonight, and then on to Paris. Our flights are the day after tomorrow. We're to land at Orly an hour apart." He took another cookie and crushed it between his fingers. "I've been filled with such excitement, I can hardly breathe. Haven't been able to sleep or eat. All I do is think of us there. Silly things like buying a newspaper at a kiosk, drinking espresso at Café de Flore, listening to jazz music, watching the rain. I think of our life, what it could be, what we could be, how much better we are together than apart. Now she suddenly breaks it off when everything is finally in place."

"I didn't know," Tamar said, shaken. Hadas had left that part of the story out, which made her wonder what else she hadn't told her. "I'm so sorry, Daoud. You're a good man. Don't waste your life here waiting for Hadas. Go to France. Find a wife, start a family of your own. Let her go, let the past go."

"No." He shook his head and took a deep pull on the cigarette. "She'll come round. She always does. Just needs a bit more time, you'll see."

"Oh, Daoud, I'm afraid you don't see. Hadas will never leave her family, her children. How could she? She wouldn't be the woman you love if she did."

"I know that," he snapped. "They're meeting us in France."

"You think Moti will let his children go? That will never happen. In all the years you've been together, why didn't she leave with you? Why not leave Israel before she married Moti when it would have made the most sense? She loves him, you know. Not like she loves you, but enough to stay. She'll never leave him."

"Yes, she will." He ground the cigarette into the ashtray, and then more quietly, "She has to. We share a history, a culture, language. I know how unhappy she is with him. What we have is primal, deeper than religion or nationality. We understand each other in a way that Moti never will. Do you know how many meals we've had together, how often we've shared a bed, how we've fought and made up? Last year when her husband received an award at some fancy bank dinner, do you know where she was?"

"Yes, home with a fever." Tamar remembered that dinner. She'd been there with Salim, who'd picked at his chicken, worried Hadas needed a doctor.

"She was with me at our house in Kafr Ma'an. When Tehila won a spelling contest in school, she was with me. When Barak lost his first tooth, she was with me. She's put me ahead of everything and everyone. Why do you think we've stayed together? No one loves me the way she does. No one loves her as I do. Apart we're ashes, together we're kings."

"I wish it was different for both of you. I do," Tamar said, reeling at the thought of so many lies. She remembered the times Hadas said she was going to help her mother in Beersheva, and after her mother died, it was a sick friend in Ramat Gan, and then it was volunteer work at the absorption center. Was any of it true? She recalled how often Salim gazed at his sister with such admiration and pride that it made Tamar ashamed she didn't do more for other people; instead she hoarded her spare time to read, to walk on the beach, to embroider.

"Do you know why she married Moti?" Before he could answer, she rushed on, "Because Salim told her to. He introduced them, said it would be an advantageous marriage, and it has been. For the most part, she's been content with Moti. They've built a good life together; one she can be proud of. One, the whole family is proud of."

He shook his head. "Stop it," he said.

"Daoud, I'm not saying this to hurt you, but you have to know she'll never defy Salim. He gave her everything, sacrificed everything in Syria and here. Their parents could barely make enough money for food. He stole to feed her, took care of her when she was sick. He left school at thirteen so he could work and make sure she received an education."

"I know how she feels about Salim," he said.

"I don't think you do. They have"—and here she hesitated, trying to find the right words to describe what she had envied for years—"a special and complicated relationship. You'd have to see them together to understand what I mean. I've never seen siblings that close except maybe twins I've read about. Hadas always knows what he wants, what he's thinking, and he knows what she needs." She placed her hand on his arm. "She'll never leave her children or Moti, not because she doesn't love you enough, but because she knows it would destroy Salim."

He sat back, his face pale, eyes closed. "The first time I saw her, she was in the garden picking lemons. I was bleeding."

He had cut his hand on a piece of barbed wire and asked her in Hebrew if she had something to stanch the blood. She heard his accent and spoke to him in Arabic, then helped clean his wound. They talked for hours. At dusk, she fed him an omelet. He told her things about his family, about the village. She wanted to know everything, who his neighbors were, what he was like as a child. She told him about her life in Syria. "We were poor; no better than dogs," she said. That evening when he left, he knew he had to see her again and returned the next day. She was waiting for him near the lemon tree. Salim had just started basic training. He wouldn't be home for nine weeks. Daoud and Hadas made a pact never to speak about politics and truly believed it had nothing to do with them. They were above old prejudices and hatreds. If anyone asked who Daoud was, Hadas said he was her fiancé from Damascus. After a while, they began to believe it. Every lie they told held a deeper truth. He stayed with Hadas for two months.

"Being with her was like having the ability to breathe underwater. I was weightless," he said, "without substance. I was free." They lived together as husband and wife in the house he grew up in, in the village he loved. His home became her home. Even now, he couldn't let that go. He gripped the table and lurched to his feet.

"Daoud, please give her a chance. Give yourself one," Tamar said.

"Tell her I'm waiting. We leave for France the day after tomorrow."

Five

It was the siesta hour when Tamar left the police station. Shops and boutiques were closed for the afternoon, except for the corner kiosk that sold newspapers and roasted peanuts. The owner called out to her by name. Through eyes hazy with sweat, she saw him and lifted her hand in greeting. *People know me here*; the thought sank like an anchor in her chest. In New York, no one would know her. She hurried home, chilled even in the heat, wondering what it had taken for a man like Daoud who had a reverence for life to kill Hadas and then himself. Until he'd spoken of all that he'd lost, the lies Hadas had told, of their plan to leave Israel, Tamar had naively imagined the affair as a great forbidden love. She hadn't thought about the price he paid, how he had lived suspended between the past and the impossible present. Nor had she fully considered the price she'd paid, lying to Salim all these years, hiding the truth to keep Hadas's secret.

She reached her apartment and stripped out of her damp clothes, then fell into bed. For the second time that day, she slept as if drugged. Hours later she woke to the cadence of Rachel and Ari's chatter. She listened for Salim. His absence siphoned the air from the room.

"Ima." Ari jumped to his feet when he saw her, knocking down the tower of blocks he'd built.

"I'm surprised you didn't wake me." She kissed the top of his head. He'd grown tall in the last year.

"Rachel wouldn't let me," he pouted. "She doesn't let me do anything."

"Thank you, Lady Rachel. I needed the sleep."

"That's what I told him."

"Good girl. Guess what? We're going to *Safta* Miriam's house for dinner, and then if you're very good, you can spend the night there," Tamar said, disregarding the twinge of guilt she felt at maneuvering the children out of the way so that when Salim came home, they could be alone.

"Is Baba coming?" Ari asked.

She bent to tie her shoes. "He's working late."

"Again?"

"Yes, again."

Over toasted cheese sandwiches, she told her mother about Salim's five-year plan.

"You go to America and you'll never come back," Miriam said, unknowingly echoing Moti.

"I'm worried. He hasn't been home in two days."

"Some people lose their minds with grief."

"Did you when Aba died?"

"A little, yes. Mostly, it just made me feel old, like I was next. I kept waiting for the angel of death to come waltzing through my front door. The sonofabitch just stood there, mocking me."

Tamar laughed. "I don't remember you being anything but yourself. Just as you are now."

"It's true," Miriam said, "but then one day it was over. I wasn't haunted anymore. I stopped being afraid."

"You think that's what'll happen to Salim? One day, he'll just stop grieving for Hadas, stop wanting to run from it." *From me*, she thought.

Miriam brushed the scattered breadcrumbs into a small pile. "I wouldn't count on it. He and Hadas were closer than most siblings. Between the two of them, I don't know how you managed to be your own person. Very strong personalities." Miriam took a sip of her coffee. "She was special. I'd have been jealous as hell."

"Well, I'm not you," Tamar said, cringing inwardly at her mother's astuteness.

An hour later, she returned to the apartment alone. Salim wasn't there. She found herself wandering the empty rooms. They had lived in the apartment for a decade, and yet without Salim and the children home, it felt strange and unfamiliar. What was she was clinging to here? She went out onto the balcony, the air fragrant with mint and night-blooming flowers. Hoping for calm, she sat in a folding chair, but her thoughts kept churning up the conversations she'd had with Moti and then the detective, which of course led her to Daoud, here in her house.

She wondered if she'd been cruel; she hadn't meant to be. When he left, he seemed angry and hurt but not desperate enough to kill. She had deliberately kept the conversation from Hadas, thinking it best her sister-in-law didn't know of his visit. Perhaps if she'd told her, Hadas wouldn't have gone to Kafr Ma'an. She might still be alive. Tamar sprang to her feet. Every time she closed her eyes, she saw their bodies lying side by side in the garden in Kafr Ma'an. The last time she saw them together, they clung to each other even as they fought. She had known Hadas was incapable of staying away from him and Kafr Ma'an. She just hadn't expected her to go there so soon after the breakup and had counted on Daoud leaving that night for Jordan and later for France.

By midmorning the following day, she was on a bus, gripping the chair rail, reminding herself to breathe. She'd tell Salim everything she knew about Hadas and Daoud. There would be no more secrets between them. And he'd have to forgive her. He'd have to understand why she'd kept the truth from him all these years. The radio beeped the news hour and she listened to a report about a skirmish in Gaza on the Egyptian border, the first since the war. She looked out at the buildings, at the signs that read for sale, at the new construction, at people in cafés, at life marching on.

She got off at the intersection at Derech Haifa and Rechov HaUniversita and walked up the hill to the village. Every few months another plot was cordoned off and emptied, houses demolished, trees uprooted. Years ago, when the government decided to clear the land for development, they gave the Jewish families that had settled there after 1949 financial incentives to leave. Kafr Ma'an wasn't being obliterated from the landscape so much as erased from it.

She plucked an orange from a low branch and tore open the peel. Her fingers and chin sticky as she sucked the juice, surprised by its bitterness. A wind blew through the derelict trees that stood like the signposts of a lost world. Weeds grew around the trunks and footpaths. She walked a long distance before coming to the stone house with the blue door. In the garden was the lemon tree and beneath it a wooden bench near to where Daoud had pulled the trigger. She saw it all, Hadas moving toward him, holding him, pressing her mouth to his and he, cocking the pistol, her terrible surprise at it going off. She bent to touch the grass where their bodies had fallen. Someone had torn down the garden wall. The stones were in a neat pile. The back door was open. Everything was the same as the last time she was here except for Daoud's suitcases. They were gone, taken, she imagined, by the police, returned to his family.

She moved farther into the main room. This was why she was here: Salim sitting on the window ledge, looking out at the trees the way she'd done six weeks ago while Hadas had broken it off with Daoud. Salim's hair was uncombed, his face unshaven. Orange peels littered the floor.

"Salim?"

For a moment she feared he was part of her inner landscape and then he turned to her and opened his hand to reveal a sprig of dry rosemary. "Hadas. How has it survived all these years? I miss her," he said.

"Me too."

"She was my sister, but she was also like my mother and my daughter, and I was her brother, and like her father and her son. And we were the best of friends. Can you understand that? This place, this life is impossible without her."

She laid her hand on his shoulder and felt the muscles shift beneath it and knew Hadas was right. She couldn't tell him, not now, maybe not ever. Knowing she and Hadas had kept this secret from him and that it had led to her death would destroy him.

"This village was always full of ghosts," he said. "We knew it then. Now she's here too."

He wrapped his arms around her. "You and the kids, you're my world now," he said.

She burrowed her face in the crease of his neck. "We'll go to America. Five years. But no villa in Herzliya. We keep our apartment and then we come home as if nothing's changed, as if we never left."

He kissed her. "Nothing will change."

The next morning, she woke to the comforting weight of him beside her, relieved he was there, yet she couldn't shake the dread she felt. Salim's eyes darted back and forth behind closed lids. The regal forehead creased in consternation, and the thin well-drawn lips tilted up at the corners. He was dreaming. Dawn sifted through the blinds. This was how she loved him best—in repose, vulnerable when she could gaze at him unabashed. Her brow furrowed. She'd discovered something new about him; he was capable of leaving her. No apology, no apparent remorse. He grew restless, legs treading under the summer blanket. She draped her thigh over his hips to settle him. In his sleep he drew her closer, the way she knew he would.

Later while he showered, she took Hadas's photograph from her handbag and looked at the words written on the back in Arabic, *For eternity*, just like the inscription in Daoud's book. The shower stopped. She buried the photo in a box of old letters.

"Everything all right?" Salim said.

She raised her face to his, closing her eyes when he kissed her. "Just thinking about all the things I'll need to store at my mother's house before we leave for New York."

In the coming months, every boulevard, building, park, and beach in Tel Aviv was a minefield of memories. She threw herself into housework, into mothering Hadas's children and her own, cupping guilt and grief in equal measures to her chest. But the strain of leaving began to tell. Rachel wouldn't let her out of her sight. Ruby's temper flared at the slightest provocation, and Ari, who'd always been an easygoing child, was often inconsolable. One afternoon when he couldn't find his bottle cap collection, he stomped through the house shouting that Rachel had stolen it, causing Rachel to weep. Salim came home at the height of the drama while Ari thrashed on the kitchen floor. Tamar tried to calm him, but a kind of hysteria had taken hold and she stood by helpless to stop it. Salim lifted him up by the shoulders and slapped him hard. A red welt bloomed on Ari's cheek and Tamar was stricken by the sight of it.

"What the hell is the matter with you?" Salim frowned, directing the question at her. She came out of her stupor long enough to escort a subdued Ari into the bedroom. Her son kneeled on his bed and stared out the window at the sky. And she, steeped in her own troubles, hadn't noticed that Ari had hardly spoken to anyone for days. *What kind of mother am I becoming?* A few hours later, she found his bottle cap collection in a bucket of wooden blocks.

"I'm not taking them to America," Ari declared. "They're sabras like me. They belong here."

That night Salim gathered them in the living room and said to Ari, "I'm sorry, *ayouni*, can you forgive me?" He opened his arms and Ari threw himself into them. He patted the sofa for Rachel to sit beside him and then looked at Ruby and said, "I know how hard it is to leave friends and places you love behind. I know how hard it is to leave your home. I know because I had to do it, but I promise you we're going to be all right. We're going to have the adventure of our lives."

Morning and night, she prayed their visas would be denied, that the US government, like a great falcon, would snatch Salim's dreams of grandeur. But Salim did have a job, and because Moti's cousin really did own a plastics factory in Brooklyn and could vouch for them, their visas were issued quicker than expected. They were given a date to appear at the American embassy. Salim bought their airline tickets. He spread them on the table like a winning hand of poker.

"Our fortune," he said.
"Our future," Ruby said solemnly.
Salim lifted his head and smiled.

Two weeks before their scheduled flight, they went to Jaffa to buy an extra suitcase for the trip. They dodged heavy traffic and crossed Jerusalem Boulevard, past the Alhambra cinema and the palm trees that flanked the pedestrian walk, then down an alley where Salim knew a man who sold luggage cheap. Afterward he took her to lunch at a falafel stand. The restaurant consisted of two plastic tables and chairs on the sidewalk and had an all-you-can-stuff-into-a-pita buffet that smelled of *amba*, spiced mango chutney. They watched each other eat without talking. The new suitcase set between them like a well-trained dog. A trickle of tahini ran down Salim's chin. She followed its descent into the cleft, where it mingled with sweat and the beginnings of a five o'clock shadow.

The bustle of the city oppressed her. The cars and crowds coalesced into a hazy blur. She smelled woodsmoke and charred meat. Above their heads, a bleached sun and sky. Her hands felt too big. She had difficulty concentrating. They returned home, where boxes were stacked in tall columns on either side of the living room. Each day her body went about the business of living, moving through space, feeding itself, while she remained numb beside it. The sensation of having split in two lingered through those final weeks.

On the morning of December fourth, five months after Hadas's death, they dressed carefully. Salim donned his only suit, the one he married in. She wore heels and her best navy skirt, which emphasized her hourglass figure. She twisted her hair into a chignon and carefully made up her face, hiding weeks of sleepless nights. She and Salim collected their papers and walked the few blocks to the embassy on HaYarkon

Street. When they reached it, she gazed at the American flag snapping in the breeze. The traffic light changed from red to green. Cars sped past. She couldn't move. Salim took her hand. The truth of this moment overwhelmed her. She was to blame. If she had told Hadas that Daoud had come to see her, if she had told Salim about the affair and how Hadas had insisted that Tamar not reveal it to him, if she had admitted her weaknesses, how she feared hurting him, angering and disappointing him, and yes, her jealousy, maybe he'd have understood and relented. Maybe they wouldn't be leaving home.

In the embassy, they stood in a long line next to an open window. The view of the sea, a vast rippling blue, made her breath catch. Even this late in the year, people were swimming. Others spread blankets and picnicked or walked along the shore. Children played in the surf, their laughter folding into the waves.

Remember this sweetness.

Salim took her hand. He looked happy and at peace. "Come, *habibti*, they're calling our names."

Part II

EXILE

Six

Brooklyn, New York, 1972

Early one Sunday morning in late July, Salim flung the front door open and shouted, "Get up, get the hell up." He'd just come home from an all-night shift at the TSS store on 42nd Street in Manhattan, where he moonlighted as a security guard on weekends. Tamar and the children scrambled into the living room. For the four years and seven months they'd been in America, she had anticipated this day. She had watched him go from a man in full control of his emotions to someone at the mercy of them.

Something awful must have happened: a fire, a death, or maybe he'd been robbed at gunpoint. The newspapers were full of such crimes. The children gaped and rubbed sleep from their eyes. Ruby leaned against the open window, where not a breath of air stirred the curtains. Bleary eyed and yawning, she tugged on the Betty Boop T-shirt that barely reached her thighs, a distasteful character, to Tamar's mind—all that faux innocence and cartoonish sexuality, and couldn't her daughter have put on a pair of shorts? Rachel stood in first position as if about to *jeté* out of the room. She was a serious student of ballet and had developed the muscular litheness that came from hours of practice. Ari looked ready to burst into tears; mouth dry, crusted with saliva, toes polished red. Rachel had used him as a dummy model to hone her manicuring skills. His face pudgy as an overstuffed doll. At age eleven, he towered over Rachel and was a smidgeon under Ruby's height and surpassed her in weight. When he walked, his thighs clapped and his belly jiggled. Tamar had never imagined having an overweight child. Salim said he was the same at that age, but she blamed it on harsh American winters when they were shut indoors with nothing to do but *fress* like *chazers*.

Tamar wrapped her arms around her youngest children and stood beside Ruby, letting all three know she was there to buffer Salim's anger, a role that had become more commonplace in the last few years. He looked them over, his face greased with sweat. He seemed to be searching for a signpost that would lead him out of the forest of his turmoil, and when he couldn't find it, he ordered them to clean the house. He marched into the bathroom. She followed close behind.

"Are you all right?"

He glared at his reflection in the mirror and, without warning, smashed it with his fist. The glass shattered. He grunted in pain. There was blood, but he wouldn't let her tend to him. Shocked and not a little frightened, she said, "Tell me what's wrong," and gave him a washcloth to wrap around his bleeding knuckles.

"Please. Just clean this filthy house," he said.

They had moved into the Calliope Garden Apartments eight months after they'd arrived in New York. Their first apartment was a basement on Brighton 9 Street. Salim brought them there straight from the airport. The December sky banked with nickel-hued clouds.

"Welcome to America." He had brandished the house key.

They were jet-lagged and hungry. The flight from Tel Aviv with three children endless. Winter had just begun, and the cold bit through their woolen coats. Seagulls circled above them like vultures. Tamar shuddered at their cawing. Ari and

Rachel fussed, and Ruby retreated into an accusing silence, the muscles in her face working to hold back tears.

The basement was one room with an alcove, where the landlord had installed a bathroom with a chain-pull toilet and tiny shower stall. There was a sofa bed she and Salim slept on. At night she rolled out thin foam mattresses for the kids and in the morning rolled them back up. They ate sitting on the floor. Salim laughed and said it was "just like home."

"Home? Not Frug Street. My God, not even Kafr Ma'an when we had nothing."

"Damascus." His eyes clouded and she knew he was thinking of Hadas.

She hated the basement apartment. In letters to her mother, she never alluded to the way the walls iced over in winter or that in summer the humidity was so thick, mosquitoes feasted on them at night and the children woke swollen-eyed and blinded until the antihistamine took effect.

At least now they had decent rooms and neighbors they liked. The Calliope Garden Apartments were a collection of four attached buildings, four stories high with glossy black fire escapes on their facades, stacked one on top of the other. The first time she saw them, she mistook the ladders and rails for balconies that connected the apartments to one another. Later she learned they were an escape route in case of fire. Those first weeks she'd lived in a state of anxiety, waiting for flames to engulf them, and spent nights formulating the quickest route to safety.

There was no garden at the Calliope Garden Apartments. Nothing grew in the patches of dirt on either side of the entrance doors to any of the buildings. In the back of Buildings A and B was a communal courtyard and a staircase that led to a cellar where tenants stored old furniture and suitcases with stickers from European cities and state fairs. There was a washing machine that jitterbugged a dozen inches during a rinse cycle and a porcelain laundry sink crackled with age. It was the same layout for Buildings C and D. Like Frug Street, the tenants' lives drifted into theirs. Each apartment was its own country and her neighbors' affairs bled out their borders into hers. She knew when Mrs. Kantor's baby was colicky and when Mrs. Eliopoulos's toy poodle, Zeus, needed a walk. Helena Eliopoulos was her closest friend in the building. A widow, a childless mother, an immigrant.

The command to clean the house mobilized them. Rachel and Ari started in their bedroom. Ruby tackled the kitchen, and Tamar the living room. Salim watched them with the same intensity he reserved for customers browsing the aisles at the TSS store, or the employees he managed at the plastics factory where he was the day foreman. When the apartment shone, he went to bed and she sent Rachel and Ari downstairs to play in the courtyard. Ruby left without telling her where she was going. Ruby worried her. Her daughter had become secretive and always smelled of cigarettes. Last week, she caught a whiff of alcohol on her breath. There was no knowing who she was hanging around with and what she was doing because she never brought anyone home. When she asked why, Ruby said, "Who'd want to meet a bunch of refugees?"

Tamar gathered the pieces of bathroom mirror and caught the dozen reflections of herself, each differing depending on the angle of the shard, not one a true replica.

Salim didn't eat dinner that night. He didn't come out of their bedroom and she didn't take him a plate. When she went to bed, she found the blinds open, the courtyard lights on, and Salim stretched out, looking toward the window. Long shadows bisected the ceiling.

"I'm sorry," he said.

"I expect you are." She stripped out of her clothes and lay beside him, unyielding.

He pulled her on top of him, kneading her lower back. "I love you."

She resented the way her body softened against his. "Well, I hate you," she said.

"Me too." He pressed his forehead to hers. "Forgive me."

When they'd applied for their visas to America, Salim said all he'd have to do was work hard and dollars would rain on him and the rain would cleanse him and make him whole again. But it had been nearly five years of ten-hour workdays, six, sometimes seven days a week.

He sat up and lit a cigarette. "Last night I caught a fourteen-year-old stealing a pack of diapers for his baby sister. It was like seeing myself at that age. I must've stolen milk at least ten times from Salach's grocery when my mother couldn't afford it. He finally gave me a job stacking shelves so he could keep an eye on me. I paid for the diapers and told the kid to get the hell out and never come back."

"You did a mitzvah. Is that what upset you?"

He closed his eyes.

"Salim?"

"The D train this morning."

"What about it?"

"The car was empty except for an old man sleeping it off. *Ya'Allah*, he stank. Clothes filthy, mouth wide open."

"Did he wake up, bother you?"

"He didn't wake up, but he bothered me." He threw his legs over the side of the bed. "I was tired. My mind wasn't right."

"What do you mean?"

He pulled the blinds up farther. His body illuminated by the courtyard lights. "Promise not to laugh?"

71

"Of course."

"He reminded me of my father. You know he worked as a *sabal* in Damascus and then again in Haifa. Until the day he died, he hauled scrap metal on his back. I stared at that old man's mouth, and watched it turn into my father's. The longer I stared, the wider it became. I felt like I was falling inside him, slipping into that disgusting old man's body, into my father's body. I was afraid and felt like I was choking. Had to open my collar button just to get a breath, and then another, and before I knew it, the shirt was off and then the train stopped at the station before ours. I burst out of there and ran home. Don't know how many miles. I couldn't feel anything. I couldn't hear my footsteps hit the concrete or my breath or feel my heart beating. It was like I was dead."

She came to him and pressed her lips to his chest. "Your heart beats strong. You're exhausted. Anybody working like you do would feel the same."

He put his arms around her. "Tell me you love me and that I'm not crazy."

"I love you so much and you're not crazy, Salim."

He kissed the top of her head.

"I think . . ." She hesitated.

"What?" He planted a kiss on her shoulder.

"It's time to stop, *ya habibi*," she said, using the Arabic endearment, foreign on her tongue.

"Working?" He gave her earlobe a gentle bite.

She shivered. "Working so hard. The hours you put in. For what? All those days turning into weeks and months. Years, Salim. We've saved enough money. Let's go home."

He dropped his arms from around her waist.

"My father used to say time was a tyrant. You leave when it's dark, come home when it's dark, and there's always more work, more time away from us that we'll never get back."

He hung his head. "Why do you do that?"

"What?"

"Undermine me."

"No, *habibi*, that's not what I was doing."

"Forget I said anything."

"Salim," she implored, but he was already climbing back into bed.

By Friday, the incident was nearly forgotten, absorbed the way the body absorbs a blow. She prepared for Shabbat, washed the floors in a manner Salim disliked, on her hands and knees, too reminiscent of his mother cleaning the homes of rich Ashkenazim in Tel Aviv.

"Be an American," he said. "Use a mop."

She scrubbed so hard, polish chipped off the wood. Wood wasn't like stone. It could burn and warp. Larvae could be writhing below the surface, carpenter ants gnawing highways that stretched from one room to another, leaving the planks beneath her hollow. At home, the floor was made of stone tiles, something she could plant her feet on and wouldn't give way.

She washed out the rags, pinned them to the clothesline outside the kitchen window, unrolled the area rug in the living room, and returned the coffee table and end tables to their place. She wiped down the doorposts and lintels, window casements and radiators, cove bases where dust collected like snow. She had just climbed onto a chair to rehang curtains in the dining room when a car pulled up to the curb with a flurry of horns and shouts: *mabruk, ya salam.* The Arabic words were so unexpected, she nearly fell; her hand pressed against the windowpane for support. Shaken, she gripped the chairback and stepped down, the curtain rod clattering to the floor.

Two teenage boys, brothers she assumed, sprang out of the station wagon. The older, stockier of the two wrapped his arm around the younger boy and drilled a knuckle into the top of his head. He shrieked and the older one released him. From her perch two stories above, she worried her children would get underfoot of these boys and called down to Ruby on the front stoop.

"Where's Rachel and Ari?"

Ruby pointed to the vestibule. Tamar signaled for her to come upstairs but her daughter resumed watching the boys, who were now wrestling. The two laughing, grunting, grappling, and rolling. Their T-shirts high on their torsos. A man, whom she took to be the boys' father, barked an order and the boys came apart like puzzle pieces and began to unload the car.

It was past four and Salim would be home from the factory soon. She climbed back up on the chair and attached the curtain rod to the post. The Shabbat meal was cooked and waiting on the stove. His TSS uniform pressed. Everything was prepared.

Tamar saw the boys' mother emerge from the car. She wore a navy blue djellaba and hijab and pointed to the mattresses that flopped over the roof of the station wagon and to the assortment of table lamps and chairs peeking through the open windows. The parents supervised while the boys removed the items from the car. Cardboard boxes listed drunkenly next to empty dresser drawers on the sidewalk. Their father stood beside them. He was tall and well built, graying hair cut close to the temples. The mother checked the lamps for damage.

Salim turned the corner, the lunch pail swinging in one hand, a bouquet of flowers in the other. Her heart squeezed at the sight of them. He used to bring flowers home every Friday, but that was in Israel. Here they saved every penny to take back with them. Until then she lived in two countries, in two tenses. In America, it was always the present tense, as if she'd been born that day fully formed. Israel was where the past sheared into the future. Salim greeted the family and shook hands with the father and the sons. They spoke in Arabic. Fragments of their conversation drifted through the window. The man, the woman, and Salim threw their heads back and laughed. Tamar bit her lip and returned to her chores. She snapped the white tablecloth into place, setting the table with the embroidered napkins from home and the cutlery she'd found on sale in a shop on Church Avenue.

A short while later, Salim's footsteps rang on the stairs. She ran to open the door so he wouldn't have to search for his key. He was surprised to see her there. She took his lunch pail and the flowers. "Thank you," she said, and raised her lips for a kiss. The smell of machine oil and sweat clung to his shirt. He brushed his mouth against hers.

"Want something to drink first or a shower?"

"Shower. Come talk to me," he said.

After putting the flowers in a vase, she followed him into the bathroom, telling him how well Ari did on his math test, looking at her feet when he stripped off his shirt, marveling that after so many years, she could still feel shy around him. His name tag on the pocket was frayed at the edges and needed mending. Sal was his American name. People at work called him Sal. The neighbors called him Sal. They called her Tammy. Sal and Tammy, like two characters in a play.

"I saw you talking to that family," she said.

"They're moving in upstairs, but only for a year."

"How come?"

"Because, *motek*, they're waiting for their house to be built on Long Island. Man, they really made it." He stepped out of his trousers.

75

"What do you mean?"

"They own a good business and they're building a house. Doing it up just the way they want."

She frowned. "Who are they?"

"Mahmoudi, Ibrahim, and Radwa. The older boy is Hussein. The younger is Faisal. He's Ruby's age."

"Muslims," she said.

"You'll never guess from where." He grinned.

"Home?"

"Yaffa. God, it was good to speak Arabic again. I forgot how much I missed it."

She picked up his clothes and it struck her that every conversation he had with her was filtered through a screen from Arabic to Hebrew and lately even English.

"So our new neighbors are really our neighbors." She straightened up.

He chuckled.

Her shoulders relaxed. "I'll put these in the wash."

His body was paler now away from the Israeli sun. Still, he was beautiful. His muscles roped around bone, joints locking and unlocking with precision, flanks long and powerful, with only a slight softness to a once articulated belly. He turned on the water and vapor gathered at the edges of the new mirror he'd installed the day after he had smashed it.

"I'm sorry I put you through that," he'd said, barely looking at her.

"It's all right," she'd said.

Water cascaded against the shower curtain. The steam laced with the Pine Sol she'd used to clean the tub. He stepped into the shower, and something of the old Salim was there in the way he ran the soap over his torso and looked at her with a roguish grin. "Like what you see?"

Flushed, she held his clothes against her chest and imagined his lips covering hers, the clothes dropping to the floor as he pulled her into the shower. Water pounding their backs. The curtain shuddering and he down on his knees stripping her, pressing his mouth to her until her legs quaked.

The kids barreled through the front door.

"Ask me later." She sped away.

She tried to time everything so he wouldn't have to rush through dinner to get to his next job. After the meal, she thought they'd stroll on Ocean Parkway, walk to the subway station, stand under the streetlamp, and kiss like young lovers. But he'd sent Ruby out for cigarettes, and God only knew what took her so long. By the time she returned, he was livid. He barely had an hour.

"Where were you?" Tamar hissed.

"Sorry, I stopped in at the library and lost track of time."

The library closed at five on Friday, and it was already past six. There was no time to question her daughter.

"Get anything good?" Ari asked.

"Nah." Ruby bent over her plate.

There was a bit of talk around the table, Tamar mostly and the kids piped in now and then about the stray cat they'd adopted. Salim remained silent.

"What cat?" Tamar asked.

"A kitten," Rachel said excitedly. "We made a bed for him in a cardboard box."

"Where is it?"

"In the hallway in Building A, next to Sarah's apartment. We named him *Chatool* for cat in Hebrew."

"Well, don't forget summer arts and crafts classes begin at the synagogue on Monday. No time for pets." She turned to Ruby. "Mrs. Eliopoulos asked me to go with her to the social security office. I don't know how long I'll be, so you'll need to take the kids. I don't want them going on their own yet."

Salim frowned. "Why do you have to go with Mrs. E?"

Tamar spooned beets onto his plate. "She doesn't have anyone else."

"Tell her you don't have time."

"I've already promised to help her."

"You want to help someone?" His voice rose. "Help your family."

She gripped the stem of her wineglass. Ari shoved a forkful of mashed potatoes into his mouth.

Salim slammed his knife down on the table. "Help me, goddamn it."

Everything grew quiet.

"I don't know what more I can do," she said. In a way, she was relieved. The flirtatious banter in the shower, the laughter downstairs with the Mahmoudis, felt like a trick of light, a sleight of hand, obfuscating the real Salim Abadi.

Rachel heaved a sob.

"Sha, sha," he said, patting her hand. "It's okay."

The light grew brighter and objects lost their definition; the silver wine goblet, the bowls of food, the platters all blurred.

"Did something happen today?" Tamar asked, unsure if she wanted to know.

"I can pick up the kids." Ruby dredged a piece of challah in the gravy on her plate.

Salim picked up his knife and fork. "I feel like I'm drowning. Don't you see what's going on?" he asked.

Tamar folded her napkin and placed it on the table beside her plate. The inside of her cheek grisly from gnawing on it. "I'm sorry. But I don't want to see. I just want to be us again. I don't care about the money or the villa you want to buy. I want to go home." Her voice climbed. The children sank farther in their chairs.

Salim hunched over his plate. "I can't. Not yet." His breath came fast in between bites.

"Why?"

He didn't answer.

Whatever stopped him from returning home, she thought, had little to do with the realities there and everything to do with his need to succeed here. He was terrified that he'd fail at the one thing he'd set out to do—become a rich man in America. Money, he was desperate to believe, would soothe the pain of loss and guarantee passage into a land with no memory, a land without Hadas. Hadas was his connection to Israel, not her, not the children. Tamar looked around the table at them and smiled, hoping to alleviate the worry she saw on their faces. She caught Ruby's eye. A soft light fell across her daughter's cheek, and the heavy sweep of hair recalled Hadas's beauty. She remembered the first time seeing Hadas run deep into the village, toward the river, toward Daoud. Her blue dress like a bolt of sky that had fallen to earth. The two disappearing into the trees. Tamar stared at her hands, rough with housework, the skin calloused, nails chipped, and hid them in her lap. She'd always thought that, of all her children, Ruby resembled her the most.

"Ima," Ruby said. "Don't worry, I'll take care of the kids. You go with Mrs. E."

The Shabbat candles burned low, and night closed in. An orchestra of crickets chirped, and from far away came the sounds of boys running. Their shouts, their sneakered feet bashing the pavement, echoed through the streets. A car whipped down Avenue C like a dream sailing by. The flowers Salim had brought home were beginning to wilt. They picked at the food congealing on their plates. Salim rose, his foot caught on the leg of the chair. There was an uncustomary twitch in his shoulders. He straightened his back and stepped away from the table. His fork scraped the china. Rachel winced at the sound.

"Forgive me." He caressed her cheek, then glanced around the table.

Tamar felt sorry for him, to be so driven he couldn't see what he was losing.

She entered the bedroom behind him. Dressed in his security uniform, he swung the nightstick and looked at himself in the full-length mirror. Her muscles coiled with the strain of having to appear normal. Everything they were was more tenuous now. A word, an action, could ruin them. She had to remember that; she had to keep herself in check because in time his outburst would dissolve like salt in rain, while her words would drill into the foundation of their marriage. She couldn't say, for instance, *I don't trust you to make the right decisions for this family.*

"Never expected to wear a uniform here," he said.

Resting her forehead in the valley between his shoulders, she felt him relax and lean against her. A well of mercy rose in her, and she thought this, too, was love.

"I can barely stand to wear it. Just putting it on . . ." He seemed baffled, but she understood. It was too reminiscent of home, of the war, of Hadas and Kafr Ma'an. The world took bits out of them, whittled them down.

She straightened Salim's lapel. "I miss you. I miss us."

From the courtyard, she heard someone call Ruby's name, and went to see who it was. The yard lights were on, and in a bright pool stood the young Mahmoudi boy, Faisal, tall, lanky, curly hair. He gazed up at their kitchen window. Tamar turned to find Ruby pressed against the glass like a moth pinned to a screen. Salim must not have heard him. He bent to rub the nose of a shoe with his sleeve.

"I'm scared that one day I'll stop missing you," she said.

He bounced the nightstick on the tip of his shoe. "I have to go."

"Don't you worry about what's happening to us?"

"Every day."

"Then let's go home. Moti says he'll help you find another job. A desk job at the bank, or you could return to the defense plant. You had a good position there. You can't really like what you're doing here, manufacturing plastic tablecloths and guard duty in a dime store."

"You spoke to Moti?' He gripped the club. "How could you talk to him about me? That traitor. Married six months after my sister was killed. Not even cold in her grave."

"It was eighteen months," she said. "What else could he do? He needed help with his household, with his children. Tehila couldn't take it all on. She's just a kid. We weren't there for them, Salim."

He flinched.

"He called to get your permission, begging you to understand that he was lonely and desperate for help. People can go mad with such loneliness. That woman he married will never replace your sister. I feel sorry for her."

He left without a word, his silence a contrail that filled the rooms. The kids were relieved and turned on the television. Ruby cleared the table and said, "I don't ever want to be like you." Tamar filled the sink, her face drawn, her hands diving for the silverware.

Midnight she checked on the children. Rachel had the blanket pulled to her chin. Ari muttered in his sleep. Their beds, a high-rise and trundle, were on one side of the room. Ruby was on the opposite end, reading with a flashlight. Her bed near the window gave her full view of the courtyard and the neighbors' apartments in Building A.

"Remember when we moved here?" Ruby whispered, the flashlight illuminating the bottom half of her face.

"Sure."

"You said we'd go home. Think we ever will?"

"Of course." Then needing to apologize for Salim's behavior at dinner, she said, "Your father's tired, overworked."

"I know." Ruby looked at the open pages of her book.

Tamar was surprised to find it was the collection of Amos Oz stories she'd brought to New York. She thought her children read only in English now. Their ability to assimilate, to adopt American customs like hot dogs on the Fourth of July, Thanksgiving, and Santa Claus, to sing "This Land Is Your Land" with the same feeling as *Hatikvah*," made her aware of how powerless she was against the lure of America.

"Was that the Mahmoudi boy calling your name?"

Ruby took her time closing the book. "Who?"

"The Mahmoudi boy, Faisal. Did Baba introduce you?"

"How did you know?"

"*Motek*, I don't think Baba wants you to be friends with those boys. He was just being polite. It's their custom," Tamar said.

Ruby turned off the flashlight. The room sank into darkness. "Are they really from Jaffa?"

"Yes."

"Weird. We come all the way to America to live next door to a family from Jaffa."

"Ironic," Tamar said, her eyes adjusting to the dark. "Nobody cares where you're from here, only how much money you make."

"Having them upstairs makes me homesick." Ruby waved the book in the air.

They heard a toilet flush.

"It isn't fair," she said, her voice tight with emotion. "Tehila's grown up without me. She's going to the army at the end of the year."

"You'll be going soon enough."

"Won't be the same. We don't know each other anymore." Ruby leaned her head against the window. "I'm not even sure I should go to the army. What if I don't fit in? What if I'm not Israeli enough?"

"You'll fit in. You're a sabra."

"Funny how you think we can just go back, pretend nothing's changed when everything has."

"It'll be hard at first, but we'll go home and resume the life we had there."

"Why's it so important I go to the army anyway? You didn't."

"Precisely. I married too young. Hadas served. Most of her friends were people she met in the army. You'll go, and within a few weeks, it'll be like you never left home."

"Sure, Ma."

"You'll see."

Hours later the apartment was stifling. She took a quilt out to the fire escape, recalling hot summer nights when she and Salim slept on their balcony on Frug Street. Light spooled out of the Mahmoudis' living room window. A pair of moths destroyed themselves against the screen and dropped to the sill. Except for the occasional car, Avenue C was quiet. Streetlamps emitted a green fluorescence; a bacchanal of insects danced in the glow. In the blackest parts of the sky, stars glittered like hard candy.

She heard a man clear his throat and the creak of a bed-spring. Upstairs the light snapped shut in the Mahmoudis' apartment. The windows, black and opaque, reminded her of Salim's description of his subway ride. Like Salim, she saw herself plummeting into the darkness, gaining speed, lost the way Jonah was lost inside the belly of the whale, far from home. She bolted upright just as the sky began to turn to ash.

Seven

The Mahmoudis' lives permeated the building. Arabic echoed through the hall and the scent of warm spices hung in the stairwell. Tamar knew when the family was home and when they were out. She saw the boys' jeans hanging on the clothesline and Mr. Mahmoudi's crisp white button-downs fluttering in the breeze. She heard the couple's animated conversations and the brothers cheering when they watched sports on the television. Every night at six thirty the family sat down to dinner. On the weekend the Mahmoudis entertained guests and played Mohamed Abd al-Wahab and Umm Kulthoum on the stereo. Tamar caught Salim listening to the music, murmuring the lyrics to himself with an expression of such intimate pleasure, she had to turn away, ashamed of her envy.

Ten days after they moved in, Ruby said, "Isn't it time we welcomed them to the building?" Her daughter perched on the kitchen counter, dressed in blue jeans with a sunburst patch covering a hole in the knee and a white Hanes T-shirt, her face a picture of bland innocence. Tamar eyed her with suspicion. Ruby never wanted to visit the neighbors, nor did she want to spend time with her. That more than anything had her agreeing.

"How about Saturday?" she said.

Ruby flushed and jumped off the counter.

On Saturdays, Tamar often visited her elderly neighbors. Ruby called it her guilt trip for leaving *Safta* Miriam alone in Tel Aviv. Sometimes her daughter had an uncanny knack for zeroing in on painful truths. Twice a month Tamar received aerograms from her mother asking when they were coming home, complaining she couldn't be expected to manage their apartment alone for so many years, and why weren't they rich already? In her most recent letter, she wrote: *The tenants want to know if you're interested in selling the apartment. I don't want to alarm you, but it gave me a schreck, the thought of you never coming home. How could that be, my only child living in the galut when you know what your father and I went through to get here? To arrive in Haifa before the continent was consumed by war was a miracle. I told the tenants no. I was right to tell them no, wasn't I?*

"Muslims," she told Ruby, "don't drink alcohol," so they made sure to dip the biscuits for the refrigerator cake into coffee instead of the wine the recipe called for. They climbed the stairs to the Mahmoudis' apartment. Tamar wore a modest A-line dress that reached her knees. The stairwell window was open, and from the next building, a radio blasted a baseball game. There was the sound of the bat striking the ball and then the spectators' cheers filled the air. She wrinkled her nose at the fried fish smell in the hall. Children's voices echoed through the courtyard. A child's bicycle bell rang, and then the ping of a Spaldeen ball and a girl singing: *A, my name is Alice and my husband's name is Al.* A breeze cooled the back of her neck. She closed her eyes at the pleasant sensation. Ruby bumped into her as she climbed the next stair; her daughter's arm caught on the plaster wall.

"You all right?"

Ruby clutched the cake pan and nodded.

They rang the bell and Mrs. Mahmoudi cried, "It's open." Tamar noticed the previous tenant's mezuzah was no longer on the doorjamb. She turned to Ruby. Her daughter's face was tight with anticipation. Tamar's own heart drummed in her chest. They stepped into the apartment like thieves. There were moving boxes set against the back wall of the living room. The furniture was polished to a high shine. Mrs. Mahmoudi came out of the kitchen, wiping her hands on a dishtowel, surprised to see them. Tamar apologized and patted her chignon in place. A ring of perspiration dampened her armpits and she sniffed furtively, mortified by the thought that Mrs. Mahmoudi could smell her.

She invited them to sit down, sweeping aside a stack of laundered shirts from the sofa and placing them on an armchair.

Tamar took the cake pan from Ruby and gave it to Mrs. Mahmoudi. "For you and your family."

"Thank you." Mrs. Mahmoudi looked bemused. "I didn't expect visitors today." She placed the pan on the coffee table.

Tamar gave her a pained smile. "I hope we are not intruding. We can come another day."

"No, no." Mrs. Mahmoudi waved away her concern. "You are welcome. Please sit."

Tamar motioned for Ruby to sit beside her. Her daughter craned her neck toward the back bedrooms.

"They're not home," Mrs. Mahmoudi said.

Ruby blinked. "Oh, I wasn't . . ." A blush crept up her neck. She settled on the couch and picked at the embroidered patch on her jeans. Above their heads a ceiling fan clicked with each revolution. Tamar perched on the edge of the plastic-covered sofa, tugging the hem of her dress over her knees, hands clasped like a schoolgirl. She was dismayed at the immediate suction of her thighs to the plastic. The humiliating sound her skin would make breaking contact with it was unbearable; she held herself so still, her feet went numb.

Mrs. Mahmoudi sat in the matching loveseat across from them and introduced herself as Radwa. She turned on a table lamp, diffusing the late afternoon gloom.

"I am Tamar. This is my daughter Ruby."

"You're lucky to have a daughter to help you," Mrs. Mahmoudi said. "I have two sons." Her voice surged with pride. "They're with my husband, bringing the rest of our things. I thought you were them."

Tamar searched for something to say. "You know my husband, Salim."

"Salim is your husband?" Radwa clapped a hand to her heart and began to speak to her in Arabic.

Embarrassed, Tamar shook her head, "No, no. I am sorry I do not speak Arabic."

"Oh," Radwa said, a slight frown marring her brow. "Salim is a good man. He helped Ibrahim carry a dresser upstairs. I tried to give him something to drink, to eat, but he said you had dinner all prepared. It was your Sabbath."

"Yes, he told me. Thank you."

"Where are you from?" Radwa crossed her ankles and leaned toward her.

Tamar looked down at her hands. She'd forgotten her wedding ring on the kitchen counter and worried the white band mark. "My parents were from Poland."

"So you're Polish?"

Tamar flushed. "No. I've never been there."

"I don't understand."

"They went to Israel a few years before the war."

"Which war? 'Forty-eight?" Radwa looked at her in consternation.

"No. Second World War in Europe."

"Ah." She settled her hands on her lap. "You're from Europe."

"No, I was born in Tel Aviv," Tamar said, her voice strained.

"Me too," Ruby piped in.

"Israeli." Radwa sat back in her chair, her lips pursed as if she'd bitten into a piece of chalk.

"Yes," Tamar rushed on, all in one breath, "everyone here is from somewhere else. We have a nice Greek neighbor upstairs. You been in America long?"

"Eighteen years," Radwa said. "My youngest, Faisal, was born in Brooklyn."

Ruby, who'd been slumping in the corner of the sofa, perked up at the sound of his name.

"Salim says you are building a house. *Mabrouk*, congratulations."

"Thank you. He told us you've been here five years."

Tamar nodded and wiped the perspiration off her neck. "Too long from home." She gave Radwa a hesitant smile. "Salim tells me you are from Israel too."

Radwa bristled. "Yaffa. Same as my husband and oldest boy, Hussein. Same as my mother and grandmother." She raised her chin a notch.

Tamar bit her lip, then gave Radwa a steady look. "So we are neighbors here and there."

Radwa laughed, and Tamar sighed in relief.

"I'll make coffee and we'll try your cake."

There was no more mention of birthplace. Ruby sat stiffly as Tamar and Radwa drank Turkish coffee. At the first sip, Tamar bowed her head. The coffee strong and infused with cardamom tasted just the way Hadas used to prepare it. They talked about the new house. They swapped recipes. Tamar spotted a bit of plaster on Ruby's blouse and brushed it off. Ruby scowled then gave a thin smile. They were discussing a recipe for tabouli when Tamar saw the angry graze on Ruby's elbow. With a bit of spit, she cleaned the trace of blood.

89

"Ma!" Ruby cried, rising off the couch.

"What?" Tamar was shocked to see Ruby so upset. Her daughter squeezed her eyes shut and dropped back onto the couch.

"Oh, *mitukah*, I embarrassed you? I was afraid your blood would go on the furniture."

"Don't worry, it's old. Your girl doesn't like when you treat her like a child. At her age I was already married."

"Me too." Tamar wished she could dive under the stack of clothes. "You are right. I am sorry, Ruby."

"There, you see, all better." Radwa patted Ruby's knee. "Now give your mother a kiss. She's the only one you've got."

Ruby tugged on her sleeves and turned to look out the window. Radwa sighed. An evening breeze stirred the curtains. A key turned in the lock. Tamar finished her coffee; the fine grounds sank between her teeth. The oldest boy, Hussein, bounded in. His straight black hair was closely cropped like his father's, and his eyes, the color of toffee, flashed at the sight of Ruby. He put a box down in the center of the room.

"Knew you couldn't keep away." He smiled.

Tamar wondered what that was about, but Ruby's focus was all on Faisal, who carried in a large picture frame.

There it was, her daughter's face pale as stone, eyes wide, pupils dilated, and a soft tremor in her lips as if all her feelings were concentrated there. She'd seen that look before on her own face. She'd seen it on Hadas's.

"We got company," Mrs. Mahmoudi admonished. "Behave yourselves."

"And cake." Hussein grinned.

"We go; your family is home." She signaled to Ruby.

"First, meet my boys. Hussein, my oldest. He's in college now, second year. A real good head for business, like Ibrahim."

Hussein raised his hand in mock salute. "Who needs advertising when I've got you, Ma."

Though she shot him a warning glance, Tamar could tell Radwa was pleased.

"And this is my youngest, Faisal." A smile hovered on her lips. "The artist in the family. Our dreamer."

Radwa then pinched each of them on the arm, and when they cried out, she rubbed the sore spots and said, "*Ayouni*," my eyes. "You know I hurt you only so the devil won't get jealous."

The boys groaned, and yet when she kissed them, they didn't turn away, not like Ruby did when she was in a mood. Tamar eased off the couch, the backs of her thighs sticky. She was grateful for the chatter that covered the embarrassing noise. Hussein shook her hand.

"You have a beautiful family," Tamar said to Radwa.

After greeting them, Faisal whispered something to Ruby and then pulled the window curtains aside. His face reflected in the glass, the halo of curls, the deep-set eyes, and sharp cheekbones. He was handsome, almost beautiful. Without a word, he slipped out onto the fire escape.

Radwa sucked in a breath. "That boy scares me to death."

Ruby leaned on the window casement, ready to climb out after him.

"Ruby," Tamar said, "time to go home."

They heard the muffled ring of Faisal's feet on the iron treads. He sat on a rung between the third and fourth floors and lit a cigarette. His silhouette etched into the darkening sky.

Hussein bit into a slice of cake. A spot of cream remained on the corner of his mouth. "Delicious," he said.

Tamar gripped Ruby's hand and thanked Radwa for her hospitality. To her surprise, Radwa pulled them into an embrace, wrapping them in warm flesh and rose oil.

"Good neighbors are good." She patted Ruby's cheek. "In America, everybody's the same."

Radwa was right. Here they had the chance to be friends. On their way out, they stopped to look in the boys' room. The Mahmoudis had given their children the larger bedroom just as Tamar and Salim had. The beds were set against opposite walls. Above one bed was a framed high school diploma and a certificate for the honor roll. Above the other was a set of pencil drawings.

"Are those Faisal's?" Ruby asked.

"Every year he gets excellent in art. His teacher says he's got real talent."

"They're gorgeous, aren't they, Ima?" Ruby said, her face glowing.

"Yes." She recalled Hadas's excitement over Daoud's poetry, *Scenes from a Village*, and remembered the day he presented the Hebrew translation to her. Tamar looked at the small landscape of the churchyard across the street, the lilac bushes drawn with exquisite care. "Very good."

Radwa beamed.

They were at the front door when Ruby said, "Please tell him I love them," then practically flew down the stairs.

Tamar saw Radwa's worried expression, knowing it mirrored her own. "I think maybe we got trouble," Radwa said.

Tamar squeezed her hand. "Let's hope not."

It was late afternoon by the time she coaxed Ruby out of the house. There was the Sabbath shopping to complete, and Tamar had no intention of letting her stay home while Faisal rode his bicycle in aimless circles in the courtyard, creating a kind of gravitational pull that drew her daughter to him. After balking all morning, Ruby finally agreed to accompany her. As soon as they stepped outside, a blanket of heat and humidity settled over them. They walked on the shady side of East Fifth Street, where it was cooler under a canopy of maple trees. Her nose twitched at the fecund scent rising off the trunks. Lichen clung to the bark. Victorian homes with deep porches and flagstone walks lined the street. Tiger lilies and daisies lolled their heads, drunk on the sodden air. Ruby pointed to a red cardinal perched on a branch while cicadas droned. Tamar felt ragged in the heat.

There was a line of customers at Korn's Delicatessen on Church Avenue. Women conferred over slabs of lox, and trays of herring in sour cream and onions. Mr. Korn sold home-made sides like *kasha varnishkas* and *farfel* to go with the brisket and broilers. Pickled cucumbers floated in a barrel of brine. Salamis dangled from the ceiling, their skins rippling with fat. The aromas stirred Tamar's appetite. Her stomach growled. Ruby eyed her curiously.

"I forgot to eat lunch. Anyway, it's too hot."

"Steamy." Ruby wiped the back of her neck with a scarlet bandanna. Faisal had one hanging out of his back pocket, and now her daughter did too. An industrial-grade fan in the corner of the deli blasted a stream of pastrami-scented air. When Mr. Korn wasn't busy, he usually gave her a free sample, his white apron accentuating his generous girth. Today, he didn't look up for more than a minute, his hands expertly pushing a hunk of roast beef through the meat slicer.

"I'll get us a number." Ruby stretched an arm to reach the ticket tape machine.

"Forty-nine." She held up the ticket. *She looks happy*. Yesterday, Tamar caught her watching Faisal kicking a soccer ball in the street, her feelings on full display. She had to fight the urge to throw a pillowcase over Ruby's head and hustle her inside.

Twenty minutes later, they emerged from Korn's with three shopping bags of deli meats, smoked fish, and canned goods. Tamar carried one on her hip.

"We should've brought the cart," Ruby grumbled, a bag in each arm.

"Cart's broken, which is why I'm glad you're here. We still need to go to the bakery."

"Well, you did promise that if I came shopping today, I wouldn't have to clean tomorrow." Ruby grinned.

"Did I say that?"

"Ma."

"Oy, everything's a negotiation." Tamar pinched her lightly on the arm.

"Not fair. I can't retaliate." Ruby wiggled her fingers.

"Who said life was fair?" She found herself grinning, feeling for the first time in a long while close to Ruby, a sense of aliveness that she'd forgotten. She'd been so focused on performing her duties, on getting through each day, that she'd overlooked the joy her children gave her, and how that joy reinforced her sense of purpose.

Feingold's Bakery was one of the few stores on the avenue that had air-conditioning. Tamar's body drooped with relief when they entered. She breathed in the fragrance of baked goods and freon. Except for the lighted display cases crammed with an assortment of cakes and cookies, the shop was dingy, encased in a subterranean half-light. Above the shelves stacked with breads was a teetering pile of cake boxes and, beside the cash register, a giant spool of candy cane string. Mr. Feingold wiped down the counter. His white baker's uniform was splattered with cherry and chocolate sauces.

"What can I get for you, Mrs.?" His Yiddish accent, thick and familiar, reminded her of Miriam and gave her a pang.

"Large challah and rye bread sliced," Tamar said, "and give me, please, a nice piece of marble cake. I have no time to bake this week. Don't cut from the end, I want only from the middle of the sheet."

"Of course, Mrs." He cleaned off his hands and, with a glint in his eye, said to Ruby, "Maybe your sister would enjoy a black-and-white?" He wrapped the iced cookie in wax paper and gave it to her, revealing an A followed by a row of numbers tattooed on his forearm.

Tamar shot him a glance, secretly amused by his compliment. "You know this is my daughter, Mr. Feingold. How is your wife today?"

"At the heart doctor with her mother, thanks for asking."

"I hope her mother is well." She watched Feingold cut a large slice of cake.

"Believe me, that woman will outlive us all." He wrapped the string around the cake box.

With a slight bow, he presented Tamar with a marzipan in the shape of a pineapple and watched her take a bite as he put her purchases into a bag.

"Good, no?" he said.

"Delicious." Tamar hid her revulsion behind a smile. The yellow-dyed almond paste crumbled like plaster in her mouth. She placed the money on the counter and was about to pick up her shopping bags when they heard angry shouts coming from the street.

Mr. Feingold frowned.

"What is it?" Tamar said.

"A fight. Lock the door. I've seen this too many times."

"Here?" Tamar was surprised.

"Here, Lodz, what does it matter? Bullies are the same everywhere." He looked grim. Ruby decided to investigate.

"Come back," Feingold shouted, but her daughter charged ahead and Tamar lunged after her.

"Have you gone crazy?"

In the time they'd spent in the bakery, a crowd had gathered outside the pizza parlor next door. They formed a circle around the pizzeria owners, Louie and Joey Caprini. It took her a moment to register what was happening. They were kicking a body on the ground. She couldn't see who it was. Their movements appeared choreographed, almost balletic; arms raised, legs swinging, and then the fierce thrust into a wall of flesh. Their grunts of satisfaction punctured the air. She stood on tiptoe and saw a skinny young man, about twenty, with long stringy blond hair huddled on the pavement in fetal position.

Tamar pressed a hand to her throat. His shirt was torn. He didn't make a sound. She wanted to cry out and tell the Caprini brothers to stop, to scream at the crowd to help him, but she said nothing, afraid they might turn on her and Ruby next. The man could be a foreigner like them. She tried to shield Ruby from the sight, but her daughter was mesmerized by the violence the way they all were. The Caprini brothers kept kicking and cursing the man. She thought they'd kill him. One of the brothers landed a blow on his cheek, splitting it open like fruit, blood running along the concrete. It seemed ludicrous now to think that she'd felt almost safe in this corner of Brooklyn, waiting out the five-year sentence Salim had imposed on them.

The crowd grew larger. Even Mr. Feingold stood in the doorway of his store, registering a look of horror. Almost everyone shopping on Church Avenue gathered there, spilling onto the road, bringing cars to a halt. She studied the faces of those nearest her, the lust they exhibited as they watched the man whimpering on the ground, then turned to Ruby, whose eyes were fixed not on the victim, but on the edge of the circle where someone was pushing his way through. A shout went up.

"Stop."

It was Faisal Mahmoudi.

Ruby gasped.

Tamar took hold of her wrist, intending to pull her inside the bakery. Faisal charged through the crowd and slammed into the Caprini brothers, sending Louie, the shorter and older of the two, to his knees. Joey stumbled backward, catching himself before toppling into the crowd. That element of surprise gave Faisal the time he needed to help the young man up.

"Look, Ma." Ruby's voice was full of wonder. Faisal lifted the man to his feet. The Caprini brothers bellowed, "That bastard tried to steal from us." Faisal shot them a look of disgust and tossed a dollar bill on the ground. The young man stumbled, his face swollen and bloody. Faisal held him up. A police car came into view.

"You wanna tell the cops what happened?" Faisal said.

The guy shook his head, "Man, just get me outta here."

Faisal began to lead him away when Ruby called his name. Their eyes locked and then he and the man crossed McDonald Avenue and disappeared into the Buzz-A-Rama, the racing car shop on the corner.

They'd already started for home when Tamar remembered their shopping bags in Feingold's.

"Oof," Mr. Feingold said when Tamar and Ruby returned for them. "You're lucky they didn't get you, too, those two Mussolinis. Did ya hear what happened in the synagogue last *shabbos*?"

Tamar shook her head, her heart still pounding from the excitement.

"Swastika big as a man someone painted on the wall. Think anyone was arrested?"

It was obvious he was speaking rhetorically, so Tamar remained silent.

"Janitor cleaned off the paint like nothing happened. Now they beat this *shlemazel*. Five minutes later it's like nothing happened. Few weeks ago, kids from the Catholic school knocked a Yid off his bike, stole his money, his bicycle, and for good luck, knocked out a tooth. I read about it in the *Jewish Week*. Here everybody's your enemy and everybody's your friend." He took the bags from under the counter, clicking his tongue.

"Thank you for keeping the packages safe," Tamar said, wanting only to get home.

"Watch yourselves, this is a dangerous place. On the outside, looks good. On the inside, *ganifs* and murderers. A *gutt shabbos*," he said, then winked. "I gave you a little something extra."

"Thank you." Tamar felt his eyes on them as they stepped out the door. A block away, she peered into the bag and found the box with the marble cake, the breads, and the little something extra, three black-and-white cookies and a strawberry marzipan. They crossed Beverly Road.

"Faisal's a hero," Ruby said. "What he did was brave."

"What he did was crazy. He could've been killed or started a riot. He should've waited for the police," Tamar said, unable to pry the image of the young man on the ground out of her head. She closed her eyes against the violence, hearing again the grunts and groans, the excitement of the crowd, and nearly tripped on a crack in the sidewalk.

"He's a hero," Ruby insisted.

"All right, so he did a good turn, but it was foolish. What was he thinking busting into the crowd like that?"

"Come on, Ma, you saw those men. They wanted to kill that guy. What Faisal did took real courage." She shifted the bags in her arms.

"I don't care. I don't want you hanging around him. He's not . . ."

"What?" Ruby lifted her chin.

Tamar recognized the look of defiance and bit her lip. "You know very well what."

"I want to hear you say it."

"I know what you think I'm going to say, but this has nothing to do with him being Muslim. He's just not for you." She blinked away the sweat about to drip into her eyes.

"Why? He's brave, good looking, smart."

"Pshhht, you talk like a child. Don't forget who you are and where you come from."

"What does that mean?"

Tamar gripped the shopping bags. The combined smells of deli meats, smoked fish, and baked goods nauseated her. "Hadas isn't dead so long that you can forget how she died, or forget that your cousin, Tehila, goes to the army in a few months." The moment the words raced out of her mouth, she wanted to call them back.

"Oh my God, I knew it. It's because he's Muslim. You're a racist." Ruby stomped off.

Tamar rushed after her. "No, a realist. This is not about race. It's about tribes, religion, land, history. I want an easy life for you. I'm sure he's a good boy, special even, but to be with him means that you will always have to choose between love and duty to your family, to your country, and think, Ruby, who will accept you? Your people? His people? You know I'm right. I'm sure his family feels the same." The whole time she was speaking, she thought of Hadas and Daoud. Fifteen years they were together, sneaking around, unable to live out in the open. Their ending seemed inevitable now. That Ruby might have a similar fate terrified her.

"It's different here," Ruby cried.

"You can say that after what you just witnessed. *Motek*, it's the same everywhere. People love and hate and sometimes it gets all tangled up and ends in tragedy."

"What are you talking about?"

Tamar shook her head. "Nothing. Forget it. We thought we were safe here, but the only safe place for us is home. Israel. At least there they don't beat you in the streets like a dog."

"Unless you're Muslim," Ruby shot back.

"You know that isn't true. The situation is more complicated than what you suggest."

"Hate is hate, Ima, and there's no such thing as my people or his people, not here."

Tamar squinted into the setting sun. There was no use arguing with her. Salim would be home soon, and she still had to put the groceries away and prepare dinner. By the time they reached Avenue C, the silence between them was freighted with all that was left unsaid. She put the packages down to open the entrance door just as a paper airplane sailed through the air and landed at Ruby's feet. Tamar joined her at the curb. They looked up and saw Faisal on the roof, bathed in sunlight. Ruby unfolded the sheet of paper. The page was blank but for one Hebrew word: *Ohev*, Love. Tamar saw the garden in Kafr Ma'an as she had last seen it, barren and bloodstained.

Eight

A shift occurred in their lives, an uptick in energy, like a change in frequency that vibrated below the surface, and it was all Ruby's fault. Ruby, who was incandescent, filling every room with an ebullience Tamar found alarming. One evening Tamar spied her in the churchyard across the street, certain she was there to meet Faisal. Ruby stood alone near the lilac bushes he'd sketched and began to move to some internal music, contracting her torso, lifting her limbs. Her body expressing something Tamar had no words for. A cloud of fireflies rose in the twilight, illuminating her daughter's haunting dance. Late the following night, she found Ruby on the roof, gazing at a corridor of black sky. The child was so still, Tamar couldn't help thinking of Lot's wife turned into a pillar of salt because she'd dared to look back with longing at a burning Sodom, at the ruin of her city.

Sometimes Tamar reacted to the change the way she imagined horses do before lightning strikes, a raise of the head in the direction of the storm, a snort to determine its power, and then realizing it was far in the distance, going back to the task at hand. She began experiencing blinding headaches where she could do nothing except go to bed, her mind flitting from one grisly image to another of Hadas and Daoud, of the young man Faisal saved on Church Avenue, beaten bloody by the Caprini brothers, and then Faisal on the rooftop appearing godlike and Ruby pushing past her through the entrance doors and up the stairs until she was beside him, the bags of groceries abandoned. Her body brimming with pain, Tamar finally slept. When she awoke, Rachel and Ari were stationed on either side of her like janissaries guarding the palace gate. "We're hungry."

She stumbled into the kitchen, hands groping for the knife, a block of cheese, the bread. "You can do this on your own."

"Tastes better when you make it, Ma," Rachel said, and Ari agreed. They looked apprehensive, like they'd won a prize and worried she'd take it from them.

She felt the same helplessness as after Hadas's death. Only then she had no clear vision of the path they were on. Now she did and what she saw frightened her. Ruby had no idea of the danger she was in, of how love could turn into despair, of how fragile identity was. Her mother, after meeting Salim, had said, *Cross a border and you're lost.* Now all of these years later, Tamar reluctantly agreed with her. From the moment she met Salim, elements of her identity, her culture had been subsumed by his. She worried it would be the same for Ruby if she were with Faisal.

Ruby was restless. She had trouble sleeping and gave in to crying jags. The only cure for Tamar's own wretchedness had been to leave her mother's house against Miriam's wishes and join Salim in Kafr Ma'an after he'd threatened to break things off, saying it was time she chose between being a child in her mother's house or a woman in his. They married nine weeks later at the Rabbinate in Ramat Gan. Her mother was there, elegant in her green wool coat, her makeup pristine, her mouth a line of resignation. Tamar was the same age as Ruby was now.

If there was one thing she was grateful for, it was that Salim was too busy to notice this new development. He was working overtime in the factory. Though something of Ruby's behavior must have registered because one morning in late August he said, "What's the matter with her?" when Ruby appeared at the breakfast table rumpled, a fuzzy smile on her face. She snagged a slice of toast and shuffled back to her room without greeting them.

Rachel smirked. "She gets weirder every day."

"I like her this way," Ari said, spooning blackberry jam onto his toast. "She lets me borrow her colored pencils."

Tamar pretended she hadn't heard Salim's question. She didn't think it wise to tell him Ruby was in love with Faisal. She wasn't sure how he'd react to the news, whether he'd read it as teenage infatuation, or a betrayal of the family honor. Hadas's words were branded in her heart. He'd despise Ruby for being with someone outside of their faith and hate Tamar for keeping it from him. It was one thing to be friendly with your Muslim neighbors, speak their language, eat their food, attend their weddings and funerals, but quite another to allow your daughter to associate with their son.

With the summer at an end, the school year began, which left Ruby little time to spend with Faisal, who worked most afternoons and weekends in his father's import company downtown. Mr. Mahmoudi sold delicacies from the Levant. Tamar was almost certain this would end the summer romance. She knew an unaccustomed leisure now that the children were in school and relished the quiet solitude that marked her days. She made the beds, shopped, and prepared dinners, did the laundry, worked on her mending, and listened to her favorite music. She had time now to work on her Gobelin, needlepoints depicting European landscapes and paintings of the masters. Sometimes she wondered what life would have been like if her father hadn't died when she was fourteen, if her mother hadn't left her alone so often, if after his death, her mother hadn't brought home men, formless, faceless, their quiet laughter, the swift curse of pain when they stumbled into a chair in the dark. They left nothing but the sound of the door closing behind them at dawn. Her mother sitting on the balcony smoking, the air wet with dew. Sometimes Tamar wondered what her life would've been like if she'd married someone else, someone who wasn't compelled to leave home to make a fortune.

It was mid-September and she decided to treat herself. The day was bright and warm. She had a good book and made her way to Ocean Parkway, where cars sped by. She sat beneath a leafy canopy. Men and women on nearby benches chatted and munched on sunflower seeds. She opened her book but was distracted by the pigeons pecking at the seed shells on the ground. A yellow leaf landed in her lap. She looked up to see from where it had fallen and saw Ruby and Faisal on a bicycle, racing toward her. Her daughter sat on the horizontal crossbar, encircled in his arms. He stood on the pedals. Ruby's head fit neatly beneath his rib cage. They were going too fast to see her. Ruby's hair rippled behind her. She bent low over the handlebars. They barreled past her. Tamar dropped the book onto the bench and chased after them, calling Ruby's name. The light was red, but instead of waiting for it to change, Faisal wended around the cars. She saw her daughter pivot and grab the neckline of his shirt. Their faces golden in the sunlight. They turned a corner and disappeared.

She couldn't settle after that. The two had looked so young and strong, so right together, so much like Hadas and Daoud on those afternoons they'd charge through the *pardes*. Their laughter gilding the treetops. It was too early for the kids to be out of school. She blamed Faisal for that, though she supposed Ruby could have instigated that bit of truancy. After all, what did she really know about her daughter now that she was an American? She picked up her book and hurried back to the Calliope Garden Apartments. It was hideous the way life persisted as if nothing untoward had happened. The sun shone, the sky cloudless, the flowers and trees lush in their final days of summer, welcoming autumn with naive eagerness.

She didn't want to run into her neighbors, especially Helena, who'd know something was amiss and demand an explanation. How could she say she was terrified for her child because of a past Ruby knew nothing about? She took the cellar stairs, thinking to enter the building through the courtyard entrance and found the cellar door open. The smell of something long dead hung in the air. She stepped around the stored bicycles and furniture. An old sofa without seat cushions propped against a cinderblock wall. The chair beside it, an orphan from a once-expensive dining set missing a leg.

Daylight pressed against a small window near the ceiling. She washed her face in the laundry sink in the back. Her legs quivering as if she'd run a race. The water tasted of chlorine, but she drank it anyway, then wiped her hands and face on her blouse. She heard the scrape of a shoe. Someone tripped and giggled.

"Klutz."

Ruby and Faisal; she recognized his voice and tiptoed behind an old bureau, where she remained hidden but able to see them.

He ruffled Ruby's hair. Her daughter finger-combed her bangs. She'd cut them with Tamar's pinking shears the night before.

"Thanks for the ride."

"I like it," he said.

"What?"

"Your hair."

Ruby ducked.

He pulled her hand from her face. "You don't ever have to hide from me."

Tamar thought they were going to kiss, but all Faisal did was rest his cheek against Ruby's, which was almost worse. The intimate gesture made her aware of just how far things had progressed between them.

"You ever think about how close we are," he said, "you downstairs, me up? Almost like we're living together."

"All the time," she said.

"Meet me tomorrow night?"

"Where?"

"The roof."

"Okay." Ruby cupped his jaw. He kissed her then, cradling her face.

They left soon after. Tamar stood there a long time before climbing the cellar stairs. The sounds of her neighbor's lives' and the aromas of their dinners cooking coalesced in the yard. Mrs. Kantor's baby cried and her daughter, Sarah, Rachel's best friend, practiced the recorder. A cat mewled near the garbage bins in the alley. Gooseflesh rose on her arms. The air was cooler now, dusk had closed in.

"Ma?" Ari leaned out the bedroom window. "Where were you?" She heard the panic in his voice. His hair fell into his eyes. She barely recognized him from that angle. "Coming." The kids had gotten home before her. Shaken, she walked past Faisal's bicycle sprawled on the ground like a body that had fallen through the sky.

The kiss haunted her all night. While she ate dinner, the family around her, Ruby guarding her secret behind a smile. "Ma, this tastes so good." Tamar wanted to shake her daughter and say, *Don't do it. They'll brand you a traitor.* It's what Hadas always feared. Tamar thought of Hadas and Daoud in Kafr Ma'an. Like the village itself, they were doomed from the beginning. Her sister-in-law unsuspecting, arriving there with hope and regret, shame and guilt, a Gordian knot of hopeless love. Daoud and his gun waiting for her. Her photograph in his wallet. *For eternity.* Because of them, they were in America. Because of them, her daughter loved Faisal. Because of them, they were in exile.

She had trouble sleeping. Every time she closed her eyes, she saw Ruby and Faisal sailing past her on the bicycle, disappearing, resurfacing in the cellar. Once she fell asleep, only to be jerked awake after dreaming that she was in the house in Kafr Ma'an, watching from behind the shutters Daoud and Hadas in the garden kissing, the lemon tree burgeoning with fruit. The next moment she saw the revolver, but when she opened her mouth to warn Hadas, it was Ruby she was warning, urging her to run.

Tamar turned on her side and faced Salim. He slept undisturbed until dawn, then gathered his clothes. She heard the torrent of shower water.

"I'll make breakfast," she said when he came into the bedroom.

"Don't bother. I'll get something on the way."

He was almost at the door.

"Kiss me?" She closed her eyes, not waiting to see if he'd make the trek across the room.

"I thought you wanted to sleep." He hovered above her.

She wrapped her arms around his neck. He gave her a peck on the cheek.

"You can do better than that."

She couldn't remember the last time he'd really kissed her. He was always rushing off to work.

"I love your mouth," she said, tracing his lips.

"I love yours too," he said and kissed her, his tongue soft against hers, and for a moment she forgot to be afraid. For a moment she believed he'd take care of everything.

"I need to talk to you," she said, the words melting into breath.

"Now?"

"About Ruby."

He sighed and sat at the edge of the bed. "What's wrong?"

She wished his arms were still around her. It would be easier to tell him what she'd witnessed on the parkway and in the cellar. She stammered a bit and then managed to get the story out. He leaned his elbows on his knees and stared at the floor. Pulling the sheet up over her breasts, she wondered what he was thinking. A shaft of sunlight warmed the tops of her feet. "I've tried talking to her," she said. "She won't listen to me but maybe if you speak to her . . ." The words trailed off as he stood up.

"I don't think that's a good idea." He looked down at his watch. "Ach, I'm late for work."

"What about Ruby?"

"Let it go, Tami. I'm sure it's nothing. Ruby's a smart girl. In six months, the Mahmoudis will move into their new house far away in Long Island."

"But we don't know how serious things are between them."

"I'm sure if you don't make a big deal about it, it'll go away."

"And what if it doesn't?" She swung her legs off the bed. "I think you have to stop her."

"If I tell her to stop seeing Faisal or that they can't be friends or she can't love him, what do you suppose is going to happen? She'll stick to him just to stick it to us. Don't be stupid here. Better to leave it alone. This little summer romance you're afraid of will fade away. In a month it'll be like nothing happened."

"But Salim," she entreated.

"Forget it. Promise me," he said.

"I . . ."

"Good," he smiled, and then gave her an affectionate flick on the nose. She winced.

Once the door had closed behind him, her thoughts became a battering ram. The situation with Ruby and Faisal dredged up all the old anxieties. The worry that Salim would find out about Hadas and Daoud, the secret she'd kept from him. She would certainly lose him if he learned Daoud had sat in their kitchen angry and hurt that Hadas had broken it off with him two days before they were to leave for France. Salim would want to know why she hadn't stopped Daoud, why she hadn't gone to the authorities, why she hadn't warned Hadas that Daoud was waiting for her at Kafr Ma'an. She had no real answer except that she hadn't thought Hadas would go to Kafr Ma'an, hadn't ever imagined Daoud with a gun. She had just wanted, as Salim wanted now, to forget about it, to believe it would go away. Daoud would go to France and Hadas's life, all of their lives, would return to normal.

It was clear to her that since Salim was unwilling to do something about Ruby, she had to. Otherwise, she'd lose her too. In her mind, Salim and Ruby were connected. Losing them was rooted in a world where she was a foreigner. The place where the Mahmoudis lived, where Radwa sent delicious treats each week, reminding Salim of his mother's house in Damascus, of his beloved sister, Hadas. Delicacies Tamar didn't dare attempt on her own, *lachma bjeen* and *kibbeh*. Losses that were about more than the music, language, and food they shared, but about a primal code that said, *This is who we are.* She was the outsider. Ruby was given entrée into that world now. What would happen when her daughter realized she couldn't straddle both, the way Hadas had finally understood it?

That afternoon she waited for Mr. Mahmoudi to come home. The boys ran up ahead of him, their footsteps a drumroll on the stairs. She intercepted him on the landing.

"*Salaam alaikum*, Mr. Mahmoudi." Her smile hesitant and unsure.

He bowed his head. "*Shalom*, Tamar."

"I know you must want to get home. Forgive me for stopping you," she began. "Maybe you have a minute to speak?" Her mouth was dry. She licked her lips.

"Of course. And call me Ibrahim. We're neighbors." He smiled, his eyes disappearing into their sockets, gazing at her like a pair of high beams in a tunnel.

"Thank you." She was relieved the hall light was dim, hoping Mr. Mahmoudi could not see her nervousness. She clutched the handkerchief in her skirt pocket. "I'm sorry." Her facial muscles felt stiff.

"Are you all right?"

"Please excuse me, I hesitate to speak. What I have to say is . . ." She searched for the word in English, had looked it up that afternoon in the Hebrew-English dictionary when she'd made up her mind to talk to him. "Awkward." She let out a breath. "I hope you can forgive my foolish tongue. But I believe you will understand why I come to you when I tell you..." She wasn't sure where to begin.

"Go on."

"Well." She reflexively smoothed a hand over her skirt. She had dressed modestly to confront him and wore her hair up. She questioned now if she should have covered her head,

110

or if her efforts to show respect were silly and in vain. "Our children," she began.

"Yes?" He looked at his watch and with an apologetic smile said, "Tamar, my wife is holding dinner for me. I'd rather not anger her."

"Of course. It's just that this is so difficult to say." She closed her eyes.

"You're beginning to worry me. Has something happened?"

Her stomach knotted. "They cut school yesterday." She blurted out the words, too late to call them back.

"Who?"

"Your son Faisal and my daughter Ruby. I saw them on Ocean Parkway when they should have been in school."

"You're sure?"

"Yes," she said. "Was Faisal at work?"

He thought for a moment. "Yesterday? No. There was a test."

She twisted the handkerchief in her hands. "I called the school. No test. He was with my daughter. They rode a bicycle together. They looked . . ." Again, she searched for the right word, finding it hard to squeeze out, *free*. "I haven't told my husband yet." Having to lie to him because Salim was unwilling to do what needed to be done filled her with shame. If only he were having this conversation with Mr. Mahmoudi. "I'm sure you understand how delicate and complicated the situation is. Ruby has never done anything like this before."

"You think my son has?"

Her gaze fell to the black and white mosaic tiles on the landing. "No. Of course not." *How well do any of us know what our children are capable of?*

"What worries you? That they cut school, or that they're friends?"

She pitched her voice just above a tight whisper. "The problem, sir, is that they're more than friends."

He shifted from one foot to the other, the first indication that he was uncomfortable. "You have proof?"

"I saw them. They came into the cellar. Imagine my embarrassment. They didn't know I was there. Like a child, I hid." She looked down at her hands. "They kissed." Her cheeks felt hot.

Mr. Mahmoudi's face went blank. "Oh."

She blundered on, "I'm sure your son is a good boy and that they're only having a bit of fun together, but my daughter will be returning to Israel next year, to the army. How would it look? You must see the problem."

Mr. Mahmoudi pursed his lips.

"This never would've happened if we were home. Lines are clearly drawn there, but here everything is so open." She faltered for a moment. When he didn't respond, she continued, telling herself she was doing this for Ruby. "You can't possibly condone your son lying to you and cutting school."

He raised his chin a notch, the muscle in his jaw working. When he finally spoke, he looked past her. "I don't think you know me well enough to know what I condone and what I don't. I do wonder why you're making so much of this. My wife would say they're children and that in America there are no lines, no enemies." His expression was grim. "You are nothing like my wife."

Her eyes welled up as if she'd been slapped. "I'm sorry for being so blunt, perhaps even a bit crass. Please accept my apologies. Your wife is a lovely person, a woman to be admired. But surely you can see that I want only to protect my daughter and your son from the pain that such a union would cause. With respect, Mr. Mahmoudi, I was sixteen when I met my husband, younger than my daughter is now." She swallowed past the

ache in her throat. "A year later we married. Our children"—
she looked at the crushed handkerchief in her palm—"aren't
children anymore. They're almost adults and you know very
well what can happen," and then in a more conciliatory tone
she said, "How would it work between them? A Muslim and
a Jew, even in America. Don't you think it's better to finish it
now before anyone is hurt?"

Long minutes passed before he spoke, each word a knife
prick. "I like your husband. I consider Salim a friend. We
speak the same language, and I don't just mean Arabic. We
understand each other. I might even say that we're alike in all
the ways that make us men. Maybe this is what bothers you.
Not our differences as you point out, but our similarities." He
drew a long breath. "You don't need to worry. I have other
plans for Faisal. I'll take care of it."

"Thank you," she sighed. "I know this was hard and I'm
sorry if I insulted you or your family in any way. That wasn't
my intention."

"I know very well your intention, Mrs. Abadi." He climbed
the stairs.

"Please give my regards to your wife."

He slammed the door shut.

There was still an hour of daylight left when the courtyard
lights flickered on. Rachel and Ari were in the building next
door, visiting the Kantors. She went in to check on Ruby and
saw her staring out the window at Mr. Mahmoudi and Faisal
in the yard.

"What's going on?" she asked.

Ruby said nothing. Her face strained and pale, her eyes on
Mr. Mahmoudi undoing his belt buckle. The air outside still
like before a heavy rain.

"He was waiting in the yard for us." Ruby wiped her nose on her sleeve. "He told me to go home."

Mr. Mahmoudi snapped the belt; it gave a loud report. Faisal placed his hands on the wall. Even from two stories up, Tamar could see the boy was trembling. Her heart sank and she felt ill. Mr. Mahmoudi took something out of his shirt pocket and placed it in Faisal's mouth. When Faisal tried to turn around, his father told him to face front. Ruby whimpered. Mr. Mahmoudi raised the belt in the air and let it fall. Faisal jerked. Ruby jolted as if she'd been the one struck. Animal-like grunts emerged from deep in the boy's throat. He gripped the wall harder and pressed his forehead to it. All her life she had seen men pray that way, entreating God. Five times that belt rose and fell on the boy's back. The sound of the strop like the thwack of a sail collapsing and filling. When it was over, Ruby lay curled on her bed. Tamar glanced across the courtyard and saw Rachel and Ari in the Kantors' apartment, framed in the window, their faces crushed against the glass.

"I'm so sorry," Tamar said.

She heard footsteps on the staircase and slowly opened the front door. Mr. Mahmoudi had his arms around Faisal and was half carrying him up the stairs. When they reached the landing, he stopped and brushed the hair off his son's damp brow. Tamar refrained from looking at the anguish on Mr. Mahmoudi's face. Faisal hung his head. She noticed the length of his neck, the shade of his skin the same hue as her children's. Mr. Mahmoudi's stare burned through her.

"Keep your daughter away from my son," he hissed and led Faisal upstairs, their footfalls ringing on the marble. "Straighten up, boy."

Faisal did as he was told.

Nine

They had just begun dinner when Ruby said, "Baba, tell Mr. Mahmoudi that Faisal did nothing wrong. My shoe broke. He gave me a ride on his bicycle, that's all."

Salim shot Tamar a scorching glance.

Cringing inwardly, she kept her eyes on her plate.

There were too many dishes on the table for a weeknight. A frenzy had overtaken Tamar after she'd witnessed Mr. Mahmoudi punishing Faisal in the courtyard. She suspected Ibrahim had chosen the spot deliberately, knowing she would have a clear view. The man had a Machiavellian flair. No one could have turned away from such a spectacle, least of all the one who'd unwittingly instigated it. He knew how thin the membrane between parent and child was when it came to pain. Ruby's suffering was her own, just as Faisal's was his. Her daughter was inconsolable afterward. Guilt, Tamar discovered, was like quicksand. The evening wore on and she sank deeper with no chance of escape or redemption. Her stomach churned as Salim grew tenser beside her.

The lights of the cheap chandelier glinted off the plates and the jelly glasses of Coca-Cola. Something Hadas once said felt like a hurricane coursing through her: *Love comes without invitation.* Had it come for Ruby the way it had come for Hadas? Ruby's voice emerged as if out of a fog.

"I swear there was a test that morning and then the school released us after fourth period lunch."

Tamar refused to look at Salim and tried to ease the tension from her shoulders. She pictured Ibrahim calling the school, proving she'd lied to him. Why had she told that stupid lie?

"Enough, Ruby. Now isn't the time for this discussion. Let Baba eat." She rubbed her temples and then stuffed a forkful of chicken into her mouth, her throat working to get it down.

"Someone has to do something," Ruby cried. "His father beat him with a belt. Isn't that against the law in America?"

With a resolute if somewhat desperate smile, Tamar turned to Rachel. "How was your ballet class?" Then to Ari, "Wasn't there a trip to the library today or is that tomorrow?"

Salim patted Ruby's hand. "I'm sorry that happened to Faisal. Ibrahim's a good man. I don't think he'd do something like this unless he had a solid reason. Where did he get the idea you and Faisal played hooky?" He looked straight at Tamar with a grim expression.

"I don't know." Ruby's eyes filled with tears.

Growing bored with the conversation, Ari threw a heel of bread at Rachel. She smothered a laugh and tossed a napkin at him.

"Stop it." Tamar felt a headache crowding behind her eyes. They continued bickering until Salim delivered a withering glance.

Ruby went on. "Faisal says his father threatens to send him to Israel to his grandparents. They live in Ajami. Do you know it?" Ruby sawed her schnitzel in half.

Salim nodded. "Sure, Yaffa. Outside the old city." He dipped a slice of bread into a pool of tahini. "Near Andromeda Hill."

Ruby shivered. "Sounds like that horror movie."

"No. Just a bit run down. Parts of it are beautiful. It overlooks the sea." He lit a cigarette and blew a succession of smoke rings. Ari delighted in poking his finger through the holes.

"I'd like to see this place for myself," Ruby said.

Tamar cleared her throat. "Please, can we finish dinner now? I'm sure Baba wants to watch the news."

Salim looked at Tamar with pity, then kissed Ruby's hand.

When had they become so close? The last few years Ruby's anger at being forced to live out the "American Misadventure" collided with Salim's determination to live out his dream of becoming rich.

"Did I tell you Faisal taught me to say *keef halak*, and *hamdulillah*. Of course, I already knew what they meant."

Salim laughed, "Good for you." Then with a warm smile he said, "*Ana b'hebek*."

"I love you too, Baba," she said, "so will you speak to Mr. Mahmoudi and tell him Faisal and I didn't cut school?"

"Let me think about it," he said.

Tamar groaned.

It was Rachel and Ari's turn to wash the dishes. Instead of watching television in the living room with Salim and keeping an eye on them to make sure they did a thorough job, Tamar retreated into the bedroom with the excuse that she had mending to do. She shut the door behind her and then peered into the courtyard to the spot where Faisal was punished. Salim came up behind her.

Startled, she said, "Oof, you scared me."

He wrapped his arms around her waist, his breath in her ear. She almost sighed in relief. Maybe he wasn't angry after all. Her body softened against his and she imagined herself a speck of phosphorous floating through his bloodstream, illuminating each organ, each chamber of his heart.

"You told Ibrahim about the kids," he said, squeezing her waist.

"No," the lie instinctive, self-preservatory. She stepped out of his arms.

He shifted back on his heels. "Why did you do it? After I told you to leave it alone."

She climbed into bed, pulling the sheets high. "You know why. I'm tired. I'll save the mending for tomorrow. Ari can go another day without a button on his cuff."

"Tamar," he said in the same tone he used to admonish the kids.

She bit her lip. "Let's not get into it now." She tried to steel herself against feeling like a child. "They're involved and you refused to stop Ruby from seeing him. You ran off to work. What was I supposed to do?"

He opened a fresh pack of cigarettes. "Please don't blame this on my job."

Her expression earnest, she said,"You left me no choice."

"Poor Ibrahim."

"I didn't tell him to beat his son."

"What exactly did you say to him?"

She clutched the pillow to her chest. "We talked about many things."

"So why did he punish Faisal?"

"I don't understand you. I thought you'd be furious with Ruby. Yet all you care about is Ibrahim."

"What did you say to him?" He lit a cigarette and squinted at her through a veil of smoke.

"I asked if he condoned having his son lie to him and cut school." Before Salim could respond, she lifted a hand and said, "I hoped he would tell him to stay away from Ruby."

Salim looked at her in disbelief. "You know nothing. Not only did you dishonor him and his family, leaving him no recourse but to beat his son, you made me look weak. Like a man who has no control over his wife and children."

"I'm sorry but they were kissing."

"They're kids."

"So were we once."

He didn't respond to the sour note in her voice, only shoved his feet into a pair of sandals. "Another week or two and this love affair you're so afraid of would've fizzled out." He ground the half-smoked cigarette into an ashtray.

"I don't think so." Alarmed, she said, "What are you doing?"

"I'm going to apologize to Ibrahim and his son and beg them to forgive my wife for her ignorance. Maybe then he'll be able to look at me with respect again." He pointed a finger at her, "Tell Ruby the truth."

"Salim." She rushed after him. "Please don't do this. Please stand with me on this."

"I'll tell her myself."

"Baba?" Ruby came out of her room.

"Come." He held out his hand.

Tamar watched them go, tasting blood in her mouth. She'd bitten her tongue.

For three days, Ruby refused to speak to her. On the fourth day, she knocked on Ruby's door while Rachel and Ari were in the courtyard.

"Please, *motek*." She knocked again. When she received no answer, she turned the knob.

The bedroom smelled of scrambled eggs. Ruby's breakfast dishes were piled on the floor, dirty clothes strewn on the bed. Between the rank odor and the drawn curtains, the room had the shadowy, humid feel of an overcrowded fish tank. Ruby sat with her back to the wall. She wore an olive romper Tamar disliked. The outfit too short and baggy. She'd worn it since the day she and Salim had visited the Mahmoudis to apologize for Tamar's behavior. Now it seemed a kind of rebel uniform. Ruby lifted her head out of her book.

"I'm sorry," Tamar said. "I know I overstepped. Forgive me?"

"No, I won't. Not this time."

Tamar blinked into the gloom. "*Motek*, please. I said I was sorry."

"You need to leave my room."

"Not until this is resolved. You're my daughter. We have to fix this. Our relationship is more important than any . . ." She faltered. Ruby's expression was mutinous. "Don't let this boy come between us. Please," she said quietly.

Ruby slapped the book shut. "You think this is about Faisal?" She rose off the bed in one fluid motion.

"What else?"

"Trust."

"I trust you."

"Well, I don't trust you."

Tamar took a step back. "Ruby?"

Her daughter continued, "You went straight to Mr. Mahmoudi. You didn't even have the courtesy of speaking to me about Faisal."

"You're right. I shouldn't have gone to Mr. Mahmoudi. That was a bad mistake. But I did try talking to you about Faisal. Many times. You wouldn't listen."

Ruby went on as if Tamar hadn't spoken. "You didn't ask me if we cut school. You assumed. And telling me what to do isn't a discussion," she cried. "You don't understand, Ima. He's the first real friend I've had here, and you tried to destroy that friendship."

Tamar heard the pain in Ruby's voice, saw it etched in her face, and for the first time, realized Ruby felt betrayed by her. *Had she betrayed her daughter?* "I never meant to hurt you, *mami.*" She tried to embrace her.

"No," Ruby pushed her way out of Tamar's arms and scooted back onto the bed. "Your affection isn't going to work this time." She shook a finger at her, "You don't get off that easy."

"What can I do to make it better? Do you want me to tell Mr. Mahmoudi that I was wrong? To apologize to Faisal? I will if that's what you want."

Ruby hugged her knees.

"At least tell me how much longer you're going to punish me?"

Ruby picked at the green polish on her big toe. "I don't know. All you talk about is how great it's going to be when we go home, like it's paradise over there, but you forget we live here now. You have your friends, Mrs. E and the other old farts in this building. Well, I need friends too. But you won't let me have Faisal."

"It's not the same thing."

"Of course you'd say that. Well, I'm not going to forgive you, not for a long time, maybe not ever."

Tamar bent to pick up Ari's shirt, eyes stinging. "I've never known you to be cruel."

"Me? He was whipped because of you."

"I know and I feel terrible about it, but doesn't his father have any responsibility here? I never said, please, Mr. Mahmoudi, flog your son, and do it publicly so we could all watch."

"Well Baba agrees with me."

Tamar nodded, clutching the shirt to her chest. "Maybe. I know he's angry because I talked to Ibrahim, but please don't fool yourself into thinking he condones a romantic relationship between you and Faisal." She opened the curtains. Sunlight and a warm breeze sifted into the room. Below, Ari and Rachel played a game of skelly. The scratch of bottle caps against concrete, their laughter filled the courtyard. "Like me, he wants to spare you the pain of having to tell Faisal you can't have a relationship with him."

"Why? Because you say so?"

She turned to her. "Oh, *motek*, don't be naive."

Ruby's face took on a hard, unfamiliar cast. "God, I hate you," she said. "I don't want to talk to you, don't want to hear anything you have to say ever again. You're so stupid. Everyone knows it, especially Baba." She shouted and pounded the mattress.

Tamar gave a small cry. After a long moment in which Ruby eyed her warily, she said, "I'm sorry you feel that way."

The room seemed to shrink. She felt something icy spread under her skin. Shaken, she saw what her need to protect Ruby had done. She had caused her daughter pain, had caused Faisal to suffer, and Ibrahim—he had whipped his son out in the open, not just to punish him, but as retribution against her. He had put her in her place, held up a mirror so she could see the woman she'd become. She could no more protect Ruby from loving the wrong boy than she could protect Hadas from Daoud.

The wall clock in the kitchen read 1:40 a.m. She woke gasping, covered in sweat, having dreamed she was drowning in a lake where tiny creatures lived in the reeds. Sour, stinking, desperate for air, she slipped out of the apartment into the deep silence of the hallway. The stairwell was cool, a relief from the heat in her apartment. She reached the third-floor landing and stopped at the Mahmoudis' door, laid her hand on the jamb. What dreams did they have, she wondered. She'd never thought to understand the families that lived in Ajami or the day laborers that tended their gardens in Tel Aviv and swept their streets or Daoud and his parents, not even when she'd lived in Kafr Ma'an, not even after she learned Daoud was Hadas's lover, especially not then. Unlike Hadas, she never felt the weight of the ghosts in that village until now. She caught sight of her reflection in the hall window, a specter in a white nightgown, plaited hair reaching the middle of her back, and shivered at how insubstantial she appeared.

A moon the color of old teeth hung in the sky. She walked to the edge of the roof and looked down at the fire escapes. From that angle they looked like a giant steel lizard clinging to the facade. The dark street below hazy except where the fluorescent lights glowed. She remembered Faisal's paper airplane drifting through the air, carrying the word *Ohev*, love, to her daughter. Tamar sat with her back against the perimeter wall. There was only sky above her. Like desert sand, the rooftop absorbed the day's heat, warming her. She listened to the far-off chirp of crickets, feeling miles away from the world below. The wind blew and the leaves on the oak trees rustled. She thought of Faisal with regret and imagined him sitting beside her in a shaft of moonlight. *I'm sorry*, she'd say. *I never meant* . . . What, she asked herself, had she meant? What had she expected when she told Ibrahim Mahmoudi about that kiss?

It was nearly dawn when she went back to bed. Salim pulled her close. "Where were you?"

"Thirsty."

"Did you have a dream? Tell me." He nuzzled her neck.

"I was in a lake," she began. His breath condensed on her shoulder; he was asleep.

Ten

Tamar woke to rain, the apartment empty. The kids had gone to school without waking her, without the ritual hug and kiss at the door and an off-you-go *mitukim*. She had the urge to chase them down, but it was too late. The bedside clock read nine. They were already in class. Until their return, she'd feel restless, incomplete, the distress of not having said goodbye. Still, she remained unmoving in a tangle of sheets as damp light funneled into the bedroom. The rain came in slanted sheets, pounding against the window. She imagined disappearing into the bedding, her bones thinning to dust.

The day passed in a haze of cooking, a load of laundry that she hung on the ceiling rack. She baked for the weekend, though Shabbat was days away. She didn't go to the market or visit her neighbors and was relieved when Rachel and Ari returned.

"Where's your sister?"

"How should I know?" Rachel said. "Probably at the library. Where she always goes."

After a quick snack, Rachel collected her ballet gear.

"Take an umbrella in case it rains again."

But Rachel had already skipped out the door. Tamar then turned to Ari parked in front of the television, watching *The Flintstones*, wholly absorbed. *Wasn't he too old for cartoons?* She went back into the kitchen and sliced open an end-of-season cantaloupe, inhaling the sweet musk. She scooped the innards out with a spoon and resolved not to argue with Ruby about

Faisal anymore. At seventeen, her daughter was old enough to go to the library on her own. For the past three weeks, Ruby had spent every afternoon there working on a school project, something to do with the sack of Rome.

Two hours later, Tamar peered out the dining room window. The sun was setting, and the sky was the color of a wound. Leaves were beginning to collect in small middens at the curb. Radwa strode up and down the block, her body pulsing with energy. Tamar called down, "Everything all right?"

Radwa tilted her head up. "Have you seen him?"

She didn't need to ask who. "Isn't he at work with Ibrahim?"

"Never showed up. Is Ruby home?"

And there it was, the anxiety she'd been suppressing all day. "The library. I expect her soon."

"Maybe Faisal is with her."

"Maybe." Tamar's heart sank further.

Radwa continued her vigil.

She found herself in front of the stove, fingers hovering over the knobs, picturing blue flames catching on Salim's shirts. She tore the clothes off the ceiling rack and tossed them into a basket. A key turned in the lock. Salim.

"What's wrong?"

"Was Ruby downstairs?"

"No, why?" He removed his shoes in the foyer, cupping the small of his back. She saw the flash of pain and realized with a start that one day he'd be old.

"She didn't come home from school. Rachel said she might be at the library."

"So what's the problem?" He set his lunchbox on the counter and washed his hands in the sink. The clock above the refrigerator ticked off the seconds.

"Library closed an hour ago."

"She's probably with a friend," he said, wiping his hands on a dishtowel.

"On a school night? Who?"

"I don't know, one of her girlfriends."

"What girlfriends? The only girl I ever saw her with lived in the building next door, Mary something, but she and her family moved months ago. Faisal's her best friend now."

"Why are you so worried?"

She noticed the lines of fatigue around his eyes and couldn't remember if they were there yesterday. "Faisal isn't home yet either. Radwa doesn't know where he is. The boy didn't show up for work. I think they're together."

"What are you implying?" He sat at the table.

Tamar placed a dish of stewed beef and rice in front of him.

He took his time cutting the meat. "Ruby swore to me they're just friends. So even if they are together, what's the big deal? What have you got against him? He's a good boy. Ruby told me how he saved that guy from the pizza owners. In my corner of the world, that kind of courage is everything." He took a bite and sat back, chewing with his eyes closed. He shoved another forkful into his mouth. "Better not jump to conclusions. Any beer?"

She took a can of Schlitz out of the refrigerator, using the time to empty her face of expression.

He snapped open the tab and drank. "She's a big girl. I'm sure she's fine."

"You're right." If only she'd kissed Ruby goodbye that morning, she wouldn't feel so bereft.

An hour later, the apartment closed like a vise around her. She felt the same claustrophobia she'd experienced during the Six-Day War when sirens battered the city and she and the kids hid in the bomb shelter with the rest of the women and children in their building. All the men had gone to war. Salim's unit was the first to cross the Suez Canal. She'd had the uncanny sense that she could keep him safe if she held on to his image. She felt the same about Ruby now, certain that if she let her go for even a minute, her daughter could vanish, slip through the maternal net woven at birth.

"I'm going out to look for her," Tamar said.

"It isn't necessary. She rarely misses curfew, especially on a school night." Salim lifted the tab off another can of beer. The TV flickered, casting him in a blue wash. Before she left the apartment, she popped into the kids' room to make sure they were doing their homework.

"Where's your brother?"

"Shower."

"Good. Don't leave the house."

"I won't." Rachel bent over her books.

The rain had stopped. Pavements glittered under the streetlamps. The cross above the parish in the Church of the Annunciation was dazzlingly lit. She walked fast, calling Ruby's name, trying to appear casual and unalarmed when what she wanted was to tear through the streets, keening like the women of ancient Jerusalem. What sort of mother didn't know where her daughter was after nine o'clock? A stitch in her side brought her to a stop. She glanced at the sky where the clouds had parted and revealed an impenetrable darkness.

The lights in the school gymnasium blared. A cadre of male voices and the sharp ping of a basketball smacking a wooden floor was followed by a stampede of sneakered feet rushing from one end of the court to the other. She banged hard on the locked metal doors. By the time the janitor answered, her palms throbbed. He toddled to the curb carrying a bag of garbage in each fist. *Anything could be in there.*

"Please, mister." She explained the situation to him.

He looked sympathetic but told her there were no girls in the building. "Not even the cheerleading squad," he said.

"Can I look?" She didn't trust that he'd searched all the classrooms, the girls' locker room, the bathrooms. What if Ruby was hurt?

"Sorry, lady." The door slammed shut behind him.

The stench of half-eaten lunches and sour milk straddled the curb. She charged toward Church Avenue. The only other place she could think of was the library. Even at night the building inspired awe with its elaborate cornice and Doric columns. The gate was locked and there was no way to scale the fence. She'd hoped to find Ruby loitering on the steps, but they were as empty as the building. She continued on Church Avenue, past the synagogue, where floodlights glowed, exposing the faint lines of a swastika on the wall. She ran toward Ocean Parkway, remembering Ruby and Faisal sailing past her on his bicycle. A stabbing pain under her ribs forced her onto a bench. Music poured out the windows of cars racing by.

She didn't know where else to look. Ruby must have been lonely for years, with only a handful of acquaintances who'd disappeared or moved on. She never said a word about it, only sometimes that she missed Tehila, the Scouts, and home. There were so many friends back then. Each week another party, each month another holiday celebration. She blamed herself for this mess with Faisal. How many times had she said, *Don't get too attached here; we'll be leaving soon*, and pretended Ruby's sullenness was something she'd get over, denying her sadness, believing it was all just an adolescent phase, along with the cigarettes and alcohol as if those vices would disappear once they'd return to Tel Aviv.

"Ruby!" she called and shot off the bench, nearly slipping on the wet pavement, righting herself and running full out.

She returned to the apartment panting and out of breath. Rachel and Ari met her at the door.

"Is she here?" Tamar asked.

Ari shook his head. Salim was dozing on the couch, the television on.

"Where'd you go, *Ima*?" Ari said.

It was years since her children had used the Hebrew word for "mother." "Looking for Ruby."

Rachel stretched on the area rug, legs in a wide split. Ari was at the window, a pad and pencil in his hand. "I'll be the watchman and write down who comes and goes, so when the cops get here, I can help them solve the case."

"No police," Tamar said.

"This isn't a crime," Rachel said.

But it felt like a crime. Her daughter gone. She jumped at the sound of a car backfiring.

"Maybe Ruby's visiting the neighbors," Ari suggested. "We should interview them."

"I bet she's with Faisal," Rachel said.

"What?" Tamar said sharply.

Rachel sat back, sheepish. "They're together a lot."

"Where? When?"

"School mostly."

"How would you know that? They don't go to your school."

"They pick us up on the way home."

"Why didn't you tell me?"

Rachel tugged an afghan over her lap. "What's the big deal? We all walk in the same direction."

"I thought he worked with his father after school. Were they together today?"

"I don't remember." Rachel picked a stray piece of yarn.

"Rachel," Tamar warned.

Her eyes filled. "They said they'd meet at the library. He's really nice, Ma, and funny. Ruby's always laughing at his jokes. Even the stupid ones."

Tamar scowled. "We'll talk about this tomorrow. Go to sleep."

"Where are you going?"

"Taking Ari's advice, interviewing the neighbors. Maybe someone has seen your sister."

"But it's after ten."

"Do I have a choice? Next time"—she took a firm hold of Rachel's chin—"you tell me when your sister's hanging around with Faisal."

The only person she felt close enough to disturb at that hour was Helena Eliopoulos. She went downstairs. After a light tap on the door, Tamar listened to a series of locks opening and the yelp of Helena's dog, Zeus.

"I hope it's not too late," she began.

Helena waved her in. They settled on the couch. She lifted Zeus onto her lap. "My boy's always hungry," she said, and fed him pieces of milk-soaked bread.

Tamar faced the large cross on the wall and wondered if she'd made a mistake. Helena loved gossip. She and Mrs. Orsatti across the hall dissected the lives of every tenant in the building. Adding to that, everywhere she looked, there were images of the dead. Helena's late husband, Stavos; her son, Georgie, who died of polio six months after they arrived in New York; the statue of the Virgin Mary and Jesus in his glorious suffering. She and Helena had little in common, but they shared the plight of women who'd followed their husbands to America. After twenty-two years in Brooklyn, Helena rarely spoke of Greece, as if that chapter belonged to someone else.

"You got husband trouble?" Helena chuckled. For a big woman, she had a surprisingly high-pitched laugh. "Go on, tell me." Her eyes were full of warm concern.

Tamar got straight to the point and asked if she'd seen Ruby. She couldn't keep her voice from cracking and surprised herself by saying, "I'm so ashamed."

"For what? Bringing up a beautiful, healthy girl? We've all run away, haven't we? Our mothers didn't die because of it. Neither will you. Don't worry, she'll be back tonight, tomorrow, the day after, soon as the money runs out, or when she isn't so angry. She's angry, right? Why else would she go?"

"A day or two?" Tamar repeated, stricken by the idea that Ruby might not return home tonight. She hadn't even thought of money. Ruby had about forty dollars saved from babysitting. "Please let me know if you see her."

Helena squeezed Tamar's hand. "I'll make tea. Still got Easter bread in the freezer."

Tamar didn't say no.

At midnight, Ibrahim Mahmoudi knocked on their door, a grim look on his face. "I know where they might be. There's a gazebo in Prospect Park. The kids call it Heaven."

"You think they're together too," Tamar said loud enough for Salim to hear.

Salim met them at the door.

"We'll take my car." Ibrahim walked ahead. "How are you at nighttime reconnaissance?"

Salim laughed. "Been trained by the best."

"That's what I thought."

She listened to their footsteps fade, then spent the next hours pacing the apartment, plucking cigarette after cigarette from Salim's pack, smoking them out the kitchen window, where their clothes hung like scarecrows on the line. She opened the bottle of Johnny Walker Black that Salim had got for Christmas last year from his boss and poured herself a glass, shuddered at the taste, but liked how it burned and worked the tight, cinched feeling out of her throat. At 2:00 a.m., strung out on nicotine and alcohol, she heard Salim's and Ibrahim's footsteps on the stairs and rushed to the door, eye at the peephole. They were alone. Salim stepped in and, glancing at her with a look of helplessness, bolted the door. He then went straight into their bedroom.

She followed him, stomach roiling from the liquor, the cigarettes, the worry. "What happened? Where is she?"

"We searched, drove through the park. They weren't there." He sounded exhausted. "I'm going to sleep. I've got to be at work in six hours."

She turned on the bedside lamp, their shadows gargantuan on the ceiling.

Her head pounded. "But our daughter's missing."

He placed his wallet on the dresser. "She isn't missing." He took the change out of his pocket. "We both know she's with Faisal. She'll be all right. Faisal will take care of her."

"*We* should be taking care of her. He's just a kid. They're both just kids." She felt nauseous with worry and yet was grateful that Salim didn't say what they both knew to be true: This mess was her doing. Why else would Ruby leave home?

"They could be anywhere. This country is so big," she whispered.

He went to the closet and took out his uniform, and draped it on the back of the chair in preparation for the morning.

"Don't be so dramatic," he said, "Besides, Ibrahim and I don't think they've gone very far."

The man who never put his clothes away was suddenly opening drawers, peering inside them at the socks and folded shirts, sniffing the fragrant soaps she placed there to keep his clothes smelling fresh. He strode to the window and gripped the casement, searching out some distant point in the square patch of sky overhead. A ripple of muscle like a strong current moved across his shoulders. "They'll be back tomorrow."

"Tomorrow?"

"Tomorrow!"

"You're her father, her baba. You need to find her."

"I know what I am." He pressed his forehead to the glass. "That means she'll be out all night with Faisal."

"Tamar."

"How could you come home without her?"

He swung round. "*Khalas!* You've done enough, said enough. This never would have happened if you'd come to me and discussed this properly."

She wanted to defend herself and say, *I did come to you. I wish you had listened to me.* But before she could open her mouth, he said, "I should've known with a mother like yours, you weren't fit to bring up my children."

"How can you say that?" She swiped at the tears on her face. "My mother?"

"You heard me."

She looked around the room, feeling something ugly and frightening sweep through it. "You think your family's so pure?"

He scowled. "My family? You've dishonored my family. You've brought shame on us."

She felt dizzy and grabbed hold of the bedpost. "That would be Hadas who brought shame on you, not me."

His hands curled into fists. "Don't start," he warned.

"Oh, *hamudi*, you think she was innocent." She pushed past him, wanting only to leave the room.

"What are you talking about? He grabbed hold of her arm.

She splayed her hands on his chest and pushed hard. He didn't budge.

"Nu?"

"Let me go, Salim, it's late."

"Tell me." His fingers dug into her flesh.

"No." She tried wresting out of his grip.

"Talk."

She closed her eyes. "I can't. She made me promise."

"What promise?"

"To keep her secret. From you. You're hurting me." She slumped against him. "Salim, please, let me go. I don't feel well."

"After you tell me."

"Okay."

He relaxed his grip. "I'm listening," he said in an almost reasonable tone.

She was aware of the last traces of his cologne coupled with his sweat, of how his body curved toward hers, as if all of him was listening now. She didn't want to hurt him. "Hadas had an affair."

"I don't believe it."

"For fifteen years."

He laughed in disbelief. "With who, the mailman?"

"An Arab man from Kafr Ma'an."

He stepped back, searched her face. "No."

"She loved him. Very much."

"She loved Moti," he said in a way that made her wonder if he believed his own words.

Tamar shook her head. "No, *hamudi*. She married Moti to please you."

"You're lying."

"I would never lie about something like this."

He turned to the nightstand and dug for a cigarette in the drawer. "If it's true, tell me his name."

The lights in the courtyard flickered. "Daoud Hamid. He was an engineer and a poet."

He recoiled. "What?"

"He lived in our house. That is, we lived in *his* former house in the village."

Salim shook his head. "Not possible. It can't be him. That was the name on the crime report. I saw it when I went back to the police station. The man from Qalqilya. It can't be the same man."

She walked to the window and opened it wider. "He loved her so much, Salim. Too much." A cool breeze rustled the sheer curtains.

"What are you saying?"

"It's why I've been so worried about Ruby. It feels like what Hadas went through all over again." She turned, startled to find him close behind her. "I'm scared, Salim. We have to protect Ruby. Because it can happen again. The horrible tragedy of it. Maybe not now, but years from now when he gets so angry and hurt because one day he will. He'll blame her for the whole mess, the way Daoud blamed Hadas for ruining his life, for not running off with him. They were supposed to leave for France but Hadas broke it off. Don't you see, this is why Ruby mustn't be with Faisal."

Salim backed away. "Daoud Hamid killed my sister. You knew about their affair and never told me, not even afterwards?"

"I couldn't tell you. Hadas made me swear not to. She told me over and over that if I said anything, you'd hate me. Blame me for it. She said you'd never forgive me. I believed her. Please," she beseeched, walking toward him.

"Don't." He raised his hands. "All this time you knew her killer and never said a word to me. How *can* I forgive you? *Elohim aderim*, you could have stopped it. Saved her. All you had to do was tell me. But you didn't."

"I—I know," she stammered. "I'm so sorry. I don't want to make the same mistake again. That's why you have to find Ruby."

He opened the door. "Go, please just go."

"Salim." She stood on the threshold.

He gave her a light shove, locking the door behind him.

She knocked, hoping he'd relent, and stood in the dark for a long time, ear to the panel. It was so quiet, she thought she could hear him breathing.

Eleven

Ari had thrown off his blanket. Rachel was wrapped snug in hers. Tamar's gaze rested a moment on Ruby's empty bed. Then she searched the dresser for an old blue sock Ruby kept her money in. As she suspected, it was gone. Never having traveled beyond Manhattan, she had no idea how far the kids could get on forty dollars. She got into Ruby's bed and hugged her pillow, breathing in the slight feral musk, and pictured Ruby not as she was now, but as she'd been before they'd left Israel—sensitive, defiant. A battery of memories crushed her into the mattress. One of their last days on Frishman Beach, Ruby stood rigid at the shore, her feet sinking into the sand.

"What are you doing?" Tamar asked.

"Collecting sounds," Ruby said. "So I won't forget. In case we don't come back."

"Of course we're coming back." Tamar had been convinced Salim couldn't stay away, that within a few months they'd return and regale their family and friends with their New York adventures. After Ruby "collected" her sounds, she joined her cousin Tehila.

She turned on her side. Something from under the pillow fell to the floor. Her hand closed over Ruby's diary. Ari mumbled in his sleep. She waited before turning on the flashlight, hoping it wouldn't wake him. She squelched the guilt she felt at invading Ruby's privacy, surprised to see the pages neatly filled in Hebrew, not just the early entries, which was to be expected, but the recent ones when English came to her easily. She opened to the pages at the back. Faisal's name appeared on every one. There was nothing about why they left, or where they might have gone. One passage caught her attention, dated a month ago, around the time she'd seen them kissing in the cellar.

We went to the zoo. I told Faisal I didn't like seeing animals caged. He said it wasn't so much for us to see them but for them to see us. They needed the company to know they existed. I guess he was right cause when we stepped inside their den the lions roared a hello. But then the roar changed to a wail. It was the loneliest sound I'd ever heard. Faisal saw that it upset me. We went out into the sunshine. He kissed me in the boathouse and then we walked around the lake.

All afternoon there was a weight on my chest as if love were stones collecting there. He loves me. He told me so. And it makes me so happy, and I'm so sad because of what Ima will say and Baba too, though he pretends to like Faisal, but I know it's all an act. If you ask me, he does it to drive her crazy. Sometimes I think he hates her cause she reminds him that Hadas is dead and that he ought to be home instead of here. Mr. Mahmoudi isn't any better and Radwa looks at us with pity. She knows what we're in for. I tell Faisal we're like ghosts haunting these skins. He tells me it's only skin that separates us. I tell him its two thousand years of history. He says fuck that shit. I say yeah. But then I think about Tehila and how she lost Hadas and that now she's getting ready to join the army. I think about what she would say if she knew I loved a Muslim boy, and I feel sick and think maybe I'll never go home again.

Tamar closed the diary. It's what she'd feared, her daughter torn between love and duty, love and family.

Dawn pressed against the windowpanes when she awoke to a knock on the front door. She had fallen asleep in Ruby's

138

bed. Stomach heaving, head pounding, she struggled to her feet. Ari and Rachel were asleep. The shower ran. Salim was still home. Helena, dressed in her usual mourning black, was at the door. Her dog, Zeus, was tucked under her arm like a handbag.

"I thought you should know that while I was out this morning, I saw the young Mahmoudi boy going into the cellar."

"Cellar?" Tamar said.

"In C and D Buildings."

"You saw Faisal?"

"Well, it's still a bit dark, so I can't be sure, but I think it was him. I didn't go down there myself. Zeus doesn't like the dark."

Yesterday's rain had seeped in through the cellar window above the laundry sink, causing a damp chill in the room. Tamar wrinkled her nose at the sharp smell of mold. A water bug scampered across the concrete floor. She flicked the switch and blinked at the fluorescent light. In dimension and purpose, the cellar was identical to the one in their building. Someone had left a brooch, a bow tie, and gaudy earrings in a brass bowl near the laundry sink. A Playbill from the Broadway musical *No, No, Nanette* lay on a metal chair. At the back of the cellar there was a Japanese screen, concealing what appeared to be an alcove or a small room. A brown tweed sofa bed open and unmade, sheets the color of buttermilk, and at the foot, Ruby's blue jeans with the sunburst patch on the knee. Faisal's shorts on the floor beside a shag rug. The Betty Boop T-shirt Ruby slept in was draped across a pillow. She recognized the blanket as one she'd seen on Radwa's laundry line. The kids must have just left; the sheets were still warm.

The room tipped like a ship that had hit the shoals. She felt off-kilter and lay on the bed. Her shoes soiling the sheets.

Like the bomb shelter on Frug Street, the ceiling was lower in this part of the cellar. They must have felt safe, cocooned. There was a desk and oak chair with small brass wheels on its legs. Leafing through pages of Faisal's drawings, she recalled the ones taped to the wall of his bedroom. These were different. The landscape barren, beautiful, with deep craters and wide sky that reminded her of the Negev Desert. Two large creatures inhabiting a lonely planet, barely human, but clearly male and female. And at the bottom, words in Ruby's hand. A story, a creation. There was a three-legged stool with a lamp on it, an alarm clock, the Amos Oz collection Ruby had been reading, and the blue sock she kept her money in. How long had it taken them? Hours every day after school to build their little nest. Ruby's library project. Another lie. They were like children playing house. No, they were like newlyweds, a bride and groom.

She banged her knee on the edge of a steamer trunk on her way out. By the time she reached the apartment, she was sweating and breathless. Ari and Rachel were just beginning to stir. Salim was in the bedroom. He wore his foreman's uniform, the dark green work pants and gray shirt. The name *SAL* sewn over the breast pocket. He frowned when he saw her.

"I know where they've been," she said. "Ruby and Faisal. I know where they spent the night."

Salim rushed to share the news with Ibrahim, and the two men ran down to the cellar. She had a hunch where the kids were and climbed the stairs to the roof of Building D. Hadn't she and Salim watched the sunrise on the roof of their house in Kafr Ma'an? Each morning of that first year they'd felt the world open its arms to them.

She found the pair sitting with their backs to the door. "I'm sorry," she said.

"Ma?" Her daughter managed to look frightened and rebellious at the same time.

"It's my fault." Faisal stood and tucked Ruby behind him. "I asked her to spend the night. We're okay."

"They know about the room in the cellar," she said to them quietly. "Your father and Ibrahim are there now."

"You told them," Ruby fumed.

Tamar shook her head. "Someone was bound to see you," she said, but Ruby and Faisal were already running past her, taking the stairs two at a time.

They charged into the cellar. Tamar was close behind them. The Japanese screen crashed to the floor.

"Stop," Ruby shouted.

Faisal wrapped an arm around her. "It's no use. They're not going to listen. They can't even hear you."

He was right. Ibrahim and Salim were ripping the sheets and pillows off the bed. They flung the mattress against the wall. It caught on the stool, sending the lamp crashing to the floor. The alarm clock rang. Ibrahim brought his foot down upon it. The ringing stopped and the two men, grunting with exertion, worked together to flip the sofa onto its side. The only thing left upright was the desk.

"No, Baba, please don't," Ruby cried.

The men hesitated and then mangled and tore the drawings. They overturned the desk and the chair, the brass wheels spinning maniacally.

"Enough," Tamar said. "*Bass,*" she shouted in Arabic.

Ibrahim and Salim stopped, out of breath. They looked at what they'd done, the ruin they'd committed. They looked at the faces of their children, who in that moment were no longer children, and then at each other. Ibrahim straightened his spine. "You're finished here," he said, and pushed Faisal out the door.

When they were gone, Salim said, "We will never speak of this again." His eyes shot from Ruby to Tamar.

In a matter of days, Faisal was packed and sent to live with his grandparents in Jaffa. Tamar thought she'd feel relieved, but all she felt was empty. The irony was not lost on her. This was what it took to be shipped home: her poison in Ibrahim's ear and a little room in a cellar, and all of it in the name of love. She hated her part in it and wished it could have played out—as it certainly would have—without her involvement. She went with Ruby to visit Faisal on the day of his departure. Radwa opened the door. A jet stream of heat and spices engulfed them. She opened her arms and Ruby sank into them.

Radwa cupped Ruby's face. "What are we gonna do without my boy?" She walked them down the hall to his room. "Faisal, you got company."

Radwa turned to her. "This one," she said, "knows how to break my heart."

Faisal lay on his bed. The blanket that had been in the cellar was folded over the back of a chair. "I have a going-away present for you," Ruby said and removed a stack of papers out of her bag. She sat beside him. Tamar remained in the doorway.

"Open your hands." She gave him the drawings their fathers had torn and the ones safe inside the desk drawer. She'd gone back and collected the pieces, taping them together, ironing them smooth. "We're going to finish this someday."

Perhaps it was the lighting that gave Faisal's skin an ashy hue or the sadness that leached into the room. Tamar cleared her throat. "I wanted to wish you safe journey."

He sat up. "Maybe I'll see you in Israel one of these days." He gazed at Ruby. "It's my first trip there or anywhere."

"I'll be there next year. We'll see each other all the time, even when I'm in the army." Ruby held his hand. Then she turned to Tamar. "Please leave us alone." Ruby looked ready to cry.

Ruby stayed with the Mahmoudis until it was time for Faisal to go to the airport. Ibrahim carried the boy's suitcase downstairs. Radwa held her son's hand. Just then, Hussein turned the corner, carrying a carton of cigarettes. His jaunty stride came to a stop when he saw them. He waved and Faisal lifted his head, and then after a moment in which they could hear a bird twittering in the branches of an oak tree, Faisal ran to him and they embraced.

"You're not getting rid of me that fast." Hussein grinned. "I'll see you on the next buying trip."

Faisal returned to Ruby and cradled her in his arms. Tamar remained on the stoop, feeling as if she were standing on the other side of a canyon watching a landslide.

Avenue C was empty at that hour of the evening. Cars were parked along the curb like a circus train waiting to leave town. Streetlights tugged at the bits of glass lodged in the road. Before Ibrahim got in the car, he looked straight at Tamar and said, "This could have turned out differently, you know. We could have been the exception." He slammed the door and drove off.

Ruby carried a sack in her arms.

"What's that?" Tamar asked.

"A present from Faisal."

He'd given her a five-pound bag of red pistachio nuts. Ruby refused to share them and ate every last one. For months her hands and lips were stained pink. Pink fingerprints marked the doors and window casements. Pink on the refrigerator, the sinks, and walls. Pink on the books and clothing, the bedding, the television. Everywhere Ruby touched, the faint impression of Faisal remained.

Part III

DISMANTLING

Twelve

Mid-October an unexpected heat wave had the neighbors gathering on the stoops of the Calliope Garden Apartments. From her second-story window, she heard their conversations. Rachel and Ari were playing kickball with the neighborhood kids. Salim brought the dinner plates into the kitchen.

"Are you going downstairs to watch them?"

"I don't think so." She stacked the dishes in the sink, feeling him behind her, weighing his next move. Her body tensed as one of his hands climbed up over her breasts, the other splayed on her collarbone, thumb curving into the hollow at the base of her neck, softly and then with a bit of pressure, enough to let her feel the strength in his hands. This was where they were now—the secret she'd revealed was a loaded pistol between them. It could frighten them together or drive them apart.

"None of this makes sense without you," he said. The belt buckle on his chinos, the blades of his hips against her back, his warm breath at her temple. She knew he did this because he needed her for something.

This is me truly alive, she thought with despair.

He gave her butt a squeeze. "I want us to have everything."

"I know."

Yesterday he'd taken her to see a house for sale on the other side of the borough in a new development east of Canarsie. Steering her mind from the house and all that it implied, she soaped the forks, ran the sponge over the bellied spoons. She heard Rachel and Ari squabbling and wondered if Ruby was off sulking somewhere. When she wasn't trailing through the apartment like a wraith in a Yiddish play, she gave into bouts of shouting and weeping.

A plate slipped from her hands. With her back to him, she said, "We had everything once."

The front door closed behind him. She leaned against the sink, the ire draining from her. All day the heat had made her homesick. This morning she thought she smelled the jasmine in their front garden in Tel Aviv, but it was only the fabric softener. The fragrance burst out of the washing machine. She hung the clothes on the line and thought home was no longer rooted in one place but existed in the scents of a thousand objects. She dried her hands and on impulse unbraided her hair. The unruly waves far from the Israeli sun had deepened to a dark blond. The sweep of it across her back reminded her of the summers on kibbutz when she was in the Scouts harvesting fruit, dancing around a campfire. She put on her favorite dress and kicked off her slippers. Before she could talk herself into a pair of shoes, she descended the stairs barefoot to join Salim.

Outside, the warm dusk engulfed her. A few people had set out folding chairs near where the children played. Rachel led the youngest ones, a group of four- and five-year-olds in a game of Red Light, Green Light. Ari was a giant next to them. The children fell in giggles when he froze mid-stride, hands clawing the air, a goofy grin on his face. She waved and he beamed at her. Salim greeted her with a nod. His gaze rested on her hair before sliding down her figure, stopping at her feet. His smile slow and knowing as it traveled up her body. He turned to the cluster of men, dark and foreign, their laughter gruff, their accented talk wrapped in cheap cigarillos.

"Tammy," the women called to her. The anglicized version of her name with its long and flattened "a" made her grind her teeth. Only Radwa ignored her. The day after Faisal left, Tamar knocked on Radwa's door. No one answered, though she could have sworn someone peered through the peephole. After a week of silence, she confronted Radwa in the stairwell.

"Have I done something to offend you?" She shifted her shopping bag onto her hip.

"You can ask me that?" Radwa said.

"I'm sorry. I thought we were good neighbors and friends." Tamar widened her smile, trying to appear at ease.

"We were never that." Radwa's hands clenched at her sides. "Ibrahim told me you called my son a liar and accused him of skipping school. You thought he was a bad influence on your daughter. Ibrahim wouldn't tell me why he punished Faisal. Neither would my son. For weeks they kept it from me. But I know now. You shamed my boy. You disapproved of him and he was punished. If that wasn't enough, you sent our husbands down to that room where our children made a home, a safe place where they could be together. Something we are not capable of doing. When I first met Salim and then you, I wanted to imagine we could be different. But then you spoke to my husband. You sent them down there. You pushed them to it, knowing they would destroy what our children had built. It's what you wanted."

Tamar blanched. "No. I didn't know what they would do," she insisted. But somewhere inside her, she must have known that neither man would stand for Ruby and Faisal's defiance and that they'd never accept an unsanctioned love. She couldn't tell Radwa why she tried to separate the children, that even here, thousands of miles away, Hadas and Daoud's deaths haunted her. She blundered on, "Believe me, I had no idea Faisal would be punished that way. I was sure you knew that I'd spoken to Ibrahim, that he told you about our conversation, about my concern for the children."

"My husband tries to spare me when he can. He knew what you did would break my heart. Now my family is broken. My youngest child far from me in a place I cannot protect him, where I know he will be hurt by more people like you. I was a fool to believe we had to send him away. And all because you don't want your daughter to love my son."

"I'm sorry," Tamar said, but Radwa had already turned to climb the stairs.

Later that same day when Tamar asked Ruby if Faisal had arrived safely in Israel, her daughter said, "Please don't pretend you care. I don't think I could stand it," and left the apartment.

Tamar found Helena reclining in a beach chair, her expression wistful as she observed the children playing. She stood beside her until Helena looked up and said, "Wow, I don't think I've ever seen you with your hair down. You look like a teenager. I had no idea it was so long and wild," she laughed.

A flush stained Tamar's cheeks as she took in Helena's appearance: the ubiquitous widow's black, hair coiffed into a brunette helmet each week at the beauty parlor.

Helena pointed to an empty folding chair beside her.

"I was saving this for you," she said. "You all right?"

"Sure," Tamar said, and then greeted another neighbor before Helena could probe further.

She wasn't ready to tell her about the house for sale. Yesterday, they left the kids home with Ruby. The day was overcast and the stench of sewage drifted out of the sanitation plant on Flatlands Avenue near the Paerdegat Basin. She held her breath until Salim said, "What are you doing?" Then he pointed to the strip mall that lined Ralph Avenue. "They have everything here."

There was a supermarket, an International House of Pancakes, a bank, Woolworth's, and a Chinese restaurant. The stores were big and over-bright, something she'd come to expect of American shops, where merchandise was always on display and she was reduced to being just another consumer, one of the masses, anonymous and unseen, her money the only thing speaking for her.

Helena took her hand and stared at Tamar's bare feet. "What's going on, you a hippie now?"

"It's so warm, I didn't feel like putting on shoes." To get her friend off the topic of her attire, she said, "Do you need to go back to the Social Security office?"

"Those bloodsuckers"—Helena struggled to sit up—"they want to keep my money. Twenty-two years Stavos worked in this country. Now they're giving me a hard time again. He's dead six years and six years I fight with them until they give me what's mine. You come with me, I take you to lunch after. Good Greek food." She clutched Tamar's wrist.

"You don't need to do that."

"We're friends, right?" Helena said.

"Yes." She glanced at Radwa.

A car gunned its engine. She followed its path to McDonald Avenue, catching sight of the oak trees and the Dutch colonial houses across the street, the Church of the Annunciation on the corner with its green lawn spanning half a block, tempting her the way the kibbutz had tempted her to run barefoot through fields of tall grass. Farther along Avenue C was the school where Ari and Rachel were in the fifth and sixth grades, and a few streets beyond, the high school Ruby attended. She knew this neighborhood almost as well as she knew Tel Aviv. She'd even come to like their apartment though she'd hated it at first, the dark foyer and two mean bedrooms. Seeing her reaction, Salim had cradled her face and said, "What did I promise you?"

"A fortune in five years and then home."

Until yesterday the words had been her mantra but then he'd taken her to that new development with its model homes and identical two-family townhouses with screen doors and pitched roofs. Acres of derelict lots heaped with slabs of concrete, twisted steel girders, and weeds as tall as men.

"This was once a landfill site. Amazing what they can do with garbage here."

They drove down roads where bulldozers had exhumed broken toasters and busted television sets. The smell was a combination of sewage, rusted pipes, tarred pilings, and the primal stink of excavated earth. He stopped the car on a block where there was a row of attached houses on one side and a weed-ridden lot on the other. Each house had a driveway and a garage. Abutting the garage was a ground-floor rental apartment. At the corner of the block, a hill of sand she knew Ari would love to climb. She pictured it full of sharp objects and imagined how and where he would be cut, the length and depth of the wounds, the blood difficult to stanch.

Salim came up behind her, his hands on her shoulders. "Can you see it?" he said, his chin a pendulum swinging across her scalp. "Our future here."

Her toes curled on the concrete as she speculated on that future. A breeze blew across the avenue. Her neighbors chattered on about whose child was sick with mumps, whose husband had lost his job, who was pregnant, who had died, and had anyone seen the latest Vogue pattern? Salim was deep in the circle of men. His stance indolent, one hand in his trouser pocket, the other holding a cigarette. She was sixteen the first time he'd kissed her. They were on Kibbutz Ein Gev. After a night of folk dancing, he took her into the banana grove and tossed his shirt on the ground for her to lie on. They faced each other shivering. He tasted of smoke and caramelized banana; their toes burrowed into the soil like worms.

He'd practically dragged her into that house for sale, through the kitchen with its fancy dishwasher, up the short flight of stairs to the master bedroom, private bath, and walk-in closet.

"Tell me you can resist this," he said.

When had she ever wanted such things? When had he?

He crossed the hall. "This can be Ari's." He pointed to a small room. "He'll be a bar mitzvah in two years. I can't see him sharing with his sisters forever. Can you?"

His logic was a serpent.

They went down a short flight of stairs to "Rachel's bedroom," where a sliding glass door opened onto a tiny patio and a cement yard with a narrow strip of dirt.

"Remember the garden we had on our balcony in Tel Aviv? We could do that here, only better."

Sturdy weeds marked the perimeter of a three-foot fence, not the lush dahlias and lilies that had grown in terra-cotta planters on their balcony or the bougainvillea that greeted them at the entrance to their apartment building.

"Is it safe?" she asked, apprehensive at how easy it would be for someone to climb the fence and molest her daughters. "People could break in."

"You always look for the hair in the soup." He gave her a gentle shake. "You know what the best part of this place is? The rental. We'll be landlords, put a little extra aside." He took hold of her hands. "Think of it, Tamar." And then he whispered in her ear, "I put a binder down."

Now she felt Salim's attention on her.

153

"Anything wrong?" He mouthed the words.

She shook her head, and he resumed his conversation with Ibrahim Mahmoudi. The men spoke in Arabic. Before they married, she had asked Salim what it was like to be an Arab Jew in an Arab land. He shrugged. "Somedays not much different from being an Arab Jew in a Jewish land." Then he changed the subject, as if she couldn't grasp what it meant to be an outsider. The truth was she hadn't then; she did now.

Salim and Ibrahim were the same height, though Ibrahim was a bit thicker around the middle. He was right about one thing: It did disturb her to see their similarities, but not for the reasons he thought. His presence made her see Salim more distinctly, closer to how Hadas had seen him, what she'd warned her about—that way they had of speaking with authority on all subjects, how they behaved with their wives and children—patronizing, cautious, with a touch of tyranny. Neither appeared too comfortable in their skin, not even Salim, who was ready to put good money down on a house where the carpeting smelled of naphthalene and the living room sported a wall of floor-to-ceiling mirrors. Their reflections had caught half a dozen times.

"Why you standing?" Helena patted the seat next to her. "I have a crick in my neck from looking up at you."

Tamar dropped into the chair, the homesickness like a low-grade fever she couldn't shake. Darkness fell in increments, and the sky turned a deep cerulean. The children played tag. Ari always last, his legs lagging while his torso lunged forward. His head craned at an awkward angle. Some of the younger children were dressed in pajamas ready for bed, moist from their baths, not wanting to miss a second of the evening with its symphony of crickets and insects that singed their wings on the lamps above the lintel.

Ruby sauntered toward her. Tamar gripped the arms of the chair, squinting at her daughter's choice of wardrobe—a black Led Zeppelin T-shirt tied at the midriff and cutoff jean shorts. An homage to Faisal.

"I wish you could've worn something a bit more decent," Tamar whispered so no one would hear.

Ruby cast a withering glance at Tamar's bare feet and said, "Didn't know this was a dressy affair."

She hid her feet under the chair.

"I'm going to the pizza shop for ices. Dad gave me money." She flashed a set of bills

"Are you bringing some back for the kids?"

"Yeah."

"Fine, then you can go."

Ruby glared at her. "I wasn't asking for your permission. Baba just wanted me to tell you that I was going." She left before Tamar could formulate a response.

"Give her time," Helena said.

Tamar frowned at her daughter's receding figure, so bright and tall, a newly minted American girl.

Ari hurtled past, startling her. He was no longer running with the pack of children whose shouts pierced the evening sky but running from them in a new game. She looked to see if Rachel was part of the small mob; her younger daughter was on the stoop of Building A with her friend, Sarah Kantor.

Nine or ten children ranging from ages eight to thirteen were in pursuit of Ari. They chanted his name. Ari, hair hanging in his eyes in thorny spikes, waved his arms as if he were stopping a bus. When they reached the corner of East Fourth Street, one of the older boys leapt into the air and slapped the street sign, making it ring, alarming the adults. The other children spun around so fast, Ari had to perform a quick two-step, swerving on the balls of his feet, righting himself before toppling onto the concrete and then racing off ahead of the pack. She was surprised by his agility. His hands pummeled the air, footfalls thundering, belly lifting and dropping like a sack of flour. Terrorizing shrieks of joy filled the avenue each time the kids drew close enough to touch him.

On the third turn when the children reached Building D, Ari stumbled and dropped to his knees, his palms breaking his fall, his chest heaving as he tried to catch his breath. Tamar rose out of the chair as the children swarmed around him. They're too close, she thought, worrying he was hurt. He stayed on all fours. A small red-haired boy from Building C poked him in the stomach with a stick.

"Hey," she called out, "stop that."

"Look at it jiggle," the boy cried. "Jiggle boy, jiggle boy."

Ari tugged his shirt down. Another child around the same age ruffled his hair but Ari shook him off. One by one the boys took their turn pulling and jabbing.

"Stop that," she shouted, her voice drowned out by the children's screeching laughter.

"Leave them," Helena counseled. "They're playing."

"Too rough," Tamar said.

"They're boys."

She turned to Salim, hoping he'd put an end to the game, but he was still in deep conversation with Ibrahim. Also, Ari didn't seem to mind their antics. He giggled and smacked their hands away until the ringleader, the oldest boy in the group, who looked as if he belonged on a recruitment poster—tall, square-jawed, blond with a military crew cut, shouted, "Hunters, prepare for phase two." The children stood at attention. "Ride him, Mikey," he said, and the youngest child climbed onto Ari's back. Her son attempted to rise to his feet, but the boy bounced up and down as though riding a bronco, bringing Ari to his knees. When Ari tried to toss him off, the child squeezed his legs around his torso and held on to the collar of his shirt. Her son hooted with pained laughter as two others tickled him mercilessly, their fingers drilling into his flesh, under his arms, until the boy with the military crew cut gave the command for them to halt. Mikey slid off with a thump.

The leader said, "Get up," and Ari got up. "Run!" he shouted.

Ari shook himself off and ran. The pack gave chase. At first, her son galloped up and down the block, but soon he tired, and each lap became shorter than the last until there was nowhere left for him to go. When the leader called "Circle," she watched with growing dread the children looping their arms, trapping Ari in the center. In one voice they cried: "Jiggle boy, jiggle boy." Ari lunged right, then left, trying to break free. When he saw no way out, he came to a standstill, head bowed, his breath labored.

Though Helena tried to hold her back, Tamar marched to the periphery of the circle. Her voice unnaturally shrill, she said, "Get away from him." She thought they'd disband when they saw her, but the children continued undeterred. Their voices grew louder, and the air thickened with their excitement. Ari crouched on the ground, belly spilling out of his shirt. Her son looked helpless. As if they'd been waiting for this moment, the boys converged on him, their silence menacing. Her neighbors stared at the ring of children, at her son's mortification; not one came to his aid and she hated them for it.

"Ari, come here."

He didn't appear to hear her and tucked his chin into his chest, wrapping his arms around his head, waiting for whatever punishment the boys would mete out.

"Leave him alone." Her throat was raw.

He let out a cry. Tamar charged ahead, ready to tear them off him, not caring who she hurt, but a pair of arms lifted her into the air. She swallowed a scream.

"Let him be," Salim hissed.

"He's hurt."

"He'll be fine." Salim's expression was grim as he held her back.

She struggled, looking up just in time to see Radwa watching them.

Tamar went limp in his arms. "Get him out of there, please."

"Not yet. He's got to learn to fight for himself."

"Ari, get up," she said, and then to Salim, "Your son needs help."

Ari staggered to his feet, deflecting the kicks and the punches aimed at him, dodging like a bull in an arena. His T-shirt ripped. Scratches on his arms and legs. The children continued their assault; their numbers swelling as even the littlest ones who an hour ago had played with Ari entered the game. To her complete surprise, Ari rose to his full height and roared. He stretched his arms into the air and roared again. The sound reverberated through her. Like an outraged bear, he swiped at the crowd that jeered at him. Her eyes filled; her body tensed. Mothers shooed their youngest ones inside. Women called to their husbands. She struggled to break free of Salim's hold, but he held her tight. His voice gravel in her ear, "Let him be a man."

"He's eleven, damnit."

Ari lifted his fists into the air and whipped his arms round in windmill fashion. The boys nearest him scattered, but not before Ari landed a swift punch. The ringleader with the military crew cut howled and grabbed hold of his face.

"That's enough," Salim said at last. "Time for everybody to go home." As if shaken out of a sack, the children scampered into their buildings.

There was blood on her son's chin.

"I'm proud of you," Salim said, and Ari grinned. Tamar wanted to pull her son into an embrace, but Salim stepped in front of her and whispered, "Not now. The boy needs his father, not his mother's coddling."

Radwa called to Salim, "You've got a brave boy there."

Salim bowed his head. "I hope one day he'll be as brave as your sons."

Ruby came down the block, carrying a cardboard tray of Italian ices. "What happened?"

"Ari beat up that kid, Mitchell, from around the corner. He punched him right in the jaw. You should've seen it," Rachel said. Tamar swung round. She had no idea Rachel was even behind her.

"We played hunter and I was the prey, and when they caught me, they tried to beat me up, but I got a good punch in, didn't I, Baba? Just like Bruce Lee," Ari said.

Salim laughed. "Yeah, you beat up the biggest boy in the group."

"Hurray you." Ruby handed Ari a rainbow ice. "About time someone kicked his ass. That kid acts like a drill sergeant."

"Where's my ice?" Rachel said.

"Right here, *motek*."

The three stood licking their treats unfazed, while Tamar remained shaken, trying to understand what had happened.

Neighbors said good night and left with folding chairs tucked under their arms.

Helena waved to her. "See you tomorrow. You got a big, strong boy."

"Ruby, take the kids upstairs," Salim said. "I'll be there in a minute to help Ari clean up."

Without a murmur, the three disappeared into the building.

"Don't be mad," Salim said.

"Why would I be mad?" She lifted her chin, hoping the tremor in it went undetected.

He threw his arm across her shoulders. "Because when it comes to the kids, you like to be the one in charge, and I've let you until now but we both know that sometimes you overdo it."

"That's unfair."

"Is it?" He rubbed his cheek against hers, the burr scratching her skin. "You can thank me later."

"For what? Not taking our son out of harm's way?"

"Forget Ari, he's fine. He was never in any real danger and he needed to know he could handle himself. Now he does."

"So you say."

He gave her hair a gentle tug. "We got more important things to look forward to. We're in contract. The house is ours or will be when the mortgage comes through."

"The house?" She stumbled—a pebble dug into the sole of her foot.

"After what just happened with those *mamzerim,* I bet you'll be happy to get away from here." His breath warm on her cheek. "It's fate, *ayouni.* The house came to us just in time. You'll see, it'll be better for all of us. Ruby, the kids. I'll go check on Ari. He's gonna be damn sore tomorrow." He grinned and strode into the building.

She wanted to call him back to tell him what she thought of the house, how another move seemed so precarious, uprooting the family again, investing their life savings in something that rested on little more than sand. Most of all, she wanted to tell him how he'd reneged on his promise to her, but she knew what he'd say—"You owe me this"—and given all that had transpired between them, maybe she did.

Except for the faint crackle of the streetlights and the rumble of cars on Ocean Parkway, everything hushed. Radwa waited for her husband at the entrance. Tamar thought they'd already gone upstairs. She thought she ought to apologize to Radwa again, but the words stayed trapped in her throat. Ibrahim stopped beside her.

"Don't worry, your son's fine. It's a part of nature. You have to let them go. Especially when you see that sometimes they're better off without you." He walked through the entrance door, Radwa close behind him.

Thirteen

On the first of March 1973, they drove across Brooklyn in a car crammed with almost everything they owned. A truck hauling their furniture trailed behind them. For months she and Salim had argued over the move. Even so, six weeks before the closing date, she and Salim presented a united front and gathered the children in the living room. They told them about the new house in Canarsie. As he sat them down, she recalled the last time he did this when he convinced them that moving to America was going to be a grand adventure. She wasn't so sure he could do so now that they were older. What had become clear to her since the night she'd revealed Hadas's secret was that she'd lost purchase in her marriage. She'd lost his trust. Salim spoke the truth when he said they wouldn't discuss it again. Yet that was all she wanted, to explain, to make him understand how conflicted she'd been, to ask for forgiveness and receive it.

Ari was the first to cry out and say the move was unfair, especially now that he'd garnered some respect and was no longer the target of bullies.

Rachel accused them of not caring. "You never ask us what we want."

Salim said something about how good it was going to be to own a home. "We'll have the freedom to do what we want." He strode around the room, rubbing his hands together as if he were hoping the friction would generate the excitement he wanted, rather than the pall that had settled over them.

Tamar turned to Ruby, who'd remained quiet throughout the discussion. "What do you think about all this?"

"Me?" Ruby said, "Why bother asking *me* when you've already made the decision? Nothing we say will change anything. You'll do whatever you want. Neither of you gives a shit if we're happy."

"Hey," Salim said. "You know that isn't true. I work hard to make your lives better. Life doesn't stop because we're moving. You can have your friends over anytime. You'll have your own rooms and I'm sure your friends will love the yard. I'm going to put in a swimming pool, and you can have parties and barbecues. How about that?"

"Whatever you say, Baba," Ruby said, and left the room.

Ari asked, "Are you really going to put in a pool?"

"You bet," Salim said, then tugged on Rachel's ponytail. "What about you, Ruchie?"

"I'll tell you later."

"Why not now?"

"'Cause I have to see if Sarah can sleep over before I make my decision."

Salim turned to Tamar and smiled. "Thank you for standing with me on this. He grabbed her hand. "I know you're afraid this means we'll never go home again, but we will someday. I promise. You'll see, we're going to be happy now."

"Oh, Salim, I know you believe that. Maybe it's better we stop promising things we can't keep. That way no one gets hurt."

A month later they were driving into the new development, past a crane parked in a field and tarp-covered hills of sand. They arrived to find a stranger on their stoop. The young man of average height dressed in blue jeans and a peacoat rose to his feet as they pulled into the driveway. His duffel bag at the bottom of the stairs.

"Who's that?" Ruby asked.

"Our new tenant, Gadi Azoulay." Salim put the car into park. "He's a friend of my boss's son."

Tamar frowned. "I thought he was coming in April."

"And lose a month's rent?"

"We haven't even moved in yet."

"What does that matter? He's not living with us. You won't even know he's here."

Salim introduced them to Gadi, who revealed a charming overlap of his two front teeth when he smiled. He had a prominent nose and shaggy light brown hair. Salim handed him the key in exchange for an envelope of cash. Before going into the rental, he lifted two boxes out of the trunk without being asked and deposited them on the porch.

Tamar struggled to open the door, jiggling the key in the lock.

"Mind if I try?" Gadi said.

She stepped aside. With one quick turn, he unbolted the lock, then dug into his pocket for cigarettes and offered her one.

"Thanks. Where in Israel are you from?" She bent over the flame.

"Originally, Bat Yam. More recently, Tel Aviv."

She blew a trail of smoke over her shoulder, looking down at Salim pulling blankets out of the back seat. His shirt lifting, the dimples in his lower back a set of quotation marks.

"I better go." He descended the stairs as Salim came up.

"Did you know he lived in Tel Aviv?"

"Yeah, small world. Hey, help me bring these in." He pointed to the boxes Gadi had stacked near the entrance. "Since when do you smoke before dinner?"

Tamar shrugged. "I don't." She took a long drag then crushed it under her heel.

Hours later when the furniture was in place, she left the children to continue unpacking and took the shopping cart out of the garage. She peered into Gadi's window. He was in the kitchen, bowed over the sink, scooping water up with his hands. He turned abruptly and saw her there. She flushed with embarrassment and raised her hand in greeting. He didn't return the gesture.

Hills was the biggest supermarket she'd ever seen. Only in America, she thought, where there was an abundance of space could there be a grocery store a block long. Half-drunk on fluorescent lighting and towering wagons of produce, she journeyed through the aisles, reading the labels on bottles and cans. She breathed in the fermented air in the dairy section, stuffed the cart with ice cream and tater tots, then followed the aroma to baked goods and the deli counter. Hills sold everything from eggs to paperback novels. As she stood at the checkout, the enormity of what she'd agreed to filled her to choking. They'd bought a house in the middle of a landfill. On the way back, she dragged the cart over uneven sidewalks, some cracked, others buckling. The ground beneath her sinking.

That spring the lots were covered with dandelion and clover, bindweed and thistles, and everywhere there were the sounds of construction, the rhythmic hammering, the whine of the saw. Each day a fleet of cement trucks poured new foundations. Men in hard hats bellowed over the din. The scent of raw wood filled the air. The neighborhood burgeoned around them. Houses sprang up like mushrooms after a rainstorm. The children attended the neighborhood schools—modern edifices with courtyards and rotundas and a hundred windows that didn't open. Everyone in her family seemed to be settling in. Except her. To her, the house felt like a railway station where their lives had stalled.

One night while they were getting ready for bed, Salim said, "I left the factory."

"What?" She felt a jolt of excitement, of hope, perhaps now they could go home.

"I'm the new manager of Eli's laundromat."

"Your boss, Eli? When did this happen?"

"Last week."

"Why didn't you tell me?"

"I'm telling you now." He tossed his shirt across a chair.

"How could you not tell me something like this?"

"There's lots of things we don't tell each other."

"Salim, that isn't fair. There was ever only one thing I didn't tell you."

He undid his trousers. "Anyway, it's the perfect solution for us."

"Solution? How?" She slipped into bed.

"We get twenty-five percent of the profits, plus a salary, and I learn how to run a business on his money. In six or seven months, he'll sell it to me. Don't look at me like that."

She focused on a thin crack in the ceiling that ran from the light fixture to the door. "Like what?"

"Like it's Yom Kippur."

"I'm tired." She turned on her side. A paltry show of defiance that he didn't even notice. He just kept talking about how this was his big chance to prove what he'd always known about himself: He was a businessman—a *macher*—not an employee.

Early each morning she saw them off. Salim and the children striding down the block, turning the corner, disappearing from view. She remained by the window until Gadi left for work. She watched him walk to the curb and light a cigarette. He pulled his shoulders back as if bracing for the day. A breeze lifted the hair off his neck. She had no idea what made him turn around, but he always did. He looked at her framed in the window, clutching the neck of her robe, then raised his hand in greeting and she spread her palm on the pane. They didn't speak. They didn't even smile, but somehow his acknowledgment that she was there made it a little more possible for her to move through her day.

It didn't take long for Salim to see the potential of owning his own business. A few weeks after he began running the laundromat, he declared the only way to guarantee his success was if he had extra capital.

"We've already got two mortgages," she pointed out.

"There's the apartment in Tel Aviv," he said. "Just sitting there, making a couple of lira a month. It could give us the opportunity to make a fortune."

"Don't even joke about it."

A month went by before he brought the subject up again, this time at the dinner table with the children present.

"Just imagine what we can do with the money if we sell it," he said.

"What can we do?" Ari asked.

"Well, instead of driving around in that *taranteh* we've got now, we can buy a new car and . . ."

"And what?" Ruby said.

"I can start my own business."

Tamar could see the thought elated him. She found it difficult to swallow the food in her mouth and spat it into a napkin.

"What kind of business, Baba?" Rachel asked.

"A store or I can even go into manufacturing. Something like what my boss does."

"Plastics?" Tamar said, incredulous. "You hated that job."

"I wouldn't hate it if the business were mine."

She picked at a sauce stain on the tablecloth. "Why even bring it up? We can't sell. We've got to have some place to live when we go home. Don't we?"

Salim's face was inscrutable. The children bowed their heads. That night unable to sleep, she walked through the house. The dim glow of the streetlamp spilled into the living room. She opened the door to Ruby's room in the basement and stood on the landing. Between the landing and the door to the garage was the party wall they shared with Gadi's apartment. She pressed an ear to it and heard the television set he'd recently purchased. She pictured him sitting on the sofa he'd dragged in off the street, the TV light flickering across his face.

The next morning, she awoke at dawn and filled a box with a set of old dishes, two stout glasses, a worn tea kettle, and a *finjan* she no longer used. On impulse, she added a package of Elite Turkish coffee. Then she dressed in a pair of slacks and a green knit blouse. She applied lipstick and rebraided her hair then waited for Salim and the children to leave before she took the box downstairs to Gadi. When he opened the door, she said, "This is for you," and held the carton out like it was a prize he'd won. He ran a hand through his hair, grimacing when his fingers caught on a knot. His face unshaven, his blue jeans riding low on his hips. He held a T-shirt in his hands and blinked at her before pulling it over his head.

"Sorry, did I wake you?"

"No. What have you got there?"

"Dishes and a few things I thought you could use. I should've given them to you weeks ago, but it took me a while to unpack. I wasn't sure if you'd want them. I can take them back." She was rambling. He looked older in the morning light. Twenty-eight or -nine. He had a way of looking at her that made her uncomfortably aware of herself. She sucked in her stomach. He peered into the box. His head close to hers. He smelled of Necca Sheva, an Israeli soap he must've brought from home. She sniffed and closed her eyes. "This is getting heavy."

"Sorry," he said, yet still didn't take the box from her.

"Should I just leave it here on the doorstep?"

"Nah." He hefted it onto his shoulder. "*Yallah,*" he said, expecting her to follow.

He placed the box on the kitchen counter.

She looked around the spartan room. A stack of books against the wall next to the TV. "Will you be staying long in the U.S.?"

"About a year, 'til I've saved enough money for university back home."

"What do you plan to study?" There wasn't a thing on the walls. The folding chair they'd given him was used in lieu of a coffee table.

"Film." He lit a cigarette. "Want one?"

She shook her head. "You work in the plastic factory with your friend?"

He threw the match into the sink. "God no. I'd rather be dead." He shot a train of smoke over her shoulder.

She blinked. "So where do you work?"

He opened the box. "While I was in Italy, I met a man there who owns a frame shop in Coney Island. He offered me a job. I took it."

"You were in Italy?"

"I was in a lot of places." He stacked the dishes in the cabinet. "Thanks for these, especially this—" He held up the *finjan* and the coffee. "I'll make us a cup."

"Don't you have to go to work?"

He looked at his wristwatch. "Not yet."

She sat on the edge of the sofa, a hideous orange corduroy, and wondered why he didn't cover its ugliness with a sheet. He placed two glasses on the chair, half filled with *cafe botz*, the type of coffee soldiers made in the field, then sat beside her, their knees almost touching.

"Do you like it here?" She took a sip and winced. "Hot," she said, the roof of her mouth scorched.

He cocked his head. "Honestly?"

She nodded, rubbing her tongue along the ridge of her teeth, thinking how comfortable it was to slip into Hebrew with someone outside of her family.

"Not really. I can't seem to find the beauty in it. Are you all right?"

"Fine." She attempted a smile, her lips wobbly. "It's getting late." She rose to put the glass in the sink. He took it from her, then plucked a strand of hair off her face. Instinctively, she turned and for a moment her cheek rested in his palm. She felt his chest rise and fall.

"Sorry. It was about to go into your eye," he said.

On impulse she said, "Come for Shabbat dinner. Salim would love the company. We all would."

"If I can. Thanks for the dishes," he replied and led her to the door.

All day she thought about Gadi alone in his apartment, sitting on the orange sofa, his books and TV for company, and ran her tongue over the roof of her mouth where the flesh had peeled. She didn't see much of him after that. He didn't come for Shabbat dinner. He left the house earlier and came home later. He didn't wave goodbye or check to see if she was standing at the window. There were nights he didn't come home at all.

The weather warmed, causing the carpet to smell of naphthalene. Vapors rose out of the pile—a killing field for moths. She kept the windows open and vacuumed each day, attempting to suction the foulness out, but the odor remained.

"Don't you smell it?" she asked Salim.

They had just finished eating their Sabbath lunch. She played a record on the stereo. He lit a cigarette. For the first time in days, they weren't arguing over selling their Tel Aviv apartment. The hopeful strains of Debussy's *Arabesque* filled the room. They were alone. Ruby had taken the kids to the mall. Satiated and feeling lazy, they sat on the sofa. Soon they'd withdraw into the sweetness of a Sabbath nap, tuck into crisp sheets. The breeze would almost make it feel like home. She took out her Gobelin. Salim lit a cigarette.

"We've got to be smart about this. We've got to be like sharks," he said.

She cut a length of peach floss.

"Keep moving or die."

She forced herself to relax and focused on the large tapestry of Degas's dancers. She'd forgotten how satisfying needlework could be, filling an empty space with uniformed stitches, watching the slow emergence of an image surface.

"I'm sorry, what are we talking about?" She tried to project a sense of calm.

"What we've been talking about for months. A business," he said. "Our business."

She stuck the needle into the canvas. "Please, not on Shabbat."

"It's the only way for us to succeed."

How emphatic he was; how sure of himself. She pressed a hand to her stomach, feeling it roil under her palm. The smell from the carpet made her light-headed.

"I must have seemed so gullible to you," she said. "I believed everything you told me."

The music continued with its cascade of soft, deliberate notes.

He frowned. "What do you mean? Don't you want a business? You complain about how much I work. This way I can close on Shabbat, take a vacation. I'll finally be my own boss."

"What I mean," she enunciated with care, "is that you've gone back on every promise you've ever made to me. You've taken us away from everything we know and brought us here. This isn't where we ultimately belong. It's a stopover."

"So you keep saying. The rest of us don't feel that way."

"If you sell the apartment, Salim, we have nothing to return to."

He shot off the couch, brimming with energy. "Don't you want me to be successful?" The cigarette was tucked into the corner of his mouth. A trail of smoke lurked behind him.

She looked down at her hands crushing the Gobelin in her lap. "Of course. But you'd be successful anywhere, especially back home."

"Tamar"—he ground the butt into the ashtray—"if I sell the apartment, I can buy my own business here. Do you have any idea what that means?"

The thought appalled her. It was worse than buying the house.

"You already have a business with Moti's cousin, Eli."

"If I have to settle for quarters and dimes, I want all the profits, not just a percentage of them. He lied to me; said I could buy him out slowly. Now he wants all the money up front. I don't want to be some glorified employee."

"Glory in a laundromat?"

His lips tightened. "That's why I have to sell the apartment and use the money to invest here. I'll buy him out and then have enough for a down payment on another business. See? I'll own two."

"Then when will we go home? Six years and we're still in this godforsaken—"

"Godforsaken? Look around you. I'm partners in a laundry business. We own a house in America. We're landlords."

"We're in debt," she interjected.

"Gadi Azoulay pays good money to rent the apartment downstairs. A few more years and we'll pay down the mortgage. What do I have to do to satisfy you?"

"Think of the kids," she said.

"I am. They're doing great. Ari's got friends. Rachel loves her new ballet school, and Ruby's happy again. Why would you want to ruin what they have here?"

"Ruby happy? You see what you want to see, Salim."

Her head was buzzing, the naphthalene overwhelming. She got up to open the window wider and took a deep breath. Her gaze fell on the empty lot across the street where a blue plastic detergent container glowed in the sunlight, the color teasing a memory—Hadas in her blue dress, running into the *pardes*, Daoud stepping out of the row of trees into the path, catching her in his arms.

Salim picked up the pack of cigarettes on the coffee table, the lighter in his other hand, flicking it on and off. They faced each other. "How do I convince you this is what's best for us?"

A sedan pulled into the driveway next door. Their new neighbors, the Rosens, had moved in a week ago. Mrs. Rosen stepped out of the car carrying a Macy's shopping bag.

She turned back to Salim. "Please let's go home before it's too late, before we ruin everything. Let's sell this house, take our money, and start a business in Tel Aviv. We'll be with our family, Hadas's family, and you'll get what you want. We'll be happy again. Please, Salim."

He placed his hands on her shoulders and searched her face. She leaned against him. He kissed her and she relaxed, thinking it would be all right now.

He pressed his forehead to hers. "Tamar, you have to stop fighting me. I'm selling the apartment. I'm not going to let you destroy our chances of a good life here because you're scared."

Her eyes welled; she pushed her way out of his arms. "You're right. I am scared. One day you'll regret this. Just think what Hadas would say. She'd be so disappointed. She'd want us to go home, to be there for her children."

He stiffened at the mention of his sister. "I told you we don't talk about her. You've said some miserable things to me that I've had to excuse over the years because I was the one who forced you to come here. And I know how hard it's been. But then you bring up Hadas, thinking I'll give in to you. From the beginning, she warned me that when the time came for you to be strong, you'd fold like a cardboard house."

"I don't believe you." She flicked her hand. "She wouldn't say that. She respected me. She loved me."

"I know my sister. She loved you as long as you kept her secret. If you'd done the right thing and told me, she'd have hated you; I wouldn't have. I'd have thanked you." He marched upstairs.

Fourteen

His absence was numbing. Salim called on Friday mornings to speak to the children and give her an update on the sale of the apartment. Each day she roamed through the house, gathering the detritus: the dirty cups in the children's rooms, empty bags of Fritos under the beds, a sweater that had fallen off the back of a chair. She adjusted the painting of a boat tossed in a storm at sea. She'd bought it on layaway from the shop Gadi worked in the same week Salim left for Israel. Owing them an outing, she'd taken Rachel and Ari to the Brooklyn Aquarium. They'd spent every day in the small yard playing with the water hose, bounding through the spray like puppies. Ruby had a job as a mother's helper babysitting two children, but even if she'd had the time, it would have been futile to ask her along. Ruby wanted little to do with her. Besides, she had friends now, girls and boys that loitered in parks and on street corners. They went to church dances on Saturday nights. They ate grilled cheese and bacon sandwiches at the Greek Diner. Tamar smelled the pork on her daughter's clothing. There was a time when Ruby was too ashamed to bring anyone home, yet these new friends skipped through the foyer and greeted her, *How ya doin', Mrs. Abadi*, in their twangy accent. They shuffled past the kitchen and down to Ruby's room. She glared at them through a haze of cigarette smoke from the top of the stairs. Their laughter, their rock music, their curses punctuating every line of conversation, all of them more foreign to her than Faisal had ever been.

It took her and the children two hours to arrive at the Brooklyn Aquarium. At each leg of the journey, they looked at her with reproach. When they reached the boardwalk, they gripped the railing and gaped at the ocean. A tanker was anchored at sea, gulls rode the waves and scavenged for food. Sunbathers glistened like gems on the sand.

The children asked, "Can we swim?"

"Next time." She paid the entrance fee and they walked through a maze of dank corridors. They studied the dolphins and the seals. They watched with faces pressed against the glass the quiet grace of whales floating in tanks. On the walk back to the train station, Ari said he preferred the life of seagulls.

"They're scavengers."

"Exactly. They take what they want and want what they get."

"Who told you that?"

"Baba."

Her mouth formed a sullen *Oh* and then, seeing what street they were on, said, "I think the frame shop where Gadi works is around here."

"Can we say hello?" Rachel said.

"Can we, Ma? He promised to show me how to frame a picture if I came by." Ari took two pieces of Juicy Fruit from the pack in his pocket and stuffed them into his mouth.

"Ask your sister if she'd like a piece."

Ari rolled his eyes. "Why? She hardly eats anything."

"Gum isn't food, stupid," Rachel said.

"Enough," Tamar said. "Just give her a piece."

While they continued to bicker, she took out her compact and applied a fresh coat of lipstick.

"What are you doing that for?" Rachel asked.

She ignored her and returned the compact to her bag. "Did you get a piece of gum?"

Rachel blew a bubble.

"Good, let's go."

The store was tucked beneath the elevated train and smelled of linseed and wood shavings. There were paintings of forest landscapes in the window.

"What a nice surprise." A smile lit Gadi's face. He was looking directly at her.

She felt her mouth go dry. It had been weeks since she'd seen him. "Is it all right if I explore?"

"Go ahead. I'll entertain these two."

An old phonograph played 1930s Russian tango music. The tune was simple, and she hummed along under her breath. Feeling self-conscious, she smoothed her hair, noting the way Gadi's hair bounced when he laughed at something Ari said. His skin tanned from mornings at the beach, his hazel eyes bright.

Rachel sorted through a tin of slogan buttons—*Vote Lindsey, Power to the People*—reading each aloud. Tamar combed through the paintings propped against the wall, finally landing on the small boat, knowing immediately that she wanted it though it had little artistic merit. The background was muddy and all of it done in yellow and ochre, colors not associated with the sea, but she was drawn to its somber pull toward destruction and the boat's unflagging hope to stay afloat.

Each week she went back to put a few more dollars down on the painting. She arrived when Gadi was in the alcove at the back of the shop. There was a cot with blue and white cotton ticking, a wooden table, and an icebox, where he kept his lunch. The man who'd given him the job was a Russian immigrant who had two more businesses in Coney Island. He came in the evenings to collect the day's earnings. From the sound of it, he was everything Salim aspired to be. Gadi closed the shop for an hour in the afternoon. He ate his lunch and then rested on the cot, one arm cushioning his head, a lit cigarette in his other hand. He used the time to think, he said, the cigarette burning down to his fingertips. "Aren't you afraid of fire?" she asked.

"Nah, I've been awake with my eyes closed since the army."

Sometimes she would get there while he was still eating. He'd answer her knock by stuffing his feet into a pair of sandals, and he'd stare at her through the warped glass pane before opening the door. He smelled of smoke and sometimes of arak.

"*Yallah, tikansee,*" he'd say, and walk ahead, his sandals slapping the linoleum. She'd feel a moment's hesitation being alone with him, but then she'd think of Salim in their apartment, selling the furniture and appliances they'd left behind, and thought no more about whether it was proper for her to be alone with Gadi.

Still, the remains of his lunch embarrassed her, intruding on him in this way. He offered her a cigarette and a cola. They sat at the table amid scraps of food, his teeth marks visible in a heel of salami. The phonograph bleated the tango as she waited for him to write a receipt for the amount. On the way out, she'd ask, "What is this music you keep playing?"

"Russian tango. Meyerkov gave it to me. There's no radio, so it's better than listening to the thoughts in my head." He gave a self-deprecating laugh. She noticed how clear the whites of his eyes were and wondered what he saw when he looked at her. A woman a decade older, time digging its trenches into her brow. Her hair in a bun like an old maid, nothing but lipstick to brighten her face.

"I never knew Russians composed tango music. You're welcome to borrow a record of mine, if you want."

He held open the door. "Thanks. I'd be happy to bring the painting home for you, so you don't have to keep making the trip."

Her eyes widened. "I hadn't even thought of that. It would make things easier."

"Unless you like coming to Coney Island."

Blushing, she said, "I do, actually. I like the boardwalk. It reminds me a little of Tel Aviv. Does it feel that way to you?"

"Not really."

She had the gnawing sense that she bored him. He never asked her to stay longer. He never even shook her hand.

"Okay then, see you next week," he said and stood in the threshold until she reached the stairs of the elevated train. That night she listened for his key in the lock and tiptoed downstairs to the landing at the top of the basement stairs. She pressed her ear to the party wall. Something dropped onto the table in his flat, possibly his keys, and then the pad of his feet crossing into the small kitchen. The sharp turn of the faucet and water running in the sink. He switched on the radio. When she heard the toilet flush, she rushed back upstairs, stunned by what she'd done. She blamed Salim for leaving her alone. She imagined him in their kitchen in Tel Aviv. A warm breeze drifting in through the balcony and the aroma of their neighbor Shula's cooking, spiced and delicious, making him homesick enough so that he wouldn't go through with the sale.

The last time she went to the frame shop, the day had been overcast. People hurried through the streets, glancing at the darkening sky. She'd forgotten her umbrella and hoped the rain would hold off until she was inside the store. The buildings under the elevated train leaned one into the other like a quorum of men in prayer. She banged on the door of the shop to be heard over the train and the thunder that boomed over the ocean. When Gadi didn't answer, she worried she'd made the trip for nothing, but then he came out of the back. The shop appeared gloomier than usual. She brought a homemade coffee cake. The only man she'd ever baked for was Salim and so the act of sifting flour, beating eggs, creaming butter and sugar had seemed almost adulterous. She wore her best skirt and her hair loose.

"Come in." He led her into the alcove. Rather than offering her a Coke, he admired her outfit, his gaze resting briefly on her hips. "This deserves something better than cola," he grinned.

She bit her lip and watched him pour a shot of arak into a jelly glass. "You haven't been home for a while," she said and then blushed.

He placed the drink on the table.

"I mean I haven't heard you there." She almost groaned. "Please don't think that I keep tabs on you. I don't. It's just that the walls are thin." If possible, her face grew redder, as she recalled all the times in the past few weeks that she had pressed her ear against the party wall. She looked away and gulped the arak

He smiled, aware of her discomfort. "My sister and her friend are visiting. They've got a place in the city. I've been spending time with them."

The liquor burned her throat and made the back of her neck ache. There was bread and the remains of a stuffed pepper on the table. She wondered whether it was his sister or her friend who had prepared the meal.

"You must be lonely here," she said.

He peered at her through the gloom. Light from the overhead turned his hair the color of caramel.

"Sorry. None of my business," she said, unable to stop, "but you do live alone, work alone. I just thought it must get lonely."

"I don't think about it." He went into the front room and put a record on. "Here's Pyotr Leshchenko, the Russian you like."

She remembered the cake and set it on the table.

"Wow," he said when she opened the tin. "May I?" He tore off a piece. There was dirt under his nails. "Delicious."

She turned away from the sight of the mashed cake between his teeth.

"Salim enjoying Israel?" He licked his fingers, then wiped them down the front of his jeans.

She sat down and smoothed the skirt over her knees. "He's there on business," she said. "Not much time for fun."

"You've gone sad suddenly. What are you thinking about?" Gadi poured another shot of arak into her glass.

"He's selling our apartment in Tel Aviv. He's found a buyer."

"You don't want him to."

"No."

"Why's he doing it, then?"

"So he can buy a business here." She tugged at a thread on her skirt; one hard pull and the hem would unravel.

"I thought he already had one."

"He's part owner in a small laundromat. Salim's ambitious. He wants something of his own."

"I can understand that."

"Can you? Are you sure it's the Russian I like?"

"Yes, but it's the B side of the record."

A clap of thunder rattled the door. "I forgot my umbrella." Her eyes filled with tears. She blinked them away.

"Don't worry, I've got an extra. Drink up," he said.

She took a cautious sip, not wanting to get drunk and do something silly. She already regretted coming here, dressed as she was.

"Do you tango?" he asked.

Startled, she said, "Not for years. You?"

"Lessons with an old girlfriend."

"Now you look sad."

He shrugged. "Dance?" And he held out his hand.

"Here?" She looked at the cramped quarters.

"It's not like there are any customers."

Maybe it was the clouds pressing against the storefront window that encouraged intimacies, or the rain beating the pavement, or the two shots of arak that allowed her to lean against him. He murmured in her ear.

"What did you say?"

"I love the rain." He clasped her waist to guide her around the edge of the cot.

"Me too."

His hand was warm against her back, his breath in her hair. She almost tripped over his feet. He closed his eyes, his cheek to hers. The scent of arak drifted from their mouths. He dipped her low and she gasped, blood rushing to her head. The needle sank into the next selection. They danced around the table and into the front room. She searched for something to say to ease the tension.

"Do you know Kafr Ma'an?" she asked.

"Sure. What about it?"

"Salim and I used to live there."

"Must've been a long time ago. Place is deserted now."

"I wish we'd never left. They tore most of it down after we did."

"What was it like?" His lips grazed her ear.

"Very sweet." She closed her eyes.

"How so?"

"We knew it wouldn't last."

He pulled her close. His mouth a centimeter above hers. She felt something hard against her hip and recoiled at the heat that flared between them. The light flickered and rain hit the window like pins. They came to a stop; the accordion flooded the room.

"I'm sorry, I have to go."

He released her. "I'll get the umbrella."

She picked up her bag and gave the store a last look. "Would you mind bringing the painting home with you?"

"Tonight?"

"Yes," and then in case he had the wrong idea, "I'll send Ari down with the rest of the money. You can give him the receipt along with the painting."

He nodded. "Okay," and he went into the back and retrieved an umbrella. "Thanks for the cake," he said.

She tugged at her skirt, knowing it would probably get ruined in the rain.

When the house was empty, it belonged to her. Until the children returned, always sooner than expected, their key in the lock, their voices in the hall, the thud of a shoe hitting the floor. Her solitude shattered. They shouted, "Ma, you home? Ma?" It took long minutes before she could summon an answer. Since the move—yes, only since the move (she clung to that)—she had a hard time summoning an emotion, even love. That was the poison they inhaled like an undetectable gas. She watched her children as if they were strangers living behind a glass case that she could only press her nose to.

She picked up Ari's dirty socks, Rachel's hair ribbon, a worn copy of Hesse's *Demian* Ruby was reading for a senior literature class. She used the ribbon to earmark the page. She took burgers out of the freezer, cleaned the white-tiled counter and red ceramic containers marked *Sucre* and *Farine*. Even when the kids weren't home, it was hard for her to expand into the space, to recline on the sofa, to listen to music, or to

183

read aloud the way she did sometimes. In high school, she'd studied elocution in a room that faced the sea, and recited the Song of Songs, the Hebrew dictionary perched on her head. *Tell me, you whom my soul loves, where you shepherd.* Hands on her waist, she breathed her ribs open and closed like a concertina, aware of the places in her body that replicated the same patulous movement open shut, open shut. Her voice a bird that flew out the open window. In this house her voice sank into the carpet, to the river of sludge that ran beneath the floor, ferrying her dreams into the Paerdegat Basin around the corner, a canal that separated Canarsie from Bergen Beach. The water gray, brown foam bobbled on the surface like ice floes. Sometimes fish that had lost their bearings ended their lives panting on the weedy shore.

Together with the painting, Gadi brought home the Russian tango album as a gift. *A sweet reminder of a rainy afternoon*, he wrote in Hebrew on the back of the receipt. She put the record on, picturing him on her sofa, laughing in the waning light. His long eyes gleaming as she walked across the room with a grace she couldn't quite muster with him. On that last visit to the frame shop, the tango had haunted her all the way home. The rhythm pulsing in time to the chugging train. The Atlantic Ocean in full view. Her body suffused with the breadth of all that boundless space. Her rib cage expanded and contracted as if she were in her elocution class, her voice winding toward the sea.

The record played and she took up the needlepoint of Degas's ballerinas. She snipped a length of red floss and split the threads. From her tapestry bin she took the postcard Salim had sent from Tel Aviv, a picture of the Jaffa Clock Tower. On the back, he'd written: *Sold*. With her embroidery scissors, she cut the word into tiny squares and sewed them into the background of the Gobelin. It took time for them to disappear into the canvas, to become part of the reflection of dancers in the mirror, time to thread the needle, to lay the stitches, time before Salim's betrayal was vanquished beneath the satin threads.

In an hour she'd hear a key in the lock. The kids charging in. Rachel would prepare for her ballet class and Ruby would dash into her room in the basement, cheeks flushed, hair mussed, trailing in the scent of some boy's cologne. Ari would snack, sit by the window, and watch clouds drift across the sky. Their grandeur reflected in his face and for a moment the great scope of the world would defeat him. *How does one begin to live when your house is not your home?* she imagined him asking. And her answer, *I wish I knew, eynayim sheli, my eyes. Ayouni, ayouni.*

Fifteen

He returned from Israel with gifts: chocolates and puzzles for the kids, a blouse and a book for Ruby, jewelry for her—a hammered silver ring with a green Eilat stone. "It's beautiful," she said, admiring the way the silver caught the light and the purity and color of the stone.

"I had it made especially for you," he said.

"Oh, Salim." She hugged him, breathed in his scent. "Thank you. I'll cherish it, always."

She wore it every day. Its presence gave her comfort, lulled her into believing that he'd forgiven her. Maybe the price for true reconciliation was the apartment, she thought. And for the first week or two it seemed so, but then she began noticing subtle changes, things she mistook for a lack of time and forgetfulness, for overwork when Salim didn't kiss her when he left in the morning, and how when he returned, he'd ward her off. "Shower," he'd say and dodge upstairs, so different from the days when he'd invite her in to talk about their day. He stopped undressing in front of her, as if he'd suddenly grown shy, and unless she took his hand when they walked together, he didn't hold hers. They didn't make love, and the lack of intimacy (an intimacy they had managed to hold on to even during the worst of times) spread from one day to the next like a virus that infected every aspect of their lives. She tried to pinpoint when the attrition began—was it before their last argument in June or when Salim returned from Israel and immersed himself in the laundromat business? She wondered if going home had reminded him why they'd left. He must have thought about Hadas and Daoud often. (How could he not?) He might even have gone to Kafr Ma'an without telling her. And she didn't ask, fearing it would stir it all up again, what she'd done, the secret she'd kept from him.

One night before bed, Tamar said, "Are you still angry with me over Hadas?"

"No." He took off his pants and carefully folded them over the chair.

"You haven't . . . we haven't in so long."

"I know. I'm just tired," he said without looking at her.

She picked at the waffle pattern on the blanket. "I guess this happens to all couples at some point."

"I guess." He climbed into bed and faced the window, his back to her.

She gave a small, pained laugh, "I just never imagined it would happen to us." Then she ran her hand over his shoulders and down his back. She missed him.

"I'm sorry, Tami, truly *habibti*." He kissed her hand, then placed it on her hip with a soft pat.

Each rejection stunned her anew. She picked through their conversations, searched for clues that would lead her to the cause of his defection. Then tried everything to win back his favor. She prepared his favorite meals, starched his shirts, took an interest in his business, in the Israeli news, even politics. She waxed the hair off her body, rubbed almond oil into her skin, wore perfume and makeup, dyed her hair, used the code they'd developed over the years: a lingering touch, laughter that slowly died, the brush of her body against his, a note placed in a strategic spot to be read, to be savored. Nothing worked. He was immune to her. He had developed amnesia, forgotten their language, their customs. He was a foreigner in their land.

Then the first letter arrived from the girl. The soldier. The twenty-year-old Salim had fallen in love with when he sold their apartment to her parents. The envelope written in the fulsome scrawl of a teenager. The number one inside a heart with an arrow shot through its center at the bottom righthand corner. There was no return address and so she'd thought it might be from Tehila, Hadas's daughter, and opened it, never expecting to read the words *Come back my love.* She immediately sealed it shut and left it on the kitchen table, where it waited like a prophecy for him.

That evening at dinner while the kids argued over something on the television, Tamar whispered to Salim, "Who was that letter from? I didn't recognize the handwriting."

His eyes latched on to hers. In them she saw a flash of fear and then a forced calm.

"The buyers' daughter," he said, spreading a thin layer of harissa on a slice of rye. "She's interested in going to college here after her service."

"But why is she writing to you? You don't know anything about the university system here."

"I'm the only person she knows in the U.S."

"She's seems very young, Salim. It would be a shame if she mistook your attentions for something more than friendly counsel from an older man. Don't you think?"

He bent over his plate. "Sometimes you talk too much."

She decided to let the matter drop but then two more letters arrived, one following the other like homing pigeons. That night she found him sitting on the stoop, drinking a beer and smoking a cigarette, cupping it in his hand like a soldier in the field, keeping the lighted tip hidden. The moon was bright, and the sky was deep and starless. It was late and the only sounds were the gentle buzzing of cicadas.

She sat beside him. "Can I have a drag?" she said.

Without a word, he passed the cigarette to her and she leaned against the railing, noticing the way his arms rested on his knees, the pull on the muscles in his back. He stared ahead at the empty lot overgrown with saplings and weeds.

"What is it with you and this girl?" she asked.

He tensed.

"Hey." She placed a hand on his shoulder.

"Nothing," he said.

"Those letters aren't nothing. She loves you or thinks she does." She exhaled a cloud of smoke.

His face filled with a tender light.

Her breath hitched. "Oh, Salim, what have you done?"

He shook his head. "I never meant . . . I'm so sorry, *ayouni*."

She stood up and ground the cigarette beneath her heel. "You have to stop it. Now. Tell her it's over. No more letters. Do you understand? You tell her it's over."

He dropped the empty beer bottle over the railing into the can below. The sound of it crashing into the aluminum bin made her flinch. His face was stark under the yellow porch light.

"You're right," he nodded. "Except," he said with a sad smile, "I'm afraid it's too late." He kissed her cheek and went inside.

On the last day of Rosh Hashanah while she breakfasted on oolong tea and honey cake, the twenty-fourth letter from the girl slid through the mail slot. She recognized the soldier's handwriting, her penchant for numerical order. The number 24 circled in red ink on the envelope fat with mementos. *Par Avion* written across the back seal in bubble letters, the rounded penmanship of a young woman in love. In her zeal, the girl pressed the pen too hard, carving confessions into blue sheets of onionskin as though she were carving them into Salim's heart.

Tamar considered tearing the letter up or hiding it beneath the basket of onions she kept in the hall closet. No one would know it was there. The kids were with Salim in the *shtiebel* on the corner in a ground-floor apartment converted into a temple by a young Lubavitcher rabbi and his pregnant wife. Poor Salim. There was no Mizrahi synagogue in the neighborhood and so he was forced to pray with the Ashkenazim during the holy days. Through the open windows she heard the cantor imploring God and the congregation's voices lifting, condensing into a single note. She chafed at the indignity and felt isolated and adrift in this place where all the houses were identical and attached like paper cutouts. She had to put up with letters that arrived every few days from a girl not much older than Ruby. Missiles that targeted her marriage with ruthless precision.

She tried to keep busy. There were still cartons she couldn't bring herself to unpack. Everything inside them was either from Israel or for Israel. When no one was home, she went into the garage and opened the boxes. She tried to imagine the items in their apartment in Tel Aviv, the Corelle dinnerware set bought with eighteen books of S&H green stamps, and the barnyard- themed kitchen towels she'd found in the dollar bin at Woolworth's, only to remember that Salim had sold their apartment for a down payment on a candy store he intended to buy. Soon the smell of rusted sewer pipes and the whiff of dead mice forced her to retreat inside. From the living room window, she eyed the empty tract of land across the street strewn with bald tires and broken bottles. When sunlight caught on the glass shards in the dry weeds, she worried fire would scorch the field, cross the asphalt, and burn down the house. She worried the animals that lived in the lots, possums and raccoons, mice and feral cats that tore the ears off one another, animals wild with rabies would bite and infect her children. She worried about disease, viruses and bacteria that festered in the Paerdegat Basin that ran parallel to the house.

She steamed the envelope open, a trick she'd learned from her mother. Miriam had opened all of Judah's letters. She maintained that a wife should know everything about her husband, but Miriam never knew Judah followed her through Tel Aviv, photographed her from a distance like a private eye. After he died, she found boxes of photos on the top shelf of his closet. He titled the photographs: *Miriam at Café Royale, Miriam reading Colette, Miriam in the souk, Miriam at the beach in a bikini drawing attention to herself, Miriam flirting with a waiter, Miriam dancing the Pasodoble in the Kings of Israel Square with a stranger.*

"I never really knew your father," she said, bemused. They'd been married seventeen years.

Her father didn't take many pictures of her and only when she was a child, like the time she skinned her knee, or chipped a baby tooth on an olive pit, or when she'd inadvertently buried a hummingbird in the hole she'd dug in the sandbox in Park Meir. By the time she realized what she'd done and tried to rescue the bird, it was dead. She was six. Her father snapped the shot at the moment of discovery when her face had registered horror and the terrible knowledge that she had the power to destroy but did not have the power to mend what had been destroyed.

When she'd finished steaming the girl's letter open, the corners were curled, and the ink smudged. For a moment, she considered resealing the envelope; a good marriage was built on trust but then she reasoned he was *her* husband, and the soldier was an infiltrator. Salim had forfeited that trust when he welcomed the girl into their camp.

She tipped the envelope over and dozens of wilted petals fluttered onto the kitchen table. The orange blossoms transported her to the house in Kafr Ma'an, where on Saturday afternoons they picnicked in the *pardes*, branches heavy with fruit and the sky achingly blue. She and Salim, snuggled on a blanket, hands sticky with juice, pith trapped under their fingernails. She remembered one winter when they took the bus to visit his mother in Beersheva. The windows were open, and on either side of the road, orchards flooded the air with that scent. They could see over the treetops to where the landscape succumbed to the hills of the Negev Desert, brown and small like the humped backs of dromedaries.

"There are signs everywhere in nature." Salim pointed to the hills, "Three hills—three children."

After Ari was born, she told him in another age he'd have been celebrated as a prophet or burned as a witch.

She opened her eyes to the petals scattered on the table. The room was still, the air thick. The first time Salim and the girl met was in the apartment on the day her parents came to see it. The second time was by chance on the Tel Aviv promenade. The sea was rough. Black flags snapped in the wind along the lifeguard stations, warning swimmers to beware of the undertow. The girl couldn't see Salim's face in the sunlight, but his sandaled feet caught her attention—the slender bones linking foot to ankle, the powerful toes poised at the edge, the long stride toward her. The shouts of noisy beachgoers receded, as did the sounds of waves pummeling the shore. The girl's Czech rifle slipped off her shoulder. A happy accident. Salim called it fate. All this and more the girl recounted in letters two and three. There was further mention of it in letter five.

By then, the soldier also referred to their encounter as fate, only she used the word *destiny*.

The soldier was relentless. Two dozen letters swollen with reminders of home: Elite chocolate wrappers, bird feathers, ficus leaves. One letter contained a white peacock feather taken, the girl said, from an albino peacock at the Ramat Gan Zoo. Tamar would have set it on fire if the children hadn't burst in. In the following letter, the girl sent a moth interred in a small matchbox, pinned to cotton batting, its wings spread in a parody of flight. She sent a vial of sand from the Judean Desert the color of gazelles. There was miniature coral that looked like bits of fossilized bone, spiraled and multihued. Each letter contained objects that triggered memories only the girl and Salim knew. Salim locked them in his nightstand and hid the key. Tamar picked the lock with a nail file and read each one. She took the mementos from one envelope and placed them in another. Pages from letter ten that told of the day the girl saved her mother from asphyxiation from a gas leak, she put in envelope six, which relayed a story about a fight with a bully in school, and the pages from envelope four she placed into letters seven, eight, and nine.

She crushed a handful of petals; the perfume smeared on her fingertips and she read, *I miss washing your shirts and seeing them dry in the sunlight, remembering the way you filled them.* There was a picture of the girl in an IDF uniform. She was beautiful: long brown hair and blue eyes too big for her face. Eyes that swallowed everything she saw. On the back of the photograph, she wrote: *Ad le'netzach, For eternity.* Tamar shuddered, recalling the inscription on Hadas's photo in Daoud's wallet. She continued reading, the tea cold, the cake a pyramid of crumbs.

Yesterday I went to our favorite ice cream shop on King George Street and ordered the same flavors you ordered for me—pistachio and banana. Flavors I hadn't eaten since childhood.

That day we stood together in the shop, the streets crowded, I asked for a simple vanilla cone and you surprised me. I didn't even know I missed those flavors until that moment.

Remember how you once told me that I brought you back to life, well ayouni, I was asleep before I met you. I'm wide awake now.

She couldn't bring herself to read the rest of the letter.

Marriage, Tamar discovered, was a land without borders. The night she defected to Ruby's basement, she dreamed she was an old woman. Her hair white, her skin a web of wrinkles. She had her embroidery and stitched a window in a stone wall that peered onto a meadow. She moved onto the faces of a man and woman sipping wine, a boy playing a violin, a girl on pointe. Everything she stitched came to life. In the center of the meadow, she faced the window, desperate to see inside, only to find she'd sewn her eyes shut.

Tamar read Salim's reply to the girl's first letter. He made the mistake of asking her to mail it. "America's the best place for people like us," he wrote and promised there was a job waiting for her at the end of her service in five months. By then he'd have his candy store. Something big and bright. He'd teach her to make a lime rickey, a cherry Coke, a malted, and egg cream, even a root beer float, a world of beverages the girl had never heard of.

He didn't tell her how he'd given up a steady salary as foreman in a plastics factory to go partners in a laundromat, or that he'd taken a second mortgage on the house, all so that he could call himself an American businessman. What he got was a cramped storefront with bad lighting and poor ventilation. He spent fourteen hours a day wrapped in the fragrance of cheap softeners and bleach, making change, cleaning out lint traps, listening to other people's clothes flail in the dryer drums. He didn't write a word about how Tamar worked beside him when the kids were in school, folding laundry, heating their lunch, washing their plates in the deep sink. Nor did he tell her it was on the same block as a poultry slaughterhouse and that the street stank and was littered with feathers, tornadoes of them swirling in the air whenever the wind blew or a car sped by or how they stood together and watched carousels of chickens with their necks cut spin in a macabre waltz as men in white coveralls hosed down the floor—bloodstained, filthy with debris, the spray ascending toward the skylight, creating a luminous rainbow. Sometimes he turned to her with a half smile and said, "There's beauty everywhere."

Now he had his sights on a candy store. "Two businesses," he crowed when he returned from Israel with cash from the sale of their apartment. "And one day two might become three. Anything's possible here."

Tamar stuffed the letter and the petals back into the envelope. She kept the picture of the girl in her apron pocket and opened a window to clear the room of the *pardes*. The prayers were ending. Soon her family would enter, the screen door slamming behind them. The kids kicking off their shoes calling, "Ma, you home?"

"Where else would I be?" She'd exit the kitchen, smiling.

"How about a walk?" Salim said after Tamar had cleared the lunch dishes.

Ruby stayed behind but Rachel and Ari joined them and ran ahead as Salim and Tamar wandered through the neighborhood, marking where new foundations had been poured, new houses built, new neighbors sitting on their porches, neighbors who waved hello when they passed.

"Lunch was delicious," Salim said.

"Thanks," she replied, aware of the tension that filled her whenever they were together now, as if he were a stranger, the unreachable object of her love. She willed herself to relax, to enjoy the day with him at her side. The sun warm on her back; the air soft on her skin. *He's with me*; the words filled her with a forgotten sweetness. She took a breath before slipping her arm through his. If he let her keep it there, then everything would be all right, and if he removed his arm from hers, then she would beg off with a headache. When he smiled and began relaying a story about something a customer did, she was so relieved, she blinked back tears. She laughed hard at something he said and could tell that her laughter, her closeness, the intimate way she clung to him, just as she'd done when they first fell in love, made him happy.

They strolled along Avenue M, where tracts on either side of the street were piled high with dirt and sand, littered with boulders and concrete slabs that had long rebar poking out of them. Rachel and Ari attempted to climb one of the sand piles.

"Watch out," Tamar shouted.

"They'll be okay," Salim said.

They continued until they reached the Paedegat stables a few blocks away, a remnant of the once rural landscape before it was turned into a dumping site and then a housing development. They stood alongside the paddock, Rachel and Ari leaned against the fence, and all four watched a young female rider lift and drop in the saddle like a piston. The pungent scent of horseflesh and manure reminded her of when she and Salim had met on the kibbutz. Salim squeezed her forearm and she wondered if he remembered that day too, so long ago, when Hadas had introduced them. They were outside the dining hall. Salim had taken Tamar's hand and turned it palm up.

"I thought so," he'd said.

"What?" she'd asked, her pulse beating in her ears so hard, she could barely hear him.

"Here"—he pointed to her love line—"I'm right here," then folded her fingers into a fist and looked at the creases along her pinky and said, "So are our children."

She tore her hand away, sure that he was mocking her.

Hadas, who'd been watching her brother, said, "Leave her alone, Salim, she's shy. Besides, she's too good for you. Come," she said to Tamar. "Let's go inside before he does something really stupid like ask you to marry him."

She felt light-headed at the thought.

Hadas laughed. "Don't look so worried. He won't do that. At least not yet." When Tamar looked back, instead of finding Salim laughing at her, his expression was serious, curious as if Hadas had planted a seed and it had taken root.

Ari sidled up to them. "Can we go to the bowling alley?"

"If Ima says it's all right," Salim said.

"Sure, if you all want to," Tamar replied.

The bowling alley was two blocks from the stables. Soon as they stepped inside, the kids rushed to the counter to rent shoes. She blinked into the gloom.

"I don't think this place has ever been exposed to daylight," she said.

The bowling alley was empty except for the man behind the shoe counter and the woman running the concession stand. The lighting was dim, and the walls were covered in nicotine stains. Music played and neon flashed above the wooden alleys. The rumble of bowling balls surging toward the pins, the booming crash before the pinsetter swooped them up and repositioned them, all made it difficult to hear each other.

Salim ordered a beer and passed Tamar a plastic cup. They sat close to one another at a table at the far end of the room, watching the kids play. She leaned toward him, about to say something innocuous into his ear about celebrating Rosh Hashanah in a bowling alley, but there was something in his face that stopped her.

"You're thinking about Hadas," she said with a sinking feeling.

He nodded.

"It's hard, isn't it? Especially on the holidays. I'm sorry, Salim."

"You didn't pull the trigger."

"No, but I didn't stop it either," she said, uncertain if he heard her above the din.

He gulped down his beer. "You couldn't have. I'm not even sure I could have, even if I'd known about the affair. Hadas did what she wanted; I realize that now. It was unfair of me to blame you."

She squeezed his hand, "Thank you, *habibi*."

"Do you mind if we go?" he said.

As she rounded up the kids, a serpent of a thought slipped through her defenses—he'd forgiven her because of the soldier. They walked home subdued, the air of festivity gone. The girl must have convinced him to do it, knowing that forgiveness was a letting go, a leaching of the poison, leaving the body spent, drained of all feeling. Once that thought took hold, Tamar couldn't shake it.

Ruby greeted them at the door.

"I know what my New Year's resolution is," she declared.

"Oh yeah? What's that?" Tamar asked, glad to have Ruby to distract her. She filled the kettle with water while Salim settled on the sofa.

"On my eighteenth birthday, I'm going home, joining the army, and there's nothing you or Baba can do about it."

"What makes you think we'd stop you?"

"Whatever," Ruby said and flounced out of the house.

As Tamar served him coffee, Salim pointed to the Israeli newspaper on his lap. "Look what we're missing over there." A corner of the girl's letter poked out of his pocket.

She already knew about the Jewish New Year events: harvest festivals on kibbutzim, folk dancing in Tel Aviv, a concert featuring Isaac Stern and the Israel Philharmonic at the amphitheater in Caesarea. There was bickering in the Knesset and a picture of Golda Meir looking like somebody's great-aunt, with her head bowed toward Moshe Dayan, his eye-patch a rogue ink spot.

Salim read to her an article about the excessive spending on the new F-15 fighter jets, and the Soviet MiGs on the ground in Damascus and Cairo, Henry Kissinger's warnings, and the southern border, where sands shifted from Ashkelon to the Gaza Strip. "Too close," he murmured, rubbing his forehead, "there's going to be a war. I can feel it here." He pointed to his sternum.

Rachel and Ari raced out the front door just as their neighbors, Gershon and Netta Rosen, entered. "*Gut Yom Tov,*" they cried, repeating the words as they walked through the foyer. Salim rolled his eyes before they appeared in the living room. He didn't like the Rosens. To him, they were *shvitzers,* show-offs interested only in money. "They think their money can wipe their memories clean, wipe the stink of the ghetto off their backs," he said of them. Tamar had stayed quiet, wondering how it was possible for Salim to be so aware of the Rosens and so blind to himself.

She offered her cheek up to Mrs. Rosen for a kiss. Mr. Rosen pumped her hand. They settled on the couch with a sigh. She served coffee and honey cake while Salim listened to their small talk, growing, Tamar noticed, bored.

She turned to them with a bright smile and asked, "How was your trip?"

"Marvelous," Mr. Rosen grinned, hitching up his pant legs.

Each year they visited relatives on kibbutz *Lohamei HaGeta'ot*, Fighters of the Ghetto Uprising, in the Western Galilee.

"Look what my cousins built," Mrs. Rosen said with excitement. "Two full-scale models. Tourists from all over the world come to see this." She spread a stack of Polaroids on the table. One set was of the Warsaw Ghetto depicting its cobbled streets, defunct trolley car, and underground bunkers. Tiny models of ghetto fighters appeared on the roofs and peered out of sewers. A German tank stood at the entrance to the ghetto amid piles of rubble. The other set of photos were of Auschwitz-Birkenau. The train tracks leading into the camp were painted steel gray, and there were prisoners in striped uniforms and Nazi guards located in strategic towers with their guns pointed at the prisoners below. There were cardboard cutouts of people in cattle cars and barbed wire fences made of real barbed wire, and a sign at the entrance that read ARBEIT MACHT FREI in tin letters. Even the crematoria were faithfully rendered with the logo of the TOPF company embossed on them. Outside the compound were tiny cherry trees someone colored in marker and a brick house with a gabled roof and a brass mailbox with the word *Commandant* written on it. It was as close to being there without being there, the Rosens said.

"Your cousins are very clever." She touched a gable on the commandant's house. "An almost gruesome likeness," Tamar said, and then, "Maybe we can put the Polaroids away before the children return."

"Certainly, my dear." Netta Rosen scooped them into her purse.

The Rosens brought sweets from the Holy Land to celebrate the New Year: blue and white Jordan almonds in tiny mesh pouches and a box of *Lokum,* Turkish delight, Salim's favorite. He pried the box open and stuffed a jellied rosewater square into his mouth. "This candy takes me back to my childhood in Damascus and later on Shabazi Street."

"Where's Shabazi Street?" Gershon asked.

"South Tel Aviv. I bet you've never been there. Not your kind of place. It's run-down. A neighborhood full of Jews from Arab lands. Poor shopkeepers, drug dealers, and prostitutes. Some as young as fourteen."

"Oh yes," he said when Mrs. Rosen sputtered in protest. "Sent out by their fathers and brothers."

"But how can they be Jews?" Netta said.

"You didn't know there were Jewish prostitutes?" Salim looked at Mr. Rosen, who kept his eyes focused on the cup in his hand, a dark flush on his cheeks. "Gershon, what secrets are you keeping from your wife?" Salim chuckled, baiting him. "There must have been Jewish whores in the German town you grew up in?"

Tamar rubbed a hand in agitated circles on her chest, wondering if the Rosens were seeing firsthand the cracks in her marriage. Salim was determined to get a rise out of them. She patted her apron pocket where the girl's photo was hidden, recalling her olive complexion and dark hair, the almond-shaped eyes. Like Hadas, the thought nipped at her; the girl was Mizrahi.

"What's the matter?" Salim said. "You look like someone kicked you."

"I'm fine." She kept her voice steady.

"But in Israel?" Mrs. Rosen continued. Her shoulders drooped. She tugged at her sleeves, drawing the fabric over her knuckles. Poor Netta had walked in buoyed by her trip, by the knowledge that her dress was expensive, that her hat with its blue feather against her cheek signaled to the green in her eyes to shine. Now those eyes appeared frightened. She had lost her footing and Tamar saw her struggle to reclaim it.

In a moment Tamar would vacate her body and float into the ether. She wished she had her needlepoint, something to occupy her hands. If being a good hostess and having respect for her elders hadn't been ingrained in her, she'd shut the conversation down and hustle the Rosens out. But it was too late; Salim was well into it again. Spilling out of his seams, Hadas would've said and laughed in a way that would've shut him up good.

Mrs. Rosen gave a slight moan and bowed her head when Salim said, "Israel's just like any other country. Wasn't sculpted out of the Ten Commandments." He stuffed another piece of Turkish delight into his mouth. Mrs. Rosen drank her coffee with a subdued slurp. Salim drew a breath, and before he could utter another word, Tamar said, "Netta, please try the cake," and after shooting Salim a dark glance, she continued, "This is Salim's sister's recipe. She added a half cup of date molasses and black coffee to the mix. Hadas was a wonderful baker. She excelled at everything."

The muscle in Salim's jaw throbbed. His hand slid into his pocket. Tamar saw his thumb caress the envelope.

"We didn't know Salim had a sister," Mrs. Rosen said.

"She died." Tamar picked a thread off her apron, the scalloped edges of the girl's photo visible through the material. "Killed by—"

Salim popped out of his chair. "Gershon, let's celebrate the New Year with a glass of arak."

Before Gershon could answer, Tamar said, "It's why we came to America, to escape what can't be escaped, the irrational, the unpredictable, the truth." Sweat dampened her back.

Netta Rosen pressed a hand to her heart. "How terrible for you."

Salim lit a cigarette. No one spoke. The clock in the kitchen ticked. The silence swelled.

Mrs. Rosen cleared her throat. "We thought only to drop in for a minute to give you the small gift and go. We're having dinner with our daughter, Selena, and her husband, the pediatric surgeon, Dr. Marvin Fruchtman." The feather on her hat quivered.

"Marvin's the assistant to the chief surgeon at Mount Sinai Hospital," Mr Rosen said.

Tamar presented the cake to them. They had become part of the mise-en-scène, props in the dumb show she and Salim were in. They demurred, glanced at the door, and blew on their coffee. Salim closed his eyes. He launched into a tale about his time in Midrash Menashe, a school in the Yemenite quarter in Tel Aviv. He studied there a year before he left to work to support himself and Hadas. Tamar cringed, knowing he was saying all of this just to needle them, to annoy and ultimately to unseat them from what he considered was their too high perch.

"I had to memorize entire *parashot* from the *Tanach*. I can still recite them."

The Rosens signaled to each other, searching, Tamar thought, for an escape. Mr. Rosen, whose thinning hair exposed a scalp festooned with freckles, urged Salim to go on, perhaps to hurry things along. Mrs. Rosen agreed. Her head bobbled like the plastic bird on the pharmacy counter that never stopped dipping its beak into a cup of water. She tugged the chiffon skirt over her dimpled knees, her face a mask of benign politeness.

"The school," Salim said, "was on the top floor of an Ottoman building. A ruin. The roof leaked. Pigeons lived in the stairwell." He paused and, after a swift look at Tamar, said, "Time can vanquish anything." Her heart gave a painful thump. She didn't know what to make of that remark, whether he meant time had vanquished their marriage, or in time this new love would be vanquished and their marriage would continue as before.

Mrs. Rosen put her cup down; her hand hovered over the honey cake. "I'm counting calories. Weight Watchers," she sighed. "Sometimes I wake up in the morning with my fingers so swollen, I can't turn my rings." Everyone looked at her pudgy fingers bejeweled with a large square sapphire on one hand and a pear-shaped diamond and platinum wedding band on the other.

"I didn't stay long," Salim said. "I joined the Palmach."

"The Palmach?" Mr. Rosen's interest peaked.

"In '46, I lied about my age. I became a squad leader two years later."

"What did you have to do to become squad leader?" Mr. Rosen leaned forward.

Salim dug into his shirt pocket for a pack of Kents.

"Anyone want more coffee? I can make tea if you prefer," Tamar said. "I didn't even have a chance to put out the fruit. Let me put out the fruit."

No one wanted fruit, coffee, or anything else. For the first time that afternoon, the Rosens sat still in their chairs. Tamar heard Rachel and Ari squabbling outside. A pale shaft of sunlight drenched the carpet. Ruby came in. Tamar felt a moment's relief at the interruption. Ruby greeted Netta and Gershon, shaking their hands, wishing them a Happy New Year. She seemed so adult, so distant.

Ruby snatched a slice of cake off the plate and skipped downstairs to her room without a word for Tamar and Salim. What the Rosens must think of them. Worse was what Ruby thought of her leaving Salim's bed. After the first night, when Tamar made some excuse about his aching back and how he needed to sleep alone for a while, Ruby didn't say anything more about it. She had no idea what was churning in her daughter's head.

Mr. Rosen cleared his throat. "So what did you do?"

Salim lit a cigarette. The smoke rose like cloud cover; when it cleared, he said, "I had to prove that I'd killed a man."

Tamar closed her eyes.

"What man?" Mr. Rosen said.

"An Arab."

"Was this before or after your sister was killed?"

Salim flicked a line of ash into the remains of his coffee. "Obviously, Gershon, it was years before my sister was murdered, because afterwards we moved to America. Tamar would have you believe that I ran away."

He sat like a pasha in the recliner. His hair swept off his forehead, his shirt unbuttoned at the throat, a hand on his knee, the brass buckle cutting into his stomach, and sticking out of his pocket the letter from that girl. *Salim the lover, the prophet. Salim the killer.*

"Don't," Tamar implored.

"What does it matter? It happened so long ago. And you forgave me, right?"

"Please, please stop talking," she begged.

Salim faced the Rosens. "We heard there might be trouble in an Arab village."

"Where?" Mr. Rosen said.

"Kafr Ma'an on the outskirts of Tel Aviv."

Tamar squeezed her eyes shut.

"By the time my unit got there, the village was deserted. We didn't have to fire a shot. They'd already packed and fled to Jordan."

"What made them leave?" Mr. Rosen asked.

Salim shrugged. "Maybe they thought we'd do to them what they'd done to us in Hebron, Jerusalem, Jaffa, Damascus, Cairo, Baghdad—all across the Arab world."

Tamar muttered his name. The Rosens sat back against the sofa. Salim drew a breath.

"I did a house-to-house search and found a man lying face down in an open doorway. He must have fallen in the rush to escape. There was a pool of blood near his head. I don't know why his people didn't bury him; maybe they didn't know what had happened to him. They left that to us. He was dead."

"So you didn't kill him," Mr. Rosen said.

"Not technically, no."

"Then what?" Mr. Rosen sounded annoyed, but Salim wasn't to be rushed.

"I checked his pockets for identification, then turned him over. He had a thick brown mustache. A young man's mustache. I don't know why it surprised me except that I thought he was old." Salim's voice faded.

"Why?" Mrs. Rosen asked.

"His feet. He wore no shoes. They were old man feet, hard and cracked. I wanted to cover them up. I was embarrassed for him."

"What did you do next?" Mr. Rosen asked.

"I told you, proof."

"What kind of proof, Baba?"

He started at the sound of Ruby's voice; she had come up for a glass of milk. He cleared his throat, stuck out his chin, and said, "I cut off his thumb and delivered it to my superiors."

Mr. Rosen set his coffee on the table. "What does the finger of an already dead man prove?"

"That I could obey orders without question. Palmach leaders needed to know that my loyalty surpassed even my conscience."

"For God's sake, you were still a boy. Besides, the man was already dead."

"What difference does it make if I killed him or someone else did? We were all to blame, including his own people. And you"—he turned to Ruby—"don't look at me like that. Two weeks earlier, men from that village attacked a kibbutz. They burned the fields and killed three people. One was a small child. You think I give a shit that I took his thumb?" He dragged on the cigarette and then stubbed it out, the movement a choreography of controlled violence.

"Oh, Baba," Ruby said. "I thought you liked the Mahmoudis."

"What do they have to do with this?" He scowled.

"I can't believe you have to ask." She turned on her heel, her footsteps hissing on the carpeted stairs.

Why, Tamar wondered, did he tell that particular story to the Rosens, to Ruby? Then she caught sight of the envelope again. Everything circled back to the girl. He must have told her. A confession in the dark, the way he'd confessed it to Tamar, devastated by what he'd done. Only the girl had sent him blossoms as a way of acceptance, of forgiveness, the washing away of a sin, something Tamar had never been able to give him. She had pushed that awful confession to the far corners of their marriage. The desecration of that man's body was an act that didn't belong to him, didn't belong to them, but was now tangled up with that soldier, and had always been tied to Hadas, who'd exonerated him by saying, "*Achi*, let it go. They made you do it."

Tamar lurched to her feet. "I'll get the fruit."

"Please don't bother. It's time we returned to the synagogue," Mr. Rosen said, unbuttoning and buttoning his vest.

"Oh yes," said Mrs. Rosen and jerked to a standing position, setting the feather on her hat into motion. She smoothed her skirt. "A shame how much they're charging for a seat on the High Holy Days. *Ganefs*, if you ask me."

Tamar couldn't wait for them to leave. "Thank you for stopping by and for the lovely gifts. Perhaps you'll take some cake?" What had possessed her to bake Hadas's recipe? Salim wouldn't touch it, not after that first bite. How he'd looked at her, like she'd resurrected a ghost. The Rosens made their way into the foyer.

"Something terrible is going to happen," Salim said. "I can taste it. Like blood in my mouth. I know what war is. How brutal it makes us. *The harvest is past; the summer has ended, and we are not saved. Can the Ethiopian change his skin, can the leopard his spots?*"

"If you mean that people don't change," Tamar said, knowing that when he quoted Jeremiah, they were in for a bad time, "then maybe you're right, but there's nothing in the newspaper to suggest there's going to be a war, so just stop it."

"Ach, what do you know? At this very moment our enemies are gathering on the border." He stalked into the kitchen.

The Rosens looked at him, bewildered. "War? What are you talking about?"

She said, "Even if it were true, there's nothing you can do. It's like trying to stop the ocean. Who has the strength for that?"

"We better have the strength." He hurled the words at her.

"No Salim, *they* better have the strength. You live here now, remember? This is what you wanted. Exile from home, from obligation, from our family."

The Rosens hurried out the door.

"I'm leaving," Ruby said, dressed in jeans and a T-shirt.

"Where are you going?" Tamar asked, wishing she wouldn't leave her alone with Salim.

"Out." The door shook on its hinges.

Salim trudged back into the living room, the folded newspaper under his arm. A car horn blared. There was the hollow smack of a ball against the stoop and the ringing of a bicycle bell. It was only a few hours ago that they'd gone for a walk, that she'd felt close to him again and had allowed herself to hope that he'd give up the girl. He had even forgiven her. That should have made things right between them.

The house was still, like the aftermath of a wreck. She wiped the counter, wrapped the uneaten cake in foil, then poured herself a glass of water. She felt Salim's presence in the kitchen. "You know how much I love you," she said, and without looking at him, placed the girl's photograph on the refrigerator, next to the kids' spelling tests. "Do you really want her between us?"

"I never meant to hurt you," he said.

He left for *Maariv*, evening prayers. The front door snapped shut. Night descended on the house like a prowler, tentative and cagey. On the table the girl's letter, the envelope open, petals spilling out its mouth. Salim had left it there for her, as if to say no more pretense, no more hiding, no more lies.

Sixteen

During the Ten Days of Awe, she dreamed about her mother: Miriam arrives for a visit. She steps inside and the floor turns to sand. She sinks so quickly, there's no time to save her. Tamar tries to sweep the sand away. She searches for her mother in the dunes in the living room, but Miriam has vanished. Desperate to find her, she floods the house, and the sand becomes mud, and the mud becomes a river. The current carries the furniture out the door. On the street the sofa bumps into a parked car. The sun is high, and vapors rise off the seat cushions. Pyramids of mud form on the sidewalk. They are totems for the missing. Her house is a ruin; her mother is gone, and she is orphaned again.

She burrowed deeper into sleep. The longer she remained asleep, the easier the fast; the longer she slept, the less likely she'd run into Salim on his way to the temple. A gust of wind smacked against the basement window. She tugged the blanket over her shoulders. Nearby, a neighbor's child practiced "Three Blind Mice" on the piano. She listened to the steady plunk of keys. Last night while brushing her teeth, she stared at her reflection. A stranger, blank and incomprehensible. She remembered that Miriam's hair had turned white after Judah's death. Like a character in a fairy tale cursed, she came into Tamar's room, pointing to her head in wonder.

"It's some kind of punishment." Miriam said.

"But why?"

"Your father's dead."

"Isn't that punishment enough?"

It had certainly felt that way to her. The place her father had occupied was reduced to a few dozen boxes of photographs. There were days she had to remind herself that he was truly gone. Any minute he could open the door and place his camera on the table, go into the kitchen, and wash the perspiration off his face. How many times had she wanted to shout, "Take a picture of me, Aba." She'd kept his camera. All her life she'd wanted to be his subject and muse, the way her mother had been. After he died, she had to concede that he'd found her uninteresting and uninspiring.

"We never should have married," Miriam sighed, lighting a cigarette, batting the smoke away from her face. "I chose badly. Not a bad man. A good man, just a bad choice for someone like me. He was one of those men that made a woman feel guilty for wanting to live."

She recalled going with her mother to the dances on Saturday nights in *Kikar Malchai Yisrael*. She was seven or eight at the time. The whole city would turn out for the event. Miriam taught her the hora, the steps to Yemenite dances, to dances that exhorted the clouds to give rain, the earth a rich harvest. At nine forty-five, a paso doble played over the loudspeakers; couples fell into rows. From the sidelines, she watched Miriam pose like a matador and then the inevitable stranger with his arms outstretched and her mother stepping into them. She looked so beautiful. When they marched past her, she'd wave but Miriam carried on as if she hadn't seen her. She felt that moment now as the gray morning crept along the basement floor, how she'd wrap her arms around herself, pinching the skin at her waist until the pain was so sharp, she couldn't breathe, and the music receded, and her vision narrowed to the spot of light over her mother's stamping feet.

211

Tamar closed her eyes. She felt out of step. Something essential evaded her; it wasn't just time passing, but the feeling that time was running out. Soon she'd be old. Like Miriam, it would overtake her all at once. Salim would be lost to her. She tucked the covers under her chin and looked at Ruby sleeping fully clothed in the next bed. She had her shoes on, for goodness' sake. Tamar suppressed the urge to wake her. What could she do? Ruby was practically an adult. What could you tell a daughter who insisted on sleeping like an infantryman ready for combat? Tamar blamed Salim, his predictions of war, his emotional desertion, and that girl, that soldier. Honestly, she didn't know what to make of her children's behavior: Rachel primping all the time, plucking her eyebrows into a fine line that gave her the appearance of a startled doe. Ari sitting by the window searching the sky. What did he expect to find there? What was he looking for? In guiltier moments, she wondered if he was searching for her. How was she to know what he wanted when he didn't tell her? No one said anything. They hardly talked to each other except in banalities: *Pass the salt, did you send my shirt to the dry cleaners, Ma where are my shoes? Can I have a dollar?* Was there a subtext she wasn't aware of, or was it just a matter of the oldest child teaching the younger two how to wield silence like a weapon?

Ruby shifted in her sleep; her shoes scraped the aluminum bedframe. Tamar held herself still so as not to wake her. Last night when the house had finally settled and Salim and the children were asleep, she went out into the yard and stood beneath the mimosa tree. The last of its blossoms carpeted the ground, and the scent shot her back into a night in Tel Aviv when she and Salim were on the balcony. She was pregnant with Rachel. Mimosa and the oily scent of diesel clotted the air. The murmuring city, their neighbors' conversations echoed through the narrow street.

212

"It's like a goddamn amphitheater," Salim said.

She treasured that echo, evidence they weren't alone. They stayed on the balcony long after their neighbors' radios broadcasted the national anthem. Theaters had let out and buses had stopped running; restaurants had closed their doors and piled chairs on tabletops. The streets were empty. She could feel the sea air on her skin. The baby moved like a porpoise in a tank. Her feet were hot, and there was that ache in her lower back as if someone were grinding their heel into it. She wanted to go to bed, but Salim got down on his knees, kissed her breasts, and pressed his hand between her legs, so that she felt herself swell, sure that her body couldn't contain both her and the baby. She thought she heard the trees whisper and the sea lapping the shore, but it was Salim telling her that he loved her.

In the small hours of the morning, she went into labor. There was no public transportation until six and cabbies had long since gone home. Salim took a bicycle out of the bomb shelter and placed a blanket across the bar. She rode the six miles to the hospital cradled in his arms, the dark a damp caress. Palm fronds shook in the wind, and shadows chased them through the dusty streets. Each contraction drew her face into the crook of his neck. Her lips found the long tendons, sucking and biting his skin as their baby readied itself for the world. They arrived in time for her to enter the delivery room. When it was done and the blood wiped clean, and the baby wrapped like a gift and placed in a bassinet, a nurse wheeled her gurney into the corridor. All the rooms were occupied. Visitors and hospital personnel walked through the hall, avoiding her gaze. She turned her face to the wall. The stench of her labor hanging in the air.

A few days later, they brought the baby home. It was late autumn, and the rains came. They named the child Rachel for

Salim's mother, Rachel the favored second wife of Jacob, and the Hebrew word for "ewe."

She was conscious of the ticking clock. In a minute, everything changed. In a minute, nothing changed. Time simply passed. When they bought this house, she had signed the deed and felt the tiny sail of hope she'd held on to collapse.

"You agreed to this," Salim said when he noticed her hesitation.

"Yes, because you said I owed it to you. Because I kept a secret from you. But you lied to me. You said we would go home."

Seven months in this house and she was still reluctant to disturb the rooms. The yard was desolate with its square of concrete and dry earth. She had planted the mimosa tree after discovering one just like it next door. Her eyes traveled the steel beam in the basement ceiling, then flicked to the posters on the wall. One of Bob Dylan, another of a Japanese Kabuki actor, and a small postcard of Leo Tolstoy in his man-of-the-people costume. She studied the bookcase Ruby had made out of found bricks and pine planks. The bedsprings creaked and she held her breath until Ruby settled. She was after all only a visitor here and had slept in this room for less than a season. Her clothes and toiletries were back in that other country where her marriage languished. All that she'd brought here was the biscuit tin with her threads and needles, the large Gobelin of Degas's dancers. She wanted no reminders of Salim here, and yet everything reminded her of him. From under the pillow, she retrieved the white moth interred in a matchbox the soldier had sent him. She felt it flutter in her chest and knew Salim would never forgive her if she destroyed it, but it was all she could think about, pulverizing its wings into dust.

Washed and dressed, she stood on the porch. The *shtiebel* was overcrowded. A sea of black-garbed men with *tallitot* draped over their heads spilled onto the road. The cantor's deep tenor rose over the worshippers. The morning sun a white disk in a bleached sky. There was a chill in the air. Mrs. Rosen waved and called her over. Tamar pretended not to notice. Something cut through the prayers. She bent over the railing and heard a broadcast coming from Gadi's apartment. The men began the silent *HaAmidah* prayer. The news came through clearly now. Surprised he had the radio on, she hurried downstairs to stand in front of his door. He saw her and came out wearing only a pair of jeans. His skin contracted in the cool air. A cigarette in his hand. His face ashen. "Have you heard?"

She shook her head and cocked her ear, hearing but not hearing, unable to absorb what was being said, and then the strange buckle in her knees. Gadi wrapped an arm around her and drew her close enough to feel his chilled skin against her cheek. His cigarette singed her hair.

"Sorry." He brushed at the ashes.

They stepped apart, embarrassed. One by one, men broke away to listen to the news. The congregants huddled in front of her house. Gadi's radio boomed into the Yom Kippur silence. The word *war* crackled like fire. Salim broke through the crowd and stood beside her, his face a mask of triumph and horror. He had predicted this moment. Men stood with bowed heads; their backs bent with the news.

At 2:00 pm in a coordinated attack, Egyptian and Syrian forces stormed Israel's borders along the Sinai Peninsula and the Golan Heights.

"Let me pass," she said, unable to listen to the rest.

The men parted for her. She dashed up the stairs and into the house. Rachel and Ari followed close behind. Ari rushed to his chair by the window.

"What are you looking at now?" Rachel said, exasperated.

"The war."

"It isn't here, stupid. You don't have to worry."

He pointed to Tamar in the kitchen. "Might as well be."

She opened the refrigerator, squinting into the glare, and took what she needed to prepare breakfast, trying to quell the tremor in her hands.

"Ma?" Rachel said.

"Yes?"

"It's Yom Kippur." She pointed to the food on the counter.

"God has other things on his mind." She grunted in pain as hot grease splattered on her forearm. In no time, she filled a platter with scrambled eggs and a large bowl with chopped salad. She sliced bread and brewed a pot of coffee. Ruby emerged from the basement, rubbing her eyes, dressed in a batik skirt and the boots she had slept in, hair uncombed.

"What's going on?" And then she saw the food. "Oh my God, you're cooking? What happened?"

"I'm sorry."

"There's a war in Israel." Rachel was proud she was the first to give her sister the news.

Ruby paled. "Holy shit, Baba was right." She slid into a chair. "So what do we do now?"

As if on cue, Salim stepped into the foyer, assaulted by the aroma of coffee and eggs. He stood unmoving, then slammed the door shut lest the odors escape out to their neighbors, all good observant Jews. His breath whistled from between his teeth.

"What the hell's going on?"

"Breakfast." Tamar put a stack of plates on the table for Ruby to set. She told Ari and Rachel to sit down.

"Does this mean we're going home?" Ruby asked.

Tamar opened her mouth; no words came, but an image of her mother alone in her apartment in Tel Aviv made her grow cold, and then she recalled the dream and looked around the room, half expecting to see it buried in sand.

Salim rubbed his hands over his face, waiting, it seemed, for the scene before him to dissolve. After a moment of indecision, he crossed to the sink and washed his hands. He washed and washed, checking his nails repeatedly for dirt, scrubbing his palms, the backs of his knuckles, his wrists.

"Please get me a towel," he said.

No one moved. He wiped his hands down the front of his slacks, then sat abruptly at the table. They lifted their knives and forks. They ate without looking at each other, without talking, swallowing audibly. Sunlight poured through the living room windows. Dust motes gyrated in the beams. Out in the street, men resumed their prayers.

In the evening the shofar trumpeted, marking the end of Yom Kippur. Worshippers walked past her house in silence, their footsteps lonely beats on the concrete. The wind moaned and shook the withering leaves to ground. She was at the counter, finishing off the last of the potato salad. She used a tablespoon, scooping up as much food as her mouth could hold. Such pleasure in a full mouth working, chewing, mashing, her throat funneling it all into her stomach, which despite all she'd consumed that day, was not yet full. She drank another cup of coffee, cut a second slice of cake, and continued to eat. She washed the dishes. No one was home and she was grateful for the solitude. She dried her hands on a dishtowel and walked through the rooms, conscious of the objects in them: the photographs of her children, the shoes in the hall, the stack of unanswered mail, and the jackets hanging off the backs of chairs like old seal skins. In spite of herself, she'd made the place a home.

She took out the Gobelin. From below she heard the scrape and thump of Gadi packing and pictured his clothes scarcely filling his duffel. He hadn't come with much. She chose blue thread and separated the strands. Now she thought he must be wrapping the snow globe of the Empire State Building he'd shown her. She licked the thread, shaped it between her teeth, and drew it through the eye of the needle. The embroidery thread snagged; she used her fingers to loosen the knot, tearing the strands. She rethreaded the needle and began the row again, only to let the canvas fall to her lap. A familiar prickle behind her eyes, she bolted off the sofa, pulled the window curtain aside, and looked at the sky, where the moon rode low on the horizon, surrounded by a platoon of clouds. She pictured Gadi in uniform, Gadi in a trench in the desert, Gadi in a tank climbing over dunes. She recalled that first celebration in Jerusalem after the '67 war, when tanks had rolled down the boulevard, and a string of fighter jets had shattered the sound barrier, leaving contrails in the sky. Why, she had wondered then, would the government flaunt its strength? Didn't they know it made them more vulnerable?

She ran a finger over the painting of the boat at sea and frowned at the layer of dust. Something fell in Gadi's apartment. She rushed to the party wall. There was another sound, this time like a slap, and she imagined an openhanded smack to the side of his head in rebuke: He was here while his comrades were crossing the Sinai. He was walking now, opening the faucet, perhaps washing his face. She worried he was shaving, the razor in his hand. News of the dead had already reached them, hundreds in the first hours. The reserves still being called. Truckloads of men filled the roads. She stuffed an apple into her mouth, chewing, half choking on its flesh as the juice went down the wrong way. She thought of Salim's girl soldier at war, in the middle of it somewhere, and prayed she wouldn't die, wouldn't become a martyr. She closed her eyes, conjuring Kafr Ma'an, the *pardes*, the blue door, the Yarkon River a vein pulsing into the sea, and at night the moon, crickets scratching, and thrushes singing, coaxing the stirring heart to calm, and then unbidden, Hadas and Daoud.

There was a knock on the door. Gadi stood on the threshold.

She was relieved to see him. "I hoped you'd come. I'll make coffee."

"I'm not here for that."

"How about a slice of cake?"

"I need a box for the rest of the dishes," he said. "Thought I'd give them to the *shul*."

"Good idea. The rabbi will know who needs them."

"Maybe a young family," he said.

"Yes."

He still hadn't moved. "Mind if I smoke?" And he drew a pack of Marlboros out of his back pocket.

"It's chilly outside. There's an ashtray in the living room." She walked ahead, tossing him an encouraging smile.

He lit a cigarette, followed her in, brow furrowed. "Want to hear something funny? There's a war and yet all I can think about is my ex. Smoke?" He offered her the pack.

"Thanks."

He struck a match, and she drew back as the flame leapt between them.

"What were you saying about your ex?"

He examined the painting, stroking a tiny yellow globule. "She's with someone else now."

"What happened, or is that too personal?"

219

He perused her record collection. "You really do like classical music."

She cleared her throat. "Was I too personal?"

He shook his head. "I was an idiot."

"Why?" The accelerated hum of the refrigerator broke into the room.

"I left her, wanted to travel. Thought the best way to experience the world was if I were free. She wanted to go to university, then get married. I wasn't ready."

She brushed the hair off her forehead. "At least you know yourself."

He turned to her, "No, I don't think I do. Everywhere I went, I thought what would Alona think of this place, of these people, of this food? I haven't been home in two years."

"I haven't been home in more than six," Tamar said.

They smoked in silence, still as cats.

"Do you have a cardboard box?"

"In the garage."

"She must be terrified," he said.

"Alona?"

He nodded. "In the Six-Day War, she refused to leave the bomb shelter until it was over." Gadi faced the window. His reflection wavered in the glass.

"You going to see her when you get back?"

"My mother says she's with someone else."

"But if you still love her?"

"Wouldn't be fair. Not with the war. I'm sure he's been drafted too."

"All's fair." Tamar shot him a tight smile.

"I don't believe that, do you?"

She thought of the girl soldier and the letters that dropped like grenades into their lives. "Depends what you're fighting for."

"Well, she's no longer in my life. Truth is, I haven't thought about her for at least a year. Well, not much." He smiled, then sat beside her on the sofa and lit another cigarette. "Had the strangest feeling today she was thinking about me too."

"Maybe she was. I'm sure you'll see her again. You might even pass her on Dizengoff Street or on Gordon Beach. She'll remember how much she loved you."

"She'll remember I left her."

Tamar patted his arm in commiseration. He looked at her, and in his face, she saw fear.

"Gadi, you'll be okay."

"Sure."

"Please don't pretend."

He shrugged his shoulders. "I don't know what I feel. I don't even know what I'm doing here. I should be going to the airport."

"When's your flight?"

"Midnight. The consulate arranged for free flights home all week."

"Is that for anyone who wants to go?"

"Reservists, I think, but maybe civilians too. Why? Thinking of going home?"

"Every day. There's still time before you have to leave."

"For what?"

"I don't know, just don't go yet, at least not before I feed you. Have you eaten today?"

"Not much."

"How about a cold chicken sandwich?"

He followed her into the kitchen.

She set about preparing the meal. With her back to him, she couldn't see what he was doing, but felt him behind her as if he were a needle and she a balloon. She sliced the chicken. He looked over her shoulder down at her hands.

"Your hands are trembling," he said.

"Silly, right?"

"No."

She spread mustard on the bread.

"Am I too close? Should I move?" Instead of taking a step back, he took a step closer.

"No. Yes." She sliced a tomato.

"I make you nervous?"

"I'm always a little nervous," she confessed with a laugh.

"How come?"

"Salim says it's faulty wiring."

"I don't believe that." He sniffed her hair, his breath on the back of her neck.

She stiffened. "What do you think it is?"

"Sensitive wiring."

Her throat clenched. "Your sandwich is ready."

She didn't turn around.

"Remember our dance?" He put his hands on her shoulders, and she leaned back just enough to feel his body heat.

"Yes."

He lifted her braid and draped it over her shoulder. She thought of Salim sitting in the *shul* listening to the board members, that parliament of old men, argue about how much money they could raise for the war effort and how many lives it would save, Salim gnashing his teeth because not one of those men had ever fought a war, though a few had escaped one. He had no idea Gadi was here.

"Thank you," he said. "Think I'll take the sandwich with me."

"No." She held on to his wrist without turning around. "Tell me something you wouldn't tell anyone else."

222

His arms snaked around her waist. "I feel so sad right now, I don't know if I can stop myself from doing something really stupid."

Her muscles slackened.

"Tell me to leave."

"I don't want to."

His mouth pressed against her temple. "Is anyone home?"

"No." She held on to the counter, afraid to face him, afraid he'd disappear if she did.

He pulled her toward him, and she pivoted in his arms and raised her face to his. He rested his forehead against hers. "I'm sorry," he said.

"For what?"

"I have to go."

"Wait," she said. "This is what I see for you. You'll go home and fight in the war and it will be terrible, but when it's over you'll find Alona waiting for you. One day the two of you will swim in the sea and feel such joy, you'll never want to go anywhere without her again."

She closed her eyes and saw him swimming in Tel Aviv beyond the breakers into open water. She saw herself there with Salim. They swim a great distance, until their skin turns slick and rubbery, until they grow gills and their feet web, and they become their real mammalian selves, capable of breathing underwater.

She let him go, and when he was at the door, she cried, "The box."

"I'll leave the dishes on the counter. Give them to the rabbi for me?"

She nodded. "Take care, Gadi."

He gave her a mock salute. "Go home," he said.

"Maybe."

223

"Don't wait too long. Even if we survive this, we'll never be the same again."

"Why do you say that?"

"They caught us by surprise."

"What difference does that make?"

"We're vulnerable now. They know it."

"Haven't we always been?"

"No. For a while we were like gods. Now they know we're human. And we do too."

In the kitchen she found Gadi's sandwich on the counter and devoured it. Her belly so bloated it was difficult to breathe. His words rang in her ears. *Go home.* The idea took root. *Go home.* Leave Salim, leave the children and this house, where her marriage was bleeding out. Then he'd feel her absence. The children would miss her, but they'd get along fine without her, and when the war was over, she'd send for them. She'd see her mother and sleep in her childhood bed. She'd be useful again, volunteer. In the city by the sea, she'd walk the winding streets, smell the wild jasmine, and pick the fruit off the trees. These thoughts raced through her, excited her. They were an ocean rising, crashing against the shores of her body. She would go home.

Tamar grabbed hold of her stomach and covered her mouth. She ran into the bathroom and purged the day's contents into the toilet. Afterward, she brushed her teeth and gulped water from the tap. Legs shaking, she looked at her reflection in the mirror and saw the wallpaper behind her: rows of silver swans embossed on pink velvet. Near the sink a corner of the paper curled. She grasped it between her fingers and gave a hard tug. With a satisfying hiss, the paper came off in a solitary sheet. She tore until the walls were bare and all that remained were islands of dried glue.

Seventeen

Ruby surprised them. Four days after the war began, she packed a bag, called Tehila with the news that she'd decided to enlist early, and used her babysitting money to buy a cheap seat on an El Al flight leaving that night for Tel Aviv. Salim waited in the car to take her to the airport. The spindly elms planted that summer along the curb shimmered in the sunset. Tamar saw him through the storm door, tapping his thumbs on the steering wheel, staring into the rearview mirror as if he were waiting for someone to materialize in the back seat. A car horn lacerated the air. His gaze remained fixed. He waited the way the old Jews in the *shtiebel* waited for the messiah to come. For the girl, Tamar thought. He was waiting for the girl, for his new life to begin.

A shout went up in the living room, where Rachel and Ari played a game of Spit. The cards smacked the coffee table in quick succession until Ari bellowed, "That's not fair. You're cheating."

"Sore loser," Rachel crowed.

"Ma?"

She turned to find Ruby in the kitchen, duffel at her feet, dressed in black jeans and a T-shirt. Her shoulders and back straight. Ruby's eyes glistened with excitement. *She looks good.* With a sense of relief and consternation, Tamar said, "Promise me you'll stay with *Safta* Miriam." She hugged her, releasing a breath when her daughter didn't resist. How good it felt to hold her, to feel the body she'd birthed all those years ago, strong and capable. The clean scent of Ruby's hair filled her with hope.

"Do you think I'll have to go to the army right away?" Ruby asked.

"No one's going to train new recruits now. It'll be a while before you're called up. In the meantime, study for your exams. A little hard work, you can get your high school diploma this term. Then you can go to the army."

"I'll take care of high school after the war. For now, Tehila says I can volunteer in the city or on a kibbutz."

"I'm proud of you." She tucked her hands into the pockets of her apron, trying to stem her anxiety.

"Thank you, Ima. Do me a favor?"

"Anything."

"Don't let her get to you."

Tamar flinched. "Who?"

"The girl with the letters."

It shouldn't have surprised her that Ruby knew about the soldier, but it did. No matter how hard she tried to hide them, the letters surfaced like bodies washed up on a shore.

She gripped Ruby's hands. "Forget everything. Start new. Pretend this never happened."

"What? Baba's girlfriend?"

She squeezed eyes shut. "America."

"That would be some trick, Ma." She swung the duffel bag over her shoulder. "I think you should come to Tel Aviv."

"Oh, *motek*, I don't know." Her resolve to return home had faltered, especially when she saw that Salim had no intention of voluntarily joining his reserve unit. He had waited for the consulate to call. But the days passed in silence and the war continued, and though neither expressed it, they were relieved that he wouldn't go into battle. But she couldn't stop thinking about it—the moment the Egyptians crossed the

Suez Canal and demolished the Bar Lev line, Syrian planes blasting the northern border, their tanks pummeling the terrain. She thought about the soldiers caught unawares, helpless in the onslaught, and about those captured, and she didn't know what was worse—captivity or death. Men who were once her neighbors, the sons and husbands of her friends. At night when she closed her eyes, she saw a thousand dead laid out and heard the boom and shriek of SAM missiles, the terrible silence before an explosion and the deafening aftermath. She recalled the bomb shelter in their Tel Aviv apartment and remembered the adrenaline pounding through her as she and the children raced down the stairs. There'd been no question then, only certainty that they were where they were supposed to be, each fighting in their own way, even if that fight amounted to nothing more than going about their daily business.

When her mind wasn't on the war, it rushed toward her mother. No matter their differences, in the end Miriam had been there for her. She could envision what it must have been like to attend the wedding of her only child, whom she'd considered too young to marry, and what it must have taken to make her peace with Salim once she was pregnant with Ruby. Miriam had wanted something else for her. She understood that now, though she still couldn't imagine what that something else might have been. Her mother never said anything more than "Do your best." She'd done an awful thing in leaving her alone and wondered if that would be her fate too. Her children rapt in the drama of their lives and she excluded because that's the way it was with children, and Salim bound to his soldier. One day that girl would want a baby of her own.

Another roar from the living room and then a peal of giggles.

"If you're worried about these two"—Ruby grinned at Rachel and Ari making faces at one another while they waited their turn to say goodbye—"don't be. They aren't babies anymore. Baba can take care of them. It'll give him something to think about when you're not here. Bet he'd miss you."

"Please." Tamar picked up the playing cards scattered on the carpet, eyes burning.

"Okay, but you know I'm right." She threw her arms out. "Come here, you animals." Ruby cuffed Ari on the chin and then gave each a fierce hug. "You little turds better visit me when the war's over." Two loud kisses later, she flung open the door. Ari and Rachel charged outside and waved to her from the porch until Salim's car disappeared from view.

Tamar fled to the basement, leaving the kids watching *Batman* reruns and eating Cheez Doodles. She lay on Ruby's bed, the words *go home* a drumbeat. Maybe Ruby was right. Maybe Salim would miss her. The kids could take care of themselves most of the time. They'd be all right. They had to be. *Go home.* She pressed her face into the pillow, breathing in Ruby's scent. If she could bottle it, she'd call it freedom.

Hours later it rained, and a dank odor seeped into the basement, like groundwater rising, saturating the landfill beneath the house, unsettling decades of buried garbage and the creatures that lived in subterranean ravines alongside cities of insects, rupturing the plastic sheathing that separated the refuse from the sand and concrete on which the house stood. The house, a wooden skeleton covered in brick and aluminum siding; she imagined it flooded, like in her dream, swimming through the rooms until they filled to capacity without a bubble of oxygen left. She sat up and wanted to tell the kids right then that she was leaving but couldn't bring herself to do it.

In the days following Ruby's departure, Tamar withdrew money from the bank and bought a one-way ticket to Tel Aviv. The few hundred dollars were small compensation for all the work she'd done in Salim's laundromat. *You owe me,* he'd said to her. Well, she'd paid her debt with her labor, her love, and years of lost promise. She wasn't sure whether going meant that she was giving up or giving in; however, she knew that if she stopped to consider it too long, she'd never leave. And she had to. Not just to make sure that Miriam was all right or that the country would survive—her lips twisted in a rueful smile, such noble aspirations—but because she'd never felt more alone and knew, if she stayed, she'd remain that way. Salim was biding his time until the soldier arrived in the U.S. Tamar saw it clearly: his abandonment, his blindness to the girl who manipulated him with stories and mementos sent across the globe, aimed at binding him to her, creating a history where none existed. And in this way, the girl haunted their lives. Tamar hoped that when she was gone, Salim would miss her. Maybe without her he'd remember who they were and follow her home. Maybe he'd give up on the idea of starting life with someone new and realize the past was never past. No matter how much he wanted to move beyond the pain of Hadas's death, life with this girl wouldn't bring him the peace he sought.

She spent the rest of the day cooking large pots of food to freeze and playing music loud enough to silence her thoughts. At dinner that night she took hold of Rachel's and Ari's hands. Avoiding Salim's gaze, she gave them the news.

"Are you crazy?" Salim said.

Rachel's eyes welled with tears. "Are we going to Israel too?"

"Not now. When the war's over, you can join me."

"Oh my God, Ma, I can't do that. I have rehearsal. It's winter recital in four weeks. Who's gonna take me to the theater?"

Tamar picked at the baked potato on her plate, pulling the skin from the flesh. "Your father." The fluorescent light buzzed and flickered. She made a mental note to remind him to change the bulb.

He sawed into his steak and then chewed as if the meat were a leather belt.

She turned to Ari. "How about you?"

He ducked his head. "Chess Club has a tournament soon." Then in an awed whisper, "I'm their best player in my age group." He cleared his throat. "Rachel's right. We can't go now."

She nodded, mindful of the fact that they were growing up and had other obligations. "These things you're involved in are important." She wiped her mouth on a napkin and placed it next to her plate. "But there are other things that are important too, like duty, helping people you care about, and those you don't even know because they're in trouble." The children sat back in their chairs. Salim went on eating, masticating his food, his jaw working like a cement grinder. She took a moment to rein in her emotions and even managed a smile. "If the war ends in time, I'll be back for both events."

Salim slammed his fork on the table. "So you intend to return."

She braced herself. "What's wrong?"

"You need to ask? What kind of mother leaves her children alone?"

Rachel and Ari stared at the carrots on their plates.

She lifted her chin. "But they're not alone, Salim. You're here." She snagged a roll out of the breadbasket. "I haven't seen my mother in six years." She pulverized the crust between her fingers. "All this time she took care of our apartment, expecting us to return. I have no idea how she's faring. Do you? No, because you didn't visit her while you were there. You didn't even make time to see Moti and Hadas's children." He was about to interrupt, but she held up her hand. "I know you had other things on your mind."

She turned to Rachel and Ari. "I need to see that *Safta* Miriam is healthy and safe." Glancing down, she was surprised to find a mound of crumbs on the table. "Salim, what I don't understand is how you don't feel the same urgency to go home, to support our family, Hadas's family, our friends. You were the one who said there'd be a war. Aren't you worried for our country? Can you imagine what would happen if—"

"Nothing will happen," he interjected, brushing off his trousers. "It's always the same shit. They start, we win, and they lose."

"Win? We've lost nearly a thousand men already. Who knows how many more? This isn't like '67. Gadi was right. We were gods then. They know we're vulnerable now."

"I don't care what Gadi said. We have a good life here. A new life."

She glanced at the refrigerator and remembered how on Rosh Hashanah she'd placed the girl's photograph there and how he had taken it down before the kids saw it. She recalled him saying to her, "I've always been up front with you. I never lied," before he tucked the photo into his back pocket.

And she had replied, "But I did, is that what you're trying to say, that I pushed you into loving this girl because I kept your sister's secret?"

He answered her quietly, as if he worried the kids would come in at any minute, "Tamar, you betrayed me. I don't blame you for it. I know you did it to help my sister, but it changed things. I didn't want it to, but it did."

"And what you're doing now isn't a betrayal?" she'd asked.

"I didn't plan on this."

"Neither did I."

He grimaced. "I know." And he had tried to embrace her.

But she'd pushed her way out of his arms, unable to bear his sympathy.

There were all sorts of betrayals in a long marriage, she'd thought at the time as she readied for bed in Ruby's room, none premeditated, but they were there, like the lies that weren't meant to hurt but did.

"Our children are happy here. Aren't you?" Salim now pinned them with a look.

"Yes, Baba." Rachel sank farther into her chair. Ari folded the napkin in his lap.

After dinner, the kids followed her into the basement. She found a deck of cards on Ruby's bookshelf. They played a few hands of rummy. She lost every round, picking up cards she didn't need, discarding the ones she did.

"Your head's not in the game, Ma," Ari complained.

"Sorry. You know I love you. I'd never leave if I thought for a minute you wouldn't be fine without me. I'm proud of how you've matured."

Neither of the children commented. Rachel dealt another hand. Salim was in the living room with the television on. When the news turned to Israel, he changed the channel before she could make out the latest casualty numbers. Since the start of the war, he'd refused to listen to the news and had stopped reading the paper. It was hard to fathom that this man who every day of his adult life had read the newspaper and listened with avid interest to the news had now stopped. His way, she thought, of disassociating from a past he no longer wanted any part of. But what really lay at the heart of his sudden aversion to the news was that he couldn't bear the thought of the girl soldier exposed to the brutality of war. The irony was that she understood him because she'd felt the same.

Time had stopped for her while he was fighting on the front lines in '67, and she imagined it stopped for him now, knowing the soldier might be close to the battle. The heart lived in the liminal space between heaven and earth when a beloved was in danger.

After another round of cards, she sent the kids off to bed and took out her needlepoint. There was only one dancer left to fill in. The background was complete. She found a measure of comfort as she separated strands of floss and threaded the needle. It was nearly midnight when she settled under the covers. The branches on the mimosa tree shook in the wind, and the Rosens' Pomeranian whimpered next door. Moths surged around the yard light. She heard the heavy tread of footsteps coming toward the basement. Her body stiffened. Minutes past and then he was there. Salim by her bedside, wearing only his briefs, hesitant, waiting for a sign. And then as if she'd expected him, had willed him there with each stitch, she lifted a corner of the blanket. He was on her, kissing her. She tasted the salt on his neck, and felt his thighs straining against hers, his hands lifting her buttocks. When they were spent, her breath raspy, his back slick with sweat, he said, "Please don't go. Don't leave us."

"What about the girl?"

He rested his forehead against hers. "I don't know. I'm sorry, I . . ."

His body, a familiar weight, retreated. Outside, the wind whipped and the rust and lead smell of the underground aquifer seeped into the room. *I'm drowning*, she thought, *we are drowning*, and heard him climb the stairs.

The next morning while the kids ate breakfast, she walked Salim to the front door, a new awkwardness between them. He was on his way to work at the laundromat. A sack of quarters hung from his wrist. "I need to be at the airport at eight. Will you take me tonight, or should I call a cab?"

Eyelids heavy from lack of sleep, he stuffed his fists into the pockets of his jacket. His mouth set in a determined line. "I've thought about it and you're not leaving."

"I'm not asking for your permission, Salim, just the way you didn't ask for mine when you sold our house and broke our marriage with that girl." She dug her heels into the floor so he wouldn't notice her legs shaking.

"Do you still love me?" He looked worn out.

"Do you?" she countered.

"Yes." He took her hand and pressed it to his chest.

"Then let her go."

He opened his mouth to answer, but no sound emerged.

"That's what I thought." She stepped away and held the storm door open for him to pass through.

A short while later, the kids left for school and she was seized by an inertia that lasted all morning. She sank into Salim's bed, their bed, and thought of last night, of the way he had loved her—as if afraid to lose her. Still, he wanted the girl. He wanted a life free of the past.

She pried open his nightstand and searched for paper and pen, knowing she'd never say to him all that she felt and found stowed in the writing tablet an envelope addressed to the soldier. On impulse she took it and every letter the girl had sent and tossed them into her suitcase. She burned blank sheets of paper in the sink and sprinkled the ashes in the drawer. Let him think she'd torched them all.

I'm counting on you to take care of our children, she wrote, and gave him a detailed schedule of their day: when they went to school, when they did their homework, Rachel's ballet classes, Ari's weekly chess meetings, his model building class in the after-school program, an upcoming parent-teacher conference. In the course of writing, it became clear that he had no idea what his children's lives were like.

Time sped, then slowed, an erratic current that left her energized one minute and wrung out the next. Her suitcase was packed. Restless and not knowing what else to do, she cleaned the house, dusted the painting of the boat at sea, thought of Gadi, her heart thudding in her chest at the thought that he might already be wounded or dead. When the house was pristine, she went into his apartment. The dishes were still on the counter. She hadn't had a chance to donate them to the rabbi and wondered if Salim would or if he'd leave them for the next tenant. She searched the cabinets, unplugged the refrigerator, and was struck by a terrible premonition that her husband intended to give the apartment to the girl. The soldier would live in this house. She would bathe in the tub and listen for Salim. They'd have a secret code, tapping messages on the party wall. She'd listen in on their family, be privy to their arguments and complaints. She'd worm her way into their lives, poisoning them at the root. With a great heave, Tamar sent the dishes sailing through the air.

An hour later, the children returned from school. She wrapped them in her arms, their faces burrowed on either side of her neck. Ari saw the suitcase propped against the wall. "Told you she was going." His chin wobbled.

"Shut up," Rachel said. "Don't go, Ima. It's dangerous."

She reassured her. "Not in the city. I promise. Maybe you'll come when the war's over. Then we'll all be together."

"Don't bother." Ari kicked off his shoes.

"Arileh, don't be angry with me. It's just for a few weeks."

Rachel tossed her backpack on the floor. "What about Baba?" She twisted the ends of her hair.

"Don't you want to go home?"

"No!" Ari shouted.

"We are home," Rachel said.

"But we always planned to go back."

Ari reached for his math text. "You planned. We figured we lived here now. You said we had to make the best of it. That's what you said."

"I know, but did we?" All these years while she'd pined for home, they'd made one here.

Rachel put a hand on her hip. "You don't know anything, and the really crappy part is you don't want to. You think we're like you but we're not."

They left her standing in the living room, their words trapped in her throat.

She ordered a cab, easier than having Salim drive her to the airport, deriding her the whole way or, worse, ignoring her. She set the table and waited for him to come home. He was late and came in glowering. He washed his hands and padded about in his stockinged feet. She could smell his sweat in them. They ate dinner and he told the kids that tomorrow, if they didn't have after-school activities, they'd meet him at the laundromat, and he'd teach them how to run the register and clean out the lint traps. "It'll all be yours one day." Then he tried to joke saying that Rachel would have to cook from now on because he could barely boil water. Tamar rolled her eyes.

"Well, that's not true." She swallowed back the memory of Tehila taking over the household duties after Hadas died, wondering if that was the fate she was leaving for her daughter. "You cooked for me when I visited you in Kafr Ma'an before we married."

"Hadas made most of those meals," he said quietly.

"Not all of them. Sometimes you'd cook something simple like *shakshuka*. You said I wasn't to touch a thing. 'A queen touches the food only after it's been served.'"

Salim lit a cigarette, eyes squinting at the smoke. "I don't remember."

"Well, I remember everything."

"That's the problem," he muttered. "For you, the past is inescapable."

"Isn't it for everyone?"

"No. Some of us move beyond it, some of us forget."

"No, you don't. You just pretend to. May I?" She pointed to his cigarette. He sank it into his water glass, where it sizzled before bobbing to the surface.

Her palms were sweating, and she shivered as if with cold. The taxi waited at the curb. She kissed Rachel and Ari goodbye, their expressions mutinous as she tried to memorize the supple muscularity of Rachel's body, the soft pillow of Ari's. For a moment Ari relented and enveloped her in a hug. He hugged her with all his being, and when he let her go, she felt a keen loss.

"I love you," she said. "That'll never change. I'm your mother. I don't know how to be anything else."

Rachel looked stricken. "You're still our mother, aren't you?"

"Of course. I just meant that while I'm away, Baba will take care of you."

"Think so?" Rachel snorted and shot her a cynical glance. "Bet he'll try to make me do everything because I'm the girl, but I won't let him."

"Good, don't. Anyway, you won't have to. There's plenty of food in the freezer, enough for a month. You won't go hungry and you won't have to cook."

"Is that how long you're going to be away?"

"Depends on the war."

Ari looked at the cab waiting by the curb. "You're leaving just when things are getting good."

The driver honked and that seemed to be the cue Rachel needed. She dashed into her room with Ari right behind her. Salim waited by the door, hands fisted at his sides, while she dragged her suitcase across the foyer. She gave him a quick hug, extracting herself from his arms before she could feel the regret that threatened to pull her under.

"I've written out the kids' schedule. It's on the refrigerator." After more than six years of exile, she was finally going home in a way she'd never imagined—alone.

"What do you think this'll prove?"

She gave the suitcase a light kick. "That I can live without you."

THE ANATOMY OF EXILE

Part IV

PILGRIMAGE

Eighteen

Tel Aviv, October 1973

Tamar awoke to the sounds of crows wheeling in and out of the sycamore trees lining Bialik Street. After two weeks in Israel, she was finally getting used to their incessant cawing. Each day when fighter jets tore open the sky and sonic booms shook clocks and mirrors off the walls, the crows dove into the nearest thicket. In the aftermath, an eerie stillness claimed the city. Tel Aviv had become a city of women, children, and old men, all of them conscious of the missing and the lost, of ghosts that roamed the streets and cafés. There were empty chairs everywhere and, on the advertisement pillars, posters alerting neighbors to the daily funerals, the shiva calls, and the words *May you be comforted among the mourners of Zion and Jerusalem* muttered in their ears. In a country so small, everyone knew someone who'd been killed.

She opened the *tris*. The damp morning carried in the aroma of Mrs. Brenner's cooking. Mrs. Brenner lived on the floor below. She rose before dawn in anticipation of her son's homecoming. Yesterday a ceasefire was signed. Today liver and fried onions assailed the building. By noon tomorrow, the war would be officially over and men, like Mrs. Brenner's son, would return home.

Her mother's apartment was far enough from Allenby Street to spare them the tumult of a busy thoroughfare. In the afternoons, children played in the rotunda outside the old city hall, adjacent to the home of the national Hebrew poet, Hayim Nahman Bialik, for whom the street was named. Their high-pitched cries reminded her of Ari and Rachel when they were small.

She called them each week from her mother's new telephone, installed a few days before the war began. Miriam hovered beside her, wringing her hands, pointing at her wristwatch, worried the price of an international call longer than three minutes would be astronomical. *Don't forget, I live on a pension.* This new anxiety of her mother's surprised and worried her. Miriam's strength and independence had seen her through wars, personal tragedy, and the austerity years in Israel when an egg was considered a luxury. She'd coped with the death of her husband and its aftermath: the fallout of a long marriage, the one-sided recriminations, the tedium of settling one's affairs, and years later, the painful realization that he would be the last man to love her.

As she dialed the code for an international line, she pondered whether her mother's anxiety was due to the latest war, or the result of living alone, giving her a heightened sense of her own vulnerability. The senior center where she volunteered was her only social outlet as far as Tamar could tell. Gone were the days when her mother went out four or five nights a week, some new man on the doorstep. She thought if Salim could see her mother now, he wouldn't have been so quick to denigrate Miriam, or blame Tamar for Ruby running off with Faisal. The phone barely rang before she heard someone breathing into the receiver. Her ears turned red.

"Salim? Salim, it's me. Please say something."

She heard him say, "It's your mother," then a pocket of dead air before Rachel pounced. "The war's over, right? Come home already."

Disoriented by Salim's continued silence—he hadn't spoken to her since she'd left—she was unprepared for Rachel's belligerence.

"They think I'm going to wash their clothes," Rachel cried.

"Who?" she said.

"Baba and Ari. He acts just like him, so superior. I punched him in his fat belly and he almost cried, the big baby."

"Rachel, what are you talking about? What's happening?"

"Ari. He's impossible to live with since he won that stupid chess match."

Ari's voice came on. "No, I'm not. I played the best. Baba was there. He bought me a new chess set. That's how good I was."

"*Mazel tov*, Ari. Good for you."

Rachel shouted, "Don't listen to him. He's a fat liar and cheat. He promised to help me with the laundry."

"Ow," Ari yelled. "Ma, tell her if she doesn't cut it out, I'm gonna give it to her good, like what I did to that bully. She thinks she's the boss of me. She's not you."

Tamar held the phone away from her ear.

"Hang up, hang up," Miriam whined.

Tamar tried to make the right soothing noises, but after a series of clicks, the line went dead.

"Eight minutes," her mother harped. "Eight minutes," like a bird pecking at the ground. Tamar was furious Miriam couldn't stop thinking about the cost.

"Don't worry, I'll pay," she snapped at Miriam.

"With what? The money your husband sends you?"

"Ima, please don't start."

"I don't know why you left him, but even I can see he's upset. You ran away." She shook a finger at her. "That's why the children behave as they do."

After a light supper, Miriam joined her on the balcony with a bottle of blackberry schnapps. They listened to soft guitar music trickling out of an apartment nearby. She wondered how her mother could bear the loneliness all these years.

"Why didn't you remarry?" Tamar said. "You were still a young woman when Aba died, and you had plenty of men hanging around."

Miriam lit a cigarette. Smoke wended toward the ceiling. "There were a few serious ones, but nothing ever came of them."

"Why not?" She lifted the snifter to her mouth and recalled blurting out the truth about Hadas and Daoud to Salim, the night Ruby didn't come home. Before then, the last time she drank was with Gadi in the shop in Coney Island. Every day of the war she searched the lists of the dead, the prisoners of war, the missing in action, for his name, for Moti's, relieved when she didn't find them. Moti was a commander of a tank company in an armored battalion in the Golan Heights. The family had no contact for weeks. He didn't even know she was in Israel.

"Well"—Miriam flicked ashes into a saucer—"let's just say I was too old for the unmarried men who wanted to start families of their own, and too young for widowers who wanted me to take care of their children." A vespa sputtered down the street. "I didn't want that for me, and I didn't want it for you. Why should my daughter compete for love and attention in a stranger's house?"

Tamar leaned back in her chair and recognized the irony in what Miriam had said. She'd always competed for her parents' love and attention. Her childhood, a string of lonely days. Both her parents worked, her father for the Davar newspaper, her mother for the Tel Aviv municipality, leaving Tamar to come home from school to an empty apartment. Many times she was gripped by the irrational fear that her parents were dead—drowned at sea, lost in a fire. She'd perceived this fear and the desire to belong as love and realized it as such when she met Salim and Hadas. With them, she'd fought against feeling like an outsider. She wondered what parts of her were erased in the process.

"You were such a sensitive child," Miriam said. "So much like your father. He didn't just observe the world, he absorbed it. You're like that, gauging the temperature in a room, then acting accordingly. Not me. I always react, mostly when I shouldn't."

"So why didn't you have more children? I would've loved a brother or sister."

Two teenage girls walked down Bialik Street singing. Their voices shimmering, rising into the trees.

Miriam sipped the schnapps. "We tried, didn't take. One miscarriage before you were born, another three after. Doctor said to stop, so I did. Judah took it hard. His father and brothers were murdered in the war. He worried there'd be no one to carry on the Posner family name. He was the last of his line. Not even a cousin survived."

"I wish you'd told me."

"He never spoke about it. Whenever I'd bring it up, he'd escape into his dark room. I found his disappointment"—she paused to grind the cigarette in the saucer—"punishing."

"I should've realized he wanted a son," Tamar said. "Never even occurred to me. I just thought he didn't find me very interesting."

"Oh, he loved you. But he needed a son and felt like a failure without one. Made me feel it too. Like I'd failed him. Each miscarriage was like he was burying his father and brothers all over again."

"Ima, I'm sorry."

"Was a long time ago."

That night she heard a convoy on the coastal road hauling artillery. A half-dozen helicopters flew the wounded and dead home. Once the rumbling faded, the streets sank into mournful silence. Ruby was out with Tehila again. Miriam was asleep. The wind echoed through the city—*We are alone.* She turned on her side, the wall cold against her back. In a half dream, she heard Salim's footsteps on the stairs, making his way to her. The weight of him pressing her into the mattress, opening her like fruit. She had left him. She had left her children.

There was comfort in routine, cleaning her room, making the bed, propping the pillows she'd embroidered long ago against the bolster cushions. The needlework was some of her finest. She'd been a teen when she'd made them, confident in her skill and design and had even sold a few to the yarn shop on King George Street. The proprietress, a friend of her mother's, had displayed them in the window. For weeks she'd walked past the store, wishing her father were alive to see her handiwork. He might have admired the precision of her stitches, the gradation of color like in a Seurat painting. She'd transferred her favorite photograph of his onto fabric—starlings in flight, delicate as black mourning lace against an electric blue sky.

The room was a diorama of her girlhood. Her father's best work still hung on the walls: a close-up of a white asphodel growing in the desert. Silver carp in shallow tanks at the supermarket, photographs of politicians and heads of state, landmark buildings, and biblical sites. The display reflected his wide range of interest. There was the rare photo of the three of them on Gordon Beach. Miriam, glamorous in a wide-brimmed hat. Judah, looking uncomfortable in front of the camera, and she sandwiched between them, all knees and elbows, and behind them the sea. She never realized how small boned he was, how elegant his hands and feet were. He had always seemed a giant to her, monumental behind his camera, teasing out shadow and light.

Her mother had kept the room just as she'd left it, yet everything felt different and everything felt the same. All that was missing were Salim and the children, the six lost years in America, and Hadas. They had spent a lot of time in this room. Hadas had taught her what to wear, what makeup to use, what European music to listen to, and what books to read. This was where Hadas had said she was a perfect match for Salim. "He needs someone like you—quiet, loving. Someone who won't try to change him." At the time, Hadas's words had elated her; now she wondered if her sister-in-law had thought her weak and unassuming, a girl who'd never challenge Salim, who'd be the perfect Syrian wife without the stigma of being an Arab Jew in a land that often looked down their noses at them.

Miriam burst into her bedroom. A cigarette gripped between her fingers, her thick white hair grazing her shoulders. The beginning of a dowager's hump formed at the base of her neck. Her mother wore old age like body armor, her indignation on continuous simmer. Miriam had yet to accept the capriciousness of life, the heartless way it had flung her across the globe, the loss of her beloved older brothers, Villy and Yakov, cut down in the forest like firewood, her parents in an ignominious heap in Birkenau. As for Judah, just as she was settling into the idea of growing old with him, he died at the kitchen table, reading his newspaper. The portrait he'd taken of Ben Gurion on the front page.

Her mother had her interrogation face on. Tamar stiffened and began pawing through the stacks of linens, searching for her embroidery bin in the closet where she'd stored it before moving to the U.S.

Miriam arched her brow. "Have you seen Ruby?"

Four words. That's all it took for her mother to set her nerves on fire.

"Isn't she in her room?"

"She didn't come home last night."

"She must have slept at Tehila's." Tamar stood up too fast, steadying herself on the back of a chair. It hadn't taken her mother long to complain about Ruby's behavior. A complaint aimed at Tamar, at her inability to control her daughter. Miriam's favorite refrain was, "A good mother needs a stiff backbone." And just yesterday, she'd fired another poison arrow.

"You're worried she won't like you. That's your problem right there. You think if she likes you, she'll do what you want; she'll be your friend. Children rarely do what you want them to and they're never really your friend. No one tells you how lonely motherhood is." Miriam puffed on her cigarette, wrapping them in a cloud of smoke.

When Ruby was home, she slept past noon, hardly ever joined them for a meal, and didn't do more than put her dishes in the sink. Tamar thought she needed time to acclimate. After all, she was volunteering for the Jewish National Fund, putting in long hours. It wasn't easy to be here in the middle of a war and to reunite with friends and family after years of separation.

Tamar wished she were around more. She'd hoped they'd grow closer here, become allies, friends even, share the special closeness they had when Ruby was a child. She shifted a stack of sheets aside to run her hands along the shelf, finding it empty. How long had she kept that lie alive? The child, like all her children, was a conduit that ran between her and Salim.

Tamar felt adrift, as if she'd landed in an alternate city, one that looked like Tel Aviv. The streets were the same but the people in them were all wrong, like extras on a movie set milling about in a cardboard town. There were new shops and boutiques where the old ones stood. Except for the folksongs they played on Friday afternoons, she didn't recognize any of the music on the radio. The old cafés had new owners, new clientele, and the artists and writers had left for the more bohemian climes of Jerusalem and Jaffa. It didn't seem to matter that Hebrew was her mother tongue. There were so many new words. Arabic words she didn't know folded into the lexicon: *sakhteyn, keefak, wallah, salamat.* The slang that had come up from the army barracks saturated the streets. She felt like an outsider. The night she'd arrived in Tel Aviv, Miriam asked, "Nu? Where are your husband and children?"

"Home," she replied, startled by the way the word could shift its geography. If place was an interior construct and not tangible ground, what had she been longing for all this time?

"You're just a little out of step," Miriam said. "We're a young country. Did you think we'd stand still while you were away or fall into a slumber like in a fairy tale until the princess returned to the kingdom?"

She'd thought having Ruby in Israel would make the transition home easier, but it only made her feel more alone.

"I wouldn't be too sure about her sleeping at Tehila's." Miriam waved the cigarette in the air. "Her stepmother, what's her name, Fanny?"

"Frieda."

"Doesn't like company unless Moti's home with her, and since he's still in the Golan . . . no, I don't think she's there. How he could have married someone like her after Hadas?" She shook her head. "Dry as day-old bread." Miriam took a final drag, then crushed the cigarette into a seashell Tamar had collected on the beach. A beam of sunlight landed on the rug, warming her.

"Ruby isn't company," Tamar said. "She's family. I'm sure Frieda understands how close the girls are. They're inseparable. Even with Tehila in the army."

"Trying to convince me or yourself?"

"Ima, enough."

Miriam sucked at her incisor. "Maybe you're right, then again maybe not."

Tamar rolled her eyes and continued looking for the embroidery bin, feeling the heat of her mother's gaze.

"You all right?" Miriam said.

"Fine. Are you taking the senior group to Ein Hod?"

"Leaving after lunch. They're giving us dinner in the artist's village and then we're off to Tiberias. What about you? The hospital?"

"I'm on the four o'clock shift," Tamar said.

Miriam squeezed her shoulder. "You're doing good work there."

She was a volunteer at the military hospital in Tel HaShomer. Her initial meeting with Batya Kadouri, the volunteer coordinator, had been uncomfortable. As was the first question she'd asked: "Where's your husband serving?"

Tamar had looked down at the clipboard in her lap. "He isn't." She wasn't like other women here, whose husbands and sons were on the battlefield. Her husband was thousands of miles away, safe, something for which she was relieved and yet angry and embarrassed. The least she could do was give comfort to the wounded and their families. Batya looked at her as though inspecting for cracks, vulnerabilities that would jeopardize the program and its patients. She said, "War is a threshing machine. Anyone that comes here does so in pieces. Even the ones who appear intact are broken. I need somebody with a strong stomach. The last two women I took on left in tears. I'll admit they were younger. Where are you from?"

Tamar shifted in her seat. "I've just arrived from New York."

"It took a war to bring you home?"

She squeezed her knees together. "Exactly."

They rotated her from one ward to another. Her job was to read to the soldiers, help them write letters, make them feel, in Batya's words, human again. The first week she couldn't look at the maimed bodies, the destroyed faces, especially those in the burn unit, the amputees, the boys with crushed spines, boys who'd lost arms and legs to artillery and land mines. Their gauze-wrapped stumps peeking out from under the bedsheets. She tried to find things to interest them: the sports page, the gossip columns, crossword puzzles. Too often their expressions remained blank. Batya suggested she read them poetry and the Psalms, play the music they liked. "Don't let them disappear," she admonished. There were patients too shattered to speak, others unable to stop. Sometimes she wished they would stop, especially when they catcalled and flirted with her, not because they liked her or found her attractive, but to deride each other, egg each other on. They dared one another to be men, shouted across the ward, "She doesn't want to fuck a mess like you." And if Batya happened to walk by, she'd retort, "You're all a fucking mess. Now give us some peace." The men would howl with laughter and bang on their bedpans. Tamar would escape to the bathroom to compose herself, to keep from crying, to practice her best smile. She was too earnest, too guilt-ridden. She needed to be more like Batya to survive, more of a sabra. Most days she had to force herself to walk through the wards, to peer behind the curtains and ignore the antiseptic smell that couldn't relieve the stench of shit and putrefied flesh. But no matter how bad it got, it was the one place where she didn't think about Salim.

There was no room for him inside her head, not there. That in itself was a kind of freedom.

Miriam lit another cigarette. "You look like you could use this."

Tamar waved it away and then said, "Oh, all right, give it here," and took a long drag, admiring the stack of starched white linens that had once been part of Miriam's trousseau. She reached for a summer blanket and found the shoebox she'd packed there before leaving for America. A stack of letters from school friends, holiday cards bound in a faded ribbon. The way they nestled all bundled together reminded her of the soldier's letters in the bottom of her suitcase. She had every intention of returning them, but each day the war raged, she assured herself it was better to wait. The soldier could be stationed anywhere, and besides, she was serving the country. It would be insensitive to confront her now. This was, she knew, an excuse, a way to evade the pain she felt at Salim's continued silence. To see the soldier—his *habibti*, his *ayouni*—would only humiliate her.

Tamar continued her search. Beneath the envelopes in the shoebox, she found the picture of Hadas that Daoud had had in his wallet. She slipped it into her pocket.

"I'll be back in a few days," Miriam said. "Don't do anything stupid while I'm away."

Three beeps signaling the news hour broke into the room. Mrs. Brenner had her radio turned up. "I'll remember to save my stupidity for when you return." She shoved the box back into place.

Miriam chuckled. "So that's where your sense of humor has been."

"What's that supposed to mean?"

"You've hardly smiled since you got here."

"That isn't true." She thought of what Miriam would say if she knew about Salim and the girl, and she gnawed on her bottom lip until the sound of a key in the door caught her attention. Ruby swept into the house chirping, "Shalom, shalom."

Tamar barreled into the living room. "I want to talk to you," she said.

"Sure, Ima, right after I shower." Ruby sprinted into the bathroom.

Miriam arched her brow. "Maybe you should make an appointment?"

"Very funny."

"You've been away so long, you forgot I have a sense of humor too."

"Dear God, leave me alone." Sometimes her mother was impossible. Always trying to worm information from her, demanding she be happy, as if her unhappiness had anything to do with Miriam, as if Miriam's dissatisfaction had anything to do with her. Tamar scowled. She didn't want to consider that her mother missed her the way she missed Ruby. There were generations of women fending off discontent, trying to fill the hours once devoted to their children.

Miriam chided, "You're a mother, for goodness' sake, act like one."

She waited for Ruby in Judah's former studio. After his death, Miriam had converted it into a bedroom. When her father was alive, the room smelled of developing solution. Now it was all Ruby— a dense female musk, like the odor that wafted up from an animal's belly. She knew it was irrational to feel betrayed by a scent, but she did. Just more proof Ruby was grown-up and didn't need her. She came in wearing a towel; her hair dripping onto her shoulders.

"Hey." She shut the door behind her. If Ruby was surprised to find her there, she didn't let on. With her back turned, she shimmied into her jeans.

"Did you talk to Rachel and Ari?" Ruby asked, slipping her arms into a T-shirt.

"Yesterday. Ari won his chess match. He won a trophy. Baba went right out and bought a fancy chess set so they could play together."

"Poor Ari," Ruby snickered. "Baba isn't exactly known for his patience."

"I wish you wouldn't say that, even if it's true."

"Whatever." She pulled on a pair of socks.

"When I spoke to her last week, Rachel was still rehearsing for the lead in the winter recital."

"Cool." Ruby tucked the shirt into her jeans and wove a belt through the loops.

Was she listening? Tamar sat on the edge of the bed. "Have you thought about what you're going to do?"

"Right now?" Ruby frowned.

"Future, after the army. Didn't you say you wanted to be a teacher?"

Ruby shook her head. "A translator. I told you."

"You mean from Hebrew to English?"

"Yeah and"—she hesitated—"Arabic. I'm going to study Arabic. I've picked up a bit just from being here."

"Arabic?" Tamar gathered the clothes on the bed into a pile. "Why?"

"It's Baba's first language. His and Hadas's. Tehila studied Arabic in high school. I would have, too, if I'd been here. Did you speak to him?" Ruby applied mascara, blinking at her reflection in the mirror.

"Not yet. I haven't seen you in days. What's that?" She gestured to the bruise on Ruby's neck. "Who did that to you?"

Ruby's hands fluttered to her throat. She stared past her reflection at Tamar. "It's nothing, Ima," she said, and slipped her feet into a pair of sneakers. "Must've happened unloading one of the supply trucks."

"You going out again?"

Ruby nodded. "I have to get back to the volunteer center."

"Why not stay home today? The war's over now. Soon the men will be back to take care of their families."

Ruby bent to tie her laces.

"We can go shopping. There's a new store on Eilat Street. You'll need a warmer coat for the winter, especially if you're stationed in the north."

"The war may be over but the struggle for so many of these families isn't. You should know that with the work you do. There's still plenty of people that need our help. We've been collecting clothes and food for weeks. I'm on the distribution committee."

"I know. You sure you're okay? You seem on edge."

The soggy curtain of hair draped on either side of Ruby's face gave her the appearance of a medieval saint. "Never better."

"Would you tell me if you weren't?"

"Of course." She flashed an ironic smile.

Tamar sensed she was missing something important here. Her daughter was keeping something from her, and with little ground to lose, she plunged ahead. "You'll never believe this, but I thought I saw Faisal last week." She hadn't thought to tell her about the incident. She hadn't wanted to give her ideas.

"Oh." Her daughter stopped digging through her jewelry case.

"A week ago, at Aboulafiya's Bakery. The one on Yefet Street."

Ruby continued her search, choosing a pair of large coin earrings. "I don't know Jaffa well." She plowed a brush through her hair, wincing when the bristles snagged on a knot. Outside, a delivery van hurtled down the road.

"He was driving a donkey cart, hauling sacks of potatoes. I followed him to a restaurant."

The brush slipped out of Ruby's hand. She bent to retrieve it.

"He didn't see me, at least not at first. I waited outside for him."

"Why would you do that?" Ruby said.

"To say hello. Turned out it wasn't him." A part of her had wanted it to be, had wanted to know he was all right, that her actions hadn't harmed him though of course they had. An American boy used to all that freedom. Here there was no escaping who you were. A Jew was a Jew, and an Arab was an Arab. Maybe he was back in the U.S. The thought gave her some relief.

Ruby braided her hair—fingers swift, breath fast.

"Have you seen him?" Tamar said.

Her daughter tied off the end with a rubber band and then pinched an angry color into her cheeks. "Ima, I don't know why you're asking." Ruby applied a coat of clear lip gloss. "It's been more than a year." Her mouth glistened.

"I'm sorry. The past should stay in the past." She pulled her into an embrace. "You okay?"

Ruby patted her back. "Great." Then she broke contact.

"I guess you are. Just me being silly. Besides, you know how it is here. What's tolerated and what isn't."

"I know exactly how it is here." Ruby slipped on a jean jacket and flung the braid over her shoulder. "You on duty tonight?"

"We're hosting a modest dinner and a bit of entertainment for the men who are well enough. Felt we ought to do something to mark the occasion."

Although they had won the war, it felt as if they'd lost. No parades, no celebrations. There were too many dead to celebrate a victory. "How's Tehila? She hasn't been around for a while." Her hand curled around Hadas's photograph in the pocket of her cardigan.

Ruby tugged at her cuffs. "Busy at headquarters. I guess peace is as complicated as war."

Tamar eyed the extra change of clothes she stuffed into her bag. "Are you sleeping out again?"

"Probably. I'm meeting Tehila for dinner, if that's all right. Do you and *Safta* Miriam need anything?"

"We're fine. You sure you're happy here?"

Ruby spun on her heel, her eyes overly bright. "Oh, Ima, I'm happy." She hugged her. "I don't want to be anywhere else."

Tamar felt her tremble. "I'm glad." She kissed her daughter's cheek, yet could not disregard the unease that filled her. After Ruby had left the house, Tamar found her mother on the balcony and said, "Which way did she go?"

"What makes you think I was watching?"

Tamar shot her a knowing look.

Miriam sighed. "Allenby Street. Volunteer center is in the other direction."

"I know that," Tamar snapped.

"What will you do?" Miriam plucked a cigarette out of a new pack of Time.

"What you would have done." She frowned and laced up her shoes.

Nineteen

The café, with its faded gold-and-black signage above the large window, had a bohemian charm. A large pot of geraniums stood at the entrance. It was the end of the siesta hour. People in their homes had radios and cooking pots on low. A fragrant murmur slipped from under their doors into the narrow, cobbled street, burnished by the late October sun. Where light failed to reach, long, conical shadows like bishops' hats appeared. Tabbies lounged in doorways; calicos perched on window ledges. The last of the café's patrons, a young couple, exited. Pink with sunburn, they wore their cameras like amulets around their necks. Many foreigners had volunteered on kibbutzim during the war to pick fruit and vegetables in the fields, to work the factories, to milk the cows, and collect the eggs. Now that it was over, they became tourists.

She stood across the street from the café, hidden in a doorway, trying to appear nonchalant as the couple passed, refraining from ducking her head when they looked at her with curiosity, before continuing their conversation in a language that sounded like Dutch. At the end of the road, they turned left in the direction of the mosque, whose minaret pierced the sky. In this part of Jaffa, it was a beacon. Soon the muezzin would call the worshippers to prayer and the street would swell with men.

The front door to the café was open. From her vantage point she had a clear view inside and watched in disbelief as Ruby filled a row of slim vases with carnations. She had followed her here and wondered if Ruby was in the café as part of her volunteer assignment aiding military families. When the vases were complete and the votives in place and the tables immaculate and ready for the next shift, her daughter poured two glasses of beer, then dropped a few coins into the jukebox. The Beatles' "Penny Lane" washed into the street. Tamar squinted to get a better look at the young man emerging from the kitchen in the back. His face concealed in a pocket of gloom. A blue bandanna covered his head, an apron at his waist, dirty with tomato and egg stains. He stepped into a cone of light, removed the head gear and apron, and shook out his hair. The curls she remembered fell to his shoulders, longer now than when he'd lived on Avenue C. He'd grown taller and, if possible, handsomer. He looked happy, not like the exiled son sitting in the back of his father's station wagon on the way to the airport.

He opened his arms and her daughter stepped into them. The two were drenched in the overhead light. A teapot whistled behind the door where Tamar stood. Two tabbies on a second-story balcony above the café stretched their sleepy forms. A car idled in a nearby street and a child's cry rose above the rooftops. There was a sense of inevitability in these random acts. Their sequence a string of sensory code awaiting a cipher, its secret pointing to Ruby and Faisal. She must have known but was so fixated on herself, she'd been blind to Ruby—in Israel, in America, maybe her whole life. It was her mother who'd alerted her to Ruby's behavior. She leaned against the doorframe. The brass handle dug into her back.

Ruby rested her head on Faisal's chest, his heart under her ear. Tamar wondered where the owner was and why the children seemed to be running things. She searched for the logo on the sign. The name of the café written in delicate English script—*Amina's*—gave her no clue. A certificate of ownership was taped to the inside of the window. She darted across the road to get a closer look, crouching low so the kids wouldn't spot her. The permit had the seal of the Tel Aviv-Yafo municipality emblazoned at the top of the page. The names of the business owners appeared in Hebrew and Arabic: Amina and Hamza Mahmoudi. This was his family's café. She scrambled back to her post in the doorway. Her legs felt like sandbags; her thoughts raced.

Faisal placed a hand on Ruby's hip, the other on her shoulder. They began to dance. The record changed to an old jazz standard, "Speak Low." They adjusted to the new rhythm and moved in unison. They danced the way she and Salem had danced at Hadas's winter salon parties in Kafr Ma'an: the smell of kerosene heating lamps combined with the sweat of partygoers and the fragrance of citrus trees carried on the wind. She wondered if Daoud had watched those parties from the *pardes*, watched those people in what used to be his home laughing and drinking, Hadas dancing with other men and he an outsider until she was with him and he felt a semblance of belonging again. Tamar remembered her intense relief when Salim saved her from being stuck in a corner all night, saved her from obscurity just by holding her hand. *Who was she without him?* She had no answer. She'd tried to ensure that Ruby wouldn't lose herself. Her daughter didn't know how easy it was to erase a woman. She gave up her name, her body, and then believed she was nothing without him; his opinions shaped hers, his desires were all that mattered. An insidious voice intruded on her thoughts: *Your life, not Ruby's.*

She was so proud when Ruby returned home. Being the mother of a patriotic daughter was better than being a forsaken wife. Ruby had given her a measure of self-worth. Though she now rued her gullibility, she acknowledged that if her daughter hadn't made the trip to Israel, she never would have followed. It was Ruby who gave her the courage to come home. The record came to an end and the kids leaned against the jukebox. From the moment she had seen that room in the cellar, she had known this thing between Ruby and Faisal would not end there. She had known just as she had known about Salim and the girl.

There was a roar in her head, rising up from her feet. Her hands shook. The roar grew louder. She tasted dust in the air. The door behind her rattled on its hinges and the ground quaked. Cats scampered. Thunder broke into the quiet after-noon, a barrage of shattering glass. She ran past the café and turned the corner to see a mob of angry men carrying sticks and beating them on the ground. They marched through the streets as pedestrians took cover in stores and restaurants. Protestors poured in from Ajami and Andromeda Hill. They surged through

Kedumim Square, down Yefet Street, past Aboulafiya's Bakery and the kiosk that sold ice cream in summer and warm *sahlab* in winter. Men wearing *kefiyahs* thrust their fists in the air. *"Free Palestine Now!"* they shouted.

A high-pitched whine bore into her ear as the mob con-verged in Kikar Hasha'on. They surrounded the clock tow-er and smashed a record shop's plate glass window. The cars parked near the square had their windshields broken. She sprinted back to the safety of the café to find Ruby and Faisal locking up.

"Shit," he said.

She hung back, reluctant for them to see her.

Ruby clung to his arm. "What's happening?"

"Must be the demonstration I told you about. Hussein's with them. He told me it was tomorrow." He had to shout the last words to be heard.

Smoke rose into the air.

"I have to get him before there's real trouble." He kissed her cheek and took off in a run.

"Faisal," Ruby shouted and started after him.

Panicked, Tamar cried, "Stop," but Ruby was already halfway down the alley. Tamar charged across the cobblestones, slippery with age, keeping Ruby in sight. The ground rushed toward her. She landed hard, hands scraped raw, knee aching and bleeding, the right pant leg torn. Tears sprang to her eyes; she scrambled to her feet and chased after Ruby until they reached a passageway that opened onto the clock tower plaza. She elbowed her way through a crowd of spectators to where Ruby stood poised to enter the square. The Dutch couple from the café were beside a stone column, cameras whirring.

"Ruby?" She placed a steadying hand on her shoulder.

Her daughter blinked at her in shock. "Ima, what are you doing here?"

"Please don't go after him." Palms stinging, she clutched Ruby's hand. Bits of debris worked deeper into the abrasions in her skin. "We have to go. It isn't safe. Hear that?" Sirens blared along Jerusalem Boulevard. Faisal was already swallowed up by the mob.

"I'm not leaving him." Ruby struggled against her.

She used all of her strength to drag her daughter back to a safe distance.

The earth heaved under their feet as a dozen policemen with pistols drawn and night sticks aloft raced out of the *Kishle*, the nearby precinct and jailhouse.

"There he is." Ruby pointed to Faisal in the center of the crowd, tugging on Hussein's arm.

"What's Hussein doing here?" Tamar asked.

"He came on a buying trip before the war started," Ruby said, "and couldn't leave."

"Not Israel. Here, right now."

"I don't know."

At the top of Yefet Street, two men poured gasoline over a stack of tires and ignited it. Blazes leapt. They rolled them down the hill to where four policemen stood guard. The police jumped out of the way. The air was black and poisonous, making it hard to breathe.

"Come." She drew Ruby deeper into the alley and banged on the door of a fabric and embroidery shop.

"Let us in." She kept up her pleas until a woman appeared, her head covered in a hijab. "Please."

The woman motioned for Tamar to step back. She spoke to her in Arabic, but Tamar didn't know if she was shooing them away or inviting them in.

"She's telling us to enter," Ruby said.

"Thank you." Tamar tugged Ruby inside with her.

"*Shukran*," Ruby said and marched to the back of the shop, where the windows faced the square. Her eyes pinned on Faisal. Tamar took in the cubbies filled with cotton threads and embroidery floss, a rack of Gobelins that at any other time she'd have loved to browse through. She tried to smile, knowing her face must be dirty and the stiff movement of her lips ghoulish. She wanted to ask to use the bathroom to clean up but was afraid Ruby would leave.

"You have a beautiful shop," Tamar said in English. "Thank you for letting us in."

"You are welcome." The woman pointed to Ruby. "She is your daughter?"

"Yes."

"She looks like you. Very pretty."

"Thank you." Tamar's heart swelled. "You have children?" She used the back of her hand to wipe the grime off her face.

From the pocket of her tunic, the woman removed a tissue and offered it to her. "Two. A son and a daughter. They are in Canada. My daughter studies business and my son is a pharmacist."

"You must be proud of them."

"I am," she said. "It's good for them there. No war, no fighting." She frowned. "Not so good here."

"No. Not so good."

The woman was at least ten years older than her, with a striking pair of hazel eyes. "My name is Tamar, and my daughter is Ruby."

"I am Nur."

The sirens stopped. Minutes later, soldiers in riot gear surrounded the mob. Nur stiffened. Even from within the confines of the store, Tamar felt the palpable wave of fury and desperation sweep through the crowd. "You do not need to watch," Nur said. "I have a room behind the counter."

"My daughter," Tamar said and took her place beside Ruby.

The soldiers set up a perimeter. One spoke into a bullhorn, calling instructions in Arabic and then in Hebrew, telling protestors to put their weapons down and lie on the ground, hands behind their heads. In response, Hussein, and two other young men, swung slingshots in a wide arc. Faisal wrested Hussein's weapon out of his hand. Two rocks hurtled through the air, catching a soldier, whose shield wasn't up, in the temple. He collapsed like an accordion. Someone shouted a command, and the soldiers and police corralled the protestors inside the square, trapping them. Ruby ran to the door.

"Don't you dare leave," Tamar cried.

"Stay," Nur said, and Tamar watched Ruby hesitate, the muscles in her back rippling with indecision. Reluctantly, she returned to her place by the window.

"Thank you." Tamar mouthed the words to Nur, who nodded and whispered, "I'm a mother too."

Tamar turned to Ruby in time to see the soldiers tossing canisters of teargas into the crowd. *When had they put on gas masks?* Faisal quickly tied a bandanna over his face. Men sank to their knees choking and vomiting, eyes streaming, and still they fought, brandishing their sticks while the police and soldiers acted as one body, pushing against them until the men became a tangle of arms and legs, some falling in a heap. Tamar covered her ears to block out the screams. Nur cried out, her eyes wide with fear. Ruby slapped her hands against the glass pane and Tamar turned her away from the scene.

"Ima, make them stop," Ruby said.

At the other end of the plaza, a protester launched a Molotov. The fiery bottle rotated above the crowd like a pinwheel then crashed onto a soldier's back and burst into flames. He dropped to the ground, his uniform ablaze. Tamar stuffed her knuckles into her mouth, the abrasions on her hands forgotten. Ruby pushed her way out of Tamar's arms as another Molotov was lobbed and hit the center of the square where Faisal and Hussein struggled to remain upright. Ruby gasped as Hussein screamed and clutched his face. Faisal tore off his shirt and wrapped Hussein in it. Nur began a low keening, moving her body as if in prayer. Tamar gripped her hand. The three women stood helpless, watching as the soldiers opened fire into the air above the crowd. The protestors tried to run, but the police and soldiers charged at them, hitting them with the butts of their guns. They crumpled like dolls, their heads and faces bloody. One soldier who'd stood on the periphery holding a walkie-talkie was hit with a stray bullet and dropped face down. His body looked no bigger than a child's.

A pall fell over the plaza and the cries she heard were no longer angry, only frightened and pained as men lay on the ground. The sun began to set and a long shadow fell across the square. It was hard to tell the dead from the living. Ruby flung open the door and would have run into the plaza if Tamar hadn't caught her by the sleeve.

"You've got to let me go, Ima," Ruby begged.

"I can't do that."

"Please just leave me alone. I have to make sure he's all right."

"*Motek*, think for a minute. The place is cordoned off. You can hear the ambulances coming. The authorities won't let you near him. Besides, he wouldn't want you there. Not if he loves you."

Ruby gritted her teeth. "God, I wish you'd just let me make my own decisions."

"I will. But right now, we have to get out of here." She turned to Nur and said, "Thank you for your kindness. I won't forget it. One day I'll come back to your shop."

"You are welcome anytime," she said in fluent Hebrew. "Ruby, she knows one of the boys? I pray for him and your daughter."

On impulse, Tamar kissed her cheek.

They walked the empty dun-colored streets. The day's garbage piled on the curb, souring in the late afternoon sun. She hadn't noticed the squalor on the way to the café, only the aged buildings; she'd been too intent on keeping Ruby in sight. They passed a knot of men near the kiosk that sold lottery tickets. Some had come from the protest, their shirts torn. Streaks of dried blood on their faces and arms. They must have left before the soldiers surrounded the mob. A hedgerow of cigarette butts at their feet. She hurried through the lane, her daughter subdued beside her. Outside the Alhambra Cinema on Jerusalem Boulevard, a taxi pulled up. They got into the back seat, shaken.

"Why did they do it?" Tamar wondered aloud, relieved to be speeding away from Jaffa. The driver turned onto HaYarkon Street, and the sea came into view. Across the street, new construction gleamed, capturing the sunset in their mirrored windows. Every few months another building went up along the strip, highlighting the waterfront decay, dwarfing the bungalows and shacks that were part of the first Jewish neighborhood established outside of Jaffa. Soon they'd be torn down to make room for luxury hotels and high-rises. Where would all these people go, she wondered.

"The soldiers?" Ruby asked.

Tamar turned to her, having forgotten what she'd said, and cupped Ruby's cheek, her daughter's face bruised from crying, mascara pooling under her eyes.

"Did you mean the soldiers?" Ruby repeated.

"No, *motek*. The men. Hussein. Why? The war's over."

Ruby loosened her braid, the wavy strands falling over her shoulders. "My God, Ima. You don't get it. For them, it isn't over."

"What don't I get? That they broke things and scared people. Injured them, maybe killed them? More of our soldiers were hurt. The war wasn't enough? You saw what happened to Hussein."

"They wanted the Egyptians to win for them," Ruby said.

"How did you want the war to end?"

Ruby turned to stare out the window. They were racing down the avenue, palm trees a blur.

"Does Faisal feel like his brother?"

"No. He thinks like I do. People matter, Ima, not states, not borders. Real people. That's why he was trying to get Hussein out of there. He was trying to protect him."

Tamar caught the driver's eye in the rearview mirror. "I know people matter. Including your own. Did you want them to win the war?"

"No, of course not," Ruby said. "All I want is Faisal."

Twenty

They arrived home as the telephone rang. Tamar turned on the lights, thankful Miriam was on holiday in Tiberias with her senior group.

"Maybe it's him." Ruby darted into the kitchen.

"He has this number?"

With an almost comical look of chagrin, she released her grip on the handset and sank to the floor. "No." The phone, forgotten, swung on its cord like a noose.

"What is it?" She knelt beside her.

Ruby panted. "I feel like I'm dying."

"You're not," Tamar reassured her. "It's nerves. Put your head between your knees."

But Ruby lifted her face to the ceiling instead, stretching her neck until the tendons bulged and the skin mottled, as if she were trying to tear herself in two. She bared her teeth, and when Tamar tried to comfort her, she rose to her feet and left the room.

In the evening light, the kitchen appeared worn and outdated. The salmon Formica cabinets matched the tabletop that bore the brunt of thirty years' use, marked with cigarette burns and coffee stains. There was the deep scratch made with a paring knife when she was angry with her mother for refusing to sign a parental release form. She'd forged Miriam's signature and attended the Scout *Shabbaton* on Kibbutz Ein Gev. That was the weekend she met Salim and Hadas.

A voice erupted out of the handset. She vacillated between answering and returning it to its cradle and thought it might be her mother or one of the children calling, or maybe even Salim. Batya Kadouri barked, "You missed your shift at the hospital."

Tamar straightened her sweater and found Hadas's picture still in the pocket, a corner wedged into the seam. "I'm sorry. We got caught in the riot. You must have heard about it on the news." She slid into a chair and leaned back until the crown of her head touched the wall behind her.

"You all right?" Batya asked.

"We were lucky."

"What about tomorrow? Can I count on you?" Batya said.

"I need a few days to take care of some things." She thought of Faisal wrapping Hussein's face in his T-shirt after the Molotov exploded. She doubted Radwa knew that Hussein was hurt, and that Faisal had tried to save him. She listened to the fan in Batya's office stirring the papers on her desk, and Tamar mentally traced the path to the burn unit down the corridor, through the double doors, the nurse's station, and smelled the peculiar odor of antiseptic and burnt hair. The last time she was on the night shift, the ward was silent except for the symphony of monitors and oxygen machines. The patients sedated on morphine drips. She'd been told under no circumstance to allow the men with extensive burns to drink water. They had no protective skin barrier, and it would lead to dehydration. So when a soldier woke up complaining of thirst, she rubbed his cracked lips with a glycerin swab. When he begged for a sip of water, she tried to ease him back to sleep. The following afternoon when she returned, he was gone. She stood by his empty bed, hearing the word that had trembled between them, *Imaleh*, Mommy, and regretted not giving him what he'd asked for.

"Are you losing your stomach for this work?" Batya asked. "I thought you'd last awhile."

She wrapped the phone cord around her fingers. "I can't leave my daughter just now, but I do need your help. It's possible one of the boys hurt today was taken to the burn unit at Tel-Hashomer."

"One of our boys?"

"No, a civilian."

"You mean an Arab."

"Yes. A boy we knew in America."

"You sure he's here?"

"I've no idea where they've taken him. We left just as the ambulances arrived. I hope he's with us. He obviously won't be in the military ward. Maybe the civilian population?" She gave Batya his name. "From what I could tell, he sustained burns on his face, neck, and possibly chest." Tamar didn't know what Batya made of her request but felt certain that, if Ruby were injured, Radwa would do what she could for her.

"Well, that narrows it down. I'll let you know if he's been admitted."

"Thanks. I owe you."

"I'm counting on it," Batya said and hung up.

She found Ruby with her face down in a pillow and sat beside her.

"We stink of burnt rubber and smoke." She stroked her back. "I put the water heater on. You shower first while I make us something to eat."

"Not hungry," she grumbled.

"Come on." A car cruised down the street. She looked out at the evening sky and felt calm for the first time that day.

"Leave me alone," Ruby muttered into the pillow.

Tamar rubbed her shoulders. "Never. I love you and I'm not ever going to leave you alone, so take a shower, eat something, then go to sleep. We'll figure things out in the morning."

The faint sounds of families eating their dinners ambled into the apartment. The murmur of Mrs. Brenner's radio. Her son not yet home, delayed another day.

Ruby turned over, eyes shut, thoughts concealed behind a curtain of fatigue.

A short while later, invigorated by the shower, Ruby wolfed down a toasted cheese sandwich.

"Tell me about Tehila and Barak," Tamar said, hoping to take her mind off Faisal.

Ruby talked about her cousins and how, for Moti's sake, they pretended to like their stepmother, Frieda.

"She's got the place covered in doilies. I mean, they're everywhere."

Tamar grinned. "Hadas would have hated that." With her index finger, she probed the long scratch carved into the kitchen table. "I haven't seen them yet. Moti's due back any day now."

She steered clear of any talk about Faisal and the protest and ignored the sadness ruffling the edges of their conversation. This was the first meal they'd had alone together in a long time, the first where talking about Hadas wasn't weighed down by tragedy. Listening to Ruby, watching thoughts flicker across her face, she imagined an alternate version of them. One that was more loving, where time expanded even as it contracted, bringing tomorrow closer and the sweetness of this moment to an end.

"You eating that?" Ruby pointed to the half sandwich on her plate.

"No, *motek*. It's yours."

"Thanks." Ruby squeezed Tamar's hand. "I know I didn't show it today, but I'm glad you were there, Ima. I don't think I would've made it out of Jaffa without you." Her eyes welled.

"Hey, it's okay. We're okay."

Ruby nodded her head and picked up the sandwich.

After her daughter went to bed, Tamar made the mistake of listening to the late news and learned that a soldier was killed in the riot and two others seriously wounded. Soldiers weren't the only casualties. Three protesters were dead. A policeman shot off his pinky and another had his arm broken. Twenty-two people were injured, two of them in critical but stable condition. She wondered how bad Hussein's injuries were. Property had been damaged, cars destroyed, a community traumatized. Over sixty men were arrested. Tamar was certain Faisal was among them. He'd been on the ground in the center of the mob, hands behind his back.

She spent most of that night on the balcony, drinking the last of the blackberry schnapps, gazing at the TV antennas planted on the opposite roof. They looked almost human in the dark, prophets raising their arms toward heaven, beseeching God. By the time she crawled into bed, the crows were whirling through the trees. Moments later, Ruby burst into her room, switching on the overhead light, momentarily blinding her.

"Ima, what if Faisal was arrested? We've got to tell the police the truth." She radiated determination. "He had nothing to do with the riot. We're key witnesses. They'll have to let him go."

Tamar had been thinking the same thing. "You're making me dizzy with all this marching."

Her daughter loomed over her. "Well, what do you think?"

Tamar tugged the duvet to her chin. "I'll call the station in the morning, find out if he's there. But I don't think you should get involved."

"Then who? His brother? Hussein's probably lying in a hospital. Should his eighty-year-old grandmother go to the police?" Her eyes already swollen from crying filled with new tears.

"What about his parents or other relatives?" She sat up. "Doesn't Ibrahim have brothers Faisal can turn to?"

Ruby flung herself on the bed, virtually trapping Tamar under the blanket. "His parents are in America. The uncles who might have supported him are probably in jail too. I'm the only one he has." She wiped her nose on the back of her hand. "Ima, please. You owe Faisal that much."

"I don't think we can just rush into the police station and demand his release. We have to be careful about this."

She stormed to the door. "I knew you wouldn't help us."

"*Motek*, don't be so impatient. Give me a chance."

"I didn't even want to ask you. Tehila insisted."

"You spoke to Tehila about this?"

"While you were in the shower."

"About Faisal?"

"Don't look so shocked. Unlike you, I'm not ashamed of my relationship with him."

"Ruby, I'm not ashamed. I'm worried. Please understand the difference."

"I do understand, but if you won't come with me, then I'll go to the station myself."

Only a few hours ago she had thought that, with a little bit of effort, they could reinvent themselves, form a closer relationship. Here they were the same as ever. "I didn't say I wouldn't go."

"Then you'll come?"

Ruby looked so eager. She didn't have the heart to tell her the authorities had probably made up their minds about Faisal and his brother. They were unlikely to listen to anything they said and would offer little besides contempt. No matter how much she wished Ruby would end their relationship, she couldn't let her daughter confront the authorities alone.

"I'll go. Now get some sleep. No one's going to talk to us before nine o'clock."

"Thanks, Ima. I'll never forget it."

A few tosses and turns later, she rose to make a pot of coffee. She drank her first cup at the kitchen table and listened to the city awaken to raucous birdsong, to liveries making their stops, to garbage trucks collecting yesterday's refuse. The sun was up when she heard the *alti-zachen* clip-clopping through the neighborhood in his horse-driven cart, collecting old clothes and household items to sell. An hour later, she retrieved the mail and the newspaper, then poured herself another cup of coffee and lit a cigarette, squinting at the sunlight coming in through the balcony. Photographs of the Kikar HaSha'on protest covered the front page. Incredibly, one was of Hussein lifting his fist in the air. Her stomach plummeted at what this would mean for him and Faisal. She wanted to telephone Salim, tell him about the riot, about Ruby. She wanted to tell him she was frightened that she'd seen the veneer of civility torn away and the violence and despair that lay beneath. But she didn't phone him.

Tamar rummaged through the mail, most of which was for her mother, except for one envelope stamped with the Israel Defense Forces insignia—a Star of David and in its center a sword and an olive branch. She slit it open and didn't know whether to be relieved or apprehensive. Ruby was to report to the induction center two weeks from today on November

15th at 8:00 a.m. She shoved the envelope into the pocket of her cardigan, where it rested against Hadas's photograph, and then called the police station.

They arrived in Jaffa at ten minutes to nine to find that Kikar HaSha'on was washed clean. Yesterday's violence gone, a minor event in the city's long and bloody history. The day was overcast. Shops and kiosks, some a century old, were open for business, selling fresh juices and ice cream, hats with Coca-Cola logos in Hebrew and Arabic script. The air spiced with salt water and the tang of Aleppo pines. Towers of honeyed pastries at the corner shop, where a woman with hennaed hair swatted at flies that landed on the sweet confection.

The Ottomans built the Kishle in the late nineteenth century. Its stone walls were two feet thick, impossible for a prisoner to chisel through or break free of. Through an open window in the reception area, there was a view of the sea, a reminder that something greater than the laws of men existed. They were asked to wait at the entrance while a guard inspected their bags.

"You brought a sandwich?" Ruby said, bemused.

"In case we get hungry." Tamar didn't return her gaze.

The same policemen who'd fired their guns into the square yesterday milled about today.

"What do we do?" Ruby gnawed her bottom lip.

Now that they were inside the Kishle, her daughter's anxiety clambered to the surface. She was ready to tear through the station to find Faisal. Tamar gripped her hand. "Patience," she said and counted five desks in the receiving area. Three of them had typewriters that clacked like wooden shoes on a marble floor. The room was large and boisterous. Though it was still early in the day, the place exuded a pastiche of body odor, cigarette butts, and mold. The ceiling fans were sluggish, phones rang, a man and woman argued in the corner.

At the counter she said, "I was told Faisal Mahmoudi was arrested yesterday. He's being held here. Can we please speak to the officer in charge of his case?"

The receptionist, half buried in a bridal magazine, gave a reluctant sigh. "Mahmoudi, Faisal?"

"Yes," Ruby said.

The woman opened a green logbook. After a few minutes of searching, she said, "Yeah, he's here."

"We have important information regarding the boy's case," Tamar said.

"You want him." The reception jerked her head in the direction of a man sitting against the back wall. He was dressed in civilian clothes, sturdy, ginger-haired. Freckles covered his face, arms, and neck. The plaque on his desk read *Detective Dani Itai.* He gestured for them to sit. A crocheted blue-and-white *kippah* covered the bald spot on his head. He looked familiar, like someone she might have gone to school with. When he stood and greeted them, a memory door cracked wide open. Her hand brushed against the pocket of her cardigan. She knew him. The police station in Tel Aviv. She remembered him sliding Hadas's photograph across his desk, asking if she knew that the Arabic script on the back meant *For eternity.*

"Shalom. Cookie?" he offered, stuffing one into his mouth. The first time they met, he was clean-shaven; now crumbs rained onto a thick ginger-and-gray beard. He grunted and washed the cookie down with a gulp of coffee. He'd put on weight.

"My wife bakes them every week. They're like lead but I don't want to hurt her feelings, so I tell her they're light as angels." He chuckled, then proceeded to scratch his chin, sending crumbs and flakes of dandruff down his shirtfront. "How can I help you?"

"We're here about Faisal Mahmoudi." Tamar held her purse like a shield to her chest.

He opened a folder. The fan revolved at a steady pace, unsettling the forms on his desk.

"Are you his relatives?"

"No."

"Names?"

Tamar gave him their names. "We're acquainted with his family. They were our neighbors in New York. The parents still live there. Faisal is staying with his grandparents and works in their café."

"I see." He took a handkerchief out of his back pocket and wiped his fingertips and the corners of his mouth with a perturbing thoroughness. "Well, I'm sorry to inform you the boy is in deep trouble."

He didn't appear sorry, only smug.

"But he didn't do anything," Ruby cried.

Detective Itai gave them a tight-lipped smile. "According to our report, he did. He was involved in the riot, maybe even organized it with his brother. We've had Hussein Mahmoudi on our radar for almost a month now. We think he's an agitator."

She had the feeling he was lying, groping for information.

"We also have witnesses who will testify Faisal and his brother used slingshots to bring down our officers."

"But it isn't true." Ruby, unable to contain herself, shot out of her chair.

"You're not helping." Tamar motioned for her daughter to sit.

"Your mother's right," Detective Itai said.

"If I may, sir. What my daughter says is true. The boy is innocent. We saw everything that happened."

"How did you come to be there? Did you take part in the protest?" He picked up the pack of cigarettes on his desk and offered one to Tamar, and when she declined, he turned to Ruby, who thanked him with saccharine politeness. Tamar rolled her eyes. "Of course not. My daughter and I were lunching at Amina Café, which belongs to the Mahmoudi family. I'm sure you know how well respected they are in the community."

Ruby sent her a sidelong glance.

He leaned back in his chair and gave his paunch a leisurely scratch. "I know all about the Mahmoudi clan. Everyone in Jaffa does."

"Can we please just concentrate on Faisal?" Ruby said. "When can he go home?"

Tamar sat a bit straighter in her chair and tugged on her collar. "We saw the protestors come down the hill toward Kikar HaSha'on. Faisal was in the café with us. He was worried about his brother and wanted to bring him back to the café, where he'd be safe. He followed the protestors to the clock tower. I watched him as he tried to pull his brother away from the plaza, but the police and soldiers surrounded them, and he was trapped with the others."

"Funny, he said the same thing." Detective Itai bit into another cookie and sent a cascade of crumbs into his lap.

"Because it's true." Ruby sailed out of her chair again.

Tamar bowed her neck to ease the tension in it. She didn't know how anyone could think with the typewriters clacking and people shouting. The fluorescent lights flickered. She felt a headache coming on.

"Maybe what you say is true," he conceded, "but all it does is place him in the center of the riot."

"Don't his intentions count for anything?" Ruby said.

He looked at her in silent speculation. "A judge will have to decide that. I presume he's more than a friend."

"We hoped"—Tamar gripped the strap on her handbag—"that after we told you what happened, you'd release him."

He gave an ugly chuckle. "You can't be that naïve."

Tamar blinked.

"One of our soldiers was killed and two are in the hospital barely hanging on. On top of that, my policemen were wounded."

"But he didn't do anything, except try to get his brother out of there," Ruby wailed.

His eyes narrowed. "As I thought, more than friends."

Out of desperation, Tamar said, "You know, I think we've met before."

He turned to her. "Really?"

"Yes. You were the officer in charge of my sister-in-law's case, Hadas Abadi. That was her maiden name, married name Ben Ami. She was killed in—"

"Kafr Ma'an." The full force of his gaze rested on her now.

"That's right."

"I remember that case. It was after the '67 war. Shot dead. Well"—he drew out the word—"so this proclivity runs in the family. Dangerous, don't you think?"

Ruby, not understanding, said, "What's he talking about, Ima?"

"Ruby." She looked at her daughter. "Please wait for me in the reception area."

"No way. He's got to do something about Faisal. I'm not leaving without him."

"Now." Tamar snapped. Ruby fell back on her heels. The detective rolled a pencil across his desk. "Trust me. I'm handling this. Go."

"But Ima."

"Go!"

"Oh, all right." She stomped off.

Tamar waited for her to take a seat in the reception area before returning her attention to Detective Itai. He placed his hands on the desk. She smelled the coffee on his breath.

"I think we're done here," he said.

"With all due respect, Detective Itai, I don't think we are." It took all her effort to keep her voice from shaking. "I recognized you immediately. I didn't say anything because my daughter was here, and I didn't want to upset her. You were kind to me at a difficult time in my life and I thank you for that. Today I'm here about a boy whose life is in danger." She wondered if her temerity to speak to him this way came from a lack of sleep or finding herself in the unlikely position of defending Faisal and, in turn, protecting Ruby. Her daughter was right. Faisal was innocent. It was unfair of Detective Itai to treat him like a criminal when he was little more than collateral damage.

"Perhaps you'd like to take our statements for the record, for the judge?" Tamar said. "Every word we've said is true. Faisal shouldn't be punished because he tried to help his brother, or because he happened to be in the middle of the violence with no way out."

It was the words *no way out* that conjured the image of Ibrahim Mahmoudi lifting the strop and bringing it down on Faisal's back. And it was those same words that reminded her of Salim and the man in Kafr Ma'an whose thumb he'd severed to prove his loyalty to the Palmach. Perhaps worse than the cruelty of those acts was the righteousness that accompanied them. Like her husband and Mr. Mahmoudi, Dani Itai had an air of superiority; he found their association with Faisal distasteful. His remark about proclivities was a perversion of the facts and his suggestion that it was Hadas's love for Daoud that had resulted in her death was more than callous; it was grotesque and wrong.

He cleared his throat. "Your friend will have a hearing. You can come back then to give your statements."

"Has he been charged?"

"We're still gathering the facts." He tapped his lighter on the desk, a signal, she thought, for her to leave. They could detain him for as long as they wanted. No habeas corpus in this instance.

Ruby returned to stand behind her chair. "Ima?"

Tamar decided to try a different tactic. "Detective, do you have children?"

He rubbed his lower back. "Two boys in the army. Both fought in the war."

"You're proud of them."

"They're good boys."

"Faisal Mahmoudi is also just a boy. He's eighteen, smart, talented, and a hard worker. A responsible person. He was just in the wrong place, but his heart, Detective Itai, was in the right one." At a nearby desk a telephone rang. The shrill sound reverberated through the room.

"You argue like my wife," he scowled and lifted a photo off his desk. "My youngest is eighteen and he's a *Golani* soldier, the infantry."

"I know what a *Golani* is." She smiled. "I think you forget that I grew up here, that I'm Israeli like you."

"I didn't forget but I think you have," he shot back.

She flinched, and then as if he hadn't just insulted her, he continued, "My son fought for our lives. He's a man, all right.

283

Your Faisal Mahmoudi and the rest of them are enemies of the state. He knew exactly what he was doing and what he was getting into. You, more than anyone, know what these people are capable of."

"But he didn't know. How could he? Faisal's an American." She gripped the edge of the desk. "I don't think just because we give a boy a gun, he suddenly becomes a man. He's just a boy doing a man's job. A man understands compassion and isn't given to blind hatred. He doesn't judge on the basis of ignorance. My husband"—she faltered—"my husband has always known this." She exhaled and retreated into the chair. "Faisal Mahmoudi is young. Flawed like the rest of us, but he's good and compassionate. He's brave and there is no one more loyal. I would hate for Faisal's compassion to be destroyed because of our narrow-mindedness."

Ruby squeezed her shoulder.

"Enough." He stood quickly, knocking the tin of cookies to the floor. Typewriters stopped their clacking and the men who'd been pecking at the keys remained poised at their desks. "I don't need to be lectured by a *yoredet*." He spat the word. "A woman who abandoned this country. We live the struggle every day. What do you know about our enemies? You're here on vacation, playing at being a citizen until you go back to your family in America. The judge will make the final decision here. I can't help you."

"That's it? You're kicking us out?" Ruby cried. "You're not going to release him even though you know he's innocent?"

He shot Tamar a contemptuous look, "Control your daughter or I might be tempted to put her in the same cell as her boyfriend."

Tamar pulled Ruby behind her. "Please don't make threats. After what we witnessed yesterday in the square, she's frightened for her friend, and I can't say that I blame her." She shook with the effort to stand her ground.

"Can I at least see him? Please. Just to make sure he's all right." Ruby drew in a breath and then another and broke into a sob when the detective said no.

He shook his head in disgust. "I feel sorry for you," he said to Tamar.

She wrapped an arm around Ruby's shoulders. "I feel sorry for all of us," she replied, and led her daughter to the water fountain in the reception area. A side door opened just as Ruby leaned over the spout to drink. Tamar peered in and saw a large cell made of thick limestone blocks and iron bars. From the stone floor rose the dank stench of piss and brackish water. Young and old men huddled together, arms limp at their sides, backs bowed. Faisal stood apart, staring blindly at the wall in front of him.

She tried to imagine what it was like for him cooped up in the cell, recalling how he'd rescued that young man on Church Avenue, how he stood on the roof afterward, arms stretched, embracing the sky. There was no sky here. He shook the bars as if testing their strength. It occurred to her that he had also saved Ruby. Her Ruby, who'd struggled to fit in, to find her place among strangers. He saw Tamar and lifted his hand in greeting and then noticed Ruby at the fountain and hid his face to spare Ruby from seeing him imprisoned.

A row of handcuffed men and teenage boys shuffled past. Everyone in the reception area stopped to look at them. Dirty, bedraggled, eyes bloodshot, the stench of piss on their clothing. The smell of men demeaned. She recognized some of them from yesterday's riot. Tamar overheard the receptionist say they were being transferred to Abu Kabir prison, a brutalist prison with concrete walls, klieg lights, and a lethal barbed wire fence. *They will destroy Faisal here.* Not just the Kishle, or Detective Itai, the country. The country she loved would destroy the boy her daughter loved. If things continued for him on this trajectory, there would be more arrests, more punishment, more thwarted dreams. Soon he'd be some twisted thing filled with despair and rage, like Daoud.

"Do you see him?" Ruby wiped her mouth on her sleeve, searching the prisoners being led out of the building. She looked exhausted.

"Wait for me outside."

"Why, what are you going to do? You think another cop will let me see him?"

"I'm afraid another cop isn't going to be any better than Detective Itai. The only thing we can do is come back tomorrow to find out if he's been arraigned. Go ahead. I'll see you in a few minutes."

"You're acting mysterious. What are you up to?"

"Right now, nothing." She looked at her pointedly.

"I don't like being kept in the dark, Ima."

"I know, but you have to trust me."

"I don't like it," she repeated and spun on her heel.

Tamar returned to the receptionist in the receiving area. "I have a sandwich for one of the inmates, may I give it to him?"

"You a relative?"

"Close friend of the family."

The girl chewed the tip of her pencil then nodded. "Better make it quick."

"Thanks." Before anyone could stop her, she slipped through the door. Faisal was crouched on his knees in the cell, rocking back and forth.

"Faisal?"

He blinked into the gloom. "Mrs. Abadi, it's really you. I thought I was hallucinating. What are you doing here? Where's Ruby?"

The air in the cell was stagnant and the lighting dim; she could barely see Faisal's face. His body no more than an outline in the gray shirt he wore, compliments of the Jaffa police. Moisture festered atolls of green and black mold across the ceiling and walls. A grime encrusted toilet stood in the back right corner beside a sink chattered with rust.

"Are you hurt?"

"No. Some of the others weren't so lucky." What he said was true. Many of the men sported some injury, bruised jaws and split lips. "I haven't spoken to anyone since the officer took my statement. They won't tell me what's going on."

"Have they contacted your grandmother to let her know you're here?"

"I don't know." He looked scared. "She must be worried."

"Ruby will call her when we get home. Have they fed you?"

He shuddered. "I'm not that hungry."

"Well, I made this for you." She handed him the sandwich she'd prepared earlier that morning. "Eat up."

"Thanks." After swallowing a bite, he said, "You still haven't told me why you're here or where Ruby is. I saw her at the fountain."

"Finish up."

He took another mouthful, but it was clear he didn't have an appetite. She handed him the wax paper. "Ruby's outside. I wanted to talk to you alone."

He carefully wrapped the sandwich.

"Do you love my daughter?"

The question surprised him. "Yeah, I do."

"I thought so." She stared at her shoes. Cold seeped in through the thin leather soles. Before she could say anymore, a man lying in fetal position in the back of the cell shouted, "Y'Allah, let me sleep."

Tamar gestured for Faisal to come closer. "Do your parents know you're together again?"

Faisal gave the bars a swift kick. "No one knows except Tehila and she isn't too happy for us. Ruby pretends it doesn't bother her. I don't want to cause her trouble," he said. "I love her. She loves me. We're tight, y'know. I'd do anything for her."

"Even if it meant leaving her, going back to the States?"

He held her gaze. "If I had to."

She stuffed her hands in her pockets, clutching Ruby's draft notice. "I saw how you turned away so Ruby wouldn't see you in here. You were sparing her. I appreciate that."

One of the men began urinating. She saw only the back of his robe but heard the stream land in the basin. Her nose wrinkled at the pungent odor. "Your family are American citizens, right?"

He nodded

"I think the best way to get you out of here is to go to the American Embassy. We'll tell them what we saw—that you had nothing to do with the riot."

"That's great." He beamed.

"I hope it works because the officer in charge here doesn't care how innocent you are. He's got you marked."

Faisal twisted the ends of his shirt. "Do you have a cigarette? I could really use a smoke."

"Faisal, please focus. Any minute someone will come in here and kick me out."

He pressed his forehead to the bars. "I'm listening."

"It's important you tell the embassy lawyer or whoever they assign to your case exactly what you told the police. They might come to some agreement with the authorities."

"What kind of agreement?" He frowned.

"I don't know. But if they offer you the opportunity to return to the U.S., take it." She followed the quick bob of his

Adam's apple and plowed on. "Your brother is considered a risk to the state. His picture is plastered on the front page of the newspaper. They already think you're guilty by association. A Molotov killed a soldier, one of those rocks hit another soldier in the head. He's in the hospital. And another was shot and in critical condition." She recalled that soldier's childlike body on the ground.

Faisal paled. "I didn't know. Does that mean Hussein's going to jail? I took the sling from him. He didn't get off a shot."

She cleared her throat and pulled the cardigan around her. "There's something else you should know." She took Ruby's draft notice from her pocket. "Ruby's been called up. If they decide to send you home, I need you to promise me something."

"What?"

"Ruby gets to choose where she wants to live. Her decision. No coercion, no ultimatums. Her choice. Full autonomy. If she wants to stay in Israel, she stays, and if she wants to return to the States after her service, because they won't let her out of the country now, then she does."

"She loves it here." He gripped the bars.

"I know."

"What if I decide to stay with her?"

"How would that work? Ruby could be stationed anywhere in the country. You'll hardly see her. And if you do, what will the army think about her being with you? Her fellow soldiers. Your presence in her life might put her in danger. As far as the authorities are concerned, you're on their radar now. Anytime something happens, they can haul you in here, keep you for days, maybe weeks. What kind of life is that? Always looking over your shoulder. In the end, it'll destroy you both." She could see he was trying to process what she said. "Just promise me. Ruby makes her own decision."

"I'd never make her do anything she doesn't want to. She loves me." Someone in the cell chuckled. Faisal closed his eyes. "What do I do?" He looked so forlorn, Tamar took his hand in both of hers.

"You let her go."

"Just like that," Faisal said.

"That's what we do for the people we love. We let them go, and if we're lucky, they come back to us one day."

"And if she returns to the States?"

"Then you'll know she chose you."

"Just one thing," Faisal said. "If I were a Jew, would we be having this conversation?"

"If you were a Jew, you wouldn't be in this cell. You'd be in uniform, fighting for your life and country."

"And here I thought," he quipped, "this was my country."

Minutes later she stood on the top step of the precinct, gulping at the sea air.

"Did you see him?" Ruby said.

"Not here." Tamar tucked her arm through hers.

"Where to?" Ruby fell in step.

"The American Embassy. I've got something for you." She took the draft notice from her pocket. They stopped on the promenade. Ruby read the letter. The wind whipped off the shore, and above them gulls circled and cawed.

"What do I do?" Ruby said.

"*Motek*, you don't have a choice now."

"God, what shitty timing."

They reached the embassy on HaYarkon Street. Six years ago, she'd entered this building to apply for a visa she didn't want. Now she was here on Faisal's behalf. The American flag bucked and waved. Children played in the sand. Clouds banked on the horizon. She gazed at the sea much as she'd done all those years ago and felt its indomitable force.

Twenty-One

The last of the casualties arrived. Men wounded in the final hours of the war were transferred from field hospitals to the Medical Center at Tel Hashomer. Tamar studied their charts, knew their serial numbers, their rank, the description of their injuries: shattered femur, blood loss, burns covering sixty percent of their bodies, shrapnel poised at the entrance to vital organs like enemies at the gate.

Every day she was given a new list of patients and prayed no one she knew would be on it. But it was only a matter of time. Even so, it shocked her to see Gadi's name on the list. There must be hundreds of Gadi Azoulays in Israel, she thought, and waited for the nurses to finish checking monitors and temperatures, for doctors to examine dressings and complete their rounds. Best not to leave the men alone, Batya warned. Who knew what harm they'd do? She distributed magazines, helped serve their dinners, played a few hands of gin rummy. She made them comfortable for the night, tucked them in the way she'd tucked her children into bed, wrapped tight enough to keep the monsters at bay. Her mind and body numb. *Easy,* she muttered to herself when the tremor in her hands grew. She approached his bed last. Her lungs turned to water at the sight of him. No one noticed that she sat beside him during the last hour of her shift, wiped the sweat from his face, stroked his hair, and whispered in his ear, "I've got you."

He couldn't hear her. The war had folded him away like a sheet on a shelf too high for her to reach. Belly wound, concussion, broken humerus. She lifted the edge of the blanket. The bruise on his stomach a landmass that spread beyond the borders of the dressing. When she lay her head lightly on his chest and felt it rise, she pictured them dancing in the frame shop in Coney Island, and when she took his hand and held it over her heart, she recalled Yom Kippur, the day the war broke, and how he stood in her kitchen frightened.

The following afternoon while she sat beside Gadi reading to him, he stirred, eyes fluttering open.

"Gadi? Can you hear me? Do you know me?"

His gaze drifted over her face. "Thirsty," he said.

She soaked a piece of gauze in a cup of water and dribbled it into his mouth.

"Leschenko," he murmured.

"What?" She leaned in.

"Russian tango."

Her smile widened. "That's right," she said, her throat tight with emotion. "You remember." And then saw that he'd fallen asleep again.

Later that evening, Batya invited her to dinner in the cafeteria. "It's schnitzel Wednesday. Only edible thing on the menu."

Tamar declined and waited for her to charge down the corridor in her usual brisk manner before walking in the opposite direction in search of Hussein Mahmoudi. She'd put off visiting him. Though she wanted to make sure Radwa's son was taken care of, she felt an irrational guilt that she was somehow betraying the boys in the wards, betraying Gadi. It was all so confusing. But she couldn't put it off any longer. A few days after Batya had located him in the civilian hospital, she asked Tamar if she'd been in to see him.

"I thought he was a friend of the family."

"We know his parents," Tamar demurred.

292

"You and your husband?"

"Yes."

"Who'll be joining you soon?"

Tamar turned abruptly toward the supply cupboard in Batya's office. "Do we have more stationery? The boys want to write letters to their sweethearts." Her voice bright; her smile drilled into place.

By the time she left the ward to see Hussein, it was after visiting hours. She was about to go into his room when she saw Radwa at his bedside, eyes riveted on her son, as if sheer will could restore him. Radwa didn't see her standing frozen outside the glass partition. An orderly asked Tamar if she was all right. She left without answering and spent the rest of her shift tending to the soldiers, helping ambulatory patients to the bathroom, and read Psalms to the men who were restless. Afterward, she sat beside Gadi, humming the Russian tango they'd danced to only a few months ago.

"Don't stop," he said.

"You're awake."

He licked his dry lips.

She swabbed his mouth with glycerin.

"What are you doing here?" He grabbed her wrist. His grip was surprisingly strong.

"Volunteering. I took your advice and came home." She used her other hand to sweep the hair off his forehead. "Did you have visitors today?"

"My mother was here this morning?" He let go of her wrist.

Tamar eyed him closely. "She must be so relieved to have you back."

He shook his head.

"What happened?"

"She cried for most of the hour and told me next time she'd bring Alona."

"And?"

"I told her not to come back."

"Oh, Gadi. I'm sorry. I doubt you can keep your mother away, and I'm sure if Alona did come, you'd be happy to see her."

"I'm a fucking wreck."

"You're wounded and you'll heal."

"Not completely." He closed his eyes.

"Hey, look at me."

"What are you doing here?"

"I told you. Volunteering."

"Did your husband kick you out? Or is it Jewish guilt that makes you come here every day to read to the invalids. Tucking us in like children."

"Don't be cruel. Besides I like tucking you in."

"Leave me alone."

"Not when you're like this."

"Get out," he hissed.

"Gadi, I'm not leaving."

"Why the fuck not?"

"Because I'm not Alona and I'm not your mother. Because I knew you when you were lost, and you knew me when I was lost." She held his hand. "And because we danced the tango together." She smiled, eyes welling. "Now can you move over just a bit." She closed the curtains around his bed.

"What for?" he scowled.

"I'm tired." She lay down beside him, her head on his chest. He stiffened and then she felt his muscles ease. He threaded his fingers through hers.

"I'm sorry," he murmured the words into her hair.

"Me too."

"Stay."

"As long as you want," she said.

The apartment was quiet, shadowed in plummy hues when she arrived home after midnight, exhausted and famished. Miriam and Ruby were asleep. She padded barefoot into the kitchen; her toes curling against the cold tiled floor. She fried an egg and ate it standing, hip flush against the counter, drowning a knob of bread in the runny yolk. The phone rang. She snatched the handset on the first ring. "Hold on," she said, and dragged the extension cord to the balcony, where no one would hear. A bracing whiff of spearmint from her mother's herb garden greeted her. She forgot her mug of chamomile tea on the table. It was supposed to help her unwind, ease the confusion she felt at seeing Radwa, the sorrow and helplessness she felt with Gadi, and if that wasn't enough, there was Batya's offer to consider, made as she was shrugging into her coat: "I need an assistant. Pay's good. Hours are better. Think about it." If she accepted the post, it would be the first job she ever had. She could rent an apartment near the hospital, send for her children, provide for them. The possibility of a different kind of future hung like fruit on a bough. All she needed was to stretch to reach it.

She was startled to find Salim on the line.

"You need to come home," he said.

Her stomach plummeted at the sound of his voice. She looked up at the night sky, where the city lights drained the stars of their brilliance. "What happened?"

"The kids need you."

"Are they all right?"

"They're miserable without you."

She shivered in the damp air. "I'm sorry. I miss them too. And you," she said and lit a cigarette. "Things must be pretty desperate for you to call me."

"You think I'm happy with the way things are? My wife left me. She kept secrets from me." He sounded petulant, angry.

"What about your soldier?"

"She's got nothing to do with us." His response was swift, rehearsed, she thought.

"Funny you can say that."

She heard the snap of a lighter and a quick inhale. "It's true. You're my family."

"And she's what exactly?" For a moment she thought the line had dropped, or that he'd hung up.

"Truth?"

"Please."

"I don't know," he said.

A cat yowled near the garbage bins. "I really have missed you and the kids." A fountain burbled in the square of the old city hall near the house of the poet Chaim Nachman Bialik. She remembered a poem of his she'd learned in school about three eggs in a nest and in each egg a baby bird. The poem had a melody she used to sing to the kids before bed.

Salim sighed. "Okay, then."

Mrs. Brenner's son came out onto the balcony below. He struck a match. The smell of sulfur crimped the air. He'd arrived home last weekend. Mrs. Brenner wept when she saw him. Neighbors opened their doors and shouted, "*Baruch ha-bah!*" Welcome! He dropped his duffel and walked into his mother's arms. He hadn't left the apartment since.

"I'll let you know," she said.

"What does that mean?"

"Just that." She hung up and stubbed out the cigarette.

Salim's voice remained with her long into the night, moving in and out of her consciousness, ushering images of Rachel and Ari swimming against a current toward her. Just as they'd reach her, the current would drag them out again. It went on for hours, leaving her exhausted, her children out of reach. Sometime around dawn she fell asleep and dreamed that Batya held the job in her palm, where it took the form of a house. The windows looked out onto an orchard like the one in Kafr Ma'an. Beyond it, a desert with rows of hospital beds stretching for miles, white sheets snapping in the wind. "There's so much to do," Batya said, "to build a country."

Over breakfast the next morning, Miriam buttered a slice of bread. "So he finally called."

Tamar stiffened. "How did you know it was him?"

"Who else but a husband who's lost a wife would call so late?"

"He hasn't lost me," she snapped.

"No? Misplaced then." Miriam stirred sugar into her tea. "What are you waiting for?"

"For him to decide what's important."

"And you hope you're what's important."

Tamar blew on her coffee. "Not me, us. Our family."

"I hope you know what you're doing," Miriam said. "In my experience when people are tested, they often fail."

That afternoon at the hospital, she received a call from Mr. Timothy Shaw, the man she and Ruby spoke to at the American Embassy. After a brief greeting, he said, "I thought you'd want to know, they're releasing Faisal Mahmoudi this afternoon. He's got a week to return to the States."

"And if he stays," she asked.

"I wouldn't recommend it," he said.

When she got home from her shift at the hospital, she woke Ruby. "You can see Faisal tomorrow." The jalousies were open, and light from a neighbor's kitchen stole into the room.

Ruby slapped a hand over her mouth to keep from shouting.

"Before you get too excited, there's more. He has until the day before you're drafted to leave."

It was almost comical the way her daughter's happiness evaporated. "But that's so unfair. Why?" She twisted the blanket round her fingers.

"You know why." She turned on the bedside lamp. Ruby's face was flushed with sleep.

"I wish I could go with him," she said.

"I know." Tamar kissed her cheek and surprised herself by saying, "You can be with him after the army if you want."

Ruby sank into the bedding. "A year isn't such a long time, is it?"

Tamar stayed quiet beside her and stroked her hair until she fell asleep. She remembered something Salim had once said: A year in the army was like an eternity.

They took Faisal to Ben Gurion Airport, where the smell of diesel and night-blooming flowers assaulted their senses. Two baby-faced soldiers stood on either side of the car at the main gate. While one soldier inspected the trunk and the undercarriage, the other asked for Faisal's passport and ticket. The usual questions were asked and would continue to be asked at different points of his departure: *Did you pack your suitcases or did someone pack them for you? Did anyone give you a package to take on the flight? Did you leave your suitcase unattended?* Each question made Faisal more nervous and more morose. Ruby, who sat beside him in the back seat, echoed his apprehension. Tamar tried to smile through it all. Only Timothy

Shaw, the American attaché responsible for Faisal's release, appeared calm. He'd been playing tennis at the country club in Herzliyah when the call came through that Faisal was granted an exit visa and had a seat on the 1:00 a.m. flight to New York. He wore his tennis whites to the farewell.

Once inside the terminal, they fell into a kind of funereal procession. The kids walked ahead, arm in arm, Tamar behind them and Mr. Shaw at the rear. Faisal answered another barrage of questions, deposited his luggage, and obtained a boarding pass. They went through security. Thanks to Mr. Shaw, she and Ruby were allowed to accompany him. They walked through the tangle of duty-free shops and passed a long train of carrier carts locked in their hold. At the far end of the terminal, the lights were dim near the gate, where sleepy passengers waited to board. They walked the long corridor. The floors were buffed and the tiles shone. Their shadows were long, reminding her of the drawings Faisal had made of two beasts lumbering side by side in a desert landscape. Now Ruby's hips brushed against his, their matched strides practiced and assured. Like participants in a mirror game, it was impossible to tell who led and who followed. This was how their bodies said goodbye. They walked. They spoke little. They reached the gate where he would board a bus to the plane. They waited. Ruby's hands never left his body. He leaned into every touch. No matter how many continents separated them, Tamar thought, they'd find each other, even in the dark, by smell and taste the way wolf pups licked and sniffed before burrowing into each other's warmth.

Mr. Shaw inquired after Hussein.

"He's okay, tired from surgery," Faisal said. "My mother is camped out in his hospital room."

"Your brother's in good hands." Shaw grinned, displaying a row of straight white teeth. The result of years of orthodontia. "Jewish doctors, y'know."

"We saw him this morning," Faisal said. "He's worried he'll look like Godzilla and no girl will want him. They're discharging him in a week or so."

"Tell him to come see me when he's out."

Tamar had joined them on that visit before her shift began. She knew it was cowardly to use the kids as a buffer, but she didn't know what kind of reception she'd get from Radwa. Ruby sat at the foot of the bed beside Faisal, watching him sketch. Radwa encouraged Hussein to finish his meal. The left side of his face was dressed in gauze, and there was a large bandage under his arm from where the skin was grafted.

She hovered at the door.

"Ima, come in," Ruby said.

"I didn't expect to see you," Radwa said.

"I volunteer in the building next door."

"Ruby told me. You take care of the soldiers." Her lips compressed into a hard line.

Tamar inched into the room. "The wounded boys, yes. You look well."

Radwa acknowledged the remark with a nod and returned her attention to Hussein, the meal forgotten.

"I'm glad to see you up," Tamar said to him. A month ago, she'd have felt awkward walking into a sick room. Her work in the military wards had inured her to the sight and smell of sickness and injury. "Brought you a magazine."

"*Vogue*," he said, bemused.

"Sorry, it's the only one I found in English. How's Ibrahim?"

"Fine," Radwa said. "He'll be here next week now that Faisal will be home to take care of the business."

"That's good."

"You didn't happen to bring any of that delicious cake with you?" Hussein said.

"The biscuit and chocolate cream?"

He nodded.

She looked at Radwa; "I can make it for you. Bring it on my next shift if your mother doesn't object."

Radwa smoothed the bedsheets. "Faisal told me what you did for him."

"It was nothing. You'd have done the same for my daughter. And he was innocent."

"I know," Radwa said. "His innocence was never in question."

Tamar felt her face flush, recalling their last conversation in the stairwell at the Calliope Garden Apartments.

"My son said I should thank you."

"That's unnecessary. I wanted to help."

Faisal caught her eye. He went back to his drawing, a caricature of Hussein with a head like a gargantuan sore thumb wrapped in bandages with two slits for eyes and a hole where his mouth should be. Faisal taped it to the wall. Everyone, including Hussein, chuckled.

She was at the door when Radwa said, "You bring the cake. I bring the coffee."

"I'll do that," she smiled.

Once they'd reached the gate, Mr. Shaw excused himself to buy a pack of Dunhill. His white figure cut a path through the passengers milling about in dark leisure wear, towing their carry-ons. The call to board sounded over the PA system. Ruby kissed Faisal's eyelids, his cheeks, and mouth. She lingered on his mouth. Tamar found it hard to look away and thought how time always moved forward, never back, sparing nothing and no one.

She dug a sheet of paper out of her bag and wrote her mother's telephone number and address on it. When it was time for Faisal to board, Mr. Shaw shook his hand and wished him luck. Faisal turned to her; his expression sober as if he was already mourning the loss of Ruby. She pressed the slip of paper into his palm, her lips close to his ear. "Call her when you land." His eyes widened and filled. "Thank you." He wrapped her in an embrace, and because Ruby had yet to let him go, Tamar snaked her arms around them both.

Twenty-Two

The following morning, she and Ruby walked to the collection point on Ibn Gabirol Street. Sunlight dappled the canopies of the sycamore trees, whose gray trunks resembled an orgy of twisted limbs. Sidewalks wet with dew glistened as café owners set out tables and chairs. The smell of coffee made her stomach rumble. They'd left the house without breakfast. The streets were filled with people on their way to work, newspapers tucked under their arms. They passed the City Hall and arrived at the Kings of Israel Square, where flocks of pigeons pecked at the ground and young draftees waited with their parents for buses to take them to the Bakum, the army base of absorption and sorting at Tel-Hashomer.

Tamar held up their entwined hands. "I'm not ready to let you go yet." A few days from now, they'd send Ruby to the Negev or Judean Desert, or some forest in the north, for basic training. She wasn't sure if her daughter would have the opportunity to call. That could mean weeks without hearing from her.

"If you can't phone, promise you'll write." She disregarded the inner voice asking where she'd be in the weeks to come.

"Ima, I'll be fine."

And though Ruby's eyes lit with excitement, Tamar detected fear. Salim and the children ought to be here seeing Ruby off. She blinked back tears. Instead, they had telephoned at 6:00 a.m. to wish Ruby well. Toward the end of the call,

Tamar got on the line and told Salim to "Send the children. They have winter break soon."

"Tamar, be reasonable. Come home."

"Just send them. You owe me that much."

When the call ended, she and Ruby had gone out on the balcony and watched the sun climb over the horizon.

"What are you going to do, Ima?"

"About what?"

"Baba."

"We'll be fine. Ari and Rachel will be here soon, and who knows, maybe Baba will surprise us and arrive with them."

"And the girl?" Ruby prodded.

Tamar still had the letters in her suitcase. It was time to take care of that too. "We'd better get dressed," she said.

She gripped Ruby's hand tighter.

"It's not forever," Ruby said.

They reached the bus stop, where a crowd of teenagers milled on the sidewalk. She ran into the *bourekas* shop nearby and bought Ruby a coffee and two pastries filled with cheese. By the time she returned, Ruby was talking to a group of draftees. Tamar waited on the sidelines with the other parents looking more lost than their children.

"It's nearly seven thirty." A father tapped his watch.

Bus engines rumbled to life. Ruby turned to her. "Ima," she said. Tamar opened her arms and her daughter stepped into them. "I love you," Ruby said, then rushed onto the bus and settled in a window seat, the bag of warm *bourekas* in her lap.

The decorative tile over the doorbell read *Carmela and Baruch Ashkenazi*. Tamar held the manila envelope crammed with the girl's letters against her breast. A delicious fragrance emerged from her former neighbor's apartment next door:

Saint Peter's fish stewed in tomatoes and green chili served over Persian rice. A Shabbat favorite. Shula had always made extra for them; however, today wasn't Shabbat. The door to the girl's apartment was unexpectedly ajar and voices extended into the hall. The ambient sounds of a party, though the decibel level was subdued. Perhaps a farewell for the girl on her way to the States. The thought made her sad.

She took it as an invitation to enter, and why not, this was once her apartment. The girl Salim had chosen like a second bride was in there. She stepped on the welcome mat, the magnetic pull of her former life drawing her in. They never should have left this house. Salim would have found his way eventually.

"Hello," she called.

A woman with hennaed hair shuffled into the hall, dressed in a black frock, her feet ensconced in the proletariat brown plaid slippers kibbutzniks wore.

"Come in," she said.

A gallery of Mizrahi rabbis in gilt frames lined the foyer. One of them she recognized as Rabbi Israel Abuhatzeira, known as the Baba Sali of Morocco, and only because Hadas had once remarked on his picture in the synagogue they'd donated clothes to. "See him." She'd pointed to a photograph of an old man with a forked beard, shrouded in a white tunic. "They say he's been touched by God. When he prays for you, God listens. Barren women from all over the world come to him. A year later they return with their fat babies, asking him to bless their child."

"It's kind of you to come. I'm Marcela Ashkenazi, Baruch's sister. My poor brother's inside. I haven't been able to get him to eat or drink anything since yesterday."

Tamar saw the hall mirror covered in a sheet. "Oh God, I'm sorry. I've come at a bad time."

"Go in," she urged, "the more people we have, the easier it is. We're still in shock. It was so unexpected and for it to happen after the war, as if it wasn't enough our cousin's son, Chemi, was killed in the Golan at the start of it. Someone said a plane fell on his head. I think they meant artillery, not that it really matters. He's dead."

Tamar clutched the envelope.

"Have something to eat."

"I should've brought cake," she said, flustered. Never in her life had she gone to a shiva empty-handed.

"There's plenty of food and drink. We've got booze in the kitchen, if you prefer."

She stopped at the entrance to the living room, where clusters of people nibbled on rugelach and fruit. She could see clear to the end of the balcony, where she and Salim had spent summer nights with family and friends. Now three female soldiers huddled there, conversing in hushed tones, leaning over the railing, smoking cigarettes.

The mourners sat on low stools in the living room: a teenage boy, a middled-aged woman, a man, an empty stool. She recognized the rent in their clothes, their bare feet, and ashen faces. The envelope trembled in her hands. A soldier approached the older woman and recited: *From heaven you will be comforted.*

Her eyes traveled the room, searching for the girl, landing on the heavy furniture and ornate lamps, a green ceramic vase in the vitrine, the overstuffed sofas. A memorial candle burning on a side table, a framed picture beside it. She stepped closer to get a better look at the photograph. It was of the girl standing beneath an almond tree in full bloom, the same as the wallet-size image she'd sent Salim during Rosh Hashanah two months ago. She recognized the uniform, the khaki skirt riding above the knee, the shirt tucked into the waistband, her beret folded and secured in the shoulder tab. The girl smiling into the camera—that glorious smile and luminous eyes, so blue.

"What happened?" she cried. The woman who'd been weeping looked up. Her head covered in a navy kerchief. Her eyes the same shade as the girl's.

"She was shot in the Jaffa riot. We were sure she'd make it. Two weeks she was in hospital. They airlifted her to Hadassah in Jerusalem. The best doctors and they couldn't save her," Carmela Ashkenazi said. "What kind of God does that?"

Tamar swayed on her feet. "I'm sorry. I didn't know."

"Sit before you faint." Carmela patted the folding chair beside her. "Who are you?"

"I used to live in this house. I was in the neighborhood and thought if it wasn't too much trouble that I might see it again." Scenes of the riot filled her head: the soldier who'd been hit with a rock, the first Molotov thrown, the second had struck Hussein.

"You're Salim Abadi's wife." She sat back to get a better look at her.

"That's right." The girl was the soldier hit by the stray bullet.

"He told us you loved this apartment." Carmela's gaze sacked the room. "Been nothing but a curse for us." *Tfoo, tfoo,* she spat over her shoulder. "My daughter wasn't the same after we moved here. Now this. Why did it happen?"

"I don't know," Tamar said. "Why does anything happen?"

Carmela gripped her wrist. "You're right. Not even the rabbis know." Her arm swept toward the photographs in the hall.

The soldier's body had looked so small on the ground. She crushed the envelope to her chest. A terrible accident. Friendly fire. Had someone said that on the radio or was it in the news article? "My condolences on your loss," Tamar stammered. "She was beautiful."

"The most beautiful girl. Happy until we came here. I said to her, '*Kapara*, why are you so sad?' You know what she said? 'It's the world, Ima. The world makes me sad.' I would have changed the world for her if I could. May she find peace in heaven, Amen."

"Amen," Tamar repeated.

"I blame the army. They made her a driver, so why send her into Kikar HaSha'on? Shouldn't she have stayed with the jeep? The day she was killed, she called to tell me she'd be home in the evening. 'I'll make *mufleta* for supper,' I said. It's her favorite. 'Don't bother, I have to put something in the mail tonight,' she said. "I told her tell me where the letter is. I'll do it for you." She screamed, 'It's private. Don't touch it, Ima.' Those were her last words to me. I didn't touch it. I haven't even gone into her room. I want her to know I'll never touch it, that in her last moments I listened."

Marcela came up to them quietly. "Carmela, eat something, Shula sent a tray. Maybe if you eat, Baruch will too." She drew her to her feet.

"You came to look." Carmela dried her eyes with a handkerchief. "So look."

Tamar made her way to the back of the apartment, where the bedrooms were, and peered first into the master. Carmela's dark furniture overwhelmed the room. The bed was a barge and the armoire a monolith in the corner. She considered how the girl must have felt living in this house, haunted by Salim and his family. No wonder she sent him feathers and vials of sand. What they had was as ephemeral as shadows on a wall, existing for an hour before disappearing in the sunlight.

She turned down the hall past the lavatory and bathroom. There was no mistaking the girl's room with its posters of pop stars. The bare mirror above the dresser attested to Carmela's promise to her daughter not to touch the letter. Tamar perused the bottles of nail polish adorning the girl's dresser, the miniature stuffed bear, the pots of blue and green eye shadow. There was an elegant atomizer that seemed out of place among the rest of the items. She picked it up, knowing Salim had given it to the girl. He'd given her the same perfume on her last birthday in this house. She sprayed a bit into the air, the scent taking her back to that night, then gazed into the mirror, imagining the soldier enjoying her reflection, her blue eyes shining like bits of sky. She could almost hear Salim whisper, *Ayouni, ayouni*, my eyes, my eyes, the way he'd said it to her so many times in this house.

The books surprised her. There were childhood copies of *HaDevorah Maya*, Maya the Bumblebee, Hebrew translations of *Little Women* and *Jane Eyre*, but the majority were Tamar's favorite Hebrew poets. Each copy was new, the spines barely cracked. The girl had every edition Tamar owned. Salim must've told her about the books Hadas had given her when she'd moved in with them. "Nothing sadder than an empty shelf," Hadas had said when Tamar arrived at Kafr Ma'an with only a suitcase of clothing.

A river of hushed voices washed through the apartment as more people arrived to pay their respects. The traffic below was a distant growl. Tamar sat on the bed, the girl's letters to Salim beside her. There was no one to return them to now. No one to warn off or rail against. She was tired. Morning was a long time ago. Faisal gone, Ruby drafted, the apprehension she'd felt as the bus pulled away from the curb filled her anew. How had she not noticed the air was thinner and more fragile in this room? Just the act of breathing could shatter it.

She lay on the pink waffle blanket, hugging the letters to her chest. The glow-in-the-dark stars Ruby had put up the year before they left for America were still on the ceiling. Poor Salim. She turned on her side, tucking a hand under her cheek. He didn't know his soldier was dead. There would be no obituary in the international edition of *Maariv*. The girl would continue to live in his mind. He would wait for her, as he would wait for Tamar, believing he could still choose between them.

She searched the closet, admiring the soldier's miniskirts, the pastel palette, taking care not to disturb anything. From the living room she heard Carmela keen as the men prayed *Mincha*. She peered under the bed and found Salim's letters in a box, his photograph glued to the lid amid hearts and stars drawn in colored pencils, his hair falling into his eyes, looking so much like Ari. The unposted letter was taped to a book wrapped in brown paper.

My love, it began, *you begged me to stop writing. So, this is the last letter I'll send before I leave for America. If you decide to break it off when I get there (I understood what you were trying to say in your last letter), I'll be all right, kapara. It's like you said, the world doesn't end when love dies, it only sleeps, though I think it mourns a little. I hope I can wake you again. Til then, forever yours.*

P.S. I found this at a secondhand bookshop on Allenby Street. I think it's about that village your sister loved so much.

Tamar opened the wrapping. The book jacket to the volume she'd seen only once was worn. *Scenes from a Village*, by Daoud Hamid. She remembered the day he'd given Hadas the Hebrew translation. The inscription read: *To my parents, to Kafr Ma'an that is lost to us, and to H.A, for eternity.*

Later, she would tell Gadi how she took it all—the letter, Daoud's book, and the contents in the box. She didn't want to risk Carmela finding them, imagining the pain it would cause her knowing her daughter was in love with a married man. She didn't want her blaming Salim for her daughter's sadness.

That night she telephoned Salim. They had a halting conversation about the children's visit. He finally agreed to send them. She didn't mention Leila Ashkenazi's death, his soldier, though he might have intuited it, the way a parent would, waking in the middle of the night with the sense that something was horribly wrong, the child missing from their bed. Or the way a lover would, knowing the beloved was gone. It was in his voice, not quite grief, just the filaments of it woven through their conversation, reminding her of how she'd kept his image alive in her mind during the Six-Day War in the hope that he'd come back to her. At the end of the call, she said, "You know you can come home with the kids, if you want." But even as she said the words, she felt his image stir; all the parts of him she'd held on to scattered like leaves in an autumn wind.

The bus dropped her off at the bottom of the hill, near the intersection at the entrance to Ramat Aviv. She walked past the Israel Planetarium, a modest building with a domed roof, tiny compared to the one they'd taken the children to in New York. Next door was the Eretz Museum, where archeological finds were displayed, some dating back to the Jewish Wars against the Romans, the destruction of the second temple, and the exile that would last two thousand years.

She crossed to where a row of palm trees lined the median. On one side of the road, there were blocks of new apartment buildings four stories high with front gardens and balconies where parents drank their morning coffee while children played near the carport. Gardens burgeoning with young citrus trees, frangipani trees, and bougainvillea. On the other side of the median, fields sloped toward the Yarkon River, which led out to sea. Straddled between the apartments and the river were the remains of Kafr Ma'an: thistles and scrub grass, a stone wall, a faded blue door toppled in the weeds. The houses and pathways were gone and so were the groves. All that remained of the *pardes* were a few gnarled trees. The rest were bulldozed to make way for a new neighborhood and the new building on the university campus at the top of the hill. In one of her letters, Leila wrote that Salim had taken her here to see the ruins of their old house. Tamar saw only a few stone blocks and a rusted gate. Was it their gate? Their stone blocks? She couldn't tell. There wasn't enough to piece a house together and nothing to mark that there had ever been a village here. Kafr Ma'an was gone just as Hadas had feared, just as she and Daoud were. The only trace of it was in the blood-soaked ground, in Daoud's poetry, and in the memory of all those who had once lived here.

She recalled one night in late December when the orange trees were ready for harvest. They had just finished supper. She, Salim, and Hadas gazed out at the *pardes*. The moon dressed the trees in silver. The smell of the winter rains in the air.

"Look," Hadas cried, "there they are," and pointed to the villagers, to Daoud and his brother, Amir, to his parents, to his aunts and uncles, who arrived in the dark with ladders and baskets to pick the fruit, to rub their hands in the soil and tell one another, *Remember this sweetness.*

Tamar closed her eyes and saw Kafr Ma'an as it had been, as it could have been.

ACKNOWLEDGMENTS

These days it takes a kind of heroism to publish a book like mine. I am grateful to my editor, Joe Olshan for being that hero and for sharing his wisdom, patience, and keen eye, and to Lori Milken, publisher of Delphinium Books for their steadfast support. Many thanks to Jennifer Ankner-Edelstein, Joan Matthews, Colin Dockrill, Elizabeth Shreve, and to everyone at Delphinium who helped shepherd this novel into the world.

I am eternally grateful to my agent, Murray Weiss, a true mensch whose persistence and belief in my work continues to sustain me. Warm thanks to Judy Sternlight for introducing us and for her unwavering support and friendship.

Thank you to everyone at Hedgebrook for embracing me with their "radical hospitality," for giving me time and space to complete a draft of this novel, and for the opportunity to meet my Hedgebrook sisters: Leslie Blanco, Drea Brown, Jaclyn Chan, Carla DuPree, Dana Fitz Gale, Jocelyn Johnson, Elaine Kim, Ashley Lucas, and Margarita Ramirez. My deep gratitude to The Center for Fiction Emerging Writer Fellowship, a turning point in my life. Thanks to the Byrdcliff Artist in Residency program in Woodstock, NY., the Sewannee Writers Conference, Tin House, and Napa Valley Writers Conference for their support. To my teachers Alice McDermott, Dinaw Megistu, and Yiyun Li for their wisdom.

Thank you to those who took the time to read this work in its various stages: to Ashley Lucas for her thoughtful feedback. To Sara Lippmann whose support makes me believe that I can do this work. To Shimon Carmi for his insights and knowledge of Israeli history and Mizrahi culture. To Khulud Khamis whose feedback on the Arab-Israeli and Palestinian perspective was essential to the writing of this novel. To Marcia Butler, Louise Marburg, and Chris Cander for their kindness and immense generosity. To my writing group for their commitment, patience, and longtime friendship: Julia Hirsch, Linda Guyette, and Rosanne Limoncello. You make me feel seen and heard.

To those whose support over the years has meant so much: Erica Dreifus, Nora Gold, Yona Zeldis McDonough, and Cole Meyer. To Joan Brady who helped me get through it. Thank you to longtime friends who knew me when this was just a dream Naomi Katz, Judy Penso, and Ghila Krajzman. To Zaire Dinzey-Flores and Eddie Paulino for the long conversations over large plates of hummus.

Thank you to my sister, Esther Bukai who gives me strength and love every day. To my brothers, Simon and David. To my daughters Shoshi and Becca Shmuluvitz, my heart and soul, to their partners, Mari Karppinen and Ian Grunert, and to my granddaughter, Alma, the light of our family. Finally, to my husband Levy, my heart, thank you for all the years, for the patience, and the love. I couldn't have gotten here without you.

ABOUT THE AUTHOR

Zeeva Bukai was born in Israel and raised in New York City. Her stories have appeared in *Smashing the Tablets: A Radical Retellings of the Hebrew Bible*, CARVE, *Lilith*, *McSweeney's, Quarterly Concern*, *Image Journal*, *December Magazine* and elsewhere. Her honors include fellowships at the Center for Fiction, Hedgebrook, and Byrdcliffe AIR program. She is the Assistant Director of Academic Support at SUNY Empire State University and lives in Brooklyn with her family.